OXFORD WORLD'S CLASSICS

SHE

HENRY RIDER HAGGARD was born in Norfolk in 1856, the son of a barrister and country gentleman, and after being educated privately and at Ipswich Grammar School began to prepare for entrance to the Foreign Office. When his father unexpectedly found him a post on the staff of Sir Henry Bulwer, Lieutenant-Governor of Natal, however, Haggard went to work in South Africa, where he spent several exciting years during the time of Britain's almost disastrous war with the Zulus, and the First Boer War which followed.

Haggard turned these experiences to good account on returning to England, when, after an unsuccessful start as a lawyer, he began writing, and he achieved a great popular and critical triumph with his adventure story *King Solomon's Mines* in 1885. Other remarkable tales soon followed, such as *Allan Quatermain* (1887), *She* (1887), and *Nada the Lily* (1892), and Rider Haggard became one of England's most popular novelists for the next forty years.

A distinguished public servant as well as a writer, Rider Haggard had an extensive knowledge of Agriculture and of Imperial Affairs, and sat on a number of Royal Commissions for which he was made a Knight Bachelor in 1912 and a Knight Commander of the British Empire in 1919. He died in 1925.

DANIEL KARLIN teaches at Boston University, where he holds appointments in the University Professors Program and the Department of English. He is the author of *The Courtship of Robert Browning and Elizabeth Barrett* (1985) and *Browning's Hatreds* (1993), and the editor of *The New Penguin Book of Victorian Verse* (1997) and Kipling's selected verse and prose in the Oxford Authors series (2000).

OXFORD WORLD'S CLASSICS

*For over 100 years Oxford World's Classics have brought
readers closer to the world's great literature. Now with over 700
titles—from the 4,000-year-old myths of Mesopotamia to the
twentieth century's greatest novels—the series makes available
lesser-known as well as celebrated writing.*

*The pocket-sized hardbacks of the early years contained
introductions by Virginia Woolf, T. S. Eliot, Graham Greene,
and other literary figures which enriched the experience of reading.
Today the series is recognized for its fine scholarship and
reliability in texts that span world literature, drama and poetry,
religion, philosophy and politics. Each edition includes perceptive
commentary and essential background information to meet the
changing needs of readers.*

OXFORD WORLD'S CLASSICS

H. RIDER HAGGARD

She

Edited with an Introduction and Notes by
DANIEL KARLIN

OXFORD
UNIVERSITY PRESS

OXFORD
UNIVERSITY PRESS

Great Clarendon Street, Oxford OX2 6DP

Oxford University Press is a department of the University of Oxford.
It furthers the University's objective of excellence in research, scholarship,
and education by publishing worldwide in

Oxford New York

Auckland Cape Town Dar es Salaam Hong Kong Karachi
Kuala Lumpur Madrid Melbourne Mexico City Nairobi
New Delhi Shanghai Taipei Toronto

With offices in

Argentina Austria Brazil Chile Czech Republic France Greece
Guatemala Hungary Italy Japan Poland Portugal Singapore
South Korea Switzerland Thailand Turkey Ukraine Vietnam

Oxford is a registered trade mark of Oxford University Press
in the UK and in certain other countries

Published in the United States
by Oxford University Press Inc., New York

Introduction, Note on the Text, Explanatory notes
© Daniel Karlin 1991
Select Bibliography © Dennis Butts and Daniel Karlin 1991
Chronology © Dennis Butts 1989

The moral rights of the author have been asserted
Database right Oxford University Press (maker)

First published as a World's Classics paperback 1991
Reissued as an Oxford World's Classics paperback 1998

British Library Cataloguing in Publication Data

Data available

Library of Congress Cataloging in Publication Data

Haggard, H. Rider (Henry Rider), 1856–1925.
She / H. Rider Haggard; edited with an introduction by Daniel Karlin.
p.   cm.— (Oxford world's classics)
Includes bibliographical references.
I. Karlin, Daniel, 1953– . II. Title. III. Series.
PR4731.S6 1990 823'.8—dc20

Typeset in Ehrhardt
by RefineCatch Limited, Bungay, Suffolk
Printed in Great Britain by
Clays Ltd., St Ives plc

ISBN 0–19–283550–5 978–0–19–283550–5

10

CONTENTS

Introduction   vii

Note on the Text   xxvii

Select Bibliography   xxviii

A Chronology of H. Rider Haggard   xxxi

SHE   I

Explanatory Notes   276

INTRODUCTION

THE narrator of *She*, Ludwig Horace Holly, is conspicuous for his lack of family. He is a bachelor don, alone in the world, 'misanthropic and sullen'. 'Like Cain, I was branded—branded by Nature with the stamp of abnormal ugliness, as I was gifted by Nature with iron and abnormal strength and considerable intellectual powers' (p. 16). The author of this Romantic orphan and outcast, Henry Rider Haggard, was, at first glance, in the opposite predicament. He had not a lack of family but a surfeit. He was the eighth of William and Ella Haggard's ten children, and the sixth son. His father was a loud, hearty, overbearing man, a blustering barrister and country squire of the old school—Haggard compared him to the *Spectator*'s Sir Roger de Coverley, but he sounds at times more like Fielding's Squire Western. Haggard was passionately fond of his mother, and starved of her time. He was a sickly child and a slow learner. His autobiography is dignified and reticent about these matters by modern standards, but something of his misery shows in such passages as the following:

Also I was stupid. Indeed, although she always indignantly denied the story in after years, I remember when I was about seven my dear mother declaring that I was as heavy as lead in body and mind.

I fear that I was more or less of a dunderhead at lessons. Even my letters presented difficulties to me, and I well recollect a few years later being put through an examination by my future brother-in-law, the Rev. Charles Maddison Green, with the object of ascertaining what amount of knowledge I had acquired at a day school in London . . .

The results of this examination were so appalling that when he was apprised of them my indignant father burst into the room where I sat resigned to fate, and, in a voice like to that of an angry bull, roared out at me that I was 'only fit to be a greengrocer'.[1]

Haggard was eventually sent to the Queen Elizabeth School, Ipswich, a grammar school; 'I dare say it was thought that to send me to a public school would be to waste money', he remarked.[2] It would be nice to think that he made a success of the 'inferior' school, and it of

---

[1] *The Days of My Life*, ed. C. J. Longman, 2 vols., 1926, i. 5.
[2] Five of Haggard's brothers went to public school. The sixth entered the Navy.

him, but the only tangible benefit Haggard seems to have derived from his time at Ipswich was the goodwill of the headmaster, Dr Holden, who was later to help him with the classical Greek inscription on the Sherd of Amenartas. Needless to say Haggard did not go to university. In the light of such an upbringing and education, the character of Holly—Cambridge don and social pariah, simultaneously 'branded' and 'gifted' by Nature—seems as though it expresses some of Haggard's most poignant wishes and anxieties.

He had other trials to cope with. After failing the Army entrance examination at Ipswich, he was sent to London to prepare for the entrance examination to the Foreign Office, first with a tutor and then at Scoones' crammer. While there he met and fell in love with a woman called Lilly Jackson, whose image haunted him all his life; their engagement was eventually thwarted (whether deliberately or not is unclear) by Haggard's father, in circumstances which Haggard never forgot.[3] In the summer of 1875, with his son's prospects of passing the Foreign Office examination not looking bright, William Haggard obtained for him a post (unpaid) on the staff of Sir Henry Bulwer, who was going to South Africa as Lieutenant-Governor of Natal. It was a sudden decision, and a fateful one for Haggard. It gave him four years of independence, responsibility, and adventure (he was in South Africa at the time of the annexation of the Transvaal in 1877 and the Zulu war in 1879); it also gave him the material for his best work. He began with journalism and travel-sketches about Africa, mostly undistinguished; he had not yet absorbed the true lesson of his African experiences. He was less quick than Kipling to see the resources conferred by distance from England: an imaginative depth of field, access to landscapes and legends beyond the provincial scope of English fiction, the scope for wildness and exoticism which would, at the same time, carry conviction with the English public.

In 1879, on his return to England, Haggard became engaged to Louisa Margitson, a Norfolk friend of his sister Mary. She had money—though it required litigation to get hold of it, since she was under age and her trustee disapproved of her marriage—and

---

[3] See *The Days of My Life*, i. 21–3. Lilly Jackson eventually made an unhappy marriage; Haggard's own marriage was based on something which fell considerably short of romantic passion. It was a relationship which lasted, but it was not the one he had wanted.

Haggard was no longer under pressure to find employment. They were married the following year, and returned to South Africa to farm in Natal. The rebellion in the Transvaal, which resulted in the province being ceded to the Boers, decided them to leave, however, and they returned to England in 1881. Haggard now began to read for the Bar, and wrote his first book, a commentary on recent events in South Africa, *Cetywayo and His White Neighbours*. It was published (at his own expense) in July 1882, received few notices, and did not sell. Then—out of the blue, in a sense, for he read little fiction and had written none—he wrote his first novel. His own account of why he did so is given in his autobiography:

Whilst we were at Norwood a little incident occurred which resulted in my becoming a writer of fiction. At the church which my wife and I attended we saw sitting near to us one Sunday a singularly beautiful and pure-faced young lady. Afterwards we agreed that this semi-divine creature—on whom to the best of my knowledge I have never set eyes again from that day to this—ought to become the heroine of a novel. So then and there we took paper, and each of us began to write the said novel. I think that after she had completed two or three folio sheets my wife ceased from her fictional labours. But, growing interested, I continued mine.[4]

As with many of Haggard's romances, the very improbability of this story points up its significance as a fable. It tells of Haggard's discovery of his wife's inadequacy as an emotional and imaginative partner, and records his drift away from her; the 'other woman', however, represents no threat to the conventional stability of his marriage, since she is 'pure-faced', a 'semi-divine creature' (seen in church) whose involvement with Haggard is sanctioned both by his wife and by her own impalpability (Haggard emphatically states that he has never seen her again). Haggard's ambivalence about the creative power of women is also acutely drawn. They may inspire (as

---

[4] *The Days of My Life*, i. 220. Haggard first told the story in an article in *The Idler* (April 1893) in a series called 'My First Book'. D. S. Higgins (*Rider Haggard: The Great Storyteller*, 1981, pp. 58–9) points out an inaccuracy—'The novel was begun at Bradenham and not at Norwood'—and an improbability: the story does not fit the 'eminently practical but unimaginative' character of Louisa Haggard. Haggard's friend and future sister-in-law, Agnes Barber, who read his early work sympathetically and later helped him with *She* (see note to p. 32), fits the story better, but Higgins points out that she was not with him at the time. But Higgins's own suggestion—that Haggard 'was forced to find a glib but acceptable answer to the question he was in later years most frequently asked: "How did you start to write fiction?" ', and that 'His career as a novelist began because of a deep but ill-comprehended need to write'—is hardly more satisfactory.

mute, unconscious muses) but they may not compete. It is an ambivalence which operates on the grand scale in *She*.

This first novel, *Dawn*, after much rewriting, found a commercial publisher in 1884; it was followed in the same year by *The Witch's Head*. These works brought Haggard to the notice of reviewers, but accomplished little else; and the reviews themselves were mixed. Then, in September 1885, he published *King Solomon's Mines*.

Haggard's new publishers, Cassell's, playing a hunch backed up by enthusiastic readers' reports, launched *King Solomon's Mines* with the kind of hype which foreshadowed today's marketing strategies:

Cassell's prepared long narrow posters—each as long as a hoarding—on which was printed in big type: KING SOLOMON'S MINES—THE MOST AMAZING BOOK EVER WRITTEN. Some nights after the publication of *King Solomon's Mines* the firm put up these posters, *after dark*, all over London. People went to their work on horse-buses in the morning to find the message at every turning. They could not get away from it. They went to their lunches—rich men and poor—with the same statement staring them in the face: KING SOLOMON'S MINES—THE MOST AMAZING BOOK EVER WRITTEN. People began to believe it. What was the book? They must know. Cassell's had put Haggard on the literary map in one night.[5]

Not surprisingly, Haggard immediately thought of capitalizing on his success. He began writing *Allan Quatermain*, a straightforward sequel to *King Solomon's Mines*, with a similar action and featuring the same heroes: the old hunter Quatermain, Sir Henry Curtis, and Captain John Good, along with the Zulu warrior Umslopogaas (who replaces Umbopa in the earlier book). But though *Allan Quatermain* was written in 1885, it was not published until July 1887. In the mean time Haggard wrote and published the second of the stories on which his enduring fame rests, *She*. Of course, *She* shares some of the characteristics of *King Solomon's Mines* and *Allan Quatermain* in its setting and characters. Foulata, the beautiful Kukuana girl with whom Captain Good falls in love in *King Solomon's Mines*, is matched by Ustane, Leo's Amahagger wife in *She*; in both *She* and *King Solomon's Mines* English travellers penetrate into a remote African country, the site of a vanished empire; in *Allan Quatermain*, as in *She*, a beautiful and imperious queen falls in love with an

English explorer; and many more such parallels could be given,
down to the seemingly obligatory presence in all the books of the
gratuitous and spectacular killing of big game.

And yet, despite such comparisons, there is something in *She*
unmatched by *King Solomon's Mines*, or indeed by anything else that
Haggard ever wrote, including the feeble sequel *Ayesha: The Return
of She* (1905) and the even feebler 'prequel' *She and Allan* (1921).
Haggard himself recognized the book's uniqueness, though it was
a source of frustration to him, as is always the case when a young
writer's work turns out to be his best or most popular. In his autobiography, lamenting the fact that critics of his later works kept on
comparing them unfavourably with *She*, Haggard exclaimed (in a
phrase interestingly reminiscent of the novel itself): 'As though a
man's brain could harbour a host of "Shes"! Such literary polygamy
is not possible. Only one love of this kind is given to him.'[6] *King
Solomon's Mines* was written in conscious rivalry with *Treasure
Island*,[7] and Haggard's own description of it, 'a book for boys',
is essentially accurate. As Edmund Gosse wrote to Haggard, 'that
exceedingly picturesque and ingenious book did not prepare me for
"*She*" '.[8] *She* is both more sophisticated and more primitive than
King Solomon's Mines, and also more disturbing: its landscapes and
episodes have an intensity and surrealistic precision which mark the
difference between daydream and nightmare.

The narrative foundations of *She* are those of Gothic romance:
particularly in its combination of purported authenticity with constant reminders of the story's fantastic or incredible features, its
recurring use of terms such as 'wonderful', 'strange', 'marvellous',
'uncanny'. The 'Editor' announces it as 'the record' of 'one of the
most wonderful and mysterious experiences ever undergone by
mortal men' and as an 'extraordinary history' (p. 11). 'Record' and

---

[6] *The Days of My Life*, i. 249–50.

[7] According to Haggard's daughter Lilias, 'Travelling up to London with one of his
brothers they started discussing *Treasure Island*, just then making a great success. Rider
said he didn't think it was so very remarkable, whereupon his brother replied, rather
indignantly: "Well, I'd like to see you write anything half as good—bet you a bob
you can't." "Done," said Rider . . .' (Lilias Rider Haggard, *The Cloak that I Left: A
Biography of the Author Henry Rider Haggard K.B.E.*, 1951, pp. 121–2). Haggard
himself wrote: 'I read in one of the weekly papers a notice of Stevenson's *Treasure Island*
so laudatory that I procured and studied that work, and was impelled by its perusal to
try to write a book for boys' (*The Days of My Life*, i. 230).

[8] Letter of 8 Jan. 1887, quoted by Haggard in *The Days of My Life*, i. 250.

'history' deny the imputation of fiction; at the same time the reader must not lose the sense of the incompatibility of the supposed facts with common experience (or even common sense). 'I have recently read with much interest a book of yours describing a Central African adventure', writes Holly, the narrator, to the 'Editor', clearly referring to *King Solomon's Mines*:

I take it that this book is partly true, and partly an effort of the imagination. However this is, it has given me an idea. It happens . . . that my ward, or rather my adopted son Leo Vincey and myself have recently passed through a real African adventure, of a nature so much more marvellous than the one which you describe, that to tell you the truth I am almost ashamed to submit it to you for fear lest you should disbelieve my tale. (p. 13)

To tell you the truth: the idiom is disarming, but also disingenuous: the truth is that the story is, indeed, a fiction. Haggard wanted his readers to be aware of this, I think, in contrast to their amusingly confused response to the cloud-Kukuanaland of *King Solomon's Mines* (Haggard received numerous letters asking for further information on how to get there). One of the most sublime jokes in *She* is that the preposterous lost civilization of Kôr worshipped Truth as its ultimate deity. Haggard's insistence on documentary evidence and literal veracity in *She* ironically points to the void or chaos of imagination out of which he evokes his fictional world, as in Holly's comment on the sculptures he sees in one of the caves of Kôr:

These sculptures, looked at merely as works of art, were so remarkable that I make no apology for describing them rather fully. They struck me also as being of surpassing interest as representing, probably with studious accuracy, the last rites of the dead as practised among an utterly lost people, and even then I thought how envious some antiquarian friends of my own at Cambridge would be if ever I got an opportunity of describing these wonderful remains to them. Probably they would say that I was exaggerating, notwithstanding that every page of this history must bear so much internal evidence of its truth that it would obviously have been quite impossible for me to have invented it. (pp. 127–8)

The joke in the last sentence has a serious point. Unlicensed imagination is dangerous; 'pure' fantasy corrupts or maddens. Its nakedness must be clothed with the garment of 'studious accuracy'; but the spectacle of this nakedness is, after all, what readers have come to see. The garment is therefore see-through. Ayesha herself is a figure for this paradox of imagination or desire, dressed in 'wrappings . . . so thin that one could distinctly see the gleam of the pink flesh beneath them' (p. 132); her beauty signifies her power, a power which Holly's narrative both acknowledges and resists.

The image of an all-powerful woman—one who can turn the tables, as it were, on the term 'ravishing'—has a tenacious hold on the male mind: the epithet *She-who-must-be-obeyed*, applied to Margaret Thatcher in recent years in a tone both jocular and anxious, shows its persistence. But Haggard's treatment of this misogynist stereotype is not one-dimensional or simple-minded: his success can be gauged from the multiple and conflicting attempts which have been made to come to terms with his creation.[9] *She* is the most parodied and filmed of Haggard's works,[10] and the one which has attracted the most sustained and serious critical attention—whether seen as an autobiographical record of his 'nightmares, suppressed desires and fantasies' (Higgins), a religious allegory (Leo Michael), or a fable about colonialism and male dread, the precursor of Conrad's *Heart of Darkness* and Eliot's *The Waste Land* (Sandra M. Gilbert and Susan Gubar).[11] Haggard began it at the end of January 1886, and finished it in six weeks: 'it was written at white heat, almost without rest', he wrote in his autobiography, adding:

I remember that when I sat down to the task my ideas as to its development were of the vaguest. The only clear notion that I had in my head was that of an immortal woman inspired by an immortal love. All the rest shaped itself round this figure. And it came—it came faster than my poor aching hand could set it down.[12]

Henry Miller, deeply stirred by this account, claimed that Haggard's

[9] These attempts start within the book itself, with the 'Editor's' speculations as to the meaning of Holly's narrative (see p. 15).

[10] According to Peter B. Ellis (*H. Rider Haggard: A Voice from the Infinite*, 1978, p. 278) there have been eleven film versions of *She* (as opposed to five of *King Solomon's Mines*), the earliest being a French silent of 1899; the first talking version was released by RKO in 1935 with Helen Gahagan in the starring role. The version which readers will probably know best was released by Hammer-Seven Arts in 1965 with Ursula Andress, Christopher Lee, Peter Cushing, and John Richardson. Parodies of *She* include one called *He* (1889), co-written by Andrew Lang (see note to the Dedication, p. 276).

[11] Higgins, *Rider Haggard*, p. 91; Michael, *She, an Allegory of the Church*, 1889; Gilbert and Gubar, *No Man's Land*, ii, *Sexchanges*, 1989, ch. 1.

[12] *The Days of My Life*, i. 245–6.

method of composition 'enabled him to tap his unconscious with freedom and depth';[13] but it is questionably Romantic to view *She* as the product of inspiration (or compulsion) over which its author had only nominal control. This would be to ignore both the cluster of its anthropological, mythological, and literary sources, the deliberateness of its fictional structure, and, perhaps even more importantly, the variability of its tone.[14] Certainly *She* is a darker book than either *King Solomon's Mines* or *Allan Quatermain*; but it is also funnier and more self-conscious. Haggard has been persistently criticized for writing sloppily, absurdly, bathetically; Robert Louis Stevenson told him bluntly that parts of *King Solomon's Mines* were beneath him (Haggard was modest enough to quote this letter in *The Days of My Life*), and Morton Cohen, in common with several contemporary reviewers, thought the choice of a Cambridge scholar as narrator in *She* a fatal error of judgement, since Haggard was unable convincingly to render such a man's intellectual character or speech.[15] That Haggard's style is frequently bathetic or clumsy cannot be denied; but the matter is not so easily settled.

At the end of Chapter XIV of *She*, the narrator, Ludwig Horace Holly, witnesses the agonized raving of Ayesha over the 2,000-year-old corpse of her lover, Kallikrates. 'There was something so horrible about the sight of this awe-inspiring woman letting loose her passion on the dead', Holly says, 'that I could no longer bear to look at it'; he creeps back to his resting-place, 'feeling in my trembling heart that I had a vision of a Soul in Hell'. What does he see when he wakes up, at the beginning of the next chapter? His English servant,

[13] Miller, *The Books in My Life*, 1952, pp. 93–4.

[14] The anthropological and mythological sources—African, Middle Eastern, and Celtic—are surveyed by Morton Cohen, *Rider Haggard*, 1960, pp. 102 ff. The closest African source suffers from the fact that Haggard specifically denied its influence, though critics have (probably rightly) ignored this disavowal. It concerns the small Lovedu tribe, a matriarchy ruled over by a white woman reputed to be immortal, though in fact the dynasty was carried on in much the same way that Ustane speculates in Ch. VII (p. 86). A fuller account of the Lovedu is given in E. Jensen and J. D. Krige, *The Realm of the Rain-Queen*, 1947. The literary sources, especially those concerning the figure of the *femme fatale*, are well documented by Gilbert and Gubar (see n. 11).

[15] Stevenson's opinion is in a letter to Haggard cited in *The Days of My Life*; Cohen's in *Rider Haggard: His Life and Works*, 1960, p. 116. Among contemporary reviewers, Augustus Moore ('Rider Haggard and "The New School of Romance"', *Time*, May 1887, pp. 513–24) is especially scathing on this point. It might be argued that Holly's implausibility is scarcely greater than that of a contemporary scholar-adventurer-hero, Indiana Jones.

Job, 'standing in the ray of light that pierced into the cave from the outer air, shaking out my clothes as a makeshift for brushing them, which he could not do because there was no brush, and then folding them up neatly and laying them on the foot of the stone couch'. Job is also annoyed by the lack of hot water 'in this beastly place'. 'I suppose these poor creatures only use it to boil each other in', he speculates.

The contrast between lurid Gothic fantasy and homely reminders of English life (including the class-system) is characteristic of *She*. So is the coarse joke. The system of representations in the book is incoherent and unstable: it is a work which contradicts itself at every level of genre, theme, and style. The 'Editor' for example, claims to have obeyed Holly's stipulation that the real names of his narrative be changed; and yet the story's documentary foundation is based on Leo's surname, *Vincey*, being an injunction to vengeance transmitted from generation to generation, beginning with Greek and passing through Latin and Norman French to English (see p. 19). To add to the inconsistency, both Billali and Ayesha pun on the names *Leo* and *Holly* as expressive of their respective lion- and tree-like qualities (pp. 101, 135). The Amahagger, to take another example, are collectively depicted as a European's racial and sexual nightmare, a demonic cannibalistic matriarchy squatting in the ruins of a lost civilization, sheltering in its tombs and using its desecrated mummies for fuel; yet Haggard has his narrator Holly give an earnest anthropological account of them, describing their artefacts and agriculture, remarking—again the touch of homely detail—that one of the breeds of cattle 'closely resembles the Norfolk red-pole strain' (p. 86). The two Amahagger who have major roles in the book, Billali and Ustane, are sympathetically presented, and the terrors of female domination are undercut by the saturnine humour with which Billali explains the system to Holly:

'We worship them [the women], and give them their way, because without them the world could not go on; they are the source of life.'

'Ah,' I said, the matter never having struck me quite in that light before.

'We worship them,' he went on, 'up to a certain point, till at last they get unbearable, which,' he added, 'they do about every second generation.'

'And then what do you do?' I asked, with curiosity.

'Then,' he answered, with a faint smile, 'we rise, and kill the old ones as an example to the young ones, and to show them that we are the strongest.

My poor wife was killed in that way three years ago. It was very sad, but to tell thee the truth, my son, life has been happier since, for my age protects me from the young ones.'

'In short,' I replied, quoting the saying of a great man whose wisdom has not yet lightened the darkness of the Amahagger, 'thou hast found thy position one of greater freedom and less responsibility.' (p. 107)

When he saw the manuscript of the book before its serialization in the *Graphic*, Andrew Lang was disturbed by such passages: 'some of the chaff in awful situations lets one down too suddenly' (again, Haggard himself cites this in his autobiography). Lang repeated his opinion, in a kinder tone, in his published review: 'the humour may not be always to his [the reader's] mind, though it is a foil to the terrible passages'.[16] The reviewer in the *Pall Mall Gazette* was harsher: 'Throughout the book we meet with ill-timed touches of flippancy'; and he went on to make the most sustained attack among contemporary critics on this feature of Haggard's style.

The conception, indeed, is so powerful that we rebel with a sense of injury against the many defects of execution. It is as though a subject roughed out by Michael Angelo had been executed with an eye to New Bond-street popularity by Gustave Doré. A style alternately flat and flamboyant, cheap philosophy, shallow sentiment, and a strain of humour which, though harmless enough in itself, is made by its surroundings to seem frivolous to the verge of vulgarity—these are the faults of Mr Haggard's work . . . he lacks distinction of touch in handling a theme which a great artist would have treated not only with distinction but with austerity. If Dante had been accompanied on his tour through the 'città dolente' by a special correspondent of the *Daily Telegraph*, the result would have been just such a book as 'She'.[17]

The double image of incongruity—Michael Angelo/Doré and Dante/*Daily Telegraph*—insistently draws attention to this critic's unease at Haggard's mixing of high and low literary language. He would have liked *She* to be all of a piece, to be sublime and, in his telling word, 'austere'; but Haggard was too canny for that. Throughout the book he uses humour, frequently combined with the literalism of his imagery, to add a note of burlesque to grandiose speculations or horrific scenes. Solemn, pseudo-biblical cadences give way to the most matter-of-fact tones. In Chapter XVI Ayesha

---

[16] Review in the *Academy*, No. 767, 15 Jan. 1887, p. 36.
[17] *Pall Mall Gazette*, No. 6802, 4 Jan. 1887, p. 5.

offers Holly a guided tour of the great catacombs of the vanished empire of Kôr.

'And now, follow thou me, and I will show thee after what fashion this great people fell when the time was come for it to fall,' and she led the way down to the centre of the cave, stopping at a spot where a round rock had been let into a kind of large manhole in the flooring, accurately filling it just as the iron plates fill the spaces in the London pavements down which the coals are thrown. (p. 163)

When, in the same chapter, Holly sees the great pit filled with skel-etons, the element of excessive horror itself precipitates a reaction:

In my astonishment I uttered an ejaculation, and the echoes of my voice ringing in the vaulted space disturbed a skull that had been accurately balanced for many thousands of years near the apex of the pile. Down it came with a run, bounding along merrily towards us, and of course bringing an avalanche of other bones after it, till at last the whole pit rattled with their movement, even as though the skeletons were getting up to greet us. (p. 166)

In Chapter IX the old Amahagger chieftain Billali shows Holly a 4,000-year-old, perfectly preserved woman's foot. 'Through what halls of Life had its soft step echoed, and in the end, with what courage had it trodden down the dusty ways of Death!' muses Holly. And then 'I wrapped up this relic of the past . . . and put it away in my Gladstone bag, which I had bought at the Army and Navy Stores—a strange combination, I thought' (p. 105). In Chapter XXV, deep in the bowels of the mountain and on their way to the place where the Spirit of Life eternally revolves, Holly lights a lamp with his 'box of Bryant and May's wax matches, [which] struck as merrily, there, in that awful place, as they could have done in a London drawing-room' (p. 244). In Chapter I Holly's college friend Vincey, revealing his fabulously ancient lineage, states that one of his ancestors was a Spartan hero and another a priest of Isis who 'broke his vows of celibacy and fled from Egypt with a Princess of Royal blood who had fallen in love with him' (p. 19). He goes on, presumably with a straight face, to explain that the recent, English scions of the family 'have preserved a dead level of respectability', and that his own grandfather 'made a considerable fortune out of brewing, and retired' (p. 20). In Chapter III, after giving the inscrip-tion on the Sherd of Amenartas in the original uncial script, together with a cursive transcription 'for general convenience in reading' (p. 38), Holly remarks that Vincey's English translation of it is, 'as the reader may easily see by comparison, both accurate and elegant' (p. 40). At the end of the same chapter Leo Vincey displays his reverence for the mysterious artefacts and documents which send him on his inherited mission of romantic revenge by saying to Holly, 'we may as well stow these things away and go up to town to see about our guns' (p. 50). Under attack by the Amahagger and likely to die, Leo, Holly, and Job exchange solemn farewells. 'At that moment, with an exclamation, Job lifted his revolver and fired, and hit a man—not the man he had aimed at, by the way: anything that Job shot *at* was perfectly safe' (p. 96). Holly does not confine his jokes to Job; he is not above making fun of the allegedly awe-inspiring-and-staggeringly-inconceivable theme of his narrative. 'True', he remarks in Chapter XXI, 'in uniting himself to this dread woman, he [Leo] would place his life under the influence of a mysterious creature of evil tendencies, but then that would be likely enough to happen to him in any ordinary marriage' (p. 215). In Chapter XVII, when Ayesha 'recognizes' Leo as Kallikrates, she at first believes that Holly has deliberately concealed his identity from her: she springs at Holly 'like a tigress', her voice is like 'the hiss of a snake', and Holly thinks she is about to kill him. Then, when she realizes that he is not to blame, 'she began to sob and to laugh, and generally to conduct herself like any other lady who is a little upset' (p. 178). Alongside these deliberate effects are moments of inspired bathos and spectacular bad taste. During the scene of Ayesha's agony in Chapter XIV, which Holly describes as gripping him with 'the power of fascinated terror', he suddenly worries about being discovered: 'Supposing she should hear me, or see me through the curtain, *supposing I even sneezed*, or that her magic told her that she was being watched—swift indeed would be my doom' (p. 150, my italics). When, in Chapter XV, Ayesha condemns the men who have attempted to murder Holly and Leo to a terrible death by torture, Holly begs her to show mercy; but in reporting her refusal, he cannot refrain from interrupting the very syntax of her reply with a learned aside on the peculiarities of her Greek accent (p. 161).

These examples conflict with the tendency of readers and critics—from Freud and Jung to, most recently, Sandra M. Gilbert and Susan Gubar—to interpret the action, characters, and landscape of *She* as symbolic or culturally symptomatic. This is not to say that such interpretations are wrong or unhelpful. Gilbert and Gubar are especially acute in defining the lineage of the 'femme fatale' to which Ayesha belongs, and in reconstructing the social and literary context in which Haggard's fantasy, overdetermined as it was by private and public anxieties about race, gender, imperial decline, and religious scepticism, proved so astoundingly popular. Nevertheless there is something disturbing about the very facility with which *She* lends itself to being read as a cultural document or case-history of neurosis and perversion. A psychoanalyst, told that *She-who-must-be-obeyed* was originally the name of a hideous rag doll which lived in a deep, dark nursery cupboard and was used by Haggard's nurse to frighten him, might be forgiven for suspecting a leg-pull.[18] This detail, of course, is outside the text; but there are plenty of equivalent give-aways inside it, as Gilbert and Gubar notice. The delightful Amahagger custom of 'hot-potting', for example, 'is such a vivid enactment of both castration fears and birth anxieties that it is hardly necessary to rehearse all its psychosymbolic overtones' (p. 14), and 'The "rolling pillar of Life" that brings Haggard's romance to its apocalyptic climax is an almost theatrically rich sexual symbol . . . it seems clear from the pillar's celestial radiance and regenerative power that this perpetually erect symbol of masculinity is not just a Freudian penis but a Lacanian phallus, a fiery signifier whose eternal thundering return speaks the inexorability of the patriarchal law She has violated in her Satanically overreaching ambition' (p. 20). The note of caution in 'almost theatrically rich', which registers the critics' sense that Haggard is making things too easy for them, is swept away by the trumpet-blast of interpretation at the end (as grand and sonorous as some of Haggard's own writing). The motive for such rhetoric may be the desire, or need, to bring otherwise inexplicably enduring works of imagination into a modern focus. As Gilbert and Gubar put it, '*She* was not only a turn-of-the-century bestseller but also, in a number of dramatic ways, one of the century's literary turning-points, a pivot on which the ideas and anxieties of the Victorians began to swivel into what has come to be called "the modern" ' (p. 21). But in the transformation of *She* from popular

---

[18] Lilias Rider Haggard, *The Cloak that I Left*, pp. 28–9. Haggard himself, in *The Days of My Life*, says that the doll was used to terrify his brothers and sisters, not himself (i. 248).

romance into exemplary text, ripe for ideological 'unmasking', something may be elided or overlooked—something to do with its odd or gratuitous details, its humour, and its uneven tone, and all centred around the figure of Holly, the book's narrator.

Take, for example, the 'apocalyptic climax' of the book, in which Ayesha bathes herself for the second time in the fire of life, in the belief that it will confirm and renew her near-immortal youth and beauty, only to find that it reverses the process and destroys her:

'Oh, *look!—look!—look!*' shrieked Job, in a shrill falsetto of terror, his eyes nearly dropping out of his head, and foam upon his lips. '*Look!—look!—look!* she's shrivelling up! she's turning into a monkey!' . . . Smaller she grew, and smaller yet, till she was no larger than a baboon. . . . She, who but two minutes before had gazed upon us the loveliest, noblest, most splendid woman the world has ever seen, she lay still before us . . . no larger than a big monkey, and hideous—ah, too hideous for words. (p. 257)

Why this insistence on the image of the monkey? For Henry Miller (pp. 91–2), what happens to Ayesha is a Darwinian inversion, a 'devolution' from a higher to a lower form, which signifies Nature's punishment of Ayesha's female presumption. Gilbert and Gubar, who agree with this judgement (though not, of course, with Miller's approval of it), add that when Holly claims to see 'the finger of Providence' in Ayesha's fate 'he begins to articulate the secret fear that really energizes Haggard's fantasy', the fear of the very principle of female power and its 'terrible priority' (p. 21). If we look back over the book, however, we find the monkey-image, and its Darwinian connotation, occupying a quite different place. It applies not to Ayesha but to Holly. With his bow-legs, deep chest, long arms, and hairy features, 'he reminded me forcibly of a gorilla' says the story's fictional 'Editor' (p. 11). In the opening scene of his narrative, Holly describes himself staring at his face in the mirror (that classic feminine pose) and *reflecting* (his own pun) on his ugliness: 'Short, thick-set, and deep-chested almost to deformity, with long sinewy arms, heavy features, deep-set grey eyes, a low brow half overgrown with a mop of thick black hair . . . Women hated the sight of me. Only a week before I had heard one call me a "monster" when she thought I was out of hearing, and say that I had converted her to the monkey theory' (pp. 16–17). Holly's nickname, conferred on him by

Billali, is 'the Baboon'. For Holly, therefore, to compare Ayesha's shrivelled form to a monkey's and a baboon's is not reducible to Haggard making an abstract ideological point. Holly's character is dramatically conceived, as is the case with all first-person narrators, and particularly those whose tales are enclosed in narrative 'frames' which distance them further from their authors—*Frankenstein*, to take a pertinent example. 'Like Cain, I was branded—branded by Nature with the stamp of abnormal ugliness, as I was gifted by Nature with iron and abnormal strength and considerable intellectual powers.' Holly's self-description fits that of the monster in Mary Shelley's romance, with whom he shares, too, his orphan state and his extreme alienation.

The 'Editor' notices the sexual bias of Holly's alienation or misanthropy, and its connection with his feelings for Leo, on the one occasion he meets him: when two ladies, one of them a 'pretty fair-haired girl', approach them in the street, Holly

stopped short in his talk, cast a reproachful look at his companion [Leo], and, with an abrupt nod to myself, turned and marched off alone across the street. I heard afterwards that he was popularly supposed to be as much afraid of a woman as most people are of a mad dog . . . I cannot say, however, that young Vincey showed much aversion to feminine society on this occasion. (p. 12)

Holly himself does not attribute his aversion to fear, but to his sense of being 'hated' for his ugliness. It gives an edge to his apparently naïve sexism, as in his 'terrifying reflection' that 'nearly all our deep love for women who are not our kindred depends—at any rate, in the first instance—upon their personal appearance' (p. 261, footnote). In another mirror-scene in Chapter I, he relates how he was jilted by a woman who had 'pretended to care for [him]':

I pleaded with her as I have never pleaded with any living creature before or since . . . and in the end by way of answer she took me to the glass, and stood side by side with me, and looked into it.

'Now,' she said, 'if I am Beauty' who are you?' (p. 17)

The poignancy of this image of Beauty and the Beast comes from the fact that it is not fixed to Holly's relations with women, but applies also to his relationship with Leo. 'When he was about fifteen', Holly tells us, 'they used to call him Beauty about the College, and me they

nicknamed the Beast. Beauty and the Beast was what they called us
when we went out walking together, as we used to do every day'
(p. 28). To go 'out walking together' is close to 'walking out
together', or courting; Leo's beauty offers Holly affection and devotion, whose filial aspect assures its propriety and allows its open
expression. Moreover, Holly has complete control over the relationship, since the child, with its mysterious provenance and destiny, has
been literally willed to him by Leo's father. 'I like you', says the five-
year-old Leo when he first sees his guardian, 'you is ugly, but you is
good' (p. 27). We should remember that this declaration is made at
the moment when Leo's nurse, an 'elderly person, who wept bitterly
at parting with him' has 'finally tor[n] herself away and left him'
(pp. 26–7). For Holly has determined to segregate Leo from female
nurture or companionship: 'I would have no woman to lord it over
me about the child, and steal his affections from me' (p. 26). The
child, who has lost his mother, now loses her surrogate: he turns to
Holly with a gesture whose spontaneity is, in the circumstances, a
little forced.

The compensation to Holly is not, however, merely that of an
erotic object which, under his legal and emotional guidance, returns
his love instead of rejecting it; Haggard has made his romance both
more complex and more interesting. For if Ayesha's final degrading
metamorphosis from divine to sub-human enacts Holly's misogyn-
istic revenge on the Beauties who have made him into a Beast, then
Leo, too, has his share in this retribution. To put it another way, Leo
might have some cause for complaint about his treatment in the
story. He is not, after all, the hero of an anonymous third-person
narrative, as his central role in the plot—his reuniting with Ayesha
after two thousand years of successive reincarnations—might have
led him to expect. Had he been such a hero, how would Holly have
appeared? In a 'best supporting' role, no more; instead of which, the
star part is Holly's *because Holly controls the narrative*. It is an object
lesson in the balance of fictional power: what matters is not your
apparent role (for Leo would then be unquestionably the star, or at
least the male lead) but who is in charge of the production.[19]

[19] There is a striking difference between the way the relationship between plain
narrator and handsome hero is handled in *She* and in the Allan Quatermain novels, *King
Solomon's Mines* and *Allan Quatermain*, where the handsome Sir Henry Curtis is given
much more respect, though still with the sense that Quatermain has something in

As it is, Leo is represented with relentless consistency as a dumb blond. Andrew Lang, in the same letter in which he spoke of his unease at the book's humour, remarked (with considerable under-statement): 'There is a difficulty about Leo. He is not made a very interesting person. Probably he was only a fine animal.' Haggard responded by adding a postscript to the 'Editor's' introductory chapter (p. 15), actually drawing attention to this evident gap in intel-lectual capacity between Leo and Holly, which would seem to make Holly a fitter mate for Ayesha; but his explanation—'that Ayesha, seeing further than we can see, perceived the germ and smouldering spark of greatness which lay hid within her lover's soul'—far from answering Lang's doubts, anticipates with sly humour the difficulty which we mere mortals are going to have in the course of the book to discern this spark, which remains well and truly 'hid'. Holly calls Leo 'brilliant and keen-witted, but not a scholar. He had not the dulness necessary for that result' (p. 28); but Leo's brilliance and keen wits are nowhere evident in the story (except in his spotting the remains of the ancient wharf in Chapter V) whereas his dullness shines out at every opportunity.

'Well,' I said . . . 'that is the conclusion of the whole matter, Leo, and now you can form your own opinion on it. I have already formed mine.'
   'And what is it?' he asked, in his quick way. (pp. 48–9)

When he does form his own opinion, he expresses it in characteristic style. 'Yes, I shall go, Uncle; and if I don't find the "rolling Pillar of Life," at any rate I shall get some first-class shooting' (p. 50). Though plunged into guilt and gloom by succumbing to Ayesha's charms over the dead body of Ustane, whom Ayesha has murdered, Leo soon recovers; the following morning he embraces Ayesha with, Holly caustically notes, 'more alacrity and fervour than in strictness courtesy required' (p. 220). Then Ayesha reveals that Holly has 'not forgotten how to turn a pretty phrase about a lady's eyes'. ' "Hulloa, old fellow!" whispered Leo, with a return of his old cheerfulness, "have you been paying compliments? I should never have thought it of you!" ' (p. 221). Leo's response to tumbling down into a dark

reserve which goes beyond looks or (in Sir Henry's case) aristocratic breeding. In the finale of *Allan Quatermain* Sir Henry takes on the role of narrator himself and 'corrects' some of the impressions given by Quatermain in the main body of the narrative; it would be unthinkable for Leo to do the same in *She*. He simply wouldn't be up to it.

cavern in the hollow of a mountain is equally hearty. ' "Hulloa, old fellow!" he called out, "are you there? This is getting interesting, is it not?" ' (p. 244). Even more noticeable than these bird-brained utterances are the things Leo is *not* given to say or think. It is Holly whose consciousness is the focus of the narrative: Holly who is the primary observer of the scene and mediator of the ideas it suggests. No descriptions of flora and fauna for Leo, no recording of curious native customs, no philosophizing about life, the universe, and everything. Holly's greater strength of mind also has a physical counterpart. It is Leo who is overcome and wounded in the fight with the Amahagger (he is saved by Ustane), and Leo who catches fever in the journey across the marshes. This illness ensures that it is Holly, not Leo, who first encounters Ayesha, Holly who first converses with her (in the majestic platitudes and archaic syntax which Haggard offers as signs of intellectual prowess), Holly who is given the first guided tour of the fallen empire of Kôr (an occasion for yet more sententious banalities about the Lot of Man and the Meaning of It All). Leo's weakness is emphasized by quite minor details, as in Chapter IV when he is knocked unconscious during the storm which wrecks the dhow, so that all the excitement of the whale-boat's passage through the reefs simply passes him by, or in Chapter V when he misses the buck and Holly kills it (despite the fact that Leo is supposed to be the better shot).[20] Nor is Leo given much to do in his sexual relationships with Ustane and Ayesha. In both cases he is chosen, or rather claimed, as their property; his role is limited to that of acceptance, and he never says anything which matches Ustane's song in Chapter VII or Ayesha's equally exalted 'epithalamium' in Chapter XX. At the end of Chapter VII it is made clear that Leo becomes Ustane's lover; and yet, in the act of drawing him to her, Ustane is described by Holly as having 'a look of the most utter tenderness . . . she took his head between her hands, and kissed him on the forehead as a mother might'. To both Ustane and Ayesha, Leo is as much a patient, or infant, to be nursed, as a lover. The relationship between Holly and Ayesha is—to the reader—far more erotic than that between her and Leo. Once again, it is Holly's position as narrator

---

[20] On one occasion only does Leo prove himself physically superior to Holly, and that is in Ch. XXVII, in the aftermath of Ayesha's destruction, when they are making their way back through the mountain; Holly fails to accomplish the leap over the gulf, and Leo has to rescue him.

which gives him the advantage: he is the one who directly describes Ayesha's irresistible body and the feelings it arouses in him; we have Leo's feelings at second hand.

If the hero of the story is treated with ambivalence by its narrator, what of the eponymous heroine? The cruelty of Holly's first beloved, who displays her beauty and shows him his own ugliness in the mirror, is magnified by that of Ayesha in proportion as her beauty is infinitely greater and her desire inalienably directed towards someone else. But as narrator, Holly is in a position of power over Ayesha which more than compensates for her power over him within the narrative. The story Holly purportedly tells is of the awe with which Ayesha inspired him, the hopeless unrequited passion he conceived for her, her incomparable physical appearance and majestic intellect. These appearances are deceptive, though. If Ayesha condescends to Holly, he is quite capable of returning the favour: 'she gave a little sob, and I saw that after all she was only a woman, although she might be a very old one' (p. 145); more important, she is subjected to Holly by virtue of being his literary subject: the Queen of Kôr is not more absolute than Holly in his narrative realm. Holly's power is evident precisely in those scenes where he describes Ayesha's physical beauty, for example when she unveils before him:

She lifted her white and rounded arms—never had I seen such arms before—and slowly, very slowly, withdrew some fastening beneath her hair. Then all of a sudden the long, corpse-like wrappings fell from her to the ground, and my eyes travelled up her form, now only robed in a garb of clinging white that did but serve to show its perfect and imperial shape, instinct with a life that was more than life, and with a certain serpent-like grace that was more than human. On her little feet were sandals, fastened with studs of gold. Then came ankles more perfect than ever sculptor dreamed of. About the waist her white kirtle was fastened by a double-headed snake of solid gold, above which her gracious form swelled up in lines as pure as they were lovely, till the kirtle ended on the snowy argent of her breast, whereon her arms were folded. (p. 143)

For all the narrator's reiterated claim to be struck dumb, to be incompetent or inadequate at his business ('How am I to describe it? I cannot—simply, I cannot! The man does not live whose pen could convey a sense of what I saw', he says in this same passage), the lingering relish of the language here—'slowly, very slowly', 'my eyes travelled up her form', 'a garb of clinging white'—exactly catches the pleasure of the eye, and of the *I* whose pleasure it is. Ayesha is made to strip for Holly; later, when he spies on her in the chamber where she mourns over the corpse of Kallikrates, he witnesses a psychic as well as physical unveiling—'the agony, the blind passion, and the awful vindictiveness *displayed upon* those quivering features' (p. 150, my italics).

The serpent motif which is so noticeable in the passage is another mark of Holly's power over Ayesha, as her interpreter or imagist. It links Ayesha both with Eve and the serpent, as primeval temptress and Lamia-figure; Holly's representation of Ayesha is here influenced by a whole tradition of male identifications of beautiful women with demons and monsters. It is always by his mediation that we see Ayesha; and this mediation is not motiveless and certainly not neutral. Holly's purpose in sending the 'Editor' his manuscript, as he announces it in his letter, is high-minded and altruistic: 'it has become a question whether we are justified in withholding from the world an account of a phenomenon which we believe to be of unparalleled interest, merely because our private life is involved' (p. 13). But the 'phenomenon' with which his narrative most eloquently deals is not 'She' in herself but his own creation of her. 'My empire is of the imagination', Ayesha tells Holly (p. 161); but the phrase applies with a vengeance to Holly. It is in the figure of his narrator that Haggard has invested his real authority. The title of a contemporary parody—*He*—has a glimpse of this ironic truth; or perhaps *I* would be even closer to the mark. After all, one of Haggard's most vivid memories of *She* was the moment when he delivered the manuscript to the office of his literary agent, A. P. Watt. 'There', he said, throwing it on the table, 'is what I shall be remembered by.'[21] He was right, too.

[21] *The Days of My Life*, i. 246.

NOTE ON THE TEXT

She was first published as a serial in the *Graphic* magazine, vols. 34–5, nos. 879–93, beginning 2 October 1886 and concluding 8 January 1887. The first English edition was published as soon as the serial had concluded. Haggard made changes between the *Graphic* text and the first edition, some of which, notably those to do with the account of the Sherd of Amenartas in Chapter III, and the death of the Arab servant Mahomed in Chapter VIII, are recorded in the notes. Further revisions were made in later editions, for example those of 1891 and 1896: these revisions were mainly concerned with correcting solecisms and polishing Holly's narrative style. Not all the revisions are improvements; in general I think the roughness of the first edition preferable to its more genteel successors, and I have therefore used it as copy-text for this edition. A small number of misprints have been silently emended; otherwise the text is unchanged.

The footnotes are by Haggard; an asterisk in the text signals an editorial note at the back of the book.

SELECT BIBLIOGRAPHY

Place of publication is London unless stated otherwise.

Editions

There is no collected edition of the works of Henry Rider Haggard, but recent editions include the following:

Allan and the Ice-Gods (Ayer: Salem, New Hampshire, 1976)
Allan Quatermain (Target Books, 1986)
Allan's Wife (Borgo: San Bernardino, California, 1981)
Ayesha (Target Books, 1986)
Cetywayo and His White Neighbours (AMS: New York, 1983)
Eric Brighteyes (Zebra: New York, 1983)
A Farmer's Year (Century Hutchison, 1987)
Heart of the World (Borgo: San Bernardino, California, 1980)
King Solomon's Mines (Oxford, 1989)
The Mahatma and the Hare (Ayer: Salem, New Hampshire, 1978)
Montezuma's Daughter (River City: Los Angeles, 1976)
Morning Star (Zebra: New York, 1978)
Mr. Meeson's Will (Ayer: Salem, New Hampshire, 1976)
Nada the Lily (Borgo: San Bernardino, California, 1980)
The Pearl Maiden (Zebra: New York, 1978)
She and Allan (Borgo: San Bernardino, California, 1980)
When the World Shook (Ayer: Salem, New Hampshire, 1975)
Wisdom's Daughter (Ayer: Salem, New Hampshire, 1978)

Letters

There is no complete edition of the letters but, in addition to those quoted in the biographical studies listed below, there are important holdings of Haggard's correspondence, manuscripts, and other holograph material in the following collections: the Cassell Collection, London; the Cheyne Collection, Suffolk; Columbia University Library, New York; the Higgins Collection, Suffolk; the Huntingdon Library, California; the Lockwood Memorial Library, Buffalo, New York; the John Murray Collection, London; the Norfolk Collection, Norfolk Record Office, Norwich; and the Watt Collection, London.

Autobiography

Haggard, Henry Rider, 'A Visit to the Chief Secocoeni', *The Gentleman's Magazine*, Sept. 1877, pp. 302–18.

Haggard, Henry Rider, 'A Zulu War-Dance', *The Gentleman's Magazine*, July 1877, pp. 94–7.

Haggard, Sir Henry Rider, *The Days of My Life*, ed. C. J. Longman, 2 vols. (Longmans, Green, 1926).

Higgins, D. S. (ed.), *The Private Diaries of Sir H. Rider Haggard 1914–1925* (Cassell, 1980).

Biography and Criticism

Cohen, Morton, *Rider Haggard: His Life and Works* (Hutchinson, 1960).

Cohen, Morton (ed.), *Rudyard Kipling to Rider Haggard: The Record of a Friendship* (Hutchinson, 1965).

Ellis, Peter Berresford, *H. Rider Haggard: A Voice from the Infinite* (Routledge & Kegan Paul, 1978).

Etherington, Norman, *Rider Haggard* (Twayne, Boston, 1984).

Freud, Sigmund, *The Interpretation of Dreams* (1906).

Gilbert, Sandra M., and Gubar, Susan, *No Man's Land, Volume 2: Sexchanges* (1989), esp. chapter 1: 'Heart of Darkness: The Agon of the Femme Fatale'.

Greene, Graham, 'Rider Haggard's Secret', *Collected Essays* (The Bodley Head, 1969), pp. 209–14.

Haggard, H. Rider, 'Fact and Fiction', *The Athenaeum*, No. 3063, 10 July 1886, p. 50.

Haggard, H. Rider, 'Fact and Fiction', *The Athenaeum*, No. 3066, 31 July 1886, p. 144.

Haggard, H. Rider, 'About Fiction', *Contemporary Review*, Feb. 1887, pp. 172–80.

Haggard, Lilias Rider, *The Cloak that I Left: A Biography of the Author Henry Rider Haggard K.B.E. by his daughter* (Hodder & Stoughton, 1951).

Hibbert, Christopher, *Africa Explored: Europeans in the Dark Continent, 1769–1889* (Penguin Books: Harmondsworth, 1984).

Higgins, D. S., *Rider Haggard: The Great Storyteller* (Cassell, 1981).

Jung, Carl, *The Development of the Personality*, trans. R. F. C. Hull; *Collected Works* 17 (Routledge & Kegan Paul, 1954).

Katz, Wendy R., *Rider Haggard and the Fiction of Empire: a Critical Study of British Imperial Fiction* (CUP: Cambridge, 1987).

Lang, Andrew, review of *She*, *Academy*, No. 767, 15 January 1987, pp. 35–6.

Lewis, C. S., 'High and Low Brows', *Rehabilitations and Other Essays* (1939), (repr. Richard West: Pennsylvania, 1978), pp. 100–5.

McClintock, Anne, 'Maidens, Maps and Mines: The Reinvention of Patriarchy in Colonial South Africa', *South Atlantic Quarterly*, 871 (Duke University Press, Durhem, NC, Winter, 1988), 147–91.

Michael, Leo, *She, an Allegory of the Church* (New York: F. F. Lowell & Co., 1889).

Miller, Henry, *The Books in My Life* (Peter Owen, 1952).

Moore, Augustus, 'Rider Haggard and "The New School of Romance" ', *Time*, May 1887, pp. 513–24.

'Ogilvy, Gavin' [J. M. Barrie], 'Mr H. Rider Haggard', *British Weekly*, 5 Aug. 1887, 218.

Paul, J. Balfour, 'Fact and Fiction', *the Athenaeum*, No. 3063, 10 July 1886, p. 50.

Pocock, Tom, *Rider Haggard and the Lost Empire* (Weidenfeld & Nicolson, 1993).

Sandison, Alan, *The Wheel of Empire: A Study of the Imperial Idea in Some Late Nineteenth and Early Twentieth-Century Writers* (Macmillan, 1967).

Scott, J. E., *A Bibliography of the Works of Sir Henry Rider Haggard 1856–1925* (Elkin Matthews: Bishop's Stortford, 1947).

Unsigned review of *She, Pall Mall Gazette*, No. 6802, 4 January 1887, p. 5.

Wilson, A., 'Fact and Fiction', *The Athenaeum*, No. 3063, 10 July 1886, p. 50.

Further Reading in Oxford World's Classics

Haggard, Rider H., *King Solomon's Mines*, ed. Dennis Butts.

A CHRONOLOGY OF H. RIDER HAGGARD

1856 Born at Bradenham, Norfolk, 22 June, sixth son of ten children of William Haggard, barrister and country gentleman.

1866 Sent to Garsington Rectory, near Oxford, to be taught by the Reverend H. J. Graham, and then to Ipswich Grammar School; Haggard has undistinguished school career, except for winning essay-writing competition, but reads traditional romances and has strange forebodings of death.

1873 Fails Army entrance examination; his father sends him to London to prepare for entrance examination for the Foreign Office, where he meets and falls in love with 'Lilith' (Lilly Jackson). He also attends spiritualist seances while living in London.

1875 Unexpectedly Haggard's father finds him a post on the staff of Sir Henry Bulwer, Lieutenant-Governor of Natal; Haggard travels to South Africa, where he meets many natives.

1877 Haggard accompanies Sir Theophilus Shepstone to the Boer Transvaal, which Britain annexes. His articles on Africa begin to be published in London magazines. He is appointed Master and Registrar of the High Court of Justice of the Transvaal, but is shattered by news of Lilly's marriage.

1879 Zulus defeat the British at Isandhlwana. Haggard serves in the Pretoria Horse, but then resigns his legal post and plans to begin ostrich farming. On a visit to England he meets Louisa Margitson, the (orphaned) daughter of the owner of the Ditchingham estate; they marry the following year.

1880 Haggard and Louisa return to South Africa as the first Boer War begins.

1881 Son Arthur John 'Jock' Rider born. Unhappy at political developments, the family return to England and Haggard begins to study law.

1882 Haggard publishes *Cetywayo and his White Neighbours, or Remarks on Recent Events in Zululand, Natal and Transvaal*.

1883 Daughter Agnes Angela Rider born. The family move to Ditchingham House where Haggard works on a novel.

1884 Haggard's first novel, *Dawn*, published, followed by *The Witch's Head* at the end of the year. Daughter Sybil Dorothy Rider born.

1885 Haggard called to the Bar, but writes *King Solomon's Mines*, a great critical and popular success. He then writes *Allan Quatermain* (published 1887), but continues legal practice.

1886 Haggard completes novel, *Jess*, and then writes *She* in six weeks.

1887 Haggard gives up legal work and takes holiday in Egypt while *She* is published to great acclaim. Elected to the Savile Club.

1888 *Maiwa's Revenge*, another Allan Quatermain story, sells 20,000 copies on day of publication. Returning from Iceland, Haggard is almost shipwrecked off Scotland.

1889 *Cleopatra* published. Haggard becomes friendly with Kipling.

1890 Haggard and Andrew Lang publish *The World's Desire*, a novel-sequel to the *Odyssey*.

1891 Haggard and Louisa visit Mexico in search of Inca treasure, but are desolated by news of Jock's death. *Eric Brighteyes*, an Icelandic tale, published.

1892 *Nada the Lily* published. Daughter Lilias Rider born.

1895 Haggard stands as Unionist and Agricultural candidate in Parliamentary election, but loses by 198 votes.

1896 Elected Chairman of the Society of Authors.

1898 *A Farmer's Year* published.

1901 Haggard tours twenty-six counties and writes articles on the state of agriculture, later published as *Rural England* (1902).

1905 Haggard visits America to report on the labour colonies set up for the poor by the Salvation Army; he becomes friendly with President Theodore Roosevelt. *Ayesha—The Return of She* published.

1906 Haggard invited to join the Royal Commission on Coast Erosion and Afforestation.

1912 Haggard made a Knight Bachelor for his public service, and invited to join the Royal Commission on the Dominions. *Marie*, the first of a Zulu trilogy, published.

1913 *Child of Storm*, the second Zulu tale, published.

1914 Haggard returns to South Africa for the Royal Commission, visits the Zimbabwe excavations, and has reunion with his old Zulu servant, Mazooku.

1916 Haggard revisits South Africa, and then travels to Australia, New Zealand, and Canada to discuss the possible settlement of soldiers and sailors in the Dominions after the Great War.

1917   *Finished*, the last of the Zulu trilogy, published.

1918   *Moon of Israel* successfully published, but sales of Haggard's books gradually decline.

1919   Haggard created a Knight Commander of the British Empire.

1921   *She and Allan* published.

1924   Haggard revisits Egypt but falls ill on his return.

1925   Dies 14 May; his ashes buried in Ditchingham Church.

SHE

FACSIMILE OF THE SHERD OF AMENARTAS

One ½ size

Greatest length of the original 10½ inches
Greatest breadth 7 inches
Weight 1lb. 5½oz

FACSIMILE OF THE REVERSE OF THE SHERD OF AMENARTAS

One ½ size

SHE

A HISTORY OF ADVENTURE

BY

H. RIDER HAGGARD

AUTHOR OF

'KING SOLOMON'S MINES' 'DAWN' 'THE WITCH'S HEAD' ETC.

𝔦𝔫 𝔢𝔞𝔯𝔱𝔥 𝔞𝔫𝔡 𝔰𝔨𝔦𝔢 𝔞𝔫𝔡 𝔰𝔢𝔞
𝔰𝔱𝔯𝔞𝔫𝔤𝔢 𝔱𝔥𝔶𝔫𝔤𝔢𝔰 𝔱𝔥𝔢𝔯 𝔟𝔢

Doggerel couplet from the Sherd of Amenartas

LONDON

LONGMANS, GREEN, AND CO.

1887

I INSCRIBE THIS HISTORY

TO

ANDREW LANG*

IN TOKEN OF PERSONAL REGARD

AND OF

MY SINCERE ADMIRATION FOR HIS LEARNING AND HIS WORKS

CONTENTS

	Introduction	11
I.	My Visitor	16
II.	The Years Roll By	24
III.	The Sherd of Amenartas	30
IV.	The Squall	52
V.	The Head of the Ethiopian	60
VI.	An Early Christian Ceremony	70
VII.	Ustane Sings	81
VIII.	The Feast, and After!	91
IX.	A Little Foot	100
X.	Speculations	107
XI.	The Plain of Kôr	116
XII.	'She'	125
XIII.	Ayesha Unveils	135
XIV.	A Soul in Hell	146
XV.	Ayesha Gives Judgment	154
XVI.	The Tombs of Kôr	162
XVII.	The Balance Turns	171
XVIII.	Go, Woman!	182
XIX.	'Give Me a Black Goat!'	192
XX.	Triumph	200
XXI.	The Dead and Living Meet	210
XXII.	Job has a Presentiment	217
XXIII.	The Temple of Truth	227
XXIV.	Walking the Plank	235
XXV.	The Spirit of Life	244
XXVI.	What We Saw	255
XXVII.	We Leap	263
XXVIII.	Over the Mountain	270

In giving to the world the record of what, looked at as an adventure only, is I suppose one of the most wonderful and mysterious experiences ever undergone by mortal men, I feel it incumbent on me to explain what my exact connection with it is. And so I may as well say at once that I am not the narrator but only the editor of this extraordinary history, and then go on to tell how it found its way into my hands.

Some years ago I, the editor, was stopping with a friend, '*vir doctissimus et amicus meus*,'* at a certain University, which for the purposes of this history we will call Cambridge, and was one day much struck with the appearance of two people whom I saw going arm-in-arm down the street. One of these gentlemen was I think, without exception, the handsomest young fellow I have ever seen. He was very tall, very broad, and had a look of power and a grace of bearing that seemed as native to him as it is to a wild stag. In addition his face was almost without flaw—a good face as well as a beautiful one, and when he lifted his hat, which he did just then to a passing lady, I saw that his head was covered with little golden curls growing close to the scalp.

'Good gracious!' I said to my friend, with whom I was walking, 'why, that fellow looks like a statue of Apollo* come to life. What a splendid man he is!'

'Yes,' he answered, 'he is the handsomest man in the University, and one of the nicest too. They call him "the Greek god"; but look at the other one, he's Vincey's (that's the god's name) guardian, and supposed to be full of every kind of information. They call him "Charon." '* I looked, and found the older man quite as interesting in his way as the glorified specimen of humanity at his side. He appeared to be about forty years of age, and was I think as ugly as his companion was handsome. To begin with, he was shortish, rather bow-legged, very deep chested, and with unusually long arms. He had dark hair and small eyes, and the hair grew right down on his forehead, and his whiskers grew right up to his hair, so that there was uncommonly little of his countenance to be seen. Altogether he reminded me forcibly of a gorilla, and yet there was something very

pleasing and genial about the man's eye. I remember saying that I
should like to know him.

'All right,' answered my friend, 'nothing easier. I know Vincey;
I'll introduce you,' and he did, and for some minutes we stood
chatting—about the Zulu people, I think, for I had just returned
from the Cape at the time. Presently, however, a stoutish lady, whose
name I do not remember, came along the pavement, accompanied by
a pretty fair-haired girl, and these two Mr. Vincey, who clearly knew
them well, at once joined, walking off in their company. I remember
being rather amused because of the change in the expression of the
elder man, whose name I discovered was Holly, when he saw the
ladies advancing. He suddenly stopped short in his talk, cast a
reproachful look at his companion, and, with an abrupt nod to
myself, turned and marched off alone across the street. I heard
afterwards that he was popularly supposed to be as much afraid of a
woman as most people are of a mad dog, which accounted for
his precipitate retreat. I cannot say, however, that young Vincey
showed much aversion to feminine society on this occasion. Indeed I
remember laughing, and remarking to my friend at the time that he
was not the sort of man whom it would be desirable to introduce to
the lady one was going to marry, since it is exceedingly probable that
the acquaintance would end in a transfer of her affections. He was
altogether too good-looking, and, what is more, he had none of that
consciousness and conceit about him which usually afflicts handsome men, and makes them deservedly disliked by their fellows.

That same evening my visit came to an end, and this was the last I
saw or heard of 'Charon' and 'the Greek god' for many a long day.
Indeed, I have never seen either of them from that hour to this, and
do not think it probable that I shall. But a month ago I received a
letter and two packets, one of manuscript, and on opening the first
found that it was signed by 'Horace Holly,' a name that at the
moment was not familiar to me. It ran as follows:—

'——College, Cambridge, May 1, 18—

'MY DEAR SIR,—You will be surprised, considering the very
slight nature of our acquaintance, to get a letter from me. Indeed, I
think I had better begin by reminding you that we once met, now
some five years ago, when I and my ward Leo Vincey were intro-
duced to you in the street at Cambridge. To be brief and come to my

business. I have recently read with much interest a book of yours describing a Central African adventure.* I take it that this book is partly true, and partly an effort of the imagination. However this is, it has given me an idea. It happens, how you will see in the accompanying manuscript (which together with the Scarab, the "Royal Son of the Sun," and the original sherd, I am sending to you by hand), that my ward, or rather my adopted son Leo Vincey and myself have recently passed through a real African adventure, of a nature so much more marvellous than the one which you describe, that to tell you the truth I am almost ashamed to submit it to you for fear lest you should disbelieve my tale. You will see it stated in this manuscript that I, or rather we, had made up our minds not to make this history public during our joint lives. Nor should we alter our determination were it not for a circumstance which has recently arisen. We are for reasons that, after perusing this manuscript, you may be able to guess, going away again, this time to Central Asia* where, if anywhere upon this earth, wisdom is to be found, and we anticipate that our sojourn there will be a long one. Possibly we shall not return. Under these altered conditions it has become a question whether we are justified in withholding from the world an account of a phenomenon which we believe to be of unparalleled interest, merely because our private life is involved, or because we are afraid of ridicule and doubt being cast upon our statements. I hold one view about this matter, and Leo holds another, and finally, after much discussion, we have come to a compromise, namely, to send the history to you, giving you full leave to publish it if you think fit, the only stipulation being that you shall disguise our real names, and as much concerning our personal identity as is consistent with the maintenance of the *bona fides* of the narrative.

'And now what am I to say further? I really do not know beyond once more repeating that everything is described in the accompanying manuscript exactly as it happened. As regards *She* herself I have nothing to add. Day by day we have greater occasion to regret that we did not better avail ourselves of our opportunities to obtain more information from that marvellous woman. Who was she? How did she first come to the Caves of Kôr, and what was her real religion? We never ascertained, and now, alas! we never shall, at least not yet. These and many other questions arise in my mind, but what is the good of asking them now?

'Will you undertake the task? We give you complete freedom, and as a reward you will, we believe, have the credit of presenting to the world the most wonderful history, as distinguished from romance, that its records can show. Read the manuscript (which I have copied out fairly for your benefit), and let me know.

'Believe me, very truly yours,

'L. HORACE HOLLY.

'P.S.—Of course, if any profit results from the sale of the writing should you care to undertake its publication, you can do what you like with it, but if there is a loss I will leave instructions with my lawyers, Messrs. Geoffrey and Jordan, to meet it. We entrust the sherd, the scarab, and the parchments to your keeping till such time as we demand them back again.—L. H. H.'

This letter, as may be imagined, astonished me considerably, but when I came to look at the MS., which the pressure of other work prevented me from doing for a fortnight, I was still more astonished, as I think the reader will be also, and at once made up my mind to press on with the matter. I wrote to this effect to Mr. Holly, but a week afterwards received a letter from that gentleman's lawyers, returning my own, with the information that their client and Mr. Leo Vincey had already left this country for Thibet, and they did not at present know their address.

Well, that is all I have to say. Of the history itself the reader must judge. I give it him, with the exception of a very few alterations, made with the object of concealing the identity of the actors from the general public, exactly as it has come to me. Personally I have made up my mind to refrain from comments. At first I was inclined to believe that this history of a woman on whom, clothed in the majesty of her almost endless years, the shadow of Eternity itself lay like the dark wing of Night, was some gigantic allegory of which I could not catch the meaning. Then I thought that it might be a bold attempt to portray the possible results of practical immortality, informing the substance of a mortal who yet drew her strength from Earth, and in whose human bosom passions yet rose and fell and beat as in the undying world around her the winds and the tides rise and fall and beat unceasingly. But as I went on I abandoned that idea also. To me the story seems to bear the stamp of truth upon its face. Its explanation I must leave to others, and with this slight preface, which circumstances make necessary, I introduce the world to Ayesha and the Caves of Kôr.—THE EDITOR.

P.S.—There is on consideration one circumstance that, after a reperusal of this history, struck me with so much force that I cannot resist calling the attention of the reader to it. He will observe that so far as we are made acquainted with him there appears to be nothing in the character of Leo Vincey which in the opinion of most people would have been likely to attract an intellect so powerful as that of Ayesha. He is not even, at any rate to my view, particularly interesting. Indeed, one might imagine that Mr. Holly would under ordinary circumstances have easily outstripped him in the favour of *She*. Can it be that extremes meet, and that the very excess and splendour of her mind led her by means of some strange physical reaction to worship at the shrine of matter? Was that ancient Kallikrates nothing but a splendid animal beloved for his hereditary Greek beauty? Or is the true explanation what I believe it to be—namely, that Ayesha, seeing further than we can see, perceived the germ and smouldering spark of greatness which lay hid within her lover's soul, and well knew that under the influence of her gift of life, watered by her wisdom, and shone upon with the sunshine of her presence, it would bloom like a flower and flash out like a star, filling the world with light and fragrance?

Here also I am not able to answer, but must leave the reader to form his own judgment on the facts before him, as detailed by Mr. Holly in the following pages.

THERE are some events of which each circumstance and surrounding detail seems to be graven on the memory in such fashion that we cannot forget it, and so it is with the scene that I am about to describe. It rises as clearly before my mind at this moment as though it had happened yesterday.

It was in this very month something over twenty years ago that I, Ludwig Horace Holly, was sitting one night in my rooms at Cambridge, grinding away at some mathematical work, I forget what. I was to go up for my fellowship within a week, and was expected by my tutor and my college generally to distinguish myself. At last, wearied out, I flung my book down, and, going to the mantelpiece, took down a pipe and filled it. There was a candle burning on the mantelpiece, and a long, narrow glass at the back of it; and as I was in the act of lighting the pipe I caught sight of my own countenance in the glass, and paused to reflect. The lighted match burnt away till it scorched my fingers, forcing me to drop it; but still I stood and stared at myself in the glass, and reflected.

'Well,' I said aloud, at last, 'it is to be hoped that I shall be able to do something with the inside of my head, for I shall certainly never do anything by the help of the outside.'

This remark will doubtless strike anybody who reads it as being slightly obscure, but I was in reality alluding to my physical deficiencies. Most men of twenty-two are endowed at any rate with some share of the comeliness of youth, but to me even this was denied. Short, thick-set, and deep-chested almost to deformity, with long sinewy arms, heavy features, deep-set grey eyes, a low brow half overgrown with a mop of thick black hair, like a deserted clearing on which the forest had once more begun to encroach; such was my appearance nearly a quarter of a century ago, and such, with some modification, is it to this day. Like Cain, I was branded*—branded by Nature with the stamp of abnormal ugliness, as I was gifted by Nature with iron and abnormal strength and considerable intellectual powers. So ugly was I that the spruce young men of my College, though they were proud enough of my feats of endurance and physical prowess, did not even care to be seen walking with me. Was it wonderful that I was misanthropic and sullen? Was it wonderful that I brooded and worked alone, and had no friends—at least, only one? I was set apart by Nature to live alone, and draw comfort from her breast, and hers only. Women hated the sight of me. Only a week before I had heard one call me a 'monster' when she thought I was out of hearing, and say that I had converted her to the monkey theory.* Once, indeed, a woman pretended to care for me, and I lavished all the pent-up affection of my nature upon her. Then money that was to have come to me went elsewhere, and she discarded me. I pleaded with her as I have never pleaded with any living creature before or since, for I was caught by her sweet face, and loved her; and in the end by way of answer she took me to the glass, and stood side by side with me, and looked into it.

'Now,' she said, 'if I am Beauty, who are you?' That was when I was only twenty.

And so I stood and stared, and felt a sort of grim satisfaction in the sense of my own loneliness; for I had neither father, nor mother, nor brother; and as I did so there came a knock at my door.

I listened before I went to open it, for it was nearly twelve o'clock at night, and I was in no mood to admit any stranger. I had but one friend in the College, or, indeed, in the world—perhaps it was he.

Just then the person outside the door coughed, and I hastened to open it, for I knew the cough.

A tall man of about thirty, with the remains of great personal beauty, came hurrying in, staggering beneath the weight of a massive iron box which he carried by a handle with his right hand. He placed the box upon the table, and then fell into an awful fit of coughing. He coughed and coughed till his face became quite purple, and at last he sank into a chair and began to spit up blood. I poured out some whisky into a tumbler, and gave it to him. He drank it, and seemed better; though his better was very bad indeed.

'Why did you keep me standing there in the cold?' he asked pettishly. 'You know the draughts are death to me.'

'I did not know who it was,' I answered. 'You are a late visitor.'

'Yes; and I verily believe it is my last visit,' he answered, with a ghastly attempt at a smile. 'I am done for, Holly. I am done for. I do not believe that I shall see to-morrow!'

'Nonsense!' I said. 'Let me go for a doctor.'

He waved me back imperiously with his hand. 'It is sober sense; but I want no doctors. I have studied medicine, and I know all about it. No doctors can help me. My last hour has come! For a year past I have only lived by a miracle. Now listen to me as you never listened to anybody before; for you will not have the opportunity of getting me to repeat my words. We have been friends for two years; now tell me how much do you know about me?'

'I know that you are rich, and have had a fancy to come to College long after the age that most men leave it. I know that you have been married, and that your wife died; and that you have been the best, indeed almost the only friend I ever had.'

'Did you know that I have a son?'

'No.'

'I have. He is five years old. He cost me his mother's life, and I have never been able to bear to look upon his face in consequence. Holly, if you will accept the trust, I am going to leave you that boy's sole guardian.'

I sprang almost out of my chair. '*Me!*' I said.

'Yes, you. I have not studied you for two years for nothing. I have known for some time that I could not last, and since I realised the fact I have been searching for some one to whom I could confide the boy and this,' and he tapped the iron box. 'You are the man, Holly; for, like a rugged tree, you are hard and sound at core. Listen; the boy will be the only representative of one of the most ancient families in the world, that is, so far as families can be traced. You will laugh at me when I say it, but one day it will be proved to you beyond a doubt, that my sixty-fifth or sixty-sixth lineal ancestor was an Egyptian priest of Isis,* though he was himself of Grecian extraction, and was called Kallikrates.[1] His father was one of the Greek mercenaries raised by Hak-Hor,* a Mendesian Pharaoh of the twenty-ninth dynasty, and his grandfather, I believe, was that very Kallikrates mentioned by Herodotus.[2]* In or about the year 339 before Christ,

---

[1] The Strong and Beautiful, or, more accurately, the Beautiful in strength.

[2] The Kallikrates here referred to by my friend was a Spartan, spoken of by Herodotus (Herod. ix. 72) as being remarkable for his beauty. He fell at the glorious battle of Platæa (September 22, B.C. 479), when the Lacedæmonians* and Athenians under Pausanias routed the Persians, putting nearly 300,000 of them to the sword. The following is a translation of the passage, 'For Kallikrates died out of the battle, he came to the army the most beautiful man of the Greeks of that day—not only of the Lacedæmonians themselves, but of the other Greeks also. He when Pausanias was sacrificing was

just at the time of the final fall of the Pharaohs, this Kallikrates (the priest) broke his vows of celibacy and fled from Egypt with a Princess of Royal blood who had fallen in love with him, and was finally wrecked upon the coast of Africa, somewhere, as I believe, in the neighbourhood of where Delagoa Bay* now is, or rather to the north of it, he and his wife being saved, and all the remainder of their company destroyed in one way or another. Here they endured great hardships, but were at last entertained by the mighty Queen of a savage people, a white woman of peculiar loveliness, who, under circumstances which I cannot enter into, but which you will one day learn, if you live, from the contents of the box, finally murdered my ancestor, Kallikrates. His wife, however, escaped, how I know not, to Athens, bearing a child with her, whom she named Tisisthenes, or the Mighty Avenger. Five hundred years or more afterwards the family migrated to Rome under circumstances of which no trace remains, and here, probably with the idea of preserving the idea of vengeance which we find set out in the name of Tisisthenes, they appear to have pretty regularly assumed the cognomen of Vindex, or Avenger. Here, too, they remained for another five centuries or more, till about 770 A.D., when Charlemagne invaded Lombardy,* where they were then settled, whereon the head of the family seems to have attached himself to the great Emperor, and to have returned with him across the Alps, and finally to have settled in Brittany. Eight generations later his lineal representative crossed to England in the reign of Edward the Confessor,* and in the time of William the Conqueror was advanced to great honour and power. From that time till the present day I can trace my descent without a break. Not that the Vinceys—for that was the final corruption of the name after its bearers took root in English soil—have been particularly distinguished—they never came much to the fore. Sometimes they were soldiers, sometimes merchants, but on the whole they have preserved a dead level of respectability, and a still deader level of mediocrity. From the time of Charles II. till the beginning of the

---

wounded in the side by an arrow; and then they fought, but on being carried off he regretted his death, and said to Arimnestus, a Platæan, that he did not grieve at dying for Greece, but at not having struck a blow, or, although he desired so to do, performed any deed worthy of himself.' This Kallikrates, who appears to have been as brave as he was beautiful, is subsequently mentioned by Herodotus as having been buried among the ἰρένες (young commanders), apart from the other Spartans and the Helots.—
L. H. H.

present century they were merchants. About 1790 my grandfather made a considerable fortune out of brewing, and retired. In 1821 he died, and my father succeeded him, and dissipated most of the money. Ten years ago he died also, leaving me a net income of about two thousand a year. Then it was that I undertook an expedition in connection with *that*,' and he pointed to the iron chest, 'which ended disastrously enough. On my way back I travelled in the South of Europe, and finally reached Athens. There I met my beloved wife, who might well also have been called the "Beautiful," like my old Greek ancestor. There I married her, and there, a year afterwards, when my boy was born, she died.'

He paused a while, his head sunk upon his hand, and then continued—

'My marriage had diverted me from a project which I cannot enter into now. I have no time, Holly—I have no time! One day, if you accept my trust, you will learn all about it. After my wife's death I turned my mind to it again. But first it was necessary, or, at least, I conceived that it was necessary, that I should attain to a perfect knowledge of Eastern dialects, especially Arabic. It was to facilitate my studies that I came here. Very soon, however, my disease developed itself, and now there is an end of me.' And as though to emphasise his words he burst into another terrible fit of coughing.

I gave him some more whisky, and after resting he went on—

'I have never seen my boy, Leo, since he was a tiny baby. I never could bear to see him, but they tell me that he is a quick and handsome child. In this envelope,' and he produced a letter from his pocket addressed to myself, 'I have jotted down the course I wish followed in the boy's education. It is a somewhat peculiar one. At any rate, I could not entrust it to a stranger. Once more, will you undertake it?'

'I must first know what I am to undertake,' I answered.

'You are to undertake to have the boy, Leo, to live with you till he is twenty-five years of age—not to send him to school, remember. On his twenty-fifth birthday your guardianship will end, and you will then, with the keys that I give you now' (and he placed them on the table), 'open the iron box, and let him see and read the contents, and say whether or no he is willing to undertake the quest. There is no obligation on him to do so. Now, as regards terms. My present income is two thousand two hundred a year. Half of that income I have secured to you by will for life contingently on your undertaking the guardianship—that is, one thousand a year remuneration to yourself, for you will have to give up your life to it, and one hundred a year to pay for the board of the boy. The rest is to accumulate till Leo is twenty-five, so that there may be a sum in hand should he wish to undertake the quest of which I spoke.'

'And suppose I were to die?' I asked.

'Then the boy must become a ward of Chancery* and take his chance. Only be careful that the iron chest is passed on to him by your will. Listen, Holly, don't refuse me. Believe me, this is to your advantage. You are not fit to mix with the world—it would only embitter you. In a few weeks you will become a Fellow of your College, and the income that you will derive from that combined with what I have left you will enable you to live a life of learned leisure, alternated with the sport of which you are so fond,* such as will exactly suit you.'

He paused and looked at me anxiously, but I still hesitated. The charge seemed so very strange.

'For my sake, Holly. We have been good friends, and I have no time to make other arrangements.'

'Very well,' I said, 'I will do it, provided there is nothing in this paper to make me change my mind,' and I touched the envelope he had put upon the table by the keys.

'Thank you, Holly, thank you. There is nothing at all. Swear to me by God that you will be a father to the boy, and follow my directions to the letter.'

'I swear it,' I answered solemnly.

'Very well, remember that perhaps one day I shall ask for the account of your oath, for though I am dead and forgotten, yet shall I live.* There is no such thing as death, Holly, only a change,* and, as you may perhaps learn in time to come, I believe that even here that change could under certain circumstances be indefinitely postponed,' and again he broke into one of his dreadful fits of coughing.

'There,' he said, 'I must go, you have the chest, and my will will be found among my papers, under the authority of which the child will be handed over to you. You will be well paid, Holly, and I know that you are honest, but if you betray my trust, by Heaven I will haunt you.'

I said nothing, being, indeed, too bewildered to speak.

He held up the candle, and looked at his own face in the glass. It had been a beautiful face, but disease had wrecked it. 'Food for the worms,' he said. 'Curious to think that in a few hours I shall be stiff and cold—the journey done, the little game played out. Ah me, Holly! life is not worth the trouble of life, except when one is in love—at least, mine has not been; but the boy Leo's may be if he has the courage and the faith. Good-bye, my friend!' and with a sudden access of tenderness he flung his arm about me and kissed me on the forehead, and then turned to go.

'Look here, Vincey,' I said, 'if you are as ill as you think, you had better let me fetch a doctor.'

'No, no,' he said earnestly. 'Promise me that you won't. I am going to die, and, like a poisoned rat, I wish to die alone.'

'I don't believe that you are going to do anything of the sort,' I answered. He smiled, and, with the word 'Remember' on his lips, was gone.* As for myself, I sat down and rubbed my eyes, wondering if I had been asleep. As this supposition would not bear investigation I gave it up, and began to think that Vincey must have been drinking. I knew that he was, and had been, very ill, but still it seemed impossible that he could be in such a condition as to be able to know for certain that he would not outlive the night. Had he been so near dissolution surely he would scarcely have been able to walk, and carry a heavy iron box with him. The whole story, on reflection, seemed to me utterly incredible, for I was not then old enough to be aware how many things happen in this world that the common sense of the average man would set down as so improbable as to be absolutely impossible. This is a fact that I have only recently mastered. Was it likely that a man would have a son five years of age whom he had never seen since he was a tiny infant? No. Was it likely that he could foretell his own death so accurately? No. Was it likely that he could trace his pedigree for more than three centuries before Christ, or that he would suddenly confide the absolute guardianship of his child, and leave half his fortune, to a college friend? Most certainly not. Clearly Vincey was either drunk or mad. That being so, what did it mean? and what was in the sealed iron chest?

The whole thing baffled and puzzled me to such an extent that at last I could stand it no longer, and determined to sleep over it. So I jumped up, and having put the keys and the letter that Vincey had left away into my despatch-box, and stowed the iron chest in a large portmanteau, I turned in, and was soon fast asleep.

As it seemed to me, I had only been asleep for a few minutes when I was awakened by somebody calling me. I sat up and rubbed my eyes; it was broad daylight—eight o'clock, in fact.

'Why, what is the matter with you, John?' I asked of the gyp* who waited on Vincey and myself. 'You look as though you had seen a ghost!'

'Yes, sir, and so I have,' he answered, 'leastways I've seen a corpse, which is worse. I've been in to call Mr. Vincey, as usual, and there he lies stark and dead!'

II

OF course, poor Vincey's sudden death created a great stir in the College; but, as he was known to be very ill, and a satisfactory doctor's certificate was forthcoming, there was no inquest. They were not so particular about inquests in those days as they are now; indeed, they were generally disliked, as causing a scandal. Under all these circumstances, as I was asked no questions, I did not feel called upon to volunteer any information about our interview of the night of Vincey's decease, beyond saying that he had come into my rooms to see me, as he often did. On the day of the funeral a lawyer came down from London and followed my poor friend's remains to the grave, and then went back with his papers and effects, except, of course, the iron chest which had been left in my keeping. For a week after this I heard no more of the matter, and, indeed, my attention was amply occupied in other ways, for I was up for my Fellowship, a fact that had prevented me from attending the funeral or seeing the lawyer. At last, however, the examination was over, and I came back to my rooms and sank into an easy chair with a happy consciousness that I had got through it very fairly.

Soon, however, my thoughts, relieved of the pressure that had crushed them into a single groove during the last few days, turned to the events of the night of poor Vincey's death, and again I asked myself what it all meant, and wondered if I should hear anything more of the matter, and if I did not, what it would be my duty to do with the curious iron chest. I sat there and thought and thought till I began to grow quite disturbed over the whole occurrence: the mysterious midnight visit, the prophecy of death so shortly to be fulfilled, the solemn oath that I had taken, and which Vincey had called on me to answer to in another world than this. Had the man committed suicide? It looked like it. And what was the quest of which he spoke? The circumstances were almost uncanny, so much so that, though I am by no means nervous, or apt to be alarmed at anything that may seem to cross the bounds of the natural, I grew afraid, and began to wish I had had nothing to do with it. How much more do I wish it now, over twenty years afterwards!

As I sat and thought, there was a knock at the door, and a letter, in a big blue envelope, was brought in to me. I saw at a glance that it was a lawyer's letter, and an instinct told me that it was connected with my trust. The letter, which I still have, runs thus:—

'SIR,—Our client, the late M. L. Vincey, Esq., who died on the 9th instant in——College, Cambridge, has left behind him a Will, of which you will please find copy enclosed, and of which we are the executors. By this Will you will perceive that you take a life-interest in about half of the late Mr. Vincey's property, now invested in Consols,* subject to your acceptance of the guardianship of his only son, Leo Vincey, at present an infant, aged five. Had we not ourselves drawn up the document in question in obedience to Mr. Vincey's clear and precise instructions, both personal and written, and had he not then assured us that he had very good reasons for what he was doing, we are bound to tell you that its provisions seem to us of so unusual a nature, that we should have felt bound to call the attention of the Court of Chancery to them, in order that such steps might be taken as seemed desirable to it, either by contesting the capacity of the testator or otherwise, to safeguard the interests of the infant. As it is, knowing that the testator was a gentleman of the highest intelligence and acumen, and that he has absolutely no relations living to whom he could have confided the guardianship of the child, we do not feel justified in taking this course.

'Awaiting such instructions as you please to send us as regards the delivery of the infant and the payment of the proportion of the dividends due to you,

'We remain, Sir, faithfully yours,

'GEOFFREY AND JORDAN.'

I put down the letter, and ran my eye through the Will, which appeared, from its utter unintelligibility, to have been drawn on the strictest legal principles. So far as I could discover, however, it exactly bore out what my friend had told me on the night of his death. So it was true after all. I must take the boy. Suddenly I remembered the letter which he had left with the chest. I fetched it and opened it. It only contained such directions as he had already given to me as to opening the chest on Leo's twenty-fifth birthday, and laid down the outlines of the boy's education, which was to include Greek, the higher Mathematics, and *Arabic*. At the bottom there was a post-script to the effect that if the boy died under the age of twenty-five, which, however, he did not believe would be the case, I was to open the chest, and act on the information I obtained if I saw fit. If I did not see fit, I was to destroy all the contents. On no account was I to pass them on to a stranger.

As this letter added nothing material to my knowledge, and certainly raised no further objection in my mind to undertaking the task I had promised my dead friend to undertake, there was only one course open to me—namely, to write to Messrs. Geoffrey and Jordan, and express my readiness to enter on the trust, stating that I should be willing to commence my guardianship of Leo in ten days' time. This done I proceeded to the authorities of my college, and, having told them as much of the story as I considered desirable, which was not very much, after considerable difficulty succeeded in persuading them to stretch a point, and, in the event of my having obtained a fellowship, which I was pretty certain I had done, allow me to have the child to live with me. Their consent, however, was only granted on the condition that I vacated my rooms in college and took lodgings. This I did, and with some difficulty succeeded in obtaining very good apartments quite close to the college gates. The next thing was to find a nurse. And on this point I came to a determination. I would have no woman to lord it over me about the child, and steal his affections from me. The boy was old enough to do without female assistance, so I set to work to hunt up a suitable male attendant. With some difficulty I succeeded in hiring a most respectable round-faced young man,* who had been a helper in a hunting-stable, but who said that he was one of a family of seventeen and well-accustomed to the ways of children, and professed himself quite willing to undertake the charge of Master Leo when he arrived. Then, having taken the iron box to town, and with my own hands deposited it at my banker's, I bought some books upon the health and management of children, and read them, first to myself, and then aloud to Job—that was the young man's name—and waited.

At length the child arrived in the charge of an elderly person, who wept bitterly at parting with him, and a beautiful boy he was. Indeed, I do not think that I ever saw such a perfect child before or since. His eyes were grey, his forehead broad, and his face, even at that early age, clean cut as a cameo, without being pinched or thin. But perhaps his most attractive point was his hair, which was pure gold in colour and tightly curled over his shapely head. He cried a little when his nurse finally tore herself away and left him with us. Never shall I forget the scene. There he stood, with the sunlight from the window playing upon his golden curls, his fist screwed in one eye, whilst he took us in with the other. I was seated in a chair, and stretched out my hand to him to induce him to come to me, while Job, in the corner, was making a sort of clucking noise, which, arguing from his previous experience, or from the analogy of the hen, he judged would have a soothing effect, and inspire confidence in the youthful mind, and running a wooden horse of peculiar hideousness backwards and forwards in a way that was little short of inane. This went on for some minutes, and then all of a sudden the lad stretched out both his little arms and ran to me.

'I like you,' he said: 'you is ugly, but you is good.'

Ten minutes afterwards he was eating large slices of bread and butter, with every sign of satisfaction; Job wanted to put jam on to them, but I sternly reminded him of the excellent works we had read, and forbade it.

In a very little while (for, as I expected, I got my fellowship) the boy became the favourite of the whole College—where, all orders and regulations to the contrary notwithstanding, he was continually in and out—a sort of chartered libertine, in whose favour all rules were relaxed. The offerings made at his shrine were simply without number, and I had a serious difference of opinion with one old resident Fellow, now long dead, who was usually supposed to be the crustiest man in the University, and to abhor the sight of a child. And yet I discovered, when a frequently recurring fit of sickness had forced Job to keep a strict look-out, that this unprincipled old man was in the habit of enticing the boy to his rooms and there feeding him upon unlimited quantities of brandy-balls, and making him promise to say nothing about it. Job told him that he ought to be ashamed of himself, 'at his age, too, when he might have been a grandfather if he had done what was right,' by which Job understood had got married, and thence arose the row.

But I have no space to dwell upon those delightful years, around which memory still fondly hovers. One by one they went by, and as they passed we two grew dearer and yet more dear to each other. Few sons have been loved as I love Leo, and few fathers know the deep and continuous affection that Leo bears to me.

The child grew into the boy, and the boy into the young man, as one by one the remorseless years flew by, and as he grew and increased so did his beauty and the beauty of his mind grow with him. When he was about fifteen they used to call him Beauty about the College, and me they nicknamed the Beast. Beauty and the Beast was what they called us when we went out walking together, as we used to do every day. Once Leo attacked a great strapping butcher's man,* twice his size, because he sang it out after us, and thrashed him, too—thrashed him fairly. I walked on and pretended not to see, till the combat got too exciting, when I turned round and cheered him on to victory. It was the chaff of the College at the time, but I could not help it. Then when he was a little older the undergraduates got fresh names for us. They called me Charon and Leo the Greek god! I will pass over my own appellation with the humble remark that I was never handsome, and did not grow more so as I grew older. As for his, there was no doubt about its fitness. Leo at twenty-one might have stood for a statue of the youthful Apollo. I never saw anybody to touch him in looks, or anybody so absolutely unconscious of them. As for his mind, he was brilliant and keen-witted, but not a scholar. He had not the dulness necessary for that result. We followed out his father's instructions as regards his education strictly enough, and on the whole the results, especially so far as the Greek and Arabic went, were satisfactory. I learnt the latter language in order to help to teach it to him, but after five years of it he knew it as well as I did—almost as well as the professor who instructed us both. I always was a great sportsman—it is my one passion—and every autumn we went away somewhere shooting or fishing, sometimes to Scotland, sometimes to Norway, once even to Russia. I am a good shot, but even in this he learnt to excel me.

When Leo was eighteen I moved back into my rooms, and entered him at my own College, and at twenty-one he took his degree—a respectable degree, but not a very high one. Then it was that I, for the first time, told him something of his own story, and of the mystery that loomed ahead. Of course he was very curious about it, and of course I explained to him that his curiosity could not be gratified at present. After that, to pass the time away, I suggested that he should get himself called to the Bar; and this he did, reading at Cambridge, and only going up to London to eat his dinners.*

I had only one trouble about him, and that was that every young woman who came across him, or, if not every one, nearly so, would insist on falling in love with him. Hence arose difficulties which I need not enter into here, though they were troublesome enough at the time. On the whole, he behaved fairly well; I cannot say more than that.

And so the time went by till at last he reached his twenty-fifth birthday, at which date this strange and, in some ways, awful history really begins.

III

THE SHERD OF AMENARTAS

On the day preceding Leo's twenty-fifth birthday we both proceeded to London, and extracted the mysterious chest from the bank where I had deposited it twenty years before. It was, I remember, brought up by the same clerk who had taken it down. He perfectly remembered having hidden it away. Had he not done so, he said, he should have had difficulty in finding it, it was so covered up with cobwebs.

In the evening we returned with our precious burden to Cambridge, and I think that we might both of us have given away all the sleep we got that night and not have been much the poorer. At daybreak Leo arrived in my room in a dressing-gown, and suggested that we should at once proceed to business. I scouted the idea as showing an unworthy curiosity. The chest had waited twenty years, I said, so it could very well continue to wait until after breakfast. Accordingly at nine—an unusually sharp nine—we breakfasted; and so occupied was I with my own thoughts that I regret to state that I put a piece of bacon into Leo's tea in mistake for a lump of sugar. Job, too, to whom the contagion of excitement had, of course, spread, managed to break the handle off my Sèvres china tea-cup, the identical one I believe that Marat had been drinking from just before he was stabbed in his bath.

At last, however, breakfast was cleared away, and Job, at my request, fetched the chest, and placed it upon the table in a somewhat gingerly fashion, as though he mistrusted it. Then he prepared to leave the room.

'Stop a moment, Job,' I said. 'If Mr. Leo has no objection, I should prefer to have an independent witness to this business, who can be relied upon to hold his tongue unless he is asked to speak.'

'Certainly, Uncle Horace,' answered Leo; for I had brought him up to call me uncle—though he varied the appellation somewhat disrespectfully by calling me 'old fellow,' or even 'my avuncular relative.'

Job touched his head, not having a hat on.

'Lock the door, Job,' I said, 'and bring me my despatch-box.'

He obeyed, and from the box I took the keys that poor Vincey, Leo's father, had given me on the night of his death. There were three of them: the largest a comparatively modern key, the second an exceedingly ancient one, and the third entirely unlike anything of the sort that we had ever seen before, being fashioned apparently from a strip of solid silver, with a bar placed across to serve as a handle, and some nicks cut in the edge of the bar. It was more like a model of some antediluvian railway key than anything else.

'Now are you both ready?' I said, as people do when they are going to fire a mine.* There was no answer, so I took the big key, rubbed some salad oil into the wards, and after one or two bad shots, for my hands were shaking, managed to fit it, and shoot the lock. Leo bent over and caught the massive lid in both his hands, and with an effort, for the hinges had rusted, leaned it back. Its removal revealed another case covered with dust. This we extracted from the iron chest without any difficulty, and removed the accumulated filth of years from it with a clothes-brush.

It was, or appeared to be, of ebony, or some such close-grained black wood, and was bound in every direction with flat bands of iron. Its antiquity must have been extreme, for the dense heavy wood was actually in parts commencing to crumble away from age.

'Now for it,' I said, inserting the second key.

Job and Leo bent forward in breathless silence. The key turned, and I flung back the lid, and uttered an exclamation, as did the others; and no wonder, for inside the ebony case was a magnificent silver casket, about twelve inches square by eight high. It appeared to be of Egyptian workmanship, for the four legs were formed of Sphinxes, and the dome-shaped cover was also surmounted by a Sphinx. The casket was of course much tarnished and dinted with age, but otherwise in fairly sound condition.

I drew it out and set it on the table, and then, in the midst of the most perfect silence, I inserted the strange-looking silver key, and pressed this way and that until at last the lock yielded, and the casket stood open before us. It was filled to the brim with some brown shredded material, more like vegetable fibre than paper, the nature of which I have never been able to discover. This I carefully removed to the depth of some three inches, when I came to a letter enclosed

in an ordinary modern-looking envelope, and addressed in the
handwriting of my dead friend Vincey.

> '*To my son Leo, should he live to open this casket.*'

I handed the letter to Leo, who glanced at the envelope, and then put
it down upon the table, making a motion to me to go on emptying the
casket.

The next thing that I found was a parchment carefully rolled up. I
unrolled it, and seeing that it was also in Vincey's handwriting, and
headed 'Translation of the Uncial Greek* Writing on the Potsherd,'
put it down by the letter. Then followed another ancient roll of
parchment, that had become yellow and crinkled with the passage of
years. This I also unrolled. It was likewise a translation of the same
Greek original, but into black-letter* Latin this time, which at the
first glance appeared to me from the style and character to date from
somewhere about the beginning of the sixteenth century. Immediately beneath this roll was something hard and heavy, wrapped up in
yellow linen, and reposing upon another layer of the fibrous material.
Slowly and carefully we unrolled the linen, exposing to view a very
large but undoubtedly ancient potsherd* of a dirty yellow colour![1]
This potsherd had in my judgment once been a part of an ordinary
amphora* of medium size. For the rest, it measured ten and a half
inches in length by seven in width, was about a quarter of an inch
thick, and densely covered on the convex side that lay towards the
bottom of the box with writing in the later uncial Greek character,
faded here and there, but for the most part perfectly legible, the
inscription having evidently been executed with the greatest care,
and by means of a reed pen, such as the ancients often used. I must
not forget to mention that in some remote age* this wonderful fragment had been broken in two, and rejoined by means of cement and
eight long rivets. Also there were numerous inscriptions on the inner
side, but these were of the most erratic character, and had clearly
been made by different hands and in many different ages, and of
them, together with the writings on the parchments,* I shall have to
speak presently.

'Is there anything more?' asked Leo, in a kind of excited whisper.

I groped about, and produced something hard, done up in a little

---

[1] *See* Frontispiece.—EDITOR.

linen bag. Out of the bag we took first a very beautiful miniature done upon ivory, and, secondly, a small chocolate-coloured composition *scarabæus*,* marked thus:—

symbols which, we have since ascertained, mean 'Suten se Rā,' which is being translated the 'Royal Son of Rā or the Sun.' The miniature was a picture of Leo's Greek mother —a lovely, dark-eyed creature. On the back of it was written, in poor Vincey's handwriting, 'My beloved wife.'*

'That is all,' I said.

'Very well,' answered Leo, putting down the miniature, at which he had been gazing affectionately; 'and now let us read the letter,' and without further ado he broke the seal, and read aloud as follows:—

'MY SON LEO,—When you open this, if you ever live to do so, you will have attained to manhood, and I shall have been long enough dead to be absolutely forgotten by nearly all who knew me. Yet in reading it remember that I have been, and for anything you know may still be, and that in it, through this link of pen and paper, I stretch out my hand to you across the gulf of death,* and my voice speaks to you from the unutterable silence of the grave. Though I am dead, and no memory of me remains in your mind, yet am I with you in this hour that you read. Since your birth to this day I have scarcely seen your face. Forgive me this. Your life supplanted the life of one whom I loved better than women are often loved, and the bitterness of it endureth yet. Had I lived I should in time have conquered this foolish feeling, but I am not destined to live. My sufferings, physical and mental, are more than I can bear, and when such small arrangements as I have to make for your future well-being are completed it is my intention to put a period to them. May God forgive me if I do wrong. At the best I could not live more than another year.'

'So he killed himself,' I exclaimed. 'I thought so.'

'And now,' Leo went on, without replying, 'enough of myself. What has to be said belongs to you who live, not to me, who am dead, and almost as much forgotten as though I had never been. Holly, my friend (to whom, if he will accept the trust, it is my intention to confide you), will have told you something of the extraordinary antiquity of your race. In the contents of this casket you will find sufficient to prove it. The strange legend that you will find inscribed by your remote ancestress upon the potsherd was communicated to me by my father on his deathbed, and took a strong hold upon my imagination. When I was only nineteen years of age I determined, as, to his misfortune, did one of our ancestors about the time of Elizabeth, to investigate its truth. Into all that befell me I cannot enter now. But this I saw with my own eyes. On the coast of Africa, in a hitherto unexplored region, some distance to the north of where the Zambesi falls into the sea,* there is a headland, at the extremity of which a peak towers up, shaped like the head of a negro, similar to that of which the writing speaks. I landed there, and learnt from a wandering native, who had been cast out by his people because of some crime which he had committed, that far inland are great mountains, shaped like cups, and caves surrounded by measureless swamps. I learnt also that the people there speak a dialect of Arabic, and are ruled over by a *beautiful white woman* who is seldom seen by them, but who is reported to have power over all things living and dead. Two days after I had ascertained this the man died of fever contracted in crossing the swamps, and I was forced by want of provisions and by symptoms of an illness which afterwards prostrated me to take to my dhow* again.

'Of the adventures that befell me after this I need not now speak. I was wrecked upon the coast of Madagascar, and rescued some months afterwards by an English ship that brought me to Aden, whence I started for England, intending to prosecute my search as soon as I had made sufficient preparations. On my way I stopped in Greece, and there, for "Omnia vincit amor,"* I met your beloved mother, and married her, and there you were born and she died. Then it was that my last illness seized me, and I returned hither to die. But still I hoped against hope, and set myself to work to learn Arabic, with the intention, should I ever get better, of returning to the coast of Africa, and solving the mystery of which the tradition has lived so many centuries in our family. But I have not got better, and, so far as I am concerned, the story is at an end.

'For you, however, my son, it is not at an end, and to you I hand on these the results of my labour, together with the hereditary proofs of its origin. It is my intention to provide that they shall not be put into your hands until you have reached an age when you will be able to judge for yourself whether or no you will choose to investigate what, if it is true, must be the greatest mystery in the world, or to put it by as an idle fable, originating in the first place in a woman's disordered brain.

'I do not believe that it is a fable; I believe that if it can only be re-discovered there is a spot where the vital forces of the world visibly exist. Life exists; why therefore should not the means of preserving it indefinitely exist also? But I have no wish to prejudice your mind about the matter. Read and judge for yourself. If you are inclined to undertake the search, I have so provided that you will not lack for means. If, on the other hand, you are satisfied that the whole thing is a chimera, then, I adjure you, destroy the potsherd and the writings, and let a cause of troubling be removed from our race for ever. Perhaps that will be wisest. The unknown is generally taken to be terrible,* not as the proverb would infer, from the inherent superstition of man, but because it so often is terrible. He who would tamper with the vast and secret forces that animate the world may well fall a victim to them. And if the end were attained, if at last you emerged from the trial ever beautiful and ever young, defying time and evil, and lifted above the natural decay of flesh and intellect, who shall say that the awesome change would prove a happy one? Choose, my son, and may the Power who rules all things, and who says "thus far shalt thou go,* and thus much shalt thou learn," direct the choice to your own happiness and the happiness of the world, which, in the event of your success, you would one day certainly rule by the pure force of accumulated experience.—Farewell!'

Thus the letter, which was unsigned and undated, abruptly ended.

'What do you make of that, Uncle Holly?' said Leo, with a sort of gasp, as he replaced it on the table. 'We have been looking for a mystery, and we certainly seem to have found one.'

'What do I make of it? Why, that your poor dear father was off his head, of course,' I answered, testily. 'I guessed as much that night, twenty years ago, when he came into my room. You see he evidently hurried his own end, poor man. It is absolute balderdash.'

'That's it, sir!' said Job, solemnly. Job was a most matter-of-fact specimen of a matter-of-fact class.

'Well, let's see what the potsherd has to say, at any rate,' said Leo, taking up the translation in his father's writing, and commencing to read:—

'*I, Amenartas, of the Royal House of the Pharaohs of Egypt, wife of Kallikrates* (the Beautiful in Strength), *a Priest of Isis whom the gods cherish and the demons obey, being about to die, to my little son Tisisthenes* (the Mighty Avenger). *I fled with thy father from Egypt in the days of Nectanebes,*[1]* *causing him through love to break the vows that he had vowed. We fled southward, across the waters, and we wandered for twice twelve moons on the coast of Libya* (Africa) *that looks towards the rising sun, where by a river is a great rock carven like the head of an Ethiopian. Four days on the water from the mouth of a mighty river were we cast away, and some were drowned and some died of sickness. But us wild men took through wastes and marshes, where the sea fowl hid the sky, bearing us ten days' journey till we came to a hollow mountain, where a great city had been and fallen, and where there are caves of which no man hath seen the end; and they brought us to the Queen of the people who place pots upon the heads of strangers,* who is a magician having a knowledge of all things, and life and loveliness that does not die. And she cast eyes of love upon thy father, Kallikrates, and would have slain me, and taken him to husband, but he loved me and feared her, and would not. Then did she take us, and lead us by terrible ways, by means of dark magic, to where the great pit is, in the mouth of which the old philosopher lay dead, and showed to us the rolling Pillar of Life that dies not, whereof the voice is as the voice of thunder; and she did stand in the flames, and come forth unharmed, and yet more beautiful. Then did she swear to make thy father undying even as she is, if he would but slay me, and give himself to her, for me she could not slay because of the magic of my own people that I have, and that prevailed thus far against her. And he held his hand before his eyes to hide her beauty, and would not. Then in her rage did she smite him by her magic, and he died; but she wept over him, and bore him thence with lamentations: and being afraid, me she sent to the mouth of the great river where the ships come, and I was carried for away on the ships where I gave thee birth, and hither to Athens I came at last after many wanderings. Now I say to thee, my son, Tisisthenes, seek out the woman, and learn the secret of Life, and if thou*

---

[1] Nekht-nebf, or Nectanebo II., the last native Pharaoh of Egypt fled from Ochus to Ethiopia, B.C. 339,—EDITOR.

mayest find a way slay her, because of thy father Kallikrates; and if thou dost fear or fail, this I say to all of thy seed who come after thee, till at last a brave man be found among them who shall bathe in the fire and sit in the place of the Pharaohs. I speak of those things, that though they be past belief, yet I have known, and I lie not.'

'May the Lord forgive her for that,' groaned Job, who had been listening to this marvellous composition with his mouth open.

As for myself, I said nothing: my first idea being that my poor friend, being demented, had composed the whole thing, though it scarcely seemed likely that such a story could have been invented by anybody. It was too original. To solve my doubts I took up the potsherd and began to read the close uncial Greek writing on it; and very good Greek of the period it is,* considering that it came from the pen of an Egyptian born. Here is an exact transcript of it:—

ΑΜΕΝΑΡΤΑΣΤΟΥΒΑΣΙΛΙΚΟΥΓΕΝΟΥΣΤΟΥΑ
ΙΓΥΓΤΙΟΥΗΤΟΥΚΑΛΛΙΚΡΑΤΟΥΣΙΣΙΔΟΣΙΕΡ
ΕΩΣΗΝΟΙΜΕΝΘΕΟΙΤΡΕΦΟΥΣΙΤΑΔΕΔΑΙΜΟ
ΝΙΑΥΓΟΤΑΣΣΕΤΑΙΗΔΗΤΕΛΕΥΤΩΣΑΤΙΣΙΣ
ΘΕΝΕΙΤΩΓΑΙΔΙΕΓΙΣΤΕΛΛΕΙΤΑΔΕΣΥΝΕΦΥΓΟ
ΝΓΑΡΓΟΤΕΕΚΤΗΣΑΙΓΥΓΤΙΑΣΕΓΙΝΕΚΤΑΝΕΒ
ΟΥΜΕΤΑΤΟΥΣΟΥΓΑΤΡΟΣΔΙΑΤΟΝΕΡΩΤΑΤΟ
ΝΕΜΟΝΕΓΙΟΡΚΗΣΑΝΤΟΣΦΥΓΟΝΤΕΣΔΕΓΡΟ
ΣΝΟΤΟΝΔΙΑΓΟΝΤΙΟΙΚΑΙΚΔΜΗΝΑΣΚΑΤΑΤΑ
ΓΑΡΑΘΑΛΑΣΣΙΑΤΗΣΛΙΒΥΗΣΤΑΓΡΟΣΗΛΙΟΥ
ΑΝΑΤΟΛΑΣΓΛΑΝΗΘΕΝΤΕΣΕΝΘΑΓΕΡΓΕΤΡΑ
ΤΙΣΜΕΓΑΛΗΓΛΥΓΤΟΝΟΜΟΙΩΜΑΑΙΘΙΟΓΟΣ
ΚΕΦΑΛΗΣΕΙΤΑΗΜΕΡΑΣΔΑΓΟΣΤΟΜΑΤΟΣΓΟ
ΤΑΜΟΥΜΕΓΑΛΟΥΕΚΓΕΣΟΝΤΕΣΟΙΜΕΝΚΑΤΕ
ΓΟΝΤΙΣΘΗΜΕΝΟΙΔΕΝΟΣΩΙΑΓΕΘΑΝΟΜΕΝΤ
ΕΛΟΣΔΕΥΓΑΓΡΙΩΝΑΝΘΡΩΓΩΝΕΦΕΡΟΜΕΘΑ
ΔΙΑΕΛΕΩΝΤΕΚΑΙΤΕΝΑΓΕΩΝΕΝΘΑΓΕΡΓΤΗΝ
ΩΝΓΛΗΘΟΣΑΓΟΚΡΥΓΤΕΙΤΟΝΟΥΡΑΝΟΝΗΜ
ΕΡΑΣΙΕΩΣΗΛΘΟΜΕΝΕΙΣΚΟΙΛΟΝΤΙΟΡΟΣΕΝ
ΘΑΓΟΤΕΜΕΓΑΛΗΜΕΝΓΟΛΙΣΗΝΑΝΤΡΑΔΕΑΓ
ΕΙΡΟΝΑΗΓΑΓΟΝΔΕΩΣΒΑΣΙΛΕΙΑΝΤΗΝΤΩΝΞ
ΕΝΟΥΣΧΥΤΡΑΙΣΣΤΕΦΑΝΟΥΝΤΩΝΗΤΙΣΜΑΓΕ
ΙΑΜΕΝΕΧΡΗΤΟΕΓΙΣΤΗΜΗΔΕΓΑΝΤΩΝΚΑΙΔ
ΗΚΑΙΚΑΛΛΟΣΚΑΙΡΩΜΗΝΑΓΗΡΩΣΗΝΗΔΕΚΑ
ΛΛΙΚΡΑΤΟΥΣΤΟΥΣΟΥΓΑΤΡΟΣΕΡΑΣΘΕΙΣΑΤ
ΟΜΕΝΓΡΩΤΟΝΣΥΝΟΙΚΕΙΝΕΒΟΥΛΕΤΟΕΜΕΔ
ΕΑΝΕΛΕΙΝΕΓΕΙΤΑΩΣΟΥΚΑΝΕΓΕΙΘΕΝΕΜΕΓΑ
ΡΥΓΕΡΕΦΙΛΕΙΚΑΙΤΗΝΞΕΝΗΝΕΦΟΒΕΙΤΟΑΓΗ
ΓΑΓΕΝΗΜΑΣΥΓΟΜΑΓΕΙΑΣΚΑΘΟΔΟΥΣΣΦΑΛ
ΕΡΑΣΕΝΘΑΤΟΒΑΡΑΘΡΟΝΤΟΜΕΓΑΟΥΚΑΤΑΣ

ΤΟΜΑΕΚΕΙΤΟΟΓΕΡΩΝΟΦΙΛΟΣΟΦΟΣΤΕΘΝΕ
ΩΣΑΦΙΚΟΜΕΝΟΙΣΔΕΔΕΙΞΕΦΩΣΤΟΥΒΙΟΥΕΥ
ΘΥΟΙΟΝΚΙΟΝΑΕΛΙΣΣΟΜΕΝΟΝΦΩΝΗΝΙΕΝΤ
ΑΚΑΘΑΓΕΡΒΡΟΝΤΗΣΕΙΤΑΔΙΑΓΥΡΟΣΒΕΒΗΚ
ΥΙΑΑΒΛΑΒΗΣΚΑΙΕΤΙΚΑΛΛΙΩΝΑΥΤΗΕΑΥΤΗΣ
ΕΞΕΦΑΝΗΕΚΔΕΤΟΥΤΩΝΩΜΟΣΕΚΑΙΤΟΝΣΟ
ΝΓΑΤΕΡΑΑΘΑΝΑΤΟΝΑΓΟΔΕΙΞΕΙΝΕΙΣΥΝΟΙΚ
ΕΙΝΟΙΒΟΥΛΟΙΤΟΕΜΕΔΕΑΝΕΛΕΙΝΟΥΓΑΡΟΥ
ΝΑΥΤΗΑΝΕΛΕΙΝΙΣΧΥΕΝΥΓΟΤΩΝΗΜΕΔΑΓΩ
ΝΗΝΚΑΙΑΥΤΗΕΧΩΜΑΓΕΙΑΣΩΔΟΥΔΕΝΤΙΜΑ
ΛΛΟΝΗΘΕΛΕΤΩΧΕΙΡΕΤΩΝΟΜΜΑΤΩΝΓΡΟΙ
ΣΧΩΝΙΝΑΔΗΤΟΤΗΣΓΥΝΑΙΚΟΣΚΑΛΛΟΣΜΗ
ΟΡΩΗΓΕΙΤΑΟΡΓΙΣΘΕΙΣΑΚΑΤΕΓΟΗΤΕΥΣΕΜ
ΕΝΑΥΤΟΝΑΓΟΛΟΜΕΝΟΝΜΕΝΤΟΙΚΛΑΟΥΣΑ
ΚΑΙΟΔΥΡΟΜΕΝΗΕΚΕΙΘΕΝΑΓΗΝΕΓΚΕΝΕΜΕΔ
ΕΦΟΒΩΙΑΦΗΚΕΝΕΙΣΣΤΟΜΑΤΟΥΜΕΓΑΛΟΥΓ
ΟΤΑΜΟΥΤΟΥΝΑΥΣΙΓΟΡΟΥΓΟΡΡΩΔΕΝΑΥΣΙ
ΝΕΦΩΝΓΕΡΓΛΕΟΥΣΑΕΤΕΚΟΝΣΕΑΓΟΓΛΕΥΣ
ΑΣΑΜΟΛΙΣΓΟΤΕΔΕΥΡΟΑΘΗΝΑΖΕΚΑΤΗΓΑΓ
ΟΜΗΝΣΥΔΕΩΤΙΣΙΣΘΕΝΕΣΩΝΕΓΙΣΤΕΛΛΩΜ
ΗΟΛΙΓΩΡΕΙΔΕΙΓΑΡΤΗΝΓΥΝΑΙΚΑΑΝΑΖΗΤΕΙ
ΝΗΝΓΩΣΤΟΤΟΥΒΙΟΥΜΥΣΤΗΡΙΟΝΑΝΕΥΡΗ
ΣΚΑΙΑΝΑΙΡΕΙΝΗΝΓΟΥΓΑΡΑΣΧΗΔΙΑΤΟΝΣΟ
ΝΓΑΤΕΡΑΚΑΛΛΙΚΡΑΤΗΝΕΙΔΕΦΟΒΟΥΜΕΝΟ
ΣΗΔΙΑΑΛΛΟΤΙΑΥΤΟΣΛΕΙΓΕΙΤΟΥΕΡΓΟΥΓΑ
ΣΙΤΟΙΣΥΣΤΕΡΟΝΑΥΤΟΤΟΥΤΟΕΓΙΣΤΕΛΛΩΕ
ΩΣΓΟΤΕΑΓΑΘΟΣΤΙΣΓΕΝΟΜΕΝΟΣΤΩΓΥΡΙΛ
ΟΥΣΑΣΘΑΙΤΟΛΜΗΣΕΙΚΑΙΤΑΑΡΙΣΤΕΙΑΕΧΩΝ
ΒΑΣΙΛΕΥΣΑΙΤΩΝΑΝΘΡΩΓΩΝΑΓΙΣΤΑΜΕΝΔ
ΗΤΑΤΟΙΑΥΤΑΛΕΓΩΟΜΩΣΔΕΑΑΥΤΗΕΓΝΩΚ
ΑΟΥΚΕΨΕΥΣΑΜΗΝ

For general convenience in reading, I have here accurately tran-
scribed this inscription into the cursive character:—

’Αμενάρτας, τοῦ βασιλικοῦ γένους τοῦ Αἰγυπ-
τίου, ἡ τοῦ Καλλικράτους Ἴσιδος ἱερέως, ἣν οἱ μὲν
θεοὶ τρέφουσι τὰ δὲ δαιμόνια ὑποτάσσεται, ἤδη τελ-
ευτῶσα Τισισθένει τῷ παιδὶ ἐπιστέλλει τάδε· συνέ-
φυγον γάρ ποτε ἐκ τῆς Αἰγυπτίας ἐπὶ Νεκτανέβου
μετὰ τοῦ σοῦ πατρός, διὰ τὸν ἔρωτα τὸν ἐμὸν ἐπιορ-
κήσαντος. φυγόντες δὲ πρὸς νότον διαπόντιοι καὶ κ΄δ΄
μῆνας κατὰ τὰ παραθαλάσσια τῆς Λιβύης τὰ πρὸς
ἡλίου ἀνατολὰς πλανηθέντες, ἔνθαπερ πέτρα τις μεγάλη,

γλυπτὸν ὁμοίωμα Αἰθίοπος κεφαλῆς, εἶτα ἡμέρας δ'
ἀπὸ στόματος ποταμοῦ μεγάλου ἐκπεσόντες, οἱ μὲν
κατεποντίσθημεν, οἱ δὲ νόσῳ ἀπεθάνομεν· τέλος δὲ
ὑπ' ἀγρίων ἀνθρώπων ἐφερόμεθα διὰ ἑλέων τε καὶ
τεναγέων ἔνθαπερ πτηνῶν πλῆθος ἀποκρύπτει τὸν
οὐρανόν, ἡμέρας ι, ἕως ἤλθομεν εἰς κοῖλόν τι ὄρος, ἔνθα
ποτὲ μεγάλη μὲν πόλις ἦν, ἄντρα δὲ ἀπείρονα· ἤγαγον
δὲ ὡς βασίλειαν τὴν τῶν ξένους χύτραις στεφανούντων,
ἥτις μαγείᾳ μὲν ἐχρῆτο ἐπιστήμῃ δὲ πάντων καὶ δὴ καὶ
κάλλος καὶ ῥώμην ἀγήρως ἦν· ἡ δὲ Καλλικράτους
τοῦ σοῦ πατρὸς ἐρασθεῖσα τὸ μὲν πρῶτον συνοικεῖν
ἐβούλετο ἐμὲ δὲ ἀνελεῖν· ἔπειτα, ὡς οὐκ ἀνέπειθεν,
ἐμὲ γὰρ ὑπερεφίλει καὶ τὴν ξένην ἐφοβεῖτο, ἀπήγαγεν
ἡμᾶς ὑπὸ μαγείας καθ' ὁδοὺς σφαλερὰς ἔνθα τὸ βά-
ραθρον τὸ μέγα, οὗ κατὰ στόμα ἔκειτο ὁ γέρων ὁ
φιλόσοφος τεθνεώς, ἀφικομένοις δ' ἔδειξε φῶς τοῦ
βίου εὐθύ, οἷον κίονα ἑλισσόμενον φωνὴν ἱέντα καθάπερ
βροντῆς, εἶτα διὰ πυρὸς βεβηκυῖα ἀβλαβὴς καὶ ἔτι
καλλίων αὐτὴ ἑαυτῆς ἐξεφάνη. ἐκ δὲ τούτων ὤμοσε
καὶ τὸν σὸν πατέρα ἀθάνατον ἀποδείξειν, εἰ συνοικεῖν
οἱ βούλοιτο ἐμὲ δὲ ἀνελεῖν, οὐ γὰρ οὖν αὐτὴ ἀνελεῖν
ἴσχυεν ὑπὸ τῶν ἡμεδαπῶν ἦν καὶ αὐτὴ ἔχω μαγείας.
ὁ δ' οὐδέν τι μᾶλλον ἤθελε, τὼ χεῖρε τῶν ὀμμάτων
προίσχων ἵνα δὴ τὸ τῆς γυναικὸς κάλλος μὴ ὁρῴη·
ἔπειτα ὀργισθεῖσα κατεγοήτευσε μὲν αὐτόν, ἀπολόμενον
μέντοι κλάουσα καὶ ὀδυρομένη ἐκεῖθεν ἀπήνεγκεν, ἐμὲ
δὲ φόβῳ ἀφῆκεν εἰς στόμα τοῦ μεγάλου ποταμοῦ
τοῦ ναυσιπόρου, πόρρω δὲ ναυσίν, ἐφ' ὧνπερ πλέουσα
ἔτεκόν σε, ἀποπλεύσασα μόλις ποτὲ δεῦρο Ἀθηνάζε
κατηγαγόμην. σὺ δέ, ὦ Τισίσθενες, ὧν ἐπιστέλλω μὴ
ὀλιγώρει· δεῖ γὰρ τὴν γυναῖκα ἀναζητεῖν ἥν πως τὸ τοῦ
βίου μυστήριον ἀνεύρῃς, καὶ ἀναιρεῖν, ἤν που παράσχῃ,
διὰ τὸν σὸν πατέρα Καλλικράτην. εἰ δὲ φοβούμενος
ἢ διὰ ἄλλο τι αὐτὸς λείπει τοῦ ἔργου, πᾶσι τοῖς
ὕστερον αὐτὸ τοῦτο ἐπιστέλλω, ἕως ποτὲ ἀγαθός τις
γενόμενος τῷ πυρὶ λούσασθαι τολμήσει καὶ τὰ ἀριστεῖα
ἔχων βασιλεῦσαι τῶν ἀνθρώπων· ἄπιστα μὲν δὴ τὰ
τοιαῦτα λέγω, ὅμως δέ ἃ αὐτὴ ἔγνωκα οὐκ ἐψευσάμην.

The English translation was, as I discovered on further investigation, and as the reader may easily see by comparison, both accurate and elegant.

Besides the uncial writing on the convex side of the sherd at the top, painted in dull red, on what had once been the lip of the amphora, was the cartouche* already mentioned as being on the *scarabæus*, which we had also found in the casket. The hieroglyphics or symbols, however, were reversed, just as though they had been pressed on wax. Whether this was the cartouche of the original Kallikrates,[1] or of some Prince or Pharaoh from whom his wife Amenartas was descended, I am not sure, nor can I tell if it was drawn upon the sherd at the same time that the uncial Greek was inscribed, or copied on more recently from the Scarab by some other member of the family. Nor was this all. At the foot of the writing, painted in the same dull red, was the faint outline of a somewhat rude drawing of the head and shoulders of a Sphinx wearing two feathers, symbols of majesty, which, though common enough upon the effigies of sacred bulls and gods, I have never before met with on a Sphinx.

Also on the right-hand side of this surface of the sherd, painted obliquely in red on the space not covered by the uncial, and signed in blue paint, was the following quaint inscription:—

> IN EARTH AND SKIE AND SEA
> STRANGE THYNGES THER BE.
> HOC FECIT
> DOROTHEA VINCEY.*

Perfectly bewildered, I turned the relic over. It was covered from top to bottom with notes and signatures in Greek, Latin, and English. The first in uncial Greek was by Tisisthenes, the son to whom the writing was addressed. It was, 'I could not go. Tisisthenes to his son, Kallikrates.' Here it is in facsimile with its cursive equivalent:—

ΟΥΚΑΝΔΥΝΑΙΜΗΝΓΟΡΕΥΕΣΘΑΙΤΙΣΙΣΘΕΝΗ
ΣΚΑΛΛΙΚΡΑΤΕΙΤΩΙΓΑΙΔΙ

οὐκ ἂν δυναίμην πορεύεσθαι.
Τισισθένης Καλλικράτει τῷ παιδί.

[1] The cartouche, if it be a true cartouche, cannot have been that of Kallikrates, as Mr. Holly suggests. Kallikrates was a priest and not entitled to a cartouche, which was the prerogative of Egyptian royalty, though he might have inscribed his name or title upon an *oval*.—EDITOR.

This Kallikrates (probably, in the Greek fashion, so named after his grandfather) evidently made some attempt to start on the quest, for his entry written in very faint and almost illegible uncial is, 'I ceased from my going, the gods being against me. Kallikrates to his son.' Here it is also:—

ΤΩΝΘΕΩΝΑΝΤΙΣΤΑΝΤΩΝΕΓΑΥΣΑΜΗΝΤΗΣ
ΓΟΡΕΙΑΣΚΑΛΛΙΚΡΑΤΗΣΤΩΙΓΑΙΔΙ

τῶν θεῶν ἀντιστάντων ἐπαυσάμην τῆς πορείας.
Καλλικράτης τῷ παιδί.

Between these two ancient writings, the second of which was inscribed upside down and was so faint and worn that, had it not been for the transcript of it executed by Vincey, I should scarcely have been able to read it, since, owing to its having been written on that portion of the tile which had, in the course of ages, undergone the most handling, it was nearly rubbed out—was the bold, modern-looking signature of one Lionel Vincey, 'Ætate sua 17,'* which was written thereon, I think, by Leo's grandfather. To the right of this were the initials 'J. B. V.,' and below came a variety of Greek signatures, in uncial and cursive character, and what appeared to be some carelessly executed* repetitions of the sentence 'τῷ παιδί' (to my son), showing that the relic was religiously passed on from generation to generation.

The next legible thing after the Greek signatures was the word 'ROMAE, A.U.C.,' showing that the family had now migrated to Rome. Unfortunately, however, with the exception of its termination (cvi)* the date of their settlement there is for ever lost, for just where it had been placed a piece of the potsherd is broken away.

Then followed twelve* Latin signatures, jotted about here and there, wherever there was a space upon the tile suitable to their inscription. These signatures, with three exceptions only,* ended with the name 'Vindex'* or 'the Avenger,' which seems to have been adopted by the family after its migration to Rome as a kind of equivalent to the Grecian 'Tisisthenes,' which also means an avenger. Ultimately, as might be expected, this Latin cognomen of Vindex was transformed first into De Vincey, and then into the plain, modern Vincey. It is very curious to observe how the idea of revenge, inspired by an Egyptian before the time of Christ, is thus, as it were, embalmed in an English family name.

A few of the Roman names inscribed upon the sherd I have actually since found mentioned in history and other records. They were, if I remember right,

> MVSSIVS. VINDEX
> SEX. VARIVS. MARVLLVS
> C. FVFIDIVS. C. F. VINDEX

and

> LABERIA POMPEIANA. CONIVX. MACRINI. VINDICIS

the last being, of course, the name of a Roman lady.

The following list,* however, comprises all the Latin names upon the sherd:—

> C. CAECILIVS VINDEX
> M. AIMILIVS VINDEX
> SEX. VARIVS. MARVLLVS
> Q. SOSIVS PRISOVS SENECIO VINDEX
> L. VALERIVS COMINIVS VINDEX
> SEX. OTACILIVS. M. F.
> L. ATTIVS. VINDEX
> MVSSIVS VINDEX
> C. FVFIDIVS. C. F. VINDEX
> LICINIVS FAVSTVS
> LABERIA POMPEIANA CONIVX* MACRINI VINDICIS
> MANILIA LVCILLA CONIVX MARVLLI VINDICIS

After the Roman names there is evidently a gap of very many centuries. Nobody will ever know now what was the history of the relic during those dark ages, or how it came to have been preserved in the family. My poor friend Vincey had, it will be remembered, told me that his Roman ancestors finally settled in Lombardy, and when Charlemagne invaded it, returned with him across the Alps, and made their home in Brittany, whence they crossed to England in the reign of Edward the Confessor. How he knew this I am not aware, for there is no reference to Lombardy or Charlemagne upon the tile, though, as will presently be seen, there is a reference to Brittany. To continue: the next entries on the sherd, if I may except a long splash either of blood or red colouring matter of some sort,

consist of two crosses drawn in red pigment, and probably representing Crusaders' swords, and a rather neat* monogram ('D. V.') in scarlet
and blue, perhaps executed by that same Dorothea Vincey who wrote,
or rather painted, the doggrel couplet. To the left of this, inscribed
in faint blue, were the initials A. V., and after them a date, 1800.*

Then came what was perhaps as curious an entry as anything
upon this extraordinary relic of the past. It is executed in black-letter,
written over the crosses or Crusaders' swords, and dated fourteen
hundred and forty-five. As the best plan will be to allow it to speak
for itself, I here give the black-letter facsimile, together with the
original Latin without the contractions, from which it will be seen
that the writer was a fair mediæval Latinist.* Also we discovered what
is still more curious, an English version of the black-letter Latin.
This, also written in black-letter, we found inscribed on a second
parchment that was in the coffer, apparently somewhat older in date
than that on which was inscribed the mediæval Latin translation
of the uncial Greek of which I shall speak presently. This I also give
in full.

Facsimile of Black-Letter Inscription on the Sherd of Amenartas.

Ista reliqia est valde misticū et myrificb
ops q̄d maiores mei ex Armorica ſſ
Brittania mīore secū cōvehebāt et q̄dm ſcs
cleriūs sꝑer p̄ri meo in manb ferebat q̄d
pēitus illvd destrueret affirmās q̄d esset ab
ipso sathana cōſſatb prestigiosa et dyabolica
arte q̄re p̄ter mevs cōfregit illvd ī dvas p̄tes
q̄s q̄dm ego Joh̄s de Ūiceto salvas servavi et
adaptavi sicbt apꝑarct die lūe p̄x post fest beate
Mrie virḡ anni gr̄e mccccxlv

Expanded Version of the above Black-Letter Inscription.

'Ista reliquia est valde misticum et myrificum opus, quod majores
mei ex Armorica, scilicet Britannia Minore, secum convehebant; et
quidam sanctus clericus semper patri meo in manu ferebat quod
penitus illud destrueret, affirmans quod esset ab ipso Sathana confla-
tum prestigiosa et dyabolica arte, quare pater meus confregit illud

in duas partes, quas quidem ego Johannes de Vinceto salvas servavi
et adaptavi sicut apparet die lune proximo post festum beate Marie
Virginis anni gratie MCCCCXLV.

*Facsimile of the Old English Black-Letter Translation of the above
Latin Inscription from the Sherd of Amenartas found inscribed upon
a parchment.*

Thys rellike ys a ryghte mistycall worke
& a marveylous þe whyche myne abn-
ceteres afore tyme dyd conveighe hider wt þm
ffrom Armoryke whe ys to seien Britayne þe
lesse & a certayne holye clerke shoulde allweyes
beare my ffadir on honde þt he owghte vttirly
ffor to ffrusshe þe same affirmynge þt yt was
ffourmyd & confflatyd off sathanas hym selffe
by arte magike & dyvellysshe wherefore my
ffadir dyd take þe same & to brast yt yn twepne
but I John de Uincey dyd save whool þe tweye
þtes therof & topeecyd þm togydder agapne soe
as yee se on þs deye mondaye next ffolowynge
after þe ffeeste of seynte Marye þe blessed
vyrgyne yn þe yeere of salvacioun ffowertene
hundreth & ffyve & ffowrti.

Modernised Version of the above Black-Letter Translation.*

Thys rellike ys a ryghte mistycall worke and a marvaylous, ye
whyche myne aunceteres aforetyme dyd conveigh hider with them
from Armoryke which ys to seien Britaine ye Lesse and a certayne
holye clerke should allweyes beare my fadir on honde that he
owghte uttirly for to frusshe ye same, affyrmynge that yt was
fourmed and conflatyd of Sathanas hym selfe by arte magike and
dyvellysshe wherefore my fadir dyd take ye same and tobrast yt yn
tweyne, but I, John de Vincey, dyd save whool ye tweye partes therof
and topeecyd them togydder agayne soe as yee se, on this daye mondaye next followynge after ye feeste of Seynte Marye ye Blessed

Vyrgyne yn ye yeere of Salvacioun fowertene hundreth and fyve and fowerti.'

The next and, save one, last entry was Elizabethan, and dated 1564, 'A most strange historie, and one that did cost my father his life; for in seekynge for the place upon the east coast of Africa, his pinnance* was sunk by a Portuguese galleon* off Lorenzo Marquez, and he himself perished.—JOHN VINCEY.'

Then came the last entry, apparently, to judge by the style of writing, made by some representative of the family in the middle of the eighteenth century. It was a misquotation of the well-known lines in Hamlet,* and ran thus: 'There are more things in Heaven and earth than are dreamt of in your philosophy, Horatio.'[1]

And now there remained but one more document* to be examined—namely, the ancient black-letter translation into mediæval Latin of the uncial inscription on the sherd. As will be seen, this translation was executed and subscribed in the year 1495, by a certain 'learned man,' Edmundus de Prato (Edmund Pratt)* by name, licentiate in Canon Law, of Exeter College, Oxford, who had actually been a pupil of Grocyn,* the first scholar who taught Greek in England.[2] No doubt on the fame of this new learning reaching his ears, the Vincey of the day, perhaps that same John de Vincey who years before had saved the relic from destruction and made the black-letter entry on the sherd in 1445, hurried off to Oxford to see if perchance it might avail to solve the secret of the mysterious inscription. Nor was he disappointed, for the learned Edmundus was equal to the task. Indeed his rendering is so excellent an example of mediæval learning and latinity that, even at the risk of sating the learned reader with too many antiquities, I have made up my mind to give it in facsimile, together with an expanded version for the benefit of those who find the contractions troublesome. The translation

---

[1] Another thing that makes me fix the date of this entry at the middle of the eighteenth century is that, curiously enough, I have an acting copy of 'Hamlet,' written about 1740, in which these two lines are misquoted almost exactly in the same way, and I have little doubt but that the Vincey who wrote them on the potsherd heard them so misquoted at that date. Of course, the lines really run:—

There are more things in heaven and earth, Horatio,
Than are dreamt of in your philosophy.—L. H. H.

[2] Grocyn, the instructor of Erasmus, studied Greek under Chalcondylas the Byzantine at Florence, and first lectured in the Hall of Exeter College, Oxford, in 1491.—EDITOR.

has several peculiarities on which this is not the place to dwell, but I would in passing call the attention of scholars to the passage 'duxerunt autem nos ad reginam *advenaslasaniscoronantium*,'* which strikes me as a delightful rendering of the original, 'ἤγαγον δὲ ὡς βασίλειαν τὴν τῶν ξένους χύτραις στεφανούντων.'

Mediæval Black-Letter Latin Translation of the Uncial Inscription on the Sherd of Amenartas.

Amenartas e gen. reg. Egyptii vxor Callicratis sacerdot Isidis quã dei fovet demonia attedbt filiol' svo Tisistheni iã moribũda ita mãdat: Effugi quõdã ex Egypto regnãte Nectanebo cũ patre tvo, ppter mei amorẽ pejerato. Fvgiẽtes autẽ v'sus Notũ trans mare et xxiiij mẽses p'r litora Libpe v'sus Oriẽtẽ errans vbi est petra quedã mgna scvlpta instar Ethiop capis, deinde dies iiij ab ost flum mgni eiecti p'tim submersi sumus p'tim morbo mortui sum: in sine autẽ a fer hõïbs portabamur pr palvd et vada. vbi aviũ m'titvdo celũ obũbrat dies x. donec advenim ad cavũ quedã montẽ, ubi olim mgna vrbs erat, cauerne quoq̃ imẽse: dvxerũt autẽ nos ad reginã Advenaslasaniscoronãtiũ que magic̃ vtebasr et peritia omniũ rer et saltẽ pvlcris et vigore ĩsẽescibil' erat. Hec mgno patr tui amore pcvlsga p'mũ q'dẽ ei conubiũ michi mortẽ parabat. postea v'ro recvsãte Callicrate amore mei et timore regine affecto nos pr magicã abduxit p'r vias horribil' vbi est puteus ille psũdus, cuius iuxta aditũ iacebat senios philosophi cadauer, et advẽiẽtib mõstravit flamã Uite erectã, ĩstar columne volutãtis, voces emittẽtẽ q̃si tonitrvs: tũc pr igne ĩpetu nociuo expers trãsiit et iã ipa sese formosior visa est.

Quib; fact iuravit se patrē tuū quoq; iṁor=
talē ostēsurā esse, si me prius occisa regine
cōtvberniū mallet; neq; enī ipsa me occidere
valuit, ꝓpter nostratū ṁgicā cuius egomet
ꝑtem habeo. Ille vero nichil huius gen
maluit, manib; ante ocuſ passis ne mulieſ
formositatē adspiceret: postea eū ṁgica ꝑcussit
arte, at mortuū efferebat īde cū fletib; et vagitib,
me ꝑr timorē expulit ad ostiū ṁgni ffiumiñ
velivoli porro in nave in qua te peperi, uix
post dies hvc Athenas invecta sū. At tu, O
Tisisthen, ne q'd quorū mādo nauci fac: necesse
enī est mulierē exqvirere si qva Vite mpsteriū
īpetres et vidicare, quātū in te est, patrē tuū
Callicraf in regine morte. Sin timore seu aliq
cavsa rē reliquis īfectā, hoc ipsū oīb; posteſ
mādo dū bonvs qs inveniatur qvi ignis lauacrū
nō ꝑrhorrescet et ꝑtentia digñ dōtabiſ hōiū.

Talia dico incredibilia qdē at mīe ficta de
reb; michi cognitis.

Hec Grece scripta Latine reddidit vir
doctus Edṁds de Prato, in Decretis Li=
cenciatus e Coll. Exon: Oxon: doctissimi
Grocyni quondam e pupillis, Id. Apr. A°.
Dūi. MCCCCLXXXXU°.

Expanded Version of the above Mediæval Latin Translation.

AMENARTAS, e genere regio Egyptii, uxor Callicratis, sacerdotis
Isidis, quam dei fovent demonia attendunt, filiolo suo Tisistheni
jam moribunda ita mandat: Effugi quondam ex Egypto, regnante
Nectanebo, cum patre tuo, propter mei amorem pejerato. Fugientes
autem versus Notum trans mare, et viginti quatuor menses per
litora Libye versus Orientem errantes, ubi est petra quedam magna
sculpta instar Ethiopis capitis, deinde dies quatuor ab ostio fluminis
magni ejecti partim submersi sumus partim morbo mortui sumus:

48 *She*

in fine autem a feris hominibus portabamur per paludes et vada, ubi avium multitudo celum obumbrat, dies decem, donec advenimus ad cavum quendam montem, uib olim magna urbs erat, caverne quoque immense; duxerunt autem nos ad reginam Advenaslasanis-coronantium, que magicâ utebatur et peritiâ omnium rerum, et saltem pulcritudine et vigore insenescibilis erat. Hec magno patris tui amore perculsa, primum quidem ei connubium michi mortem parabat; postea vero, recusante Callicrate, amore mei et timore regine affecto nos per magicam abduxit per vias horribiles ubi est puteus ille profundus, cujus juxta aditum jacebat senioris philosophi cadaver, et advenientibus monstravit flammam Vite erectam, instar columne volutantis, voces emittentem quasi tonitrus: tunc perignem impetu nocivo expers transiit et jam ipsa sese formosior visa est.

Quibus factis juravit se patrem tuum quoque immortalem ostensuram esse, si me prius occisa regine contubernium mallet; neque enim ipsa me occidere valuit, propter nostratum magicam cujus egomet partem habeo. Ille vero nichil hujus generis malebat, manibus ante oculos passis, ne mulieris formositatem adspiceret: postea illum magica percussit arte, at mortuum efferebat inde cum fletibus et vagitibus, at me per timorem expulit ad ostium magni fluminis, velivoli, porro in nave, in qua te peperi, vix post dies huc Athenas vecta sum. At tu, O Tisisthenes, ne quid quorum mando nauci fac: necesse enim est mulierem exquirere si qua Vite mysterium impetres et vindicare, quantum in te est, patrem tuum Callicratem in regine morte. Sin timore seu aliqua causa rem relinquis infectam, hoc ipsum omnibus posteris mando, dum bonus quis inveniatur qui ignis lavacrum non perhorrescet, et potentia dignus dominabitur hominum.

Talia dico incredibilia quidem at minime ficta de rebus michi cognitis.

Hec Grece scripta Latine reddidit vir doctus Edmundus de Prato, in Decretis Licenciatus, e Collegio Exoniensi Oxoniensi doctissimi Grocyni quondam e pupillis, Idibus Aprilis Anno Domini MCCCCLXXXXV°.*

'Well,' I said, when at length I had read out and carefully examined these writings and paragraphs, at least those of them that were still easily legible, 'that is the conclusion of the whole matter, Leo, and now you can form your own opinion on it. I have already formed mine.'

'And what is it?' he asked, in his quick way.

'It is this. I believe that potsherd to be perfectly genuine, and that, wonderful as it may seem, it has come down in your family from since the fourth century before Christ. The entries absolutely prove it, and therefore, however improbable it may seem, it must be accepted. But there I stop. That your remote ancestress, the Egyptian princess, or some scribe under her direction, wrote that which we see on the sherd I have no doubt, nor have I the slightest doubt but that her sufferings and the loss of her husband had turned her head, and that she was not right in her mind when she did write it.'

'How do you account for what my father saw and heard there?' asked Leo.

'Coincidence. No doubt there are bluffs on the coast of Africa that look something like a man's head, and plenty of people who speak bastard Arabic. Also, I believe that there are lots of swamps. Another thing is, Leo, and I am sorry to say it, but I do not believe that your poor father was quite right when he wrote that letter. He had met with a great trouble, and also he had allowed this story to prey on his imagination, and he was a very imaginative man. Anyway, I believe that the whole thing is the most unmitigated rubbish. I know that there are curious things and forces in nature which we rarely meet with, and, when we do meet them, cannot understand. But until I see it with my own eyes, which I am not likely to, I never will believe that there is any means of avoiding death, even for a time, or that there is or was a white sorceress living in the heart of an African swamp. It is bosh, my boy, all bosh!—What do you say, Job?'

'I say, sir, that it is a lie, and, if it is true, I hope Mr. Leo won't meddle with no such things, for no good can't come of it.'

'Perhaps you are both right,' said Leo, very quietly. 'I express no opinion. But I say this. I am going to set the matter at rest once and for all, and if you won't come with me I will go by myself.'

I looked at the young man, and saw that he meant what he said. When Leo means what he says he always puts on a curious look about the mouth. It has been a trick of his from a child. Now, as a matter of fact, I had no intention of allowing Leo to go anywhere by himself, for my own sake, if not for his. I was far too much attached to him for that. I am not a man of many ties or affections. Circumstances have been against me in this respect, and men and women shrink from me, or, at least, I fancy they do, which comes to the same thing, thinking, perhaps, that my somewhat forbidding exterior is a key to my character. Rather than endure this, I have, to a great extent, secluded myself from the world, and cut myself off from those opportunities which with most men result in the formation of relations more or less intimate. Therefore Leo was all the world to me—brother, child, and friend—and until he wearied of me, where he went there I should go too. But, of course, it would not do to let him see how great a hold he had over me; so I cast about for some means whereby I might let myself down easy.

'Yes, I shall go, Uncle; and if I don't find the "rolling Pillar of Life," at any rate I shall get some first-class shooting.'

Here was my opportunity, and I took it.

'Shooting?' I said. 'Ah! yes; I never thought of that. It must be a very wild stretch of country, and full of big game. I have always wanted to kill a buffalo before I die. Do you know, my boy, I don't believe in the quest, but I do believe in big game, and really, on the whole, if, after thinking it over, you make up your mind to go, I will take a holiday, and come with you.'

'Ah,' said Leo, 'I thought that you would not lose such a chance. But how about money? We shall want a good lot.'

'You need not trouble about that,' I answered. 'There is all your income that has been accumulating for years, and besides that I have saved two-thirds of what your father left to me, as I consider, in trust for you. There is plenty of cash.'

'Very well, then, we may as well stow these things away and go up to town to see about our guns. By the way, Job, are you coming too? It's time you began to see the world.'

'Well, sir,' answered Job, stolidly, 'I don't hold much with foreign parts, but if both you gentlemen are going you will want somebody to look after you, and I am not the man to stop behind after serving you for twenty years.'

'That's right, Job,' said I. 'You won't find out anything wonderful, but you will get some good shooting. And now look here, both of you. I won't have a word said to a living soul about this nonsense,' and I pointed to the potsherd. 'If it got out, and anything

happened to me, my next of kin would dispute my will on the
ground of insanity, and I should become the laughing stock of
Cambridge.'

That day three months we were on the ocean, bound for Zanzibar.

IV

THE SQUALL

How different is the scene that I have now to tell from that which has just been told! Gone are the quiet college rooms, gone the wind-swayed English elms and cawing rooks, and the familiar volumes on the shelves, and in their place there rises a vision of the great calm ocean gleaming in shaded silver lights beneath the beams of the full African moon. A gentle breeze fills the huge sail of our dhow, and draws us through the water that ripples musically against our sides. Most of the men are sleeping forward, for it is near midnight, but a stout swarthy Arab, Mahomed by name, stands at the tiller, lazily steering by the stars. Three miles or more to our starboard is a low dim line. It is the Eastern shore of Central Africa. We are running to the southward, before the North East Monsoon, between the main-land and the reef that for hundreds of miles fringes that perilous coast. The night is quiet, so quiet that a whisper can be heard fore and aft the dhow; so quiet that a faint booming sound rolls across the water to us from the distant land.

The Arab at the tiller holds up his hand, and says one word:—
'*Simba* (lion)!'

We all sit up and listen. Then it comes again, a slow, majestic sound, that thrills us to the marrow.

'To-morrow by ten o'clock,' I say, 'we ought, if the Captain is not out in his reckoning, which I think very probable, to make this mysterious rock with a man's head, and begin our shooting.'

'And begin our search for the ruined city and the Fire of Life,' corrected Leo, taking his pipe from his mouth, and laughing a little.

'Nonsense!' I answered. 'You were airing your Arabic with that man at the tiller this afternoon. What did he tell you? He has been trading (slave-trading probably) up and down these latitudes for half of his iniquitous life, and once landed on this very "man" rock. Did he ever hear anything of the ruined city or the caves?'

'No,' answered Leo. 'He says that the country is all swamp behind, and full of snakes, especially pythons, and game, and that no man lives there. But then there is a belt of swamp all along the East African coast, so that does not go for much.'

'Yes,' I said, 'it does—it goes for malaria. You see what sort of an opinion these gentry have of the country. Not one of them will go with us. They think that we are mad, and upon my word I believe that they are right. If ever we see old England again I shall be astonished. However, it does not greatly matter to me at my age, but I am anxious for you, Leo, and for Job. It's a Tom Fool's business, my boy.'

'All right, Uncle Horace. So far as I am concerned, I am willing to take my chance. Look! What is that cloud?' and he pointed to a dark blotch upon the starry sky, some miles astern of us.

'Go and ask the man at the tiller,' I said.

He rose, stretched his arms, and went. Presently he returned.

'He says it is a squall, but it will pass far on one side of us.'

Just then Job came up, looking very stout and English in his shooting-suit of brown flannel, and with a sort of perplexed appearance upon his honest round face that had been very common with him since he got into these strange waters.

'Please, sir,' he said, touching his sun hat, which was stuck on to the back of his head in a somewhat ludicrous fashion, 'as we have got all those guns and things in the whale-boat astern, to say nothing of the provisions in the lockers, I think it would be best if I got down and slept in her. I don't like the looks' (here he dropped his voice to a portentous whisper) 'of these black gentry; they have such a wonderful thievish way about them. Supposing now that some of them were to slip into the boat at night and cut the cable, and make off with her? That would be a pretty go, that would.'

The whale-boat, I may explain, was one specially built for us at Dundee, in Scotland.* We had brought it with us, as we knew that this coast was a network of creeks, and that we might require something to navigate them with. She was a beautiful boat, thirty feet in length, with a centre-board for sailing, copper-bottomed to keep the worm out of her, and full of water-tight compartments. The captain of the dhow had told us that when we reached the rock, which he knew, and which appeared to be identical with the one described upon the sherd and by Leo's father, he would probably not be able to run up to it on account of the shallows and breakers. Therefore we had employed three hours that very morning, whilst we were totally becalmed, the wind having dropped at sunrise, in transferring most of our goods and chattels to the whale-boat, and placing the guns, ammunition, and preserved provisions in the water-tight lockers specially prepared for them, so that when we did sight the fabled rock we should have nothing to do but step into the boat, and run her ashore. Another reason that induced us to take this precautionary step was that Arab captains are apt to run past the point that they are making, either from carelessness or owing to a mistake in its identity. Now, as sailors know, it is quite impossible for a dhow which is only rigged to run before the monsoon to beat back against it. Therefore we got our boat ready to row for the rock at any moment.

'Well, Job,' I said, 'perhaps it would be as well. There are lots of blankets there, only be careful to keep out of the moon, or it may turn your head or blind you.'

'Lord, sir! I don't think it would much matter if it did; it is that turned already with the sight of these blackamoors and their filthy, thieving ways. They are only fit for muck, they are; and they smell bad enough for it already.'

Job, it will be perceived, was no admirer of the manners and customs of our dark-skinned brothers.

Accordingly we hauled up the boat by the tow-rope till it was right under the stern of the dhow, and Job bundled into her with all the grace of a falling sack of potatoes. Then we returned and sat down on the deck again, and smoked and talked in little gusts and jerks. The night was so lovely, and our brains were so full of suppressed excitement of one sort and another, that we did not feel inclined to turn in. For nearly an hour we sat thus, and then, I think, we both dozed off. At least I have a faint recollection of Leo sleepily explaining that the head was not a bad place to hit a buffalo, if you could catch him exactly between the horns, or send your bullet down his throat, or some nonsense of the sort.

Then I remember no more; till suddenly—a frightful roar of wind, a shriek of terror from the awakening crew, and a whip-like sting of water in our faces. Some of the men ran to let go the haulyards and lower the sail, but the parrel* jammed and the yard would not come down. I sprang to my feet and hung on to a rope. The sky aft was dark as pitch, but the moon still shone brightly ahead of us and lit up the blackness. Beneath its sheen a huge white-topped breaker, twenty feet high or more, was rushing on to us. It was on the break—the moon shone on its crest and tipped its foam with light. On it rushed beneath the inky sky, driven by the awful squall behind it. Suddenly, in the twinkling of an eye, I saw the black shape of the whale-boat cast high into the air on the crest of the breaking wave. Then—a shock of water, a wild rush of boiling foam, and I was clinging for my life to the shroud, ay, swept straight out from it like a flag in a gale.

We were pooped.*

The wave passed. It seemed to me that I was under water for minutes—really it was seconds. I looked forward. The blast had torn out the great sail, and high in the air it was fluttering away to leeward like a huge wounded bird. Then for a moment there was comparative calm, and in it I heard Job's voice yelling wildly, 'Come here to the boat.'

Bewildered and half drowned as I was, I had the sense to rush aft. I felt the dhow sinking under me—she was full of water. Under her counter the whale-boat was tossing furiously, and I saw the Arab Mahomed, who had been steering, leap into her. I gave one desperate pull at the tow-rope to bring the boat alongside. Wildly I sprang also, and Job caught me by one arm and I rolled into the bottom of the boat. Down went the dhow bodily, and as she did so Mahomed drew his curved knife and severed the fibre-rope by which we were fast to her, and in another second we were driving before the storm over the place where the dhow had been.

'Great God!' I shrieked, 'where is Leo? *Leo! Leo!*'

'He's gone, sir, God help him!' roared Job into my ear; and such was the fury of the squall that his voice sounded like a whisper.

I wrung my hands in agony. Leo was drowned, and I was left alive to mourn him.

'Look out;' yelled Job, 'here comes another.'

I turned; a second huge wave was overtaking us. I half hoped that it would drown me. With a curious fascination I watched its awful advent. The moon was nearly hidden now by the wreaths of the rushing storm, but a little light still caught the crest of the devouring breaker. There was something dark on it—a piece of wreckage. It was on us now, and the boat was nearly full of water. But she was built in air-tight compartments—Heaven bless the man who invented them!—and lifted up through it like a swan. Through the foam and turmoil I saw the black thing on the wave hurrying right at me. I put out my right arm to ward it from me, and my hand closed on another arm, the wrist of which my fingers gripped like a vice. I am a very strong man, and had something to hold to, but my arm was nearly torn from its socket by the strain and weight of the floating body. Had the rush lasted another two seconds I must either have let go or gone with it. But it passed, leaving us up to our knees in water.

'Bail out! bail out!' shouted Job, suiting the action to the word.

But I could not bail just then, for as the moon went out and left us in total darkness, one faint, flying ray of light lit upon the face of the man I had gripped, who was now half lying, half floating in the bottom of the boat.

It was Leo. Leo brought back by the wave—back, dead or alive, from the very jaws of Death.

'Bail out! bail out!' yelled Job, 'or we shall founder.'

I seized a large tin bowl with a handle to it, which was fixed under one of the seats, and the three of us bailed away for dear life. The furious tempest drove over and round us, flinging the boat this way and that, the wind and the storm wreaths and the sheets of stinging spray blinded and bewildered us, but through it all we worked like demons with the wild exhilaration of despair, for even despair can exhilarate. One minute! three minutes! six minutes! The boat began to lighten, and no fresh wave swamped us. Five minutes more, and she was fairly clear. Then, suddenly, above the awful shriekings of the hurricane came a duller, deeper roar. Great Heavens! It was the voice of breakers!

At that moment the moon began to shine forth again—this time behind the path of the squall. Out far across the torn bosom of the ocean shot the ragged arrows of her light, and there, half a mile ahead of us, was a white line of foam, then a little space of open-mouthed blackness, and then another line of white. It was the breakers, and their roar grew clearer and yet more clear as we sped down upon them like a swallow. There they were, boiling up in snowy spouts of spray, smiting and gnashing together like the gleaming teeth of hell.

'Take the tiller, Mahomed!' I roared in Arabic. 'We must try and shoot them.' At the same moment I seized an oar, and got it out, motioning to Job to do likewise.

Mahomed clambered aft, and got hold of the tiller, and with some difficulty Job, who had sometimes pulled a tub upon the homely Cam,* got out his oar. In another minute the boat's head was straight on to the ever-nearing foam, towards which she plunged and tore with the speed of a racehorse. Just in front of us the first line of breakers seemed a little thinner than to the right or left—there was a gap of rather deeper water. I turned and pointed to it.

'Steer for your life, Mahomed!' I yelled. He was a skilful steersman, and well acquainted with the dangers of this most perilous coast, and I saw him grip the tiller and bend his heavy frame forward, and stare at the foaming terror till his big round eyes looked as though they would start out of his head. The send of the sea was driving the boat's head round to starboard. If we struck the line of breakers fifty yards to starboard of the gap we must sink. It was a great field of twisting, spouting waves. Mahomed planted his foot against the seat before him, and, glancing at him, I saw his brown toes spread out like a hand with the weight he put upon them as he took the strain of the tiller. She came round a bit, but not enough. I roared to Job to back water, whilst I dragged and laboured at my oar. She answered now, and none too soon.

Heavens, we were in them! And then followed a couple of minutes of heart-breaking excitement such as I cannot hope to describe. All I remember is a shrieking sea of foam, out of which the billows rose here, there, and everywhere like avenging ghosts from their ocean grave. Once we were turned right round, but either by chance, or through Mahomed's skilful steering, the boat's head came straight again before a breaker filled us. One more—a monster. We were through it or over it—more through than over—and then, with a wild yell of exultation from the Arab, we shot out into the comparative smooth water of the mouth of sea between the teeth-like lines of gnashing waves.

But we were half full of water again, and not more than half a mile ahead was the second line of breakers. Again we set to and bailed furiously. Fortunately the storm had now quite gone by, and the moon shone brightly, revealing a rocky headland running half a mile or more out into the sea, of which this second line of breakers appeared to be a continuation. At any rate, they boiled around its foot. Probably the ridge that formed the headland ran out into the ocean, only at a lower level, and made the reef also. This headland was terminated by a curious peak that seemed not to be more than a mile away from us. Just as we got the boat pretty clear for the second time, Leo, to my immense relief, opened his eyes and remarked that the clothes had tumbled off the bed, and that he supposed it was time to get up for chapel.* I told him to shut his eyes and keep quiet, which he did without in the slightest degree realising the position. As for myself, his reference to chapel made me reflect, with a sort of sick longing, on my comfortable rooms at Cambridge. Why had I been such a fool as to leave them? This is a reflection that has several times recurred to me since, and with ever-increasing force.

But now again we are drifting down on the breakers, though with lessened speed, for the wind had fallen, and only the current or the tide (it afterwards turned out to be the tide) was driving us.

Another minute, and with a sort of howl to Allah from the Arab, a pious ejaculation from myself, and something that was not pious from Job, we were in them. And then the whole scene, down to our final escape, repeated itself, only not quite so violently. Mahomed's skilful steering and the air-tight compartments saved our lives. In five minutes we were through, and drifting—for we were too exhausted to do anything to help ourselves except keep her head straight—with the most startling rapidity round the headland which I have described.

Round we went with the tide, until we got well under the lee of the point, and then suddenly the speed slackened, we ceased to make way, and finally appeared to be in dead water. The storm had entirely passed, leaving a clean-washed sky behind it; the headland inter-cepted the heavy sea that had been occasioned by the squall, and the tide, which had been running so fiercely up the river (for we were now in the mouth of a river), was sluggish before it turned, so we floated quietly, and before the moon went down managed to bail out the boat thoroughly and get her a little ship-shape. Leo was sleeping profoundly, and on the whole I thought it wise not to wake him. It was true he was sleeping in wet clothes, but the night was now so warm that I thought (and so did Job) that they were not likely to injure a man of his unusually vigorous constitution. Besides, we had no dry ones at hand.

Presently the moon went down, and left us floating on the waters, now only heaving like some troubled woman's breast, giving us leis-ure to reflect upon all that we had gone through and all that we had escaped. Job stationed himself at the bow, Mahomed kept his post at the tiller, and I sat on a seat in the middle of the boat close to where Leo was lying.

The moon went slowly down in chastened loveliness, she departed like some sweet bride into her chamber, and long veil-like shadows crept up the sky through which the stars peeped shyly out. Soon, however, they too began to pale before a splendour in the east, and then the quivering footsteps of the dawn came rushing across the newborn blue, and shook the planets from their places. Quieter and yet more quiet grew the sea, quiet as the soft mist that brooded on her bosom, and covered up her troubling, as the illusive wreaths of sleep brood upon a pain-racked mind, causing it to forget its sorrow. From the east to the west sped the angels of the Dawn, from sea to sea, from mountain top to mountain top, scattering light with both their hands. On they sped out of the darkness, perfect, glorious, like spirits of the just breaking from the tomb; on, over the quiet sea, over the low coast line, and the swamps beyond, and the mountains beyond them; over those who slept in peace, and those who woke in sorrow; over the evil and the good; over the living and dead; over the wide world and all that breathes or has breathed thereon.

It was a wonderfully beautiful sight, and yet sad, perhaps from the very excess of its beauty. The arising sun; the setting sun! There we have the symbol and the type of humanity, and all things with which humanity has to do. The symbol and the type, yes, and the earthly beginning, and the end also. And on that morning this came home to me with a peculiar force. The sun that rose to-day for us had set last night for eighteen of our fellow-voyagers!—had set for ever for eighteen whom we knew!

The dhow had gone down with them, they were tossing about now among the rocks and seaweed, so much human drift on the great ocean of death! And we four were saved. But one day a sunrise will come when we shall be among those who are lost, and then others will watch those glorious rays, and grow sad in the midst of beauty, and dream of Death in the full glow of arising Life!

For this is the lot of man.

V

THE HEAD OF THE ETHIOPIAN

At length the heralds and forerunners of the royal sun had done
their work, and, searching out the shadows, had caused them to flee
away. Then up he came in glory from his ocean-bed, and flooded
the earth with warmth and light. I sat there in the boat listening
to the gentle lapping of the water and watched him rise, till presently
the slight drift of the boat brought the odd-shaped rock, or peak,
at the end of the promontory which we had weathered with so much
peril, between me and the majestic sight, and blotted it from my
view. I still continued to stare at the rock, however, absently enough,
till presently it became edged with the fire of the growing light
behind it, and then I started, as well I might, for I perceived that the
top of the peak, which was about eighty feet high by one hundred
and fifty thick at its base, was shaped like a negro's head and face,
whereon was stamped a most fiendish and terrifying expression.
There was no doubt about it; there were the thick lips, the fat cheeks,
and the squat nose standing out with startling clearness against the
flaming background. There, too, was the round skull, washed into
shape perhaps by thousands of years of wind and weather, and, to
complete the resemblance, there was a scrubby growth of weeds or
lichen upon it, which against the sun looked for all the world like the
wool on a colossal negro's head. It certainly was very odd; so odd
that now I believe that it is not a mere freak of nature but a gigantic
monument fashioned, like the well-known Egyptian Sphinx, by a
forgotten people out of a pile of rock that lent itself to their design,
perhaps as an emblem of warning and defiance to any enemies who
approached the harbour. Unfortunately we were never able to ascertain whether or not this was the case, inasmuch as the rock was
difficult of access both from the land and the water-side, and we had
other things to attend to. Myself, considering the matter by the light
of what we afterwards saw, I believe that it was fashioned by man,
but whether or not this is so, there it stands, and sullenly stares from
age to age out across the changing sea—there it stood two thousand
years and more ago, when Amenartas, the Egyptian Princess, and the
wife of Leo's remote ancestor Kallikrates, gazed upon its devilish

face—and there I have no doubt it will still stand when as many centuries as are numbered between her day and our own are added to the year that bore us to oblivion.

'What do you think of that, Job?' I asked of our retainer, who was sitting on the edge of the boat, trying to get as much sunshine as possible, and generally looking uncommonly wretched, and I pointed to the fiery and demoniacal head.

'Oh Lord, sir,' answered Job, who now perceived the object for the first time, 'I think that the old gentleman* must have been sitting for his portrait on them rocks.'

I laughed, and the laugh woke up Leo.

'Hullo,' he said, 'what's the matter with me? I am all stiff—where is the dhow? Give me some brandy, please.'

'You may be thankful that you are not stiffer, my boy,' I answered. 'The dhow is sunk, and everybody on board her is drowned, with the exception of us four, and your own life was only saved by a miracle;' and whilst Job, now that it was light enough, searched about in a locker for the brandy for which Leo asked, I told him the history of our night's adventure.

'Great Heavens!' he said, faintly; 'and to think that we should have been chosen to live through it!'

By this time the brandy was forthcoming, and we all had a good pull at it, and thankful enough we were for it. Also the sun was beginning to get strength, and warm our chilled bones, for we had been wet through for five hours or more.

'Why,' said Leo, with a gasp as he put down the brandy bottle, 'there is the head the writing talks of, the "rock carven like the head of an Ethiopian." '

'Yes,' I said, 'there it is.'

'Well, then,' he answered, 'the whole thing is true.'

'I don't at all see that that follows,' I answered. 'We knew this head was here, your father saw it. Very likely it is not the same head that the writing talks of; or if it is, it proves nothing.'

Leo smiled at me in a superior way. 'You are an unbelieving Jew, Uncle Horace,' he said. 'Those who live will see.'*

'Exactly so,' I answered, 'and now perhaps you will observe that we are drifting across a sandbank into the mouth of the river. Get hold of your oar, Job, and we will row in and see if we can find a place to land.'

The river mouth which we were entering did not appear to be a
very wide one, though as yet the long banks of steaming mist that
clung about its shores had not lifted sufficiently to enable us to see its
exact width. There was, as is the case with nearly every East African
river, a considerable bar at the mouth, which, no doubt, when the
wind was on shore and the tide running out, was absolutely impassable even for a boat drawing only a few inches. But as things were it
was manageable enough, and we did not ship a cupful of water. In
twenty minutes we were well across it, with but slight assistance
from ourselves and being carried by a strong though somewhat vari-
able breeze, well up the harbour. By this time the mist was being
sucked up by the sun, which was getting uncomfortably hot, and we
saw that the mouth of the little estuary was here about half a mile
across, and that the banks were very marshy, and crowded with
crocodiles lying about on the mud like logs. About a mile ahead of us,
however, was what appeared to be a strip of firm land, and for this we
steered. In another quarter of an hour we were there, and making the
boat fast to a beautiful tree with broad shining leaves, and flowers of
the magnolia species, only they were rose-coloured and not white,[1]
which hung over the water, we disembarked. This done we
undressed, washed ourselves, and spread our clothes and the contents of the boat in the sun to dry, which they very quickly did.
Then, taking shelter from the sun under some trees, we made a
hearty breakfast off a 'Paysandu' potted tongue, of which we had
brought a good quantity with us from the Army and Navy Stores,
congratulating ourselves loudly on our good fortune in having
loaded and provisioned the boat on the previous day before the
hurricane destroyed the dhow. By the time that we had finished our
meal our clothes were quite dry, and we hastened to get into them,
feeling not a little refreshed. Indeed, with the exception of weariness
and a few bruises, none of us were the worse for the terrifying
adventure which had been fatal to all our companions. Leo, it is true,
had been half-drowned, but that is no great matter to a vigorous
young athlete of five-and-twenty.

After breakfast we started to look about us. We were on a strip of
dry land about two hundred yards broad by five hundred long, bor-
dered on one side by the river, and on the other three by endless

[1] There is a known species of magnolia with pink flowers. It is indigenous in Sikkim,
and known as *Magnolia Campbellii*.—EDITOR.

desolate swamps, that stretched as far as the eye could reach. This strip of land was raised about twenty-five feet above the plain of the surrounding swamps and the river level: indeed it had every appearance of having been made by the hand of man.

'This place has been a wharf,' said Leo, dogmatically.

'Nonsense,' I answered. 'Who would be stupid enough to build a wharf in the middle of these dreadful marshes in a country inhabited by savages, that is if it is inhabited at all?'

'Perhaps it was not always marsh, and perhaps the people were not always savage,' he said drily, looking down the steep bank, for we were standing by the river. 'Look there,' he went on, pointing to a spot where the hurricane of the previous night had torn up one of the magnolia trees, which had grown on the extreme edge of the bank just where it sloped down to the water, by the roots, and lifted a large cake of earth with them. 'Is not that stonework? If not, it is very like it.'

'Nonsense,' I said again, and we clambered down to the spot, and got between the upturned roots and the bank.

'Well?' he said.

But I did not answer this time. I only whistled. For there, laid bare by the removal of the earth, was an undoubted facing of solid stone laid in large blocks and bound together with brown cement, so hard that I could make no impression on it with the file in my shooting knife. Nor was this all; seeing something projecting through the soil at the bottom of the bared patch of walling, I removed the loose earth with my hands, and revealed a huge stone ring, a foot or more in diameter, and about three inches thick. This fairly staggered me.

'Looks rather like a wharf where good-sized vessels have been moored, does it not, Uncle Horace?' said Leo, with an excited grin.

I tried to say 'Nonsense' again, but the word stuck in my throat—the ring spoke for itself. In some past age vessels *had* been moored there, and this stone wall was undoubtedly the remnant of a solidly constructed wharf. Probably the city to which it had belonged lay buried beneath the swamp behind it.

'Begins to look as though there were something in the story after all, Uncle Horace,' said the exultant Leo; and reflecting on the mysterious negro's head and the equally mysterious stonework, I made no direct reply.

'A country like Africa,' I said, 'is sure to be full of the relics of long dead and forgotten civilisations. Nobody knows the age of the Egyptian civilisation, and very likely it had offshoots. Then there were the Babylonians and the Phœnicians, and the Persians and all manner of people, all more or less civilised, to say nothing of the Jews whom everybody "wants" nowadays. It is possible that they, or any one of them, may have had colonies or trading stations about here. Remember those buried Persian cities that the consul showed us at Kilwa.'[1]

'Quite so,' said Leo, 'but that is not what you said before.'

'Well, what is to be done now?' I asked, turning the conversation.

As no answer was forthcoming we proceeded to the edge of the swamp, and looked over it. It was apparently boundless, and vast flocks of every sort of waterfowl came flying from its recesses, till it was sometimes difficult to see the sky.* Now that the sun was getting high it drew thin sickly looking clouds of poisonous vapour from the surface of the marsh and from the scummy pools of stagnant water.

'Two things are clear to me,' I said, addressing my three companions, who stared at this spectacle in dismay: 'first, that we can't go across there' (I pointed to the swamp), 'and, secondly, that if we stop here we shall certainly die of fever.'

'That's as clear as a haystack, sir,' said Job.

'Very well, then; there are two alternatives before us. One is to 'bout ship, and try and run for some port in the whale-boat, which would be a sufficiently risky proceeding, and the other to sail or row on up the river, and see where we come to.'

'I don't know what you are going to do,' said Leo, setting his mouth,' but I am going up that river.'

Job turned up the whites of his eyes and groaned, and the Arab murmured 'Allah,' and groaned also. As for me, I remarked sweetly that as we seemed to be between the devil and the deep sea, it did not much matter where we went. But in reality I was as anxious to

---

[1] Near Kilwa, on the East Coast of Africa, about 400 miles south of Zanzibar, is a cliff which has been recently washed by the waves. On the top of this cliff are Persian tombs known to be at least seven centuries old by the dates still legible upon them. Beneath these tombs is a layer of *débris* representing a city. Farther down the cliff is a second layer representing an older city, and further down still a third layer, the remains of yet another city of vast and unknown antiquity. Beneath the bottom city were recently found some specimens of glazed earthenware, such as are occasionally to be met with on that coast to this day. I believe that they are now in the possession of Sir John Kirk.— EDITOR.

proceed as Leo. The colossal negro's head and the stone wharf had excited my curiosity to an extent of which I was secretly ashamed, and I was prepared to gratify it at any cost. Accordingly, having carefully fitted the mast, restowed the boat, and got out our rifles, we embarked. Fortunately the wind was blowing on shore from the ocean, so we were able to hoist the sail. Indeed, we afterwards found out that as a general rule the wind set on shore from daybreak for some hours, and off shore again at sunset, and the explanation that I offer of this is, that when the earth is cooled by the dew and the night the hot air rises, and the draught rushes in from the sea till the sun has once more heated it through. At least that appeared to be the rule here.

Taking advantage of this favouring wind, we sailed merrily up the river for three or four hours. Once we came across a school of hippopotami, which rose, and bellowed dreadfully at us within ten or a dozen fathoms of the boat, much to Job's alarm, and, I will confess, to my own. These were the first hippopotami that we had ever seen, and, to judge by their insatiable curiosity, I should judge that we were the first white men that they had ever seen. Upon my word, I once or twice thought that they were coming into the boat to gratify it. Leo wanted to fire at them, but I dissuaded him, fearing the consequences. Also we saw hundreds of crocodiles basking on the muddy banks, and thousands upon thousands of waterfowl. Some of these we shot, and among them was a wild goose, which, in addition to the sharp curved spurs on its wings, had a spur about three-quarters of an inch long growing from the skull just between the eyes. We never shot another like it, so I do not know if it was a 'sport' or a distinct species. In the latter case this incident may interest naturalists. Job named it the Unicorn Goose.

About midday the sun grew intensely hot, and the stench drawn up by it from the marshes which the river drains was something too awful, and caused us instantly to swallow precautionary doses of quinine. Shortly afterwards the breeze died away altogether, and as rowing our heavy boat against stream in the heat was out of the question, we were thankful enough to get under the shade of a group of trees—a species of willow—that grew by the edge of the river, and lie there and gasp till at length the approach of sunset put a period to our miseries. Seeing what appeared to be an open space of water straight ahead of us, we determined to row there before settling what to do for the night. Just as we were about to loosen the boat, however, a beautiful water-buck, with great horns curving forward, and a white stripe across the rump, came down to the river to drink, without perceiving us hidden away within fifty yards under the willows. Leo was the first to catch sight of it, and being an ardent sportsman, thirsting for the blood of big game, about which he had been dreaming for months, he instantly stiffened all over, and pointed like a setter dog. Seeing what was the matter, I handed him his express rifle,* at the same time taking my own.

'Now then,' I whispered, 'mind you don't miss.'

'Miss!' he whispered back contemptuously; 'I could not miss it if I tried.'

He lifted the rifle, and the roan-coloured buck, having drunk his fill, raised his head and looked out across the river. He was standing right against the sunset sky on a little eminence, or ridge of ground, which ran across the swamp, evidently a favourite path for game, and there was something very beautiful about him. Indeed, I do not think that if I live to a hundred I shall ever forget that desolate and yet most fascinating scene: it is stamped upon my memory. To the right and left were wide stretches of lonely, death-breeding swamp, unbroken and unrelieved so far as the eye could reach, except here and there by ponds of black and peaty water that, mirror-like, flashed up the red rays of the setting sun. Behind us and before stretched the vista of the sluggish river, ending in glimpses of a reed-fringed lagoon, on the surface of which the long lights of the evening played as the faint breeze stirred the shadows. To the west loomed the huge red ball of the sinking sun, now vanishing down the vapoury horizon, and filling the great heaven, high across whose arch the cranes and wild fowl streamed in line, square, and triangle, with flashes of flying gold and the lurid stain of blood. And then ourselves—three modern Englishmen in a modern English boat—seeming to jar upon and looking out of tone with that measureless desolation; and in front of us the noble buck limned out upon a background of ruddy sky.

Bang! Away he goes with a mighty bound. Leo has missed him. *Bang!* right under him again. Now for a shot. I must have one, though he is going like an arrow, and a hundred yards away and more. By Jove! over and over and over! 'Well, I think I've wiped your eye there, Master Leo,' I say, struggling against the ungenerous exultation that in such a supreme moment of one's existence will rise in the best-mannered sportsman's breast.

'Confound you, yes,' growled Leo; and then, with that quick smile that is one of his charms lighting up his handsome face like a ray of light, 'I beg your pardon, old fellow. I congratulate you; it was a lovely shot, and mine were vile.'

We got out of the boat and ran to the buck, which was shot through the spine and stone dead. It took us a quarter of an hour or more to clean it and cut off as much of the best meat as we could carry, and, having packed this away, we had barely light enough to row up into the lagoon-like space, into which, there being a hollow in the swamp, the river here expanded. Just as the light vanished we cast anchor about thirty fathoms from the edge of the lake. We did not dare to go ashore, not knowing if we should find dry ground to camp on, and greatly fearing the poisonous exhalations from the marsh, from which we thought we should be freer on the water. So we lighted a lantern, and made our evening meal off another potted tongue in the best fashion that we could, and then prepared to go to sleep, only, however, to find that sleep was impossible. For, whether they were attracted by the lantern, or by the unaccustomed smell of a white man, for which they had been waiting for the last thousand years or so, I know not; but certainly we were presently attacked by tens of thousands of the most bloodthirsty, pertinacious, and huge mosquitoes that I ever saw or read of. In clouds they came, and pinged and buzzed and bit till we were nearly mad. Tobacco smoke only seemed to stir them into a merrier and more active life, till at length we were driven to covering ourselves with blankets, head and all, and sitting to slowly stew and continually scratch and swear beneath them. And as we sat, suddenly rolling out like thunder through the silence came the deep roar of a lion, and then of a second lion, moving among the reeds within sixty yards of us.

'I say,' said Leo, sticking his head out from under his blanket, 'lucky we ain't on the bank, eh, Avuncular?' (Leo sometimes addressed me in this disrespectful way.) 'Curse it! a mosquito has bitten me on the nose,' and the head vanished again.

Shortly after this the moon came up, and notwithstanding every variety of roar that echoed over the water to us from the lions on the banks, we began, thinking ourselves perfectly secure, to gradually doze off.

I do not quite know what it was that made me poke my head out of the friendly shelter of the blanket, perhaps because I found that the mosquitoes were biting right through it. Anyhow, as I did so I heard Job whisper, in a frightened voice—

'Oh, my stars, look there!'

Instantly we all of us looked, and this was what we saw in the moonlight. Near the shore were two wide and ever-widening circles of concentric rings rippling away across the surface of the water, and in the heart and centre of the circles were two dark moving objects.

'What is it?' asked I.

'It is those damned lions, sir,' answered Job, in a tone which was an odd mixture of a sense of personal injury, habitual respect, and acknowledged fear, 'and they are swimming here to *h*eat us,' he added, nervously picking up an 'h' in his agitation.

I looked again, there was no doubt about it; I could catch the glare of their ferocious eyes. Attracted either by the smell of the newly killed waterbuck meat or of ourselves, the hungry beasts were actually storming our position.

Leo already had his rifle in his hand. I called to him to wait till they were nearer, and meanwhile grabbed my own. Some fifteen feet from us the water shallowed on a bank to the depth of about fifteen inches, and presently the first of them—it was the lioness—got on to it and shook herself and roared. At that moment Leo fired, and the bullet went right down her open mouth and out at the back of her neck, and down she dropped, with a splash, dead. The other lion—a full-grown male—was some two paces behind her. At this second he got his forepaws on to the bank, when a strange thing happened. There was a rush and disturbance of the water, such as one sees in a pond in England when a pike takes a little fish, only a thousand times fiercer and larger, and suddenly the lion gave a most terrific snarling roar and sprang forward on to the bank, dragging something black with him.

'Allah!' shouted Mahomed, 'a crocodile has got him by the leg!' and sure enough he had. We could see the long snout with its gleaming lines of teeth and the reptile body behind it.

And then followed an extraordinary scene indeed. The lion managed to get well on to the bank, the crocodile half standing and half swimming, still nipping his hind leg. He roared till the air quivered with the sound, and then, with a savage, shrieking snarl, turned round and clawed hold of the crocodile's head. The crocodile shifted his grip, having, as we afterwards discovered, had one of his eyes torn out, and slightly turned over, and instantly the lion got him by the throat and held on, and then over and over they rolled upon the bank struggling hideously. It was impossible to follow their movements, but when next we got a clear view the tables had turned, for the crocodile, whose head seemed to be a mass of gore, had got the lion's body in his iron jaws just above the hips, and was squeezing him and shaking him to and fro. For his part the tortured brute, roaring in agony, was clawing and biting madly at his enemy's scaly head, and fixing his great hind claws in the crocodile's, comparatively speaking, soft throat, ripping it open as one would rip a glove.

Then, all of a sudden, the end came. The lion's head fell forward on the crocodile's back, and with an awful groan he died, and the crocodile, after standing for a minute motionless, slowly rolled over on to his side, his jaws still fixed across the carcases of the lion, which we afterwards found he had bitten almost in halves.

This duel to the death was a wonderful and a shocking sight, and one that I suppose few men have seen—and thus it ended.

When it was all over, leaving Mahomed to keep a look out, we managed to spend the rest of the night as quietly as the mosquitoes would allow.

VI

AN EARLY CHRISTIAN CEREMONY

NEXT morning, at the earliest blush of dawn, we rose, performed such ablutions as circumstances would allow, and generally made ready to start. I am bound to say that when there was sufficient light to enable us to see each other's faces I, for one, burst out into a roar of laughter. Job's fat and comfortable countenance was swollen out to nearly twice its natural size from mosquito bites, and Leo's condition was not much better. Indeed, of the three I had come off much the best, probably owing to the toughness of my dark skin, and to the fact that a good deal of it was covered by hair, for since we started from England I had allowed my naturally luxuriant beard to grow at its own sweet will. But the other two were, comparatively speaking, clean shaved, which of course gave the enemy a larger extent of open country to operate on, though as for Mahomed the mosquitoes, recognising the taste of a true believer, would not touch him at any price. How often, I wonder, during the next week or so did we wish that we were flavoured like an Arab!

By the time that we had done laughing as heartily as our swollen lips would allow, it was daylight, and the morning breeze was coming up from the sea, cutting lanes through the dense marsh mists, and here and there rolling them before it in great balls of fleecy vapour. So we set our sail, and having first taken a look at the two dead lions and the dead alligator, which we were of course unable to skin, being destitute of means of curing the pelts, we started, and, sailing through the lagoon, followed the course of the river on the farther side. At midday, when the breeze dropped, we were fortunate enough to find a convenient piece of dry land on which to camp and light a fire, and here we cooked two wild duck and some of the waterbuck's flesh—not in a very appetising way, it is true, but still, sufficiently. The rest of the buck's flesh we cut into strips and hung in the sun to dry into 'biltong,' as I believe the South African Dutch call flesh thus prepared. On this welcome patch of dry land we stopped till the following dawn, and, as before, spent the night in warfare with the mosquitoes, but without other troubles. The next day or two passed in similar fashion, and without noticeable adventures, except that we shot a specimen of a peculiarly graceful hornless buck, and saw many varieties of water-lilies in full bloom, some of them blue and of exquisite beauty, though few of the flowers were perfect, owing to the prevalence of a white water-maggot with a green head that fed upon them.

It was on the fifth day of our journey, when we had travelled, so far as we could reckon, about one hundred and thirty-five to a hundred and forty miles westwards from the coast, that the first event of any real importance occurred. On that morning the usual wind failed us about eleven o'clock, and after pulling a little way we were forced to halt more or less exhausted at what appeared to be the junction of our stream with another of a uniform width of about fifty feet. Some trees grew near at hand—the only trees in all this country were along the banks of the river, and under these we rested, and then, the land being fairly dry just here, walked a little way along the edge of the river to prospect, and shoot a few waterfowl for food. Before we had gone fifty yards we perceived that all hopes of getting further up the stream in the whale-boat were at an end, for not two hundred yards above where we had stopped were a succession of shallows and mudbanks, with not six inches of water over them. It was a watery *cul-de-sac*.

Turning back, we walked some way along the banks of the other river, and soon came to the conclusion, from various indications, that it was not a river at all, but an ancient canal, like the one which is to be seen above Mombasa, on the Zanzibar coast,* connecting the Tana River with the Ozy, in such a way as to enable the shipping coming down the Tana to cross to the Ozy, and reach the sea by it, and thus avoid the very dangerous bar that blocks the mouth of the Tana. The canal before us had evidently been dug out by man at some remote period of the world's history, and the results of his digging still remained in the shape of the raised banks that had no doubt once formed towing-paths. Except here and there, where they had been hollowed out or fallen in, these banks of stiff binding clay were at a uniform distance from each other, and the depth of the water also appeared to be uniform. Current there was little or none, and, as a consequence, the surface of the canal was choked with vegetable growth, intersected by little paths of clear water, made, I suppose, by the constant passage of waterfowl, iguanas, and other vermin. Now, as it was evident that we could not proceed up the river, it became equally evident that we must either try the canal or else return to the sea. We could not stop where we were, to be baked by the sun and eaten up by the mosquitoes, till we died of fever in that dreary marsh.

'Well, I suppose that we must try it,' I said; and the others assented in their various ways—Leo, as though it were the best joke in the world; Job, in respectful disgust; and Mahomed, with an invocation to the Prophet, and a comprehensive curse upon all unbelievers and their ways of thought and travel.

Accordingly, as soon as the sun got low, having little or nothing more to hope for from our friendly wind, we started. For the first hour or so we managed to row the boat, though with great labour; but after that the weeds got too thick to allow of it, and we were obliged to resort to the primitive and most exhausting resource of towing her. For two hours we laboured, Mahomed, Job, and I, who was supposed to be strong enough to pull against the two of them, on the bank, while Leo sat in the bow of the boat, and brushed away the weeds which collected round the cutwater with Mahomed's sword. At dark we halted for some hours to rest and enjoy the mosquitoes, but about midnight we went on again, taking advantage of the comparative cool of the night. At dawn we rested for three hours, and then started once more, and laboured on till about ten o'clock, when a thunderstorm, accompanied by a deluge of rain, overtook us, and we spent the next six hours practically under water.

I do not know that there is any necessity for me to describe the next four days of our voyage in detail, further than to say that they were, on the whole, the most miserable that I ever spent in my life, forming one monotonous record of heavy labour, heat, misery, and mosquitoes. All the way we passed through a region of almost endless swamp, and I can only attribute our escape from fever and death to the constant doses of quinine and purgatives which we took, and the unceasing toil which we were forced to undergo. On the third day of our journey up the canal we had sighted a round hill that loomed dimly through the vapours of the marsh, and on the evening of the fourth night, when we camped, this hill seemed to be within five-and-twenty or thirty miles of us. We were by now utterly exhausted, and felt as though our blistered hands could not pull the boat a yard farther, and that the best thing that we could do would be to lie down and die in that dreadful wilderness of swamp. It was an awful position, and one in which I trust no other white man will ever be placed; and as I threw myself down in the boat to sleep the sleep of utter exhaustion, I bitterly cursed my folly in ever having been a party to such a mad undertaking, which could, I saw, only end in our death in this ghastly land. I thought, I remember, as I slowly sank into a doze, of what the appearance of the boat and her unhappy crew would be in two or three months' time from that night. There she would lie, with gaping seams and half filled with fœtid water, which, when the mist-laden wind stirred her, would wash backwards and forwards through our mouldering bones, and that would be the end of her, and of those in her who would follow after myths and seek out the secrets of nature.

Already I seemed to hear the water rippling against the dessicated bones and rattling them together, rolling my skull against Mahomed's, and his against mine, till at last Mahomed's stood straight up upon its vertebræ, and glared at me through its empty eyeholes, and cursed me with its grinning jaws, because I, a dog of a Christian, disturbed the last sleep of a true believer. I opened my eyes, and shuddered at the horrid dream, and then shuddered again at something that was not a dream, for two great eyes were gleaming down at me through the misty darkness. I struggled up, and in my terror and confusion shrieked, and shrieked again, so that the others sprang up too, reeling, and drunken with sleep and fear. And then all of a sudden there was a flash of cold steel, and a great spear was held against my throat, and behind it other spears gleamed cruelly.

'Peace,' said a voice, speaking in Arabic, or rather in some dialect into which Arabic entered very largely; 'who are ye who come hither swimming on the water? Speak or ye die,' and the steel pressed sharply against my throat, sending a cold chill through me.

'We are travellers, and have come hither by chance,' I answered in my best Arabic, which appeared to be understood, for the man turned his head, and, addressing a tall form that towered up in the background, said, 'Father, shall we slay?'

'What is the colour of the men?' said a deep voice in answer.

'White is their colour.'

'Slay not,' was the reply. 'Four suns since was the word brought to me from "*She-who-must-be-obeyed*," "White men come; if white men come, slay them not." Let them be brought to the land of "*She-who-must-be-obeyed*." Bring forth the men, and let that which they have with them be brought forth also.'

'Come,' said the man, half leading and half dragging me from the boat, and as he did so I perceived other men doing the same kind office to my companions.

On the bank were gathered a company of some fifty men. In that light all I could make out was that they were armed with huge spears, were very tall, and strongly built, comparatively light in colour, and nude, save for a leopard-skin tied round the middle.

Presently Leo and Job were bundled out and placed beside me.

'What on earth is up?' said Leo, rubbing his eyes.

'Oh, Lord! sir, here's a rum go,' ejaculated Job; and just at that moment a disturbance ensued, and Mahomed came tumbling between us, followed by a shadowy form with an uplifted spear.

'Allah! Allah!' howled Mahomed, feeling that he had little to hope from man, 'protect me! protect me!'

'Father, it is a black one,' said a voice. 'What said "*She-who-must-be-obeyed*" about the black one?'

'She said naught; but slay him not. Come hither, my son.'

The man advanced, and the tall shadowy form bent forward and whispered something.

'Yes, yes,' said the other, and chuckled in a rather blood-curdling tone.

'Are the three white men there?' asked the form.

'Yes, they are there.'

'Then bring up that which is made ready for them, and let the men take all that can be brought from the thing which floats.'

Hardly had he spoken when men came running up, carrying on their shoulders neither more nor less than palanquins—four bearers and two spare men to a palanquin —and in these it was promptly indicated we were expected to stow ourselves.

'Well!' said Leo, 'it is a blessing to find anybody to carry us after having to carry ourselves so long.'

Leo always takes a cheerful view of things.

There being no help for it, after seeing the others into theirs I tumbled into my own litter, and very comfortable I found it. It appeared to be manufactured of cloth woven from grass-fibre, which stretched and yielded to every motion after the body, and, being bound top and bottom to the bearing pole, gave a grateful support to the head and neck.

Scarcely had I settled myself when, accompanying their steps with a monotonous song, the bearers started at a swinging trot. For half an hour or so I lay still, reflecting on the very remarkable experiences that we were going through, and wondering if any of my eminently respectable fossil friends down at Cambridge would believe me if I were to be miraculously set at the familiar dinner-table for the purpose of relating them. I don't want to convey any disrespectful notion or slight when I call those good and learned men fossils, but my experience is that people are apt to fossilise even at a University if they follow the same paths too persistently. I was getting fossilised myself, but of late my stock of ideas has been very much enlarged. Well, I lay and reflected, and wondered what on earth would be the end of it all, till at last I ceased to wonder, and went to sleep.

I suppose I must have slept for seven or eight hours, getting the first real rest that I had had since the night before the loss of the dhow, for when I woke the sun was high in the heavens. We were still journeying on at a pace of about four miles an hour. Peeping out through the mist-like curtains of the litter, which were ingeniously fixed to the bearing pole, I perceived to my infinite relief that we had passed out of the region of eternal swamp, and were now travelling over swelling grassy plains towards a cup-shaped hill.* Whether or not it was the same hill that we had seen from the canal I do not know, and have never since been able to discover, for, as we afterwards found out, these people will give little information upon such points. Next I glanced at the men who were bearing me. They were of a magnificent build, few of them being under six feet in height, and yellowish in colour. Generally their appearance had a good deal in common with that of the East African Somali, only their hair was not frizzed up, and hung in thick black locks upon their shoulders. Their features were aquiline, and in many cases exceedingly handsome, the teeth being especially regular and beautiful. But notwithstanding their beauty, it struck me that, on the whole, I had never seen a more evil-looking set of faces. There was an aspect of cold and sullen cruelty stamped upon them that revolted me, and which in some cases was almost uncanny in its intensity.

Another thing which struck me about them was that they never seemed to smile. Sometimes they sang the monotonous song of which I have spoken, but when they were not singing they remained almost perfectly silent, and the light of a laugh never came to brighten their sombre and evil countenances. Of what race could these people be? Their language was a bastard Arabic, and yet they were not Arabs; I was quite sure of that. For one thing they were too dark, or rather yellow. I could not say why, but I know that their appearance filled me with a sick fear of which I felt ashamed. While I was still wondering another litter came up alongside of mine. In it— for the curtains were drawn—sat an old man, clothed in a whitish robe, made apparently from coarse linen, that hung loosely about him, who, I at once jumped to the conclusion, was the shadowy figure who had stood on the bank and been addressed as 'Father.' He was a wonderful-looking old man, with a snowy beard, so long that the ends of it hung over the sides of the litter, and he had a hooked nose, above which flashed out a pair of eyes as keen as a snake's, while his whole countenance was instinct with a look of wise and sardonic humour impossible to describe on paper.

'Art thou awake, stranger?' he said in a deep and low voice.

'Surely, my father,' I answered courteously, feeling certain that I should do well to conciliate this ancient Mammon of Unrighteousness.*

He stroked his beautiful white beard, and smiled faintly.

'From whatever country thou camest,' he said, 'and by the way it must be from one where somewhat of our language is known, they teach their children courtesy there, my stranger son. And now wherefore comest thou unto this land, which scarce an alien foot has pressed from the time that man knoweth? Art thou and those with thee weary of life?'

'We came to find new things,' I answered boldly. 'We are tired of the old things; we have come up out of the sea to know that which is unknown. We are of a brave race who fear not death, my very much respected father—that is, if we can get a little fresh information before we die.'

'Humph!' said the old gentleman, 'that may be true; it is rash to contradict, otherwise I should say that thou wast lying, my son. However, I dare say that "*She-who-must-be-obeyed*" will meet thy wishes in the matter.'

'Who is "*She-who-must-be-obeyed*?"' I asked, curiously.

The old man glanced at the bearers, and then answered, with a little smile that somehow sent my blood to my heart—

'Surely, my stranger son, thou wilt learn soon enough, if it be her pleasure to see thee at all in the flesh.'

'In the flesh?' I answered. 'What may my father wish to convey?'

But the old man only laughed a dreadful laugh, and made no reply.

'What is the name of my father's people?' I asked.

'The name of my people is Amahagger' (the People of the Rocks).

'And if a son might ask, what is the name of my father?'

'My name is Billali.'

'And whither go we, my father?'

'That shalt thou see,' and at a sign from him his bearers started forward at a run till they reached the litter in which Job was reposing (with one leg hanging over the side). Apparently, however, he could not make much out of Job, for presently I saw his bearers trot forward to Leo's litter.

And after that, as nothing fresh occurred, I yielded to the pleasant swaying motion of the litter, and went to sleep again. I was dreadfully tired. When I woke I found that we were passing through a rocky defile of a lava formation with precipitous sides, in which grew many beautiful trees and flowering shrubs.

Presently this defile took a turn, and a lovely sight unfolded itself to my eyes. Before us was a vast cup of green from four to six miles in extent, of the shape of a Roman amphitheatre. The sides of this great cup were rocky, and clothed with bush, but the centre was of the richest meadow land, studded with single trees of magnificent growth, and watered by meandering brooks. On this rich plain grazed herds of goats and cattle, but I saw no sheep. At first I could not imagine what this strange spot could be, but presently it flashed upon me that it must represent the crater of some long-extinct volcano, which had afterwards been a lake, and was ultimately drained in some unexplained way. And here I may state that from my subsequent experience of this and a much larger, but otherwise similar spot, which I shall have occasion to describe by-and-by, I have every reason to believe that this conclusion was correct. What puzzled me, however, was that, although there were people moving about herding the goats and cattle, I saw no signs of any human habitation. Where did they all live? I wondered. My curiosity was soon destined to be gratified. Turning to the left the string of litters followed the cliffy sides of the crater for a distance of about half a mile, or perhaps a little less, and then halted. Seeing the old gentleman, my adopted 'father,' Billali, emerge from his litter, I did the same, and so did Leo and Job. The first thing I saw was our wretched Arab companion, Mahomed, lying exhausted on the ground. It appeared that he had not been provided with a litter, but had been forced to run the entire distance, and, as he was already quite worn out when we started, his condition now was one of great prostration.

On looking round we discovered that the place where we had halted was a platform in front of the mouth of a great cave, and piled upon this platform were the entire contents of the whale-boat, even down to the oars and sail. Round the cave stood groups of the men who had escorted us, and other men of a similar stamp. They were all tall and all handsome, though they varied in their degree of darkness of skin, some being as dark as Mahomed, and some as yellow as a Chinese. They were naked, except for the leopard-skin round the waist, and each of them carried a huge spear.

There were also some women among them, who, instead of the leopard-skin, wore a tanned hide of a small red buck, something like that of the oribé,* only rather darker in colour. These woman were, as a class, exceedingly good-looking, with large, dark eyes, well-cut features, and a thick bush of curling hair—not crisped like a negro's—ranging from black to chestnut in hue, with all shades of intermediate colour. Some, but very few of them, wore a yellowish linen garment, such as I have described as worn by Billali, but this, as we afterwards discovered, was a mark of rank, rather than an attempt at clothing. For the rest, their appearance was not quite so terrifying as that of the men, and they sometimes, though rarely, smiled. As soon as we had alighted they gathered round us and examined us with curiosity, but without excitement. Leo's tall, athletic form and clear-cut Grecian face, however, evidently excited their attention, and when he politely lifted his hat to them, and showed his curling yellow hair, there was a slight murmur of admiration. Nor did it stop there; for, after regarding him critically from head to foot, the handsomest of the young women—one wearing a robe, and with hair of a shade between brown and chestnut— deliberately advanced to him, and, in a way that would have been winning had it not been so determined, quietly put her arm round his neck, bent forward, and kissed him on the lips.

I gave a gasp, expecting to see Leo instantly speared; and Job ejaculated, 'The hussy—well, I never!' As for Leo, he looked slightly astonished; and then, remarking that we had got into a country where they clearly followed the customs of the early Christians,* deliberately returned the embrace.

Again I gasped, thinking that something would happen; but to my surprise, though some of the young women showed traces of vexation, the older ones and the men only smiled slightly. When we came to understand the customs of this extraordinary people the mystery was explained. It then appeared that, in direct opposition to the habits of almost every other savage race in the world, women among the Amahagger are not only upon terms of perfect equality with the men, but are not held to them by any binding ties. Descent is traced only through the line of the mother, and while individuals are as proud of a long and superior female ancestry as we are of our families in Europe, they never pay attention to, or even acknowledge, any man as their father, even when their male parentage is perfectly well known. There is but one titular male parent of each tribe, or, as they call it, 'Household,' and he is its elected and immediate ruler, with the title of 'Father.' For instance, the man Billali was the father of this 'household,' which consisted of about seven thousand individuals all told, and no other man was ever called by that name. When a woman took a fancy to a man she signified her preference by advancing and embracing him publicly, in the same way that this handsome and exceedingly prompt young lady, who was called Ustane, had embraced Leo. If he kissed her back it was a token that he accepted her, and the arrangement continued till one of them wearied of it. I am bound, however, to say that the change of husbands was not nearly so frequent as might have been expected. Nor did quarrels arise out of it, at least among the men, who, when their wives deserted them in favour of a rival, accepted the whole thing much as we accept the income-tax or our marriage laws, as something not to be disputed, and as tending to the good of the community, however disagreeable they may in particular instances prove to the individual.

It is very curious to observe how the customs of mankind on this matter vary in different countries, making morality an affair of latitude, and what is right and proper in one place wrong and improper in another. It must, however, be understood that, as all civilised

nations appear to accept it as an axiom that ceremony is the touch-
stone of morality, there is, even according to our canons, nothing
immoral about this Amahagger custom, seeing that the interchange
of the embrace answers to our ceremony of marriage, which, as we
know, justifies most things.

VII

WHEN the kissing operation was finished—by the way, none of the young ladies offered to pet me in this fashion, though I saw one hovering round Job, to that respectable individual's evident alarm— the old man Billali advanced, and graciously waved us into the cave, whither we went, followed by Ustane, who did not seem inclined to take the hints I gave her that we liked privacy.

Before we had gone five paces it struck me that the cave that we were entering was none of Nature's handiwork, but, on the contrary, had been hollowed by the hand of man. So far as we could judge it appeared to be about one hundred feet in length by fifty wide, and very lofty, resembling a cathedral aisle more than anything else. From this main aisle opened passages at a distance of every twelve or fifteen feet, leading, I supposed, to smaller chambers. About fifty feet from the entrance of the cave, just where the light began to get dim, a fire was burning, which threw huge shadows upon the gloomy walls around. Here Billali halted, and asked us to be seated, saying that the people would bring us food, and accordingly we squatted ourselves down upon the rugs of skins which were spread for us, and waited. Presently the food, consisting of goat's flesh boiled, fresh milk in an earthenware pot, and boiled cobs of Indian corn, was brought by young girls. We were almost starving, and I do not think that I ever in my life before ate with such satisfaction. Indeed, before we had finished we literally ate up everything that was set before us.

When we had done, our somewhat saturnine host, Billali, who had been watching us in perfect silence, rose and addressed us. He said that it was a wonderful thing that had happened. No man had ever known or heard of white strangers arriving in the country of the People of the Rocks. Sometimes, though rarely, black men had come here, and from them they had heard of the existence of men much whiter than themselves, who sailed on the sea in ships, but for the arrival of such there was no precedent. We had, however, been seen dragging the boat up the canal, and he told us frankly that he had at once given orders for our destruction, seeing that it was unlawful for any stranger to enter here, when a message had come from

'*She-who-must-be-obeyed*,' saying that our lives were to be spared, and that we were to be brought hither.

'Pardon me, my father,' I interrupted at this point; 'but if, as I understand, "*She-who-must-be-obeyed*" lives yet farther off, how could she have known of our approach?'

Billali turned, and seeing that we were alone—for the young lady, Ustane, had withdrawn when he had begun to speak—said, with a curious little laugh—

'Are there none in your land who can see without eyes and hear without ears? Ask no questions; *She* knew.'

I shrugged my shoulders at this, and he proceeded to say that no further instructions had been received on the subject of our disposal, and this being so he was about to start to interview '*She-who-must-be-obeyed*,' generally spoken of, for the sake of brevity, as 'Hiya' or *She* simply, who he gave us to understand was the Queen of the Amahagger, and learn her wishes.

I asked him how long he proposed to be away, and he said that by travelling hard he might be back on the fifth day, but there were many miles of marsh to cross before he came to where *She* was. He then said that every arrangement would be made for our comfort during his absence, and that, as he personally had taken a fancy to us, he sincerely trusted that the answer he should bring from *She* would be one favourable to the continuation of our existence, but at the same time he did not wish to conceal from us that he thought this doubtful, as every stranger who had ever come into the country during his grandmother's life, his mother's life, and his own life, had been put to death without mercy, and in a way that he would not harrow our feelings by describing; and this had been done by the order of *She* herself, at least he supposed it was by her order. At any rate, she never interfered to save them.

'Why,' I said, 'but how can that be? You are an old man, and the time you talk of must reach back three men's lives. How therefore could *She* have ordered the death of anybody at the beginning of the life of your grandmother, seeing that herself she would not have been born?'

Again he smiled—that same faint, peculiar smile, and with a deep bow departed, without making any answer; nor did we see him again for five days.

When he had gone we discussed the situation, which filled me with alarm. I did not at all like the accounts of this mysterious Queen, '*She-who-must-be-obeyed*,' or more shortly *She*, who apparently ordered the execution of any unfortunate stranger in a fashion so unmerciful. Leo, too, was depressed about it, but proceeded to console himself by triumphantly pointing out that this *She* was undoubtedly the person referred to in the writing on the potsherd and in his father's letter, in proof of which he advanced Billali's allusions to her age and power. I was by this time so overwhelmed with the whole course of events that I had not even got the heart left to dispute a proposition so absurd, so I suggested that we should try and go out and get a bath, of which we all stood sadly in need.

Accordingly, having indicated our wish to a middle-aged individual of an unusually saturnine cast of countenance, even among this saturnine people, who appeared to be deputed to look after us now that the Father of the hamlet had departed, we started in a body—having first lit our pipes. Outside the cave we found quite a crowd of people evidently watching for our appearance, but when they saw us come out smoking they vanished this way and that, calling out that we were great magicians. Indeed, nothing about us created so great a sensation as our tobacco smoke—not even our firearms.[1] After this we succeeded in reaching a stream that had its source in a strong ground spring, and taking our bath in peace, though some of the women, not excepting Ustane, showed a decided inclination to follow us even there.

By the time that we had finished this most refreshing bath the sun was setting; indeed, when we got back to the big cave it had already set. The cave itself was full of people gathered round fires—for several more had now been lighted—and eating their evening meal by their lurid light, and by that of various lamps which were set about or hung upon the walls. These lamps were of a rude manufacture of baked earthenware, and of all shapes, some of them graceful enough. The larger ones were formed of big red earthenware pots, filled with clarified melted fat, and having a reed wick stuck through a wooden disk which filled the top of the pot, and this sort of lamp required the most constant attention to prevent its going out whenever the wick burnt down, as there were no means of turning it

[1] We found tobacco growing in this country as it does in every other part of Africa, and, although they are so absolutely ignorant of its other blessed qualities, the Amahagger use it habitually in the form of snuff, and also for medicinal purposes.—L. H. H.

up. The smaller hand lamps, however, which were also made of baked clay, were fitted with wicks manufactured from the pith of a palm-tree, or sometimes from the stem of a very handsome variety of fern. This kind of wick was passed through a round hole at the end of the lamp, to which a sharp piece of hard wood was attached wherewith to pierce and draw it up whenever it showed signs of burning low.

For a while we sat down and watched this grim people eating their evening meal in silence as grim as themselves, till at length, getting tired of contemplating them and the huge moving shadows on the rocky walls, I suggested to our new keeper that we should like to go to bed.

Without a word he rose, and, taking me politely by the hand, advanced with a lamp to one of the small passages that I had noticed opening out of the central cave. This we followed for about five paces, when it suddenly widened out into a small chamber, about eight feet square, and hewn out of the living rock. On one side of this chamber was a stone slab, about three feet from the ground, and running its entire length like a bunk in a cabin, and on this slab he intimated that I was to sleep. There was no window or air-hole to the chamber, and no furniture; and, on looking at it more closely, I came to the disturbing conclusion (in which, as I afterwards discovered, I was quite right) that it had originally served for a sepulchre for the dead rather than a sleeping-place for the living, the slab being designed to receive the corpse of the departed. The thought made me shudder in spite of myself; but, seeing that I must sleep somewhere, I got over the feeling as best I might, and returned to the cavern to get my blanket, which had been brought up from the boat with the other things. There I met Job, who, having been inducted to a similar apartment, had flatly declined to stop in it, saying that the look of the place gave him the horrors, and that he might as well be dead and buried in his grandfather's brick grave at once, and expressed his determination of sleeping with me if I would allow him. This, of course, I was only too glad to do.

The night passed very comfortably on the whole. I say on the whole, for personally I went through a most horrible nightmare of being buried alive, induced, no doubt, by the sepulchral nature of my surroundings. At dawn we were aroused by a loud trumpeting sound, produced, as we afterwards discovered, by a young Amahagger blowing through a hole bored in its side into a hollowed elephant tusk, which was kept for the purpose.

Taking the hint, we got up and went down to the stream to wash, after which the morning meal was served. At breakfast one of the women, no longer quite young, advanced, and publicly kissed Job. I think it was in its way the most delightful thing (putting its impropriety aside for a moment) that I ever saw. Never shall I forget the respectable Job's abject terror and disgust. Job, like myself, is a bit of a misogynist—I fancy chiefly owing to the fact of his having been one of a family of seventeen—and the feelings expressed upon his countenance when he realised that he was not only being embraced publicly, and without authorisation on his own part, but also in the presence of his masters, were too mixed and painful to admit of accurate description. He sprang to his feet, and pushed the woman, a buxom person of about thirty, from him.

'Well, I never!' he gasped, whereupon probably thinking that he was only coy, she embraced him again.

'Be off with you! Get away, you minx!' he shouted, waving the wooden spoon, with which he was eating his breakfast, up and down before the lady's face. 'Beg your pardon, gentlemen, I am sure I haven't encouraged her. Oh, Lord! she's coming for me again. Hold her, Mr. Holly! please hold her! I can't stand it; I can't, indeed. This has never happened to me before, gentlemen, never. There's nothing against my character,' and here he broke off, and ran as hard as he could go down the cave, and for once I saw the Amahagger laugh. As for the woman, however, she did not laugh. On the contrary, she seemed to bristle with fury, which the mockery of the other women about only served to intensify. She stood there literally snarling and shaking with indignation, and, seeing her, I wished Job's scruples had been at Jericho,* forming a shrewd guess that his admirable behaviour had endangered our throats. Nor, as the sequel shows, was I wrong.

The lady having retreated, Job returned in a great state of nervousness, and keeping his weather eye fixed upon every woman who came near him. I took an opportunity to explain to our hosts that Job was a married man, and had had very unhappy experiences in his domestic relations, which accounted for his presence here and his terror at the sight of women, but my remarks were received in grim silence, it being evident that our retainer's behaviour was considered as a slight to the 'household' at large, although the women, after the manner of some of their more civilised sisters, made merry at the rebuff of their companion.

After breakfast we took a walk and inspected the Amahagger herds, and also their cultivated lands. They have two breeds of cattle, one large and angular, with no horns, but yielding beautiful milk; and the other, a red breed, very small and fat, excellent for meat, but of no value for milking purposes. This last breed closely resembles the Norfolk red-pole strain,* only it has horns which generally curve forward over the head, sometimes to such an extent that they have to be cut to prevent them from growing into the bones of the skull. The goats are long-haired, and are used for eating only, at least I never saw them milked. As for the Amahagger cultivation, it is primitive in the extreme, being all done by means of a spade made of iron, for these people smelt and work iron. This spade is shaped more like a big spear-head than anything else, and has no shoulder to it on which the foot can be set. As a consequence, the labour of digging is very great. It is, however, all done by the men, the women, contrary to the habits of most savage races, being entirely exempt from manual toil. But then, as I think I have said elsewhere, among the Amahagger the weaker sex has established its rights.

At first we were much puzzled as to the origin and constitution of this extraordinary race, points upon which they were singularly uncommunicative. As the time went on—for the next four days passed without any striking event—we learnt something from Leo's lady friend Ustane, who, by the way, stuck to that young gentleman like his own shadow. As to origin, they had none, at least, so far as she was aware. There were, however, she informed us, mounds of masonry and many pillars near the place where *She* lived, which was called Kôr, and which the wise said had once been houses wherein men lived, and it was suggested that they were descended from these men. No one, however, dared go near these great ruins, because they were haunted: they only looked on them from a distance. Other similar ruins were to be seen, she had heard, in various parts of the country, that is, wherever one of the mountains rose above the level of the swamp. Also the caves in which they lived had been hollowed out of the rocks by men, perhaps the same who built the cities. They themselves had no written laws, only custom, which was, however, quite as binding as law. If any man offended against the custom, he was put to death by order of the Father of the 'Household.' I asked how he was put to death, and she only smiled, and said that I might see one day soon.

They had a Queen, however. *She* was their Queen, but she was very rarely seen, perhaps once in two or three years, when she came forth to pass sentence on some offenders, and when seen was muffled up in a big cloak, so that nobody could look upon her face. Those who waited upon her were deaf and dumb, and therefore could tell no tales, but it was reported that she was lovely as no other woman was lovely, or ever had been. It was rumoured also that she was immortal, and had power over all things, but she, Ustane, could say nothing of all that. What she believed was that the Queen chose a husband from time to time, and as soon as a female child was born this husband, who was never again seen, was put to death. Then the female child grew up and took the place of the Queen when its mother died, and had been buried in the great caves. But of these matters none could speak for certain. Only *She* was obeyed throughout the length and breadth of the land, and to question her command was certain death. She kept a guard, but had no regular army, and to disobey her was to die.

I asked what size the land was, and how many people lived in it. She answered that there were ten 'Households,' like this that she knew of, including the big 'Household,' where the Queen was, that all the 'Households' lived in caves, in places resembling this stretch of raised country, dotted about in a vast extent of swamp, which was only to be threaded by secret paths. Often the 'Households' made war on each other until *She* sent word that it was to stop, and then they instantly ceased. That and the fever which they caught in crossing the swamps prevented their numbers from increasing too much. They had no connection with any other race, indeed none lived near them, or were able to thread the vast swamps. Once an army from the direction of the great river (presumably the Zambesi) had attempted to attack them, but they got lost in the marshes, and at night, seeing the great balls of fire that move about there, tried to come to them, thinking that they marked the enemy's camp, and half of them were drowned. As for the rest, they soon died of fever and starvation, not a blow being struck at them. The marshes, she told us, were absolutely impassable except to those who knew the paths, adding, what I could well believe, that we should never have reached this place where we then were had we not been brought thither.

These and many other things we learnt from Ustane during the four days' pause before our real adventures began, and, as may be imagined, they gave us considerable cause for thought. The whole thing was exceedingly remarkable, almost incredibly so, indeed, and the oddest part of it was that so far it did more or less correspond to the ancient writing on the sherd. And now it appeared that there was a mysterious Queen clothed by rumour with dread and wonderful attributes, and commonly known by the impersonal but, to my mind, rather awesome title of *She*. Altogether, I could not make it out, nor could Leo, though of course he was exceedingly triumphant over me because I had persistently mocked at the whole thing. As for Job, he had long since abandoned any attempt to call his reason his own, and left it to drift upon the sea of circumstance. Mahomed, the Arab, who was, by the way, treated civilly indeed, but with chilling contempt, by the Amahagger, was, I discovered, in a great fright, though I could not quite make out what he was frightened about. He would sit crouched up in a corner of the cave all day long, calling upon Allah and the Prophet to protect him. When I pressed him about it, he said that he was afraid because these people were not men and women at all, but devils, and that this was an enchanted land; and, upon my word, once or twice since then I have been inclined to agree with him. And so the time went on, till the night of the fourth day after Billali had left, when something happened.

We three and Ustane were sitting round a fire in the cave just before bedtime, when suddenly the woman, who had been brooding in silence, rose, and laid her hand upon Leo's golden curls, and addressed him. Even now, when I shut my eyes, I can see her proud, imperial form, clothed alternately in dense shadow and the red flickering of the fire, as she stood, the wild centre of as weird a scene as I ever witnessed, and delivered herself of the burden of her thoughts and forebodings in a kind of rhythmical speech that ran something as follows:—

Thou art my chosen—I have waited for thee from the beginning!
Thou art very beautiful. Who hath hair like unto thee, or skin so white?
Who hath so strong an arm, who is so much a man?
Thine eyes are the sky, and the light in them is the stars.

Thou art perfect and of a happy face, and my heart turned itself towards
 thee.
Ay, when mine eyes fell on thee I did desire thee,—
Then did I take thee to me—thou, my Beloved,
And hold thee fast, lest harm should come unto thee.
Ay, I did cover thine head with mine hair, lest the sun should strike it;
And altogether was I thine, and thou wast altogether mine.
And so it went for a little space, till Time was in labour with an evil Day;
And then what befell on that day? Alas! my Beloved, I know not!
But I, I saw thee no more—I, I was lost in the blackness.
And she who is stronger did take thee; ay, she who is fairer than Ustane.
Yet didst thou turn and call upon me, and let thine eyes wander in the
 darkness.
But, nevertheless, she prevailed by Beauty, and led thee down horrible
 places,
And then, ah! then my Beloved——

Here this extraordinary woman broke off her speech, or chant,
which was so much musical gibberish to us, for all that we understood of what she was talking about, and seemed to fix her flashing
eyes upon the deep shadow before her. Then in a moment they
acquired a vacant, terrified stare, as though they were striving to
realise some half-seen horror. She lifted her hand from Leo's head,
and pointed into the darkness. We all looked, and could see nothing;
but she saw something, or thought she did, and something evidently
that affected even her iron nerves, for, without another sound, down
she fell senseless between us.

Leo, who was growing really attached to this remarkable young
person, was in a great state of alarm and distress, and I, to be perfectly candid, was in a condition not far removed from superstitious
fear. The whole scene was an uncanny one.

Presently, however, she recovered, and sat up with an extraordinary
convulsive shudder.

'What didst thou mean, Ustane?' asked Leo, who, thanks to years
of tuition, spoke Arabic very prettily.

'Nay, my chosen,' she answered with a little forced laugh. 'I did
but sing unto thee after the fashion of my people. Surely, I meant
nothing. How could I speak of that which is not yet?'

'And what didst thou see, Ustane?' I asked, looking her sharply in
the face.

'Nay,' she answered again; 'I saw naught. Ask me not what I saw.

Why should I fright ye?' And then, turning to Leo with a look of the most utter tenderness that I ever saw upon the face of a woman, civilised or savage, she took his head between her hands, and kissed him on the forehead as a mother might. 'When I am gone from thee, my chosen; when at night thou stretchest out thine hand and canst not find me, then shouldst thou think at times of me, for of a truth I love thee well, though I be not fit to wash thy feet. And now let us love and take that which is given us, and be happy; for in the grave there is no love and no warmth, nor any touching of the lips. Nothing perchance, or perchance but bitter memories of what might have been. To-night the hours are our own, how know we to whom they shall belong to-morrow?'

VIII

THE FEAST, AND AFTER!

ON the day following this remarkable scene—a scene calculated to make a deep impression upon anybody who beheld it, more because of what it suggested and seemed to foreshadow than of what it revealed—it was announced to us that a feast would be held that evening in our honour. I did my best to get out of it, saying that we were modest people, and cared little for feasts, but my remarks being received with the silence of displeasure, I thought it wisest to hold my tongue.

Accordingly, just before sundown, I was informed that everything was ready, and, accompanied by Job, went into the cave, where I met Leo, who was, as usual, followed by Ustane. These two had been out walking somewhere, and knew nothing of the projected festivity till that moment. When Ustane heard of it I saw an expression of horror spring up upon her handsome features. Turning, she caught a man who was passing up the cave by the arm, and asked him something in an imperious tone. His answer seemed to reassure her a little, for she looked relieved, though far from satisfied. Next she appeared to attempt some remonstrance with the man, who was a person in authority, but he spoke angrily to her, and shook her off, and then changing his mind, led her by the arm, and sat her down between himself and another man in the circle round the fire, and I perceived that for some reason of her own she thought it best to submit.

The fire in the cave was an unusually big one that night, and in a large circle round it were gathered about thirty-five men and two women, Ustane and the woman to avoid whom Job had played the *rôle* of another Scriptural character.* The men were sitting in perfect silence, as was their custom, each with his great spear stuck upright behind him, in a socket cut in the rock for that purpose. Only one or two wore the yellowish linen garment of which I have spoken, the rest had nothing on except the leopard's skin about the middle.

'What's up now, sir?' said Job, doubtfully. 'Bless us and save us, there's that woman again. Now, surely, she can't be after me, seeing that I have given her no encouragement. They give me the creeps, the whole lot of them, and that's a fact. Why, look, they have asked

Mahomed to dine, too. There, that lady of mine is talking to him in as nice and civil a way as possible. Well, I'm glad it isn't me, that's all.'

We looked up, and sure enough the woman in question had risen, and was escorting the wretched Mahomed from the corner, where, overcome by some acute prescience of horror, he had been seated, shivering, and calling on Allah. He appeared unwilling enough to come, if for no other reason perhaps because it was an unaccustomed honour, for hitherto his food had been given to him apart. Anyway I could see that he was in a state of great terror, for his tottering legs would scarcely support his stout, bulky form, and I think it was rather owing to the resources of barbarism behind him, in the shape of a huge Amahagger with a proportionately huge spear, than to the seduction of the lady who led him by the hand, that he consented to come at all.

'Well,' I said to the others, 'I don't at all like the look of things, but I suppose that we must face it out. Have you fellows got your revolvers on? because, if so, you had better see that they are loaded.'

'I have, sir,' said Job, tapping his Colt, 'but Mr. Leo has only got his hunting-knife, though that is big enough, surely.'

Feeling that it would not do to wait while the missing weapon was fetched, we advanced boldly, and seated ourselves in a line, with our backs against the side of the cave.

As soon as we were seated, an earthenware jar was passed round containing a fermented fluid, of by no means unpleasant taste, though apt to turn upon the stomach, made of crushed grain—not Indian corn, but a small brown grain that grows upon the stem in clusters, not unlike that which in the southern part of Africa is known by the name of Kafir corn.* The vase in which this liquid was handed round was very curious, and as it more or less resembled many hundreds of others in use among the Amahagger I may as well describe it. These vases are of a very ancient manufacture, and of all sizes. None such can have been made in the country for hundreds, or rather thousands, of years. They are found in the rock tombs, of which I shall give a description in their proper place, and my own belief is that, after the fashion of the Egyptians, with whom the former inhabitants of this country may have had some connection, they were used to receive the viscera of the dead. Leo, however, is of opinion that, as in the case of Etruscan amphoræ, they were placed there for the spiritual use of the deceased. They are mostly two-handled, and of all sizes, some being nearly three feet in height, and running from that down to as many inches. In shape they vary, but are all exceedingly beautiful and graceful, being made of a very fine black ware, not lustrous, but slightly rough. On this groundwork were inlaid figures much more graceful and lifelike than any others I have seen on antique vases. Some of these inlaid pictures represented love-scenes with a child-like simplicity and freedom of manner which would not commend itself to the taste of the present day. Others again were pictures of maidens dancing, and yet others of hunting-scenes. For instance, the very vase from which we were then drinking had on one side a most spirited drawing of men, apparently white in colour, attacking a bull-elephant with spears, while on the reverse was a picture, not quite so well done, of a hunter shooting an arrow at a running antelope, I should say from the look of it either an eland or a koodoo.

This is a digression at a critical moment, but it is not too long for the occasion, for the occasion itself was very long. With the exception of the periodical passing of the vase, and the movement necessary to throw fuel on to the fire, nothing happened for the best part of a whole hour. Nobody spoke a word. There we all sat in perfect silence, staring at the glare and glow of the large fire, and at the shadows thrown by the flickering earthenware lamps (which, by the way, were not ancient). On the open space between us and the fire lay a large wooden tray, with four short handles to it, exactly like a butcher's tray, only not hollowed out. By the side of the tray was a great pair of long-handled iron pincers, and on the other side of the fire was a similar pair. Somehow I did not at all like the appearance of this tray and the accompanying pincers. There I sat and stared at them and at the silent circle of the fierce moody faces of the men, and reflected that it was all very awful, and that we were absolutely in the power of this alarming people, who, to me at any rate, were all the more formidable because their true character was still very much of a mystery to us. They might be better than I thought them, or they might be worse. I feared that they were worse, and I was not wrong. It was a curious sort of a feast, I reflected, in appearance, indeed, an entertainment of the Barmecide* stamp, for there was absolutely nothing to eat.

At last, just as I was beginning to feel as though I were being mesmerised, a move was made. Without the slightest warning, a man from the other side of the circle called out in a loud voice—

'Where is the flesh that we shall eat?'

Thereon everybody in the circle answered in a deep measured tone, and stretching out the right arm towards the fire as he spoke—

'*The flesh will come.*'

'Is it a goat?' said the same man.

'*It is a goat without horns, and more than a goat, and we shall slay it,*' they answered with one voice, and turning half round they one and all grasped the handles of their spears with the right hand, and then simultaneously let them go.

'Is it an ox?' said the man again.

'*It is an ox without horns, and more than an ox, and we shall slay it,*' was the answer, and again the spears were grasped, and again let go.

Then came a pause, and I noticed, with horror and a rising of the hair, that the woman next to Mahomed began to fondle him, patting his cheeks, and calling him by names of endearment, while her fierce eyes played up and down his trembling form. I do not know why the sight frightened me so, but it did frighten us all dreadfully, especially Leo. The caressing was so snake-like, and so evidently a part of some ghastly formula that had to be gone through.[1] I saw Mahomed turn white under his brown skin, sickly white with fear.

'Is the meat ready to be cooked?' asked the voice, more rapidly.

'*It is ready; it is ready.*'

'Is the pot hot to cook it?' it continued, in a sort of scream that echoed painfully down the great recesses of the cave.

'*It is hot; it is hot.*'

'Great heavens!' roared Leo, 'remember the writing, "*The people who place pots upon the heads of strangers.*" '

As he said the words, before we could stir, or even take the matter in, two great ruffians jumped up, and, seizing the long pincers, plunged them into the heart of the fire, and the woman who had been caressing Mahomed suddenly produced a fibre noose from under her girdle or moocha, and, slipping it over his shoulders, ran it tight, while the men next him seized him by the legs. The two men with the pincers gave a heave, and, scattering the fire this way and that

---

[1] We afterwards learnt that its object was to pretend to the victim that he was the object of love and admiration, and so to soothe his injured feelings, and cause him to expire in a happy and contented frame of mind.—L. H. H.

upon the rocky floor, lifted from it a large earthenware pot, heated to a white heat. In an instant, almost with a single movement, they had reached the spot where Mahomed was struggling. He fought like a fiend, shrieking in the abandonment of his despair, and notwithstanding the noose round him, and the efforts of the men who held his legs, the advancing wretches were for the moment unable to accomplish their purpose, which, horrible and incredible as it seems, was *to put the red-hot pot upon his head*.

I sprang to my feet with a yell of horror, and drawing my revolver fired it by a sort of instinct straight at the diabolical woman who had been caressing Mahomed, and was now gripping him in her arms. The bullet struck her in the back and killed her, and to this day I am glad that it did, for, as it afterwards transpired, she had availed herself of the anthropophagous* customs of the Amahagger to organise the whole thing in revenge of the slight put upon her by Job. She sank down dead, and as she did so, to my terror and dismay, Mahomed, by a superhuman effort, burst from his tormentors, and, springing high into the air, fell dying upon her corpse. The heavy bullet from my pistol had driven through the bodies of both, at once striking down the murdress, and saving her victim from a death a hundred times more horrible. It was an awful and yet a most merciful accident.

For a moment* there was a silence of astonishment. The Amahagger had never heard the report of a firearm before, and its effects dismayed them. But the next a man close to us recovered himself, and seized his spear preparatory to making a lunge with it at Leo, who was the nearest to him.

'Run for it!' I shouted, setting the example by starting up the cave as hard as my legs would carry me. I would have made for the open air if it had been possible, but there were men in the way, and, besides, I had caught sight of the forms of a crowd of people standing out clear against the skyline beyond the entrance to the cave. Up the cave I went, and after me came the others, and after them thundered the whole crowd of cannibals, mad with fury at the death of the woman. With a bound I cleared the prostrate form of Mahomed. As I flew over him I felt the heat from the red hot pot, which was lying close by, strike upon my legs, and by its glow saw his hands— for he was not quite dead—still feebly moving. At the top of the cave was a little platform of rock three feet or so high by about eight deep,

on which two large lamps were placed at night. Whether this platform had been left as a seat, or as a raised point afterwards to be cut
away when it had served its purpose as a standing-place from which
to carry on the excavations, I do not know—at least, I did not then.
At any rate, we all three reached it, and, jumping on it, prepared to
sell our lives as dearly as we could. For a few seconds the crowd that
was pressing on our heels hung back when they saw us face round
upon them. Job was on one side of the rock to the left, Leo in the
centre, and I to the right. Behind us were the lamps. Leo bent forward, and looked down the long lane of shadows, terminated in the
fire and lighted lamps, through which the quiet forms of our would-
be murderers flitted to and fro with the faint light glinting on their
spears, for even their fury was silent as a bulldog's. The only other
thing visible was the red-hot pot still glowing angrily in the gloom.
There was a curious light in Leo's eyes, and his handsome face was
set like a stone. In his right hand was his heavy hunting-knife. He
shifted its thong a little up his wrist, and then put his arm round me
and gave me a good hug.

'Good-bye, old fellow,' he said, 'my dear friend—my more than
father. We have no chance against those scoundrels; they will finish
us in a few minutes, and eat us afterwards, I suppose. Good-bye. I led
you into this. I hope you will forgive me. Good-bye, Job.'

'God's will be done,' I said, setting my teeth, as I prepared for the
end. At that moment, with an exclamation, Job lifted his revolver
and fired, and hit a man—not the man he had aimed at, by the way:
anything that Job shot *at* was perfectly safe.

On they came with a rush, and I fired too as fast as I could, and
checked them—between us, Job and I, besides the woman, killed or
mortally wounded five men with our pistols before they were emp-
tied. But we had no time to reload, and they still came on in a way
that was almost splendid in its recklessness, seeing that they did not
know but that we could go on firing for ever.

A great fellow bounded up upon the platform, and Leo struck
him dead with one blow of his powerful arm, sending the knife right
through him. I did the same by another, but Job missed his stroke,
and I saw a brawny Amahagger, grip him by the middle and whirl
him off the rock. The knife not being secured by a thong fell from
Job's hand as he did so, and, by a most happy accident for him, lit
upon its handle on the rock, just as the body of the Amahagger being

undermost, hit upon its point and was transfixed upon it. What happened to Job after that I am sure I do not know, but my own impression is that he lay still upon the corpse of his deceased assailant, 'playing 'possum' as the Americans say. As for myself, I was soon involved in a desperate encounter with two ruffians who, luckily for me, had left their spears behind them; and for the first time in my life the great physical power with which Nature has endowed me stood me in good stead. I had hacked at the head of one man with my hunting-knife, which was almost as big and heavy as a short sword, with such vigour, that the sharp steel had split his skull down to the eyes, and was held so fast by it that as he suddenly fell sideways the knife was twisted right out of my hand.

Then it was that the two others sprang upon me. I saw them coming, and got an arm round the waist of each, and down we all fell upon the floor of the cave together, rolling over and over. They were strong men, but I was mad with rage, and that awful lust for slaughter which will creep into the hearts of the most civilised of us when blows are flying, and life and death tremble on the turn. My arms were round the two swarthy demons, and I hugged them till I heard their ribs crack and crunch up beneath my gripe. They twisted and writhed like snakes, and clawed and battered at me with their fists, but I held on. Lying on my back there, so that their bodies might protect me from spear thrusts from above, I slowly crushed the life out of them, and as I did so, strange as it may seem, I thought of what the amiable Head of my College at Cambridge (who is a member of the Peace Society) and my brother Fellows would say if by clairvoyance they could see me, of all men, playing such a bloody game. Soon my assailants grew faint, and almost ceased to struggle, their breath had failed them, and they were dying, but still I dared not leave them, for they died very slowly. I knew that if I relaxed my grip they would revive. The other ruffians probably thought—for we were all three lying in the shadow of the ledge—that we were all dead together, at any rate they did not interfere with our little tragedy.

I turned my head, and as I lay gasping in the throes of that awful struggle I could see that Leo was off the rock now, for the lamplight fell full upon him. He was still on his feet, but in the centre of a surging mass of struggling men, who were striving to pull him down as wolves pull down a stag. Up above them towered his beautiful pale face crowned with its bright curls (for Leo is six feet two high), and I saw that he was fighting with a desperate abandonment and energy that was at once splendid and hideous to behold. He drove his knife through one man—they were so close to him and mixed up with him that they could not get at him to kill him with their big spears, and they had no knives or sticks. The man fell, and then somehow the knife was wrenched from his hand, leaving him defenceless, and I thought the end had come. But no; with a desperate effort he broke loose from them, seized the body of the man he had just slain, and lifting it high in the air hurled it right at the mob of his assailants, so that the shock and weight of it swept some five or six of them to the earth. But in a minute they were all up again, except one, whose skull was smashed, and had once more fastened upon him. And then slowly, and with infinite labour and struggling, the wolves bore the lion down. Once even then he recovered himself, and felled an Amahagger with his fist, but it was more than man could do to hold his own for long against so many, and at last he came crashing down upon the rock floor, falling as an oak falls, and bearing with him to the earth all those who clung about him. They gripped him by his arms and legs, and then cleared off his body.

'A spear,' cried a voice—'a spear to cut his throat, and a vessel to catch his blood.'

I shut my eyes, for I saw the man coming with a spear, and myself, I could not stir to Leo's help, for I was growing weak, and the two men on me were not yet dead, and a deadly sickness overcame me.

Then suddenly there was a disturbance, and involuntarily I opened my eyes again, and looked towards the scene of murder. The girl Ustane had thrown herself on Leo's prostrate form, covering his body with her body, and fastening her arms about his neck. They tried to drag her from him, but she twisted her legs round his, and hung on like a bulldog, or rather like a creeper to a tree, and they could not. Then they tried to stab him in the side without hurting her, but somehow she shielded him, and he was only wounded.

At last they lost patience.

'Drive the spear through the man and the woman together,' said a voice, the same voice that had asked the questions at that ghastly feast, 'so of a verity shall they be wed.'

Then I saw the man with the weapon straighten himself for the effort. I saw the cold steel gleam on high, and once more I shut my eyes.

As I did so I heard the voice of a man thunder out in tones that rang and echoed down the rocky ways—

'*Cease!*'

Then I fainted, and as I did so it flashed through my darkening mind that I was passing down into the last oblivion of death.

IX

A LITTLE FOOT

WHEN I opened my eyes again I found myself lying on a skin mat not far from the fire round which we had been gathered for that dreadful feast. Near me lay Leo, still apparently in a swoon, and over him was bending the tall form of the girl Ustane, who was washing a deep spear wound in his side with cold water preparatory to binding it up with linen. Leaning against the wall of the cave behind her was Job, apparently uninjured, but bruised and trembling. On the other side of the fire, tossed about this way and that, as though they had thrown themselves down to sleep in some moment of absolute exhaustion, were the bodies of those whom we had killed in our frightful struggle for life. I counted them: there were twelve beside the woman, and the corpse of poor Mahomed, who had died by my hand, which, the fire-stained pot at its side, was placed at the end of the irregular line. To the left a body of men were engaged in binding the arms of the survivors of the cannibals behind them, and then fastening them two and two. The villains were submitting with a look of sulky indifference upon their faces which accorded ill with the baffled fury that gleamed in their sombre eyes. In front of these men, directing the operations, stood no other than our friend Billali, looking rather tired, but particularly patriarchal with his flowing beard, and as cool and unconcerned as though he were superintending the cutting up of an ox.

Presently he turned, and perceiving that I was sitting up advanced to me, and with the utmost courtesy said that he trusted that I felt better. I answered that at present I scarcely knew how I felt, except that I ached all over.

Then he bent down and examined Leo's wound.

'It is a nasty cut,' he said, 'but the spear has not pierced the entrails. He will recover.'

'Thanks to thy arrival, my father,' I answered. 'In another minute we should all have been beyond the reach of recovery, for those devils of thine would have slain us as they would have slain our servant,' and I pointed towards Mahomed.

The old man ground his teeth, and I saw an extraordinary expression of malignity light up his eyes.

'Fear not, my son,' he answered. 'Vengeance shall be taken on them such as would make the flesh twist upon the bones merely to hear of it. To *She* shall they go, and her vengeance shall be worthy of her greatness. That man,' pointing to Mahomed, 'I tell thee that man would have died a merciful death to the death these hyæna-men shall die. Tell me, I pray of thee, how it came about.'

In a few words I sketched what had happened.

'Ah, so,' he answered. 'Thou seest, my son, here there is a custom that if a stranger comes into this country he may be slain by "the pot," and eaten.'

'It is hospitality turned upside down,' I answered feebly. 'In our country we entertain a stranger, and give him food to eat. Here ye eat him, and are entertained.'

'It is a custom,' he answered, with a shrug. 'Myself I think it an evil one; but then,' he added by an afterthought, 'I do not like the taste of strangers, especially after they have wandered through the swamps and lived on wildfowl. When *She-who-must-be-obeyed* sent orders that ye were to be saved alive she said naught of the black man, therefore, being hyænas, these men lusted after his flesh, and the woman it was, whom thou didst rightly slay, who put it into their evil hearts to hot-pot him. Well, they will have their reward. Better for them would it be if they had never seen the light than that they should stand before *She* in her terrible anger. Happy are those of them who died by your hands.

'Ah,' he went on, 'it was a gallant fight that ye fought. Knowest thou, that thou, long-armed old baboon that thou art, hast crushed in the ribs of those two who are laid out there as though they were but as the shell on an egg? And the young one, the lion, it was a beautiful stand that he made—one against so many—three did he slay outright, and that one there'—and he pointed to a body that was still moving a little—'will die anon, for his head is cracked across, and others of those who are bound are hurt. It was a gallant fight, and thou and he have made a friend of me by it, for I love to see a well-fought fray. But tell me, my son, the baboon—and now I think of it thy face, too, is hairy, and altogether like a baboon's—how was it that ye slew those with a hole in them?—Ye made a noise, they say, and slew them—they fell down on their faces at the noise?'

I explained to him as well as I could, but very shortly—I was terribly wearied, and only persuaded to talk at all through fear of offending one so powerful if I refused to do so—what were the properties of gunpowder, and he instantly suggested that I should illustrate what I said by operating on the person of one of the prisoners. One, he said, never would be counted, and it would not only be very interesting to him, but would give me an opportunity of an instalment of revenge. He was greatly astounded when I told him that it was not our custom to avenge ourselves in cold blood, and that we left vengeance to the law and a higher power, of which he knew nothing. I added, however, that when I recovered I would take him out shooting with us, and he should kill an animal for himself, and at this he was as pleased as a child at the promise of a new toy.

Just then Leo opened his eyes beneath the stimulus of some brandy (of which we still had a little) that Job had poured down his throat, and our conversation came to an end.

After this we managed to get Leo, who was in a very poor way indeed, and only half-conscious, safely off to bed, supported by Job and that brave girl Ustane, to whom, had I not been afraid she might resent it, I would certainly have given a kiss for her splendid behaviour in saving my dear boy's life at the risk of her own. But Ustane was not the sort of young person with whom one would care to take liberties unless one were perfectly certain that they would not be misunderstood, so I repressed my inclinations. Then, bruised and battered, but with a sense of safety in my breast to which I had for some days been a stranger, I crept off to my own little sepulchre, not forgetting before I laid down in it to thank Providence from the bottom of my heart that it was not a sepulchre indeed, as were it not for a merciful combination of events that I can only attribute to its protection, it would certainly have been for me that night. Few men have been nearer their end and yet escaped it than we were on that dreadful day.

I am a bad sleeper at the best of times, and my dreams that night when at last I got to rest were not of the pleasantest. The awful vision of poor Mahomed struggling to escape the red-hot pot would haunt them, and then in the background, as it were, a veiled form was always hovering, which, from time to time, seemed to draw the coverings from its body, revealing now the perfect shape of a lovely blooming woman, and now again the white bones of a grinning skeleton, and which, as it veiled and unveiled, uttered the mysterious and apparently meaningless sentence:—

'*That which is alive hath known death, and that which is dead yet can never die, for in the Circle of the Spirit life is naught and death is naught. Yea, all things live for ever, though at times they sleep and are forgotten.*'

The morning came at last, but when it came I found that I was too stiff and sore to rise. About seven Job arrived, limping terribly, and with his face the colour of a rotten apple, and told me that Leo had slept fairly, but was very weak. Two hours afterwards Billali (Job called him 'Billy-goat,' to which, indeed, his white beard gave him some resemblance, or more familiarly 'Billy') came too, bearing a lamp in his hand, his towering form reaching nearly to the roof of the little chamber. I pretended to be asleep, and through the cracks of my eyelids watched his sardonic but handsome old face. He fixed his hawk-like eyes upon me, and stroked his glorious white beard, which, by the way, would have been worth a hundred a year to any London barber as an advertisement.

'Ah!' I heard him mutter (Billali had a habit of muttering to himself), 'he is ugly—ugly as the other is beautiful—a very Baboon, it was a good name. But I like the man. Strange now, at my age, that I should like a man. What says the proverb—"Mistrust all men, and slay him whom thou mistrustest overmuch; and as for women, flee from them, for they are evil, and in the end will destroy thee." It is a good proverb, especially the last part of it: I think it must have come down from the ancients. Nevertheless I like this Baboon, and I wonder where they taught him his tricks, and I trust that *She* will not bewitch him. Poor Baboon! he must be wearied after that fight. I will go lest I should awake him.'

I waited till he had turned and was nearly through the entrance, walking softly on tiptoe, and then I called after him.

'My father,' I said, 'is it thou?'

'Yes, my son, it is I; but let me not disturb thee. I did but come to see how thou didst fare, and to tell thee that those who would have slain thee, my Baboon, are by now well on their road to *She*. *She* said that ye also were to come at once, but I fear ye cannot yet.'

'Nay,' I said, 'not till we have recovered a little; but have me borne out into the daylight, I pray thee, my father. I love not this place.'

'Ah, no,' he answered, 'it hath a sad air. I remember when I was a boy I found the body of a fair woman lying where thou liest now, yes, on that very bench. She was so beautiful that I was wont to creep in hither with a lamp and gaze upon her. Had it not been for her cold hands, almost could I think that she slept and would one day awake, so fair and peaceful was she in her robes of white. White was she, too, and her hair was yellow and lay down her almost to the feet. There are many such still in the tombs at the place where *She* is, for those who set them there had a way I know naught of, whereby to keep their beloved out of the crumbling hand of Decay, even when Death had slain them. Ay, day by day I came hither, and gazed on her till at last, laugh not at me, stranger, for I was but a silly lad, I learned to love that dead form, that shell which once had held a life that no more is. I would creep up to her and kiss her cold face, and wonder how many men had lived and died since she was, and who had loved her and embraced her in the days that long had passed away. And, my Baboon, I think I learned wisdom from that dead one, for of a truth it taught me of the littleness of life, and the length of Death, and how all things that are under the sun go down one path, and are for ever forgotten. And so I mused, and it seemed to me that wisdom flowed into me from the dead, till one day my mother, a watchful woman, but hasty-minded, seeing I was changed, followed me, and saw the beautiful white one, and feared that I was bewitched, as, indeed, I was. So half in dread, and half in anger, she took the lamp, and standing the dead woman up against the wall there, set fire to her hair, and she burnt fiercely, even down to the feet, for those who are thus kept burn excellently well.

'See, my son, there on the roof is yet the smoke of her burning.'

I looked up doubtfully, and there, sure enough, on the roof of the sepulchre, was a peculiarly unctuous and sooty mark, three feet or more across. Doubtless it had in the course of years been rubbed off the sides of the little cave, but on the roof it remained, and there was no mistaking its appearance.

'She burnt,' he went on in a meditative way, 'even to the feet, but the feet I came back and saved, cutting the burnt bone from them, and hid them under the stone bench there, wrapped up in a piece of linen. Surely, I remember it as though it were but yesterday. Perchance they are there if none have found them, even to this hour. Of a truth I have not entered this chamber from that time to this very day. Stay, I will look,' and, kneeling down, he groped about with his long arm in the recess under the stone bench. Presently his face brightened, and with an exclamation he pulled something forth that was caked in dust; which he shook on to the floor. It was covered with the remains of a rotting rag, which he undid, and revealed to my astonished gaze a beautifully shaped and almost white woman's foot, looking as fresh and as firm as though it had but now been placed there.

'Thou seest, my son, the Baboon,' he said, in a sad voice, 'I spake the truth to thee, for here is yet one foot remaining. Take it, my son, and gaze upon it.'

I took this cold fragment of mortality in my hand and looked at it in the light of the lamp with feelings which I cannot describe, so mixed up were they between astonishment, fear, and fascination. It was light, much lighter I should say than it had been in the living state, and the flesh to all appearance was still flesh, though about it there clung a faintly aromatic odour. For the rest it was not shrunk or shrivelled, or even black and unsightly, like the flesh of Egyptian mummies, but plump and fair, and, except where it had been slightly burnt, perfect as on the day of death—a very triumph of embalming.

Poor little foot! I set it down upon the stone bench where it had lain for so many thousand years, and wondered whose was the beauty that it had upborne through the pomp and pageantry of a forgotten civilisation—first as a merry child's, then as a blushing maid's, and lastly as a perfect woman's. Through what halls of Life had its soft step echoed, and in the end, with what courage had it trodden down the dusty ways of Death! To whose side had it stolen in the hush of night when the black slave slept upon the marble floor, and who had listened for its stealing? Shapely little foot! Well might it have been set upon the proud neck of a conqueror bent at last to woman's beauty, and well might the lips of nobles and of kings have been pressed upon its jewelled whiteness.

I wrapped up this relic of the past in the remnants of the old linen rag which had evidently formed a portion of its owner's grave-clothes, for it was partially burnt, and put it away in my Gladstone bag, which I had bought at the Army and Navy Stores—a strange combination, I thought. Then with Billali's help I staggered off to see Leo. I found him dreadfully bruised, worse even than myself, perhaps owing to the excessive whiteness of his skin, and faint and weak with the loss of blood from the flesh wound in his side, but for all that cheerful as a cricket, and asking for some breakfast. Job and

Ustane got him on to the bottom, or rather the sacking of a litter, which was removed from its pole for that purpose, and with the aid of old Billali carried him out into the shade at the mouth of the cave, from which, by the way, every trace of the slaughter of the previous night had now been removed, and there we all breakfasted, and indeed spent that day, and most of the two following ones.

On the third morning Job and myself were practically recovered. Leo also was so much better that I yielded to Billali's often expressed entreaty, and agreed to start at once upon our journey to Kôr, which we were told was the name of the place where the mysterious *She* lived, though I still feared for its effects upon Leo, and especially lest the motion should cause his wound, which was scarcely skinned over, to break open again. Indeed, had it not been for Billali's evident anxiety to get off, which led us to suspect that some difficulty or danger might threaten us if we did not comply with it, I would not have consented to go.

WITHIN an hour of our finally deciding to start five litters were brought up to the door of the cave, each accompanied by four regular bearers and two spare hands, also a band of about fifty armed Amahagger, who were to form the escort and carry the baggage. Three of these litters, of course, were for us, and one for Billali, who, I was immensely relieved to hear, was to be our companion, while the fifth I presumed was for the use of Ustane.

'Does the lady go with us, my father?' I asked of Billali, as he stood superintending things generally.

He shrugged his shoulders as he answered—

'If she wills. In this country the women do what they please. We worship them, and give them their way, because without them the world could not go on; they are the source of life.'

'Ah,' I said, the matter never having struck me quite in that light before.

'We worship them,' he went on, 'up to a certain point, till at last they get unbearable, which,' he added, 'they do about every second generation.'

'And then what do you do?' I asked, with curiosity.

'Then,' he answered, with a faint smile, 'we rise, and kill the old ones as an example to the young ones, and to show them that we are the strongest. My poor wife was killed in that way three years ago. It was very sad, but to tell thee the truth, my son, life has been happier since, for my age protects me from the young ones.'

'In short.' I replied, quoting the saying of a great man whose wisdom has not yet lightened the darkness of the Amahagger, 'thou hast found thy position one of greater freedom and less responsibility.'

This phrase puzzled him a little at first from its vagueness, though I think my translation hit off its sense very well, but at last he saw it, and appreciated it.

'Yes, yes, my Baboon,' he said, 'I see it now, but all the "responsi-bilities" are killed, at least some of them are, and that is why there are so few old women about just now. Well, they brought it on themselves. As for this girl,' he went on, in a graver tone, 'I know not what to say. She is a brave girl, and she loves the Lion (Leo); thou sawest how she clung to him, and saved his life. Also, she is, according to our custom, wed to him, and has a right to go where he goes, unless,' he added significantly, '*She* would say her no, for her word overrides all rights.'

'And if *She* bade her leave him, and the girl refused? What then?'

'If,' he said, with a shrug, 'the hurricane bide the tree to bend, and it will not; what happens?'

And then, without waiting for an answer, he turned and walked to his litter, and in ten minutes from that time we were all well under weigh.

It took us an hour and more to cross the cup of the volcanic plain, and another half-hour or so to climb the edge on the farther side. Once there, however, the view was a very fine one. Before us was a long steep slope of grassy plain, broken here and there by clumps of trees mostly of the thorn tribe. At the bottom of this gentle slope, some nine or ten miles away, we could make out a dim sea of marsh, over which the foul vapours hung like smoke about a city. It was easy going for the bearers down the slopes, and by midday we had reached the borders of the dismal swamp. Here we halted to eat our midday meal, and then, following a winding and devious path, plunged into the morass. Presently the path, at any rate to our unaccustomed eyes, grew so faint as to be almost indistinguishable from those made by the aquatic beasts and birds, and it is to this day a mystery to me how our bearers found their way across the marshes. Ahead of the cavalcade marched two men with long poles, which they now and again plunged into the ground before them, the reason of this being that the nature of the soil frequently changed from causes with which I am not acquainted, so that places which might be safe enough to cross one month would certainly swallow the wayfarer the next. Never did I see a more dreary and depressing scene. Miles on miles of quagmire, varied only by bright green strips of comparatively solid ground, and by deep and sullen pools fringed with tall rushes, in which the bitterns boomed and the frogs croaked incessantly: miles on miles of it without a break, unless the fever fog can be called a break. The only life in this great morass was that of the aquatic birds, and the animals that fed on them, of both of which there were vast numbers. Geese, cranes, ducks, teal, coot, snipe, and plover swarmed all around us, many being of varieties that were quite new to me, and all so tame that one could almost have knocked them over with a stick. Among these birds I especially noticed a very beautiful variety of painted snipe, almost the size of woodcock, and with a flight more resembling that bird's than an English snipe's. In the pools, too, was a species of small alligator or enormous iguana, I do not know which, that fed, Billali told me, upon the waterfowl, also large quantities of a hideous black water-snake, of which the bite is very dangerous, though not, I gathered, so deadly as a cobra's or a puff adder's. The bull-frogs were also very large, and with voices proportionate to their size; and as for the mosquitoes—the 'musqueteers,' as Job called them—they were, if possible, even worse than they had been on the river, and tormented us greatly. Undoubtedly, however, the worst feature of the swamp was the awful smell of rotting vegetation that hung about it, which was at times positively overpowering, and the malarious exhalations that accompanied it, which we were of course obliged to breathe.

On we went through it all, till at last the sun sank in sullen splendour just as we reached a spot of rising ground about two acres in extent—a little oasis of dry in the midst of the miry wilderness—where Billali announced that we were to camp. The camping, however, turned out to be a very simple process, and consisted, in fact, in sitting down on the ground round a scanty fire made of dry reeds and some wood that had been brought with us. However, we made the best we could of it, and smoked and ate with such appetite as the smell of damp, stifling heat would allow, for it was very hot on this low land, and yet, oddly enough, chilly at times. But, however hot it was, we were glad enough to keep near the fire, because we found that the mosquitoes did not like the smoke. Presently we rolled ourselves up in our blankets and tried to go to sleep, but so far as I was concerned the bull-frogs, and the extraordinary roaring and alarming sound produced by hundreds of snipe hovering high in the air, made sleep an impossibility, to say nothing of our other discomforts. I turned and looked at Leo, who was next me; he was dozing, but his face had a flushed appearance that I did not like, and by the flickering fire-light I saw Ustane, who was lying on the other side of him, raise herself from time to time upon her elbow, and look at him anxiously enough.

However, I could do nothing for him, for we had all already taken a good dose of quinine, which was the only preventive we had; so I lay and watched the stars come out by thousands, till all the immense arch of heaven was sewn with glittering points, and every point a world! Here was a glorious sight by which man might well measure his own insignificance! Soon I gave up thinking about it, for the mind wearies easily when it strives to grapple with the Infinite, and to trace the footsteps of the Almighty as he strides from sphere to sphere, or deduce His purpose from His works. Such things are not for us to know. Knowledge is to the strong, and we are weak. Too much wisdom would perchance blind our imperfect sight, and too much strength would make us drunk, and overweight our feeble reason till it fell, and we were drowned in the depths of our own vanity. For what is the first result of man's increased knowledge interpreted from Nature's book by the persistent effort of his pur-blind observation? Is it not but too often to make him question the existence of his Maker, or indeed of any intelligent purpose beyond his own? The truth is veiled, because we could no more look upon her glory than we can upon the sun. It would destroy us. Full know-ledge is not for man as man is here, for his capacities, which he is apt to think so great, are indeed but small. The vessel is soon filled, and, were one-thousandth part of the unutterable and silent wisdom that directs the rolling of those shining spheres, and the force which makes them roll, pressed into it, it would be shattered into frag-ments. Perhaps in some other place and time it may be otherwise, who can tell? Here the lot of man born of the flesh is but to endure midst toil and tribulation, to catch at the bubbles blown by Fate, which he calls pleasures, thankful if before they burst they rest a moment in his hand, and when the tragedy is played out, and his hour comes to perish, to pass humbly whither he knows not.

Above me, as I lay, shone the eternal stars, and there at my feet the impish marsh-born balls of fire rolled this way and that, vapour-tossed and earth-desiring, and methought that in the two I saw a type and image of what man is, and what perchance man may one day be, if the living Force who ordained him and them should so ordain this also. Oh, that it might be ours to rest year by year upon that high level of the heart to which at times we momentarily attain! Oh, that we could shake loose the prisoned pinions of the soul and soar to that superior point, whence, like to some traveller looking out through space from Darien's giddiest peak, we might gaze with the spiritual eyes of noble thoughts deep into Infinity!

What would it be to cast off this earthy robe, to have done for ever with these earthy thoughts and miserable desires; no longer, like those corpse candles, to be tossed this way and that, by forces beyond our control; or which, if we can theoretically control them, we are at times driven by the exigencies of our nature to obey! Yes, to cast them off, to have done with the foul and thorny places of the world; and, like to those glittering points above me, to rest on high wrapped for ever in the brightness of our better selves, that even now shines in us as fire faintly shines within those lurid balls, and lay down our littleness in that wide glory of our dreams, that invisible but surrounding good, from which all truth and beauty comes!

These and many such thoughts passed through my mind that night. They come to torment us all at times. I say to torment, for, alas! thinking can only serve to measure out the helplessness of thought. What is the use of our feeble crying in the awful silences of space? Can our dim intelligence read the secrets of that star-strewn sky? Does any answer come out of it? Never any at all, nothing but echoes and fantastic visions. And yet we believe that there is an answer, and that upon a time a new Dawn will come blushing down the ways of our enduring night. We believe it, for its reflected beauty even now shines up continually in our hearts from beneath the horizon of the grave, and we call it Hope. Without Hope we should suffer moral death, and by the help of Hope we yet may climb to Heaven, or at the worst, if she also prove but a kindly mockery given to hold us from despair, be gently lowered into the abysses of eternal sleep.

Then I fell to reflecting upon the undertaking on which we were bent, and what a wild one it was, and yet how strangely the story seemed to fit in with what had been written centuries ago upon the sherd. Who was this extraordinary woman, Queen over a people apparently as extraordinary as herself, and reigning amidst the vestiges of a lost civilisation? And what was the meaning of this story of the Fire that gave unending life? Could it be possible that any fluid or essence should exist which might so fortify these fleshy walls that they should from age to age resist the mines and batterings of decay? It was possible, though not probable. The indefinite continuation of life would not, as poor Vincey said, be so marvellous a thing as the production of life and its temporary endurance. And if it were true, what then? The person who found it could no doubt rule the world. He could accumulate all the wealth in the world, and all the power, and all the wisdom that is power. He might give a lifetime to the study of each art or science. Well, if that were so, and this *She* were practically immortal, which I did not for one moment believe, how was it that, with all these things at her feet, she preferred to remain in a cave amongst a society of cannibals? This surely settled the question. The whole story was monstrous, and only worthy of the superstitious days in which it was written. At any rate I was very sure that *I* would not attempt to attain unending life. I had had far too many worries and disappointments and secret bitternesses during my forty odd years of existence to wish that this state of affairs should be continued indefinitely. And yet I suppose that my life has been, comparatively speaking, a happy one.

And then, reflecting that at the present moment there was far more likelihood of our earthly careers being cut exceedingly short than of their being unduly prolonged, I at last managed to get to sleep, a fact for which anybody who reads this narrative, if anybody ever does, may very probably be thankful.

When I woke again it was just dawning, and the guard and bearers were moving about like ghosts through the dense morning mists, getting ready for our start. The fire had died quite down, and I rose and stretched myself, shivering in every limb from the damp cold of the dawn. Then I looked at Leo. He was sitting up, holding his hands to his head, and I saw that his face was flushed and his eye bright, and yet yellow round the pupil.

'Well, Leo,' I said, 'how do you feel?'

'I feel as though I were going to die,' he answered hoarsely. 'My head is splitting, my body is trembling, and I am as sick as a cat.'

I whistled, or if I did not whistle I felt inclined to—Leo had got a sharp attack of fever. I went to Job, and asked him for the quinine, of which fortunately we had still a good supply, only to find that Job himself was not much better. He complained of pains across the back, and dizziness, and was almost incapable of helping himself. Then I did the only thing it was possible to do under the circumstances—gave them both about ten grains of quinine, and took a slightly smaller dose myself as a matter of precaution. After that I found Billali, and explained to him how matters stood, asking at the same time what he thought had best be done. He came with me, and looked at Leo and Job (whom, by the way, he had named the Pig on account of his fatness, round face, and small eyes).

'Ah,' he said, when we were out of earshot, 'the fever! I thought so. The Lion has it badly, but he is young, and he may live. As for the Pig, his attack is not so bad; it is the "little fever" which he has; that always begins with pains across the back, it will spend itself upon his fat.'

'Can they go on, my father?' I asked.

'Nay, my son, they must go on. If they stop here they will certainly die; also, they will be better in the litters than on the ground. By to-night, if all goes well, we shall be across the marsh and in good air. Come, let us lift them into the litters and start, for it is very bad to stand still in this morning fog. We can eat our meal as we go.'

This we accordingly did, and with a heavy heart I once more set out upon our strange journey. For the first three hours all went as well as could be expected, and then an accident happened that nearly lost us the pleasure of the company of our venerable friend Billali, whose litter was leading the cavalcade. We were going through a particularly dangerous stretch of quagmire, in which the bearers sometimes sank up to their knees. Indeed, it was a mystery to me how they contrived to carry the heavy litters at all over such ground as that which we were traversing, though the two spare hands, as well as the four regular ones, had of course to put their shoulders to the pole.

Presently, as we blundered and floundered along, there was a sharp cry, then a storm of exclamations, and, last of all, a most tremendous splash, and the whole caravan halted.

I jumped out of my litter and ran forward. About twenty yards ahead was the edge of one of those sullen peaty pools of which I have spoken, the path we were following running along the top of its bank, that, as it happened, was a steep one. Looking towards this pool, to my horror I saw that Billali's litter was floating on it, and as for Billali himself, he was nowhere to be seen. To make matters clear I may as well explain at once what had happened. One of Billali's bearers had unfortunately trodden on a basking snake, which had bitten him in the leg, whereon he had, not unnaturally, let go of the pole, and then, finding that he was tumbling down the bank, grasped at the litter to save himself. The result of this was what might have been expected. The litter was pulled over the edge of the bank, the bearers let go, and the whole thing, including Billali and the man who had been bitten, rolled into the slimy pool. When I got to the edge of the water neither of them were to be seen, and, indeed, the unfortunate bearer never was seen again. Either he struck his head against something, or got wedged in the mud, or possibly the snake-bite paralysed him. At any rate, he vanished. But though Billali was not to be seen, his whereabouts was clear enough from the agitation of the floating litter, in the bearing cloth and curtains of which he was entangled.

'He is there! Our father is there!' said one of the men, but he did not stir a finger to help him, nor did any of the others. They simply stood and stared at the water.

'Out of the way, you brutes,' I shouted in English, and throwing off my hat I took a run and sprang well out into the horrid slimy-looking pool. A couple of strokes took me to where Billali was struggling beneath the cloth.

Somehow, I do not quite know how, I managed to push this free of him, and his venerable head all covered with green slime, like that of a yellowish Bacchus with ivy leaves, emerged upon the surface of the water. The rest was easy, for Billali was an eminently practical individual, and had the common sense not to grasp hold of me as drowning people often do, so I got him by the arm, and towed him to the bank, through the mud of which we were with difficulty dragged. Such a filthy spectacle as we presented I have never seen before or since, and it will perhaps give some idea of the almost superhuman dignity of Billali's appearance when I say that, coughing, half-drowned, and covered with mud and green slime as he was, with his beautiful beard coming to a dripping point, like a Chinaman's freshly oiled pigtail, he still looked venerable and imposing.

'Ye dogs,' he said, addressing the bearers, as soon as he had sufficiently recovered to speak, 'ye left me, your father, to drown. Had it not been for this stranger, my son the Baboon, assuredly I should have drowned. Well, I will remember it,' and he fixed them with his gleaming though slightly watery eye, in a way I saw they did not like, though they tried to appear sulkily indifferent.

'As for thee, my son,' the old man went on, turning towards me and grasping my hand, 'rest assured that I am thy friend through good and evil. Thou hast saved my life: perchance a day may come when I shall save thine.'

After that we cleaned ourselves as best we could, fished out the litter, and went on, *minus* the man who had been drowned. I do not know if it was owing to his being an unpopular character, or from native indifference and selfishness of temperament, but I am bound to say that nobody seemed to grieve much over his sudden and final disappearance, unless, perhaps, it was the men who had to do his share of the work.

XI

ABOUT an hour before sundown we at last, to my unbounded gratitude, emerged from the great belt of marsh on to land that swelled upwards in a succession of rolling waves. Just on the hither side of the crest of the first wave we halted for the night. My first act was to examine Leo's condition. It was, if anything, worse than in the morning, and a new and very distressing feature, vomiting, set in, and continued till dawn. Not one wink of sleep did I get that night, for I passed it in assisting Ustane, who was one of the most gentle and indefatigable nurses I ever saw, to wait upon Leo and Job. However, the air here was warm and genial without being too hot, and there were no mosquitoes to speak of. Also we were above the level of the marsh mist, which lay stretched beneath us like the dim smoke-pall over a city, lit up here and there by the wandering globes of fen fire. Thus it will be seen that we were, speaking comparatively, in clover.

By dawn on the following morning Leo was quite lightheaded, and fancied that he was divided into halves. I was dreadfully distressed, and began to wonder with a sort of sick fear what the termination of the attack would be. Alas! I had heard but too much of how these attacks generally terminate. As I was doing so Billali came up and said that we must be getting on, more especially as, in his opinion, if Leo did not reach some spot where he could be quiet, and have proper nursing, within the next twelve hours, his life would only be a matter of a day or two. I could not but agree with him, so we got him into the litter, and started on, Ustane walking by Leo's side to keep the flies off him, and see that he did not throw himself out on to the ground.

Within half an hour of sunrise we had reached the top of the rise of which I have spoken, and a most beautiful view broke upon our gaze. Beneath us was a rich stretch of country, verdant with grass and lovely with foliage and flowers. In the background, at a distance, so far as I could judge, of some eighteen miles from where we then stood, a huge and extraordinary mountain rose abruptly from the plain. The base of this great mountain appeared to consist of a grassy slope, but rising from this, I should say, from subsequent observation, at a height of about five hundred feet above the level of the plain, was a most tremendous and absolutely precipitous wall of bare rock, quite twelve or fifteen hundred feet in height. The shape of the mountain, which was undoubtedly of volcanic origin, was round, and of course, as only a segment of its circle was visible, it was difficult to estimate its exact size, which was enormous. I afterwards discovered that it could not cover less than fifty square miles of ground. Anything more grand and imposing than the sight presented by this great natural castle, starting in solitary grandeur from the level of the plain, I never saw, and I suppose I never shall. Its very solitude added to its majesty, and its towering cliffs seemed to kiss the sky. Indeed, generally speaking, they were clothed in clouds that lay in fleecy masses upon their broad and level battlements.

I sat up in my hammock and gazed out across the plain at this thrilling and majestic sight, and I suppose that Billali noticed it, for he brought his litter alongside.

'Behold the House of "*She-who-must-be-obeyed*!" ' he said. 'Had ever a queen such a throne before?'

'It is wonderful, my father,' I answered. 'But how do we enter? Those cliffs look hard to climb.'

'Thou shalt see, my Baboon. Look now at the plain below us. What thinkest thou that it is? Thou art a wise man. Come, tell me.'

I looked, and saw what appeared to be the line of roadway running straight towards the base of the mountain, though it was covered with turf. There were high banks on each side of it, broken here and there, but fairly continuous on the whole, the meaning of which I did not understand. It seemed so very odd that anybody should embank a roadway.

'Well, my father,' I answered, 'I suppose that it is a road, otherwise I should have been inclined to say that it was the bed of a river, or rather,' I added, observing the extraordinary directness of the cutting, 'of a canal.'

Billali—who, by the way, was none the worse for his immersion of the day before—nodded his head sagely as he replied—

'Thou art right, my son. It is a channel cut out by those who were before us in this place to carry away water. Of this am I sure: within the rocky circle of the great mountain whither we journey was once a great lake. But those who were before us, by wonderful arts of which

I know naught, hewed a path for the water through the solid rock of the mountain, piercing even to the bed of the lake. But first they cut the channel that thou seest across the plain. Then, when at last the water burst out, it rushed down the channel that had been made to receive it, and crossed this plain till it reached the low land behind the rise, and there, perchance, it made the swamp through which we had come. Then when the lake was drained dry, the people whereof I speak built a mighty city, whereof naught but ruins and the name of Kôr yet remaineth, on its bed, and from age to age hewed the caves and passages that thou wilt see.'

'It may be,' I answered; 'but if so, how is it that the lake does not fill up again with the rains and the water of the springs?'

'Nay, my son, the people were a wise people, and they left a drain to keep it clear. Seest thou the river to the right?' and he pointed to a fair-sized stream that wound away across the plain, some four miles from us. 'That is the drain, and it comes out through the mountain wall where this cutting goes in. At first, perhaps, the water ran down this canal, but afterwards the people turned it, and used the cutting for a road.'

'And is there then no other place where one may enter into the great mountain,' I asked, 'except through the drain?'

'There is a place,' he answered, 'where cattle and men on foot may cross with much labour, but it is secret. A year mightest thou search and shouldst never find it. It is only used once a year, when the herds of cattle that have been fatting on the slopes of the mountain, and on this plain, are driven into the space within.'

'And does *She* live there always?' I asked, 'or does she come at times without the mountain?'

'Nay, my son, where she is, there she is.'

By now we were well on to the great plain, and I was examining with delight the varied beauty of its semi-tropical flowers and trees, the latter of which grew singly, or at most in clumps of three or four, much of the timber being of large size, and belonging apparently to a variety of evergreen oak. There were also many palms, some of them more than one hundred feet high, and the largest and most beautiful tree ferns that I ever saw, about which hung clouds of jewelled honeysuckers* and great-winged butterflies. Wandering about among the trees or crouching in the long and feathered grass were all varieties of game, from rhinoceroses down. I saw rhinoceros, buffalo (a large herd), eland, quagga,* and sable antelope, the most beautiful of all the bucks, not to mention many smaller varieties of game, and three ostriches which scudded away at our approach like white drift before a gale. So plentiful was the game that at last I could stand it no longer. I had a single-barrel sporting Martini* with me in the litter, the 'Express' being too cumbersome, and espying a beautiful fat eland rubbing himself under one of the oak-like trees, I jumped out of the litter, and proceeded to creep as near to him as I could. He let me come within eighty yards, and then turned his head, and stared at me, preparatory to running away. I lifted the rifle, and taking him about midway down the shoulder, for he was side on to me, fired. I never made a cleaner shot or a better kill in all my small experience, for the great buck sprang right up into the air and fell dead. The bearers, who had all halted to see the performance, gave a murmur of surprise, an unwonted compliment from these sullen people, who never appear to be surprised at anything, and a party of the guard at once ran off to cut the animal up. As for myself, though I was longing to have a look at him, I sauntered back to my litter as though I had been in the habit of killing eland all my life, feeling that I had gone up several degrees in the estimation of the Amahagger, who looked on the whole thing as a very high-class manifestation of witchcraft. As a matter of fact, however, I had never seen an eland in a wild state before. Billali received me with enthusiasm.

'It is wonderful, my son the Baboon,' he cried; 'wonderful! Thou art a very great man, though so ugly. Had I not seen, surely I would never have believed. And thou sayest that thou wilt teach me to slay in this fashion?'

'Certainly, my father,' I said airily; 'it is nothing.'

But all the same I firmly made up my mind that when 'my father' Billali began to fire I would without fail lie down or take refuge behind a tree.

After this little incident nothing happened of any note till about an hour and a half before sundown, when we arrived beneath the shadow of the towering volcanic mass that I have already described. It is quite impossible for me to describe its grim grandeur as it appeared to me while my patient bearers toiled along the bed of the ancient watercourse towards the spot where the rich brown-clad cliff shot up from precipice to precipice till its crown lost itself in cloud. All I can say is that it almost awed me by the intensity of its lonesome and most solemn greatness. On we went up the bright and sunny slope, till at last the creeping shadows from above swallowed up its brightness, and presently we began to pass through a cutting hewn in the living rock. Deeper and deeper grew this marvellous work, which must, I should say, have employed thousands of men for many years. Indeed how it was ever executed at all without the aid of blasting-powder or dynamite I cannot to this day imagine. It is and must remain one of the mysteries of that wild land. I can only suppose that these cuttings and the vast caves that had been hollowed out of the rocks they pierced were the State undertakings of the people of Kôr, who lived here in the dim lost ages of the world, and, as in the case of the Egyptian monuments, were executed by the forced labour of tens of thousands of captives, carried on through an indefinite number of centuries. But who were the people?

At last we reached the face of the precipice itself, and found ourselves looking into the mouth of a dark tunnel that forcibly reminded me of those undertaken by our nineteenth-century engineers in the construction of railway lines. Out of this tunnel flowed a considerable stream of water. Indeed, though I do not think that I have mentioned it, we had followed this stream, which ultimately developed into the river I have already described as winding away to the right, from the spot where the cutting in the solid rock commenced. Half of this cutting formed a channel for the stream, and half, which was placed on a slightly higher level—eight feet perhaps—was devoted to the purposes of a roadway. At the termination of the cutting, however, the stream turned off across the plain and followed a channel of its own. At the mouth of the cave the cavalcade was halted, and, while the men employed themselves in lighting some earthenware lamps they had brought with them, Billali, descending from his litter, informed me politely but firmly that the orders of *She* were that we were now to be blindfolded, so that we should not learn the secret of the paths through the bowels of the mountains. To this I, of course, assented cheerfully enough, but Job, who was now very much better, notwithstanding the journey, did not like it at all, fancying, I believe, that it was but a preliminary step to being hot-potted. He was, however, a little consoled when I pointed out to him that there were no hot pots at hand, and, so far as I knew, no fire to heat them in. As for poor Leo, after turning restlessly for hours, he had, to my deep thankfulness, at last dropped off into a sleep or stupor, I do not know which, so there was no need to blind-fold him. The blindfolding was performed by binding a piece of the yellowish linen whereof those of the Amahagger who condescended to wear anything in particular made their dresses tightly round the eyes. This linen I afterwards discovered was taken from the tombs, and was not, as I had at first supposed, of native manufacture. The bandage was then knotted at the back of the head, and finally brought down again and the ends bound under the chin to prevent its slipping. Ustane was, by the way, also blindfolded, I do not know why, unless it was from fear that she should impart the secrets of the route to us.

This operation performed we started on once more, and soon, by the echoing sound of the footsteps of the bearers and the increased noise of the water caused by reverberation in a confined space, I knew that we were entering into the bowels of the great mountain. It was an eerie sensation, being borne along into the dead heart of the rock we knew not whither, but I was getting used to eerie sensations by this time, and by now was pretty well prepared for anything. So I lay still, and listened to the tramp, tramp of the bearers and the rushing of the water, and tried to believe that I was enjoying myself. Presently the men set up the melancholy little chant that I had heard on the first night when we were captured in the whale-boat, and the effect produced by their voices was very curious, and quite indescribable on paper. After a while the air began to get exceedingly thick and heavy, so much so, indeed, that I felt as though I were going to choke, till at length the litter took a sharp turn, then another and another, and the sound of the running water ceased. After this the air got fresher again, but the turns were continuous, and to me, blindfolded as I was, most bewildering. I tried to keep a map of them in my mind in case it might ever be necessary for us to try and escape by this route, but, needless to say, failed utterly. Another half-hour or so passed, and then suddenly I became aware that we were once more in the open air. I could see the light through my bandage and feel its freshness on my face. A few more minutes and the caravan halted, and I heard Billali order Ustane to remove her bandage and undo ours. Without waiting for her attentions I got the knot of mine loose, and looked out.

As I anticipated, we had passed right through the precipice, and were now on the farther side, and immediately beneath its beetling face. The first thing I noticed was that the cliff was not nearly so high here, not so high I should say by five hundred feet, which proved that the bed of the lake, or rather of the vast ancient crater in which we stood, was much above the level of the surrounding plain. For the rest, we found ourselves in a huge rock-surrounded cup, not unlike that of the first place where we had sojourned, only ten times the size. Indeed, I could only just make out the frowning line of the opposite cliffs. A great portion of the plain thus enclosed by nature was cultivated, and fenced in with walls of stone placed there to keep the cattle and goats, of which there were large herds about, from breaking into the gardens. Here and there rose great grass mounds, and some miles away towards the centre I thought that I could see the outline of colossal ruins. I had no time to observe anything more at the moment, for we were instantly surrounded by crowds of Amahagger, similar in every particular to those with whom we were already familiar, who, though they spoke little, pressed round us so closely as to obscure the view to a person lying in a hammock. Then all of a sudden a number of armed men arranged in companies, and marshalled by officers who held ivory wands in their hands, came running swiftly towards us, having, so far as I could make out, emerged from the face of the precipice like ants from their burrows. These men as well as their officers were all robed in addition to the usual leopard skin, and, as I gathered, formed the bodyguard of *She* herself.

Their leader advanced to Billali, saluted him by placing his ivory wand transversely across his forehead, and then asked some question which I could not catch, and Billali having answered him the whole regiment turned and marched along the side of the cliff, our cavalcade of litters following in their track. After going thus for about half a mile we halted once more in front of the mouth of a tremendous cave, measuring about sixty feet in height by eighty wide, and here Billali descended finally, and requested Job and myself to do the same. Leo, of course, was far too ill to do anything of the sort. I did so, and we entered the great cave, into which the light of the setting sun penetrated for some distance, while beyond the reach of the light it was faintly illuminated with lamps which seemed to me to stretch away for an almost immeasurable distance, like the gas lights of an empty London street. The first thing that I noticed was that the walls were covered with sculptures in bas-relief, of a sort, pictorially speaking, similar to those that I have described upon the vases;—love-scenes principally, then hunting pictures, pictures of executions, and the torture of criminals by the placing of a presumably red-hot pot upon the *head*, showing whence our hosts had derived this pleasant practice. There were very few battle-pieces, though many of duels, and men running and wrestling, and from this fact I am led to believe that this people was not much subject to attack by exterior foes, either on account of the isolation of their position or because of their great strength. Between the pictures were columns of stone characters of a formation absolutely new to me; at any rate they were neither Greek nor Egyptian, nor Hebrew, nor Assyrian—that I am sure of. They looked more like Chinese writings than any other that I am acquainted with. Near to the entrance of the cave both pictures and writings were worn away, but further in they were in many cases absolutely fresh and perfect as the day on which the sculptor had ceased work upon them.

The regiment of guards did not come further than the entrance to the cave, where they formed up to let us pass through. On entering the place itself we were, however, met by a man robed in white, who bowed humbly, but said nothing, which, as it afterwards appeared that he was a deaf mute, was not very wonderful.

Running at right angles to the great cave, at a distance of some twenty feet from the entrance was a smaller, cave or wide gallery, that was pierced into the rock both to the right and to the left of the main cavern. In front of the gallery to our left stood two guards, from which circumstance I argued that it was the entrance to the apartments of *She* herself. The mouth of the right-hand gallery was unguarded, and along it the mute indicated that we were to proceed. Walking a few yards down this passage, which was lighted with lamps, we came to the entrance to a chamber having a curtain made of some grass material, not unlike a Zanzibar mat in appearance, hung over the doorway. This the mute drew back with another profound obeisance, and led the way into a good-sized apartment, hewn, of course, out of the solid rock, but to my great delight lighted by means of a shaft pierced in the face of the precipice. In this room was a stone bedstead, pots full of water for washing, and beautifully tanned leopard skins to serve as blankets.

Here we left Leo, who was still sleeping heavily, and with him stopped Ustane. I noticed that the mute gave her a very sharp look, as much as to say, 'Who are you, and by whose orders do you come here?' Then he conducted us to another similar room which Job took, and then to two more that were respectively occupied by Billali and myself.

XII

'SHE'

THE first care of Job and myself, after seeing to Leo, was to wash ourselves and put on clean clothing, for what we were wearing had not been changed since the loss of the dhow. Fortunately, as I think that I have said, by far the greater part of our personal baggage had been packed into the whale-boat, and was therefore saved—and brought hither by the bearers—although all the stores laid in by us for barter and presents to the natives were lost. Nearly all our clothing was made of a well-shrunk and very strong grey flannel, and excellent I found it for travelling in these places, because though a Norfolk jacket, shirt, and pair of trousers of it only weighed about four pounds, a great consideration in a tropical country, where every extra ounce tells on the wearer, it was warm, and offered a good resistance to the rays of the sun, and best of all to chills, which are so apt to result from sudden changes of temperature.

Never shall I forget the comfort of the 'wash and brush-up,' and of those clean flannels. The only thing that was wanting to complete my joy was a cake of soap, of which we had none.

Afterwards I discovered that the Amahagger, who do not reckon dirt among their many disagreeable qualities, use a kind of burnt earth for washing purposes, which, though unpleasant to the touch till one gets accustomed to it, forms a very fair substitute for soap.

By the time that I was dressed, and had combed and trimmed my black beard, the previous condition of which was certainly sufficiently unkempt to give weight to Billali's appellation for me, the 'Baboon,' I began to feel most uncommonly hungry. Therefore I was by no means sorry when, without the slightest preparatory sound or warning, the curtain over the entrance to my cave was flung aside, and another mute, a young girl this time, announced to me by signs that I could not misunderstand—that is, by opening her mouth and pointing down it—that there was something ready to eat. Accordingly I followed her into the next chamber, which we had not yet entered, where I found Job, who had also, to his great embarrassment, been conducted thither by a fair mute. Job had never got over the advances the former lady had made towards him, and suspected every girl who came near to him of similar designs.

'These young parties have a way of looking at one, sir,' he would say apologetically, 'which I don't call respectable.'

This chamber was twice the size of the sleeping caves, and I saw at once that it had originally served as a refectory, and also probably as an embalming room for the Priests of the Dead; for I may as well say at once that these hollowed-out caves were nothing more or less than vast catacombs, in which for tens of ages the mortal remains of the great extinct race whose monuments surrounded us had been first preserved, with an art and a completeness that has never since been equalled, and then hidden away for all time. On each side of this particular rock-chamber was a long and solid stone table, about three feet wide by three feet six in height, hewn out of the living rock, of which it had formed part, and was still attached to at the base. These tables were slightly hollowed out or curved inward, to give room for the knees of any one sitting on the stone ledge that had been cut for a bench along the side of the cave at a distance of about two feet from them. Each of them, also, was so arranged that it ended right under a shaft pierced in the rock for the admission of light and air. On examining them carefully, however, I saw that there was a difference between them that had at first escaped my attention, viz. that one of the tables, that to the left as we entered the cave, had evidently been used, not to eat upon, but for the purposes of embalming. That this was beyond all question the case was clear from five shallow depressions in the stone of the table, all shaped like a human form, with a separate place for the head to lie in, and a little bridge to support the neck, each depression being of a different size, so as to fit bodies varying in stature from a full-grown man's to a small child's, and with little holes bored at intervals to carry off fluid. And, indeed, if any further confirmation was required, we had but to look at the wall of the cave above to find it. For there, sculptured all round the apartment, and looking nearly as fresh as the day it was done, was the pictorial representation of the death, embalming, and burial of an old man with a long beard, probably an ancient king or grandee of this country.

The first picture represented his death. He was lying upon a couch which had four short curved posts at the corners coming to a knob at the end, in appearance something like a written note of music, and was evidently in the very act of expiring. Gathered round the couch were women and children weeping, the former with their hair hanging down their back. The next scene represented the embalmment of the body, which lay nude upon a table with depressions in it, similar to the one before us; probably, indeed, it was a picture of the same table. Three men were employed at the work—one superintending, one holding a funnel shaped exactly like a port wine strainer, of which the narrow end was fixed in an incision in the breast, no doubt in the great pectoral artery; while the third, who was depicted as standing straddle-legged over the corpse, held a kind of large jug high in his hand, and poured from it some steaming fluid which fell accurately into the funnel. The most curious part of this sculpture is that both the man with the funnel and the man who poured the fluid are drawn holding their noses, either I suppose because of the stench arising from the body, or more probably to keep out the aromatic fumes of the hot fluid which was being forced into the dead man's veins. Another curious thing which I am unable to explain is that all three men were represented as having a band of linen tied round the face with holes in it for the eyes.

The third sculpture was a picture of the burial of the deceased. There he was, stiff and cold, clothed in a linen robe, and laid out on a stone slab such as I had slept upon at our first sojourning-place. At his head and feet burnt lamps, and by his side were placed several of the beautiful painted vases that I have described, which were perhaps supposed to be full of provisions. The little chamber was crowded with mourners, and with musicians playing on an instrument resembling a lyre, while near the foot of the corpse stood a man with a sheet, with which he was preparing to cover it from view.

These sculptures, looked at merely as works of art, were so remarkable that I make no apology for describing them rather fully. They struck me also as being of surpassing interest as representing, probably with studious accuracy, the last rites of the dead as practised among an utterly lost people, and even then I thought how envious some antiquarian friends of my own at Cambridge would be if ever I got an opportunity of describing these wonderful remains to them. Probably they would say that I was exaggerating, notwithstanding that every page of this history must bear so much internal evidence of its truth that it would obviously have been quite impossible for me to have invented it.

To return. As soon as I had hastily examined these sculptures, which I think I omitted to mention were executed in relief, we sat down to a very excellent meal of boiled goat's-flesh, fresh milk, and cakes made of meal, the whole being served upon clean wooden platters.

When we had eaten we returned to see how poor Leo was getting on, Billali saying that he must now wait upon *She*, and hear her commands. On reaching Leo's room we found the poor boy in a very bad way. He had woke up from his torpor, and was altogether off his head, babbling about some boat-race on the Cam, and was inclined to be violent. Indeed, when we entered the room Ustane was holding him down. I spoke to him, and my voice seemed to soothe him; at any rate he grew much quieter, and was persuaded to swallow a dose of quinine.

I had been sitting with him for an hour, perhaps—at any rate I know that it was getting so dark that I could only just make out his head lying like a gleam of gold upon the pillow we had extemporised out of a bag covered with a blanket—when suddenly Billali arrived with an air of great importance, and informed me that *She* herself had deigned to express a wish to see me—an honour, he added, accorded to but very few. I think that he was a little horrified at my cool way of taking the honour, but the fact was that I did not feel overwhelmed with gratitude at the prospect of seeing some savage, dusky queen, however absolute and mysterious she might be, more especially as my mind was full of dear Leo, for whose life I began to have great fears. However, I rose to follow him, and as I did so I caught sight of something bright lying on the floor, which I picked up. Perhaps the reader will remember that with the potsherd in the casket was a composition scarabæus marked with a round O, a goose, and another curious hieroglyphic, the meaning of which signs is 'Suten se Rā,' or 'Royal Son of the Sun.' This scarab, which is a very small one, Leo had insisted upon having set in a massive gold ring, such as is generally used for signets, and it was this very ring that I now picked up. He had pulled it off in the paroxysm of his fever, at least I suppose so, and flung it down upon the rock-floor. Thinking that if I left it about it might get lost, I slipped it on to my own little finger, and then followed Billali, leaving Job and Ustane with Leo.

We passed down the passage, crossed the great aisle-like cave, and came to the corresponding passage on the other side, at the mouth of which the guards stood like two statues. As we came they bowed their heads in salutation, and then lifting their long spears placed them transversely across their foreheads, as the leaders of the troop that had met us had done with their ivory wands. We stepped between them, and found ourselves in an exactly similar gallery to that which led to our own apartments, only this passage was, comparatively speaking, brilliantly lighted. A few paces down it we were met by four mutes—two men and two women—who bowed low and then arranged themselves, the women in front and the men behind of us, and in this order we continued our procession past several doorways hung with curtains resembling those leading to our own quarters, and which I afterwards found opened out into chambers occupied by the mutes who attended on *She*. A few paces more and we came to another doorway facing us, and not to our left like the others, which seemed to mark the termination of the passage. Here two more white-, or rather yellow-robed guards were standing; and they too bowed, saluted, and let us pass through heavy curtains into a great antechamber, quite forty feet long by as many wide, in which some eight or ten women, most of them young and handsome, with yellowish hair, sat on cushions working with ivory needles at what had the appearance of being embroidery-frames. These women were also deaf and dumb. At the farther end of this great lamp-lit apartment was another doorway closed in with heavy Oriental-looking curtains, quite unlike those that hung before the doors of our own rooms, and here stood two particularly handsome girl mutes, their heads bowed upon their bosoms and their hands crossed in an attitude of the humblest submission. As we advanced they each stretched out an arm and drew back the curtains. Thereupon Billali did a curious thing. Down he went, that venerable-looking old gentleman—for Billali is a gentleman at the bottom—down on to his hands and knees, and in this undignified position, with his long white beard trailing on the ground, he began to creep into the apartment beyond. I followed him, standing on my feet in the usual fashion. Looking over his shoulder he perceived it.

'Down, my son; down, my Baboon; down on to thy hands and knees. We enter the presence of *She*, and, if thou are not humble, of a surety she will blast thee where thou standest.'

I halted, and felt scared. Indeed, my knees began to give way of their own mere motion; but reflection came to my aid. I was an Englishman, and why, I asked myself, should I creep into the presence of some savage woman as though I were a monkey in fact as well as in name? I would not and could not do it, that is, unless I was absolutely sure that my life or comfort depended upon it. If once I began to creep upon my knees I should always have to do so, and it would be a patent acknowledgment of inferiority. So, fortified by an insular prejudice against 'kootooing,'* which has, like most of our so-called prejudices, a good deal of common sense to recommend it, I marched in boldly after Billali. I found myself in another apartment, considerably smaller than the anteroom, of which the walls were entirely hung with rich-looking curtains of the same make as those over the door, the work, as I subsequently discovered, of the mutes who sat in the antechamber and wove them in strips, which were afterwards sewn together. Also, here and there about the room, were settees of a beautiful black wood of the ebony tribe, inlaid with ivory, and all over the floor were other tapestries, or rather rugs. At the top end of this apartment was what appeared to be a recess, also draped with curtains, through which shone rays of light. There was nobody in the place except ourselves.

Painfully and slowly old Billali crept up the length of the cave, and with the most dignified stride that I could command I followed after him. But I felt that it was more or less of a failure. To begin with, it is not possible to look dignified when you are following in the wake of an old man writhing along on his stomach like a snake, and then, in order to go sufficiently slowly, either I had to keep my leg some seconds in the air at every step, or else to advance with a full stop between each stride, like Mary Queen of Scots going to execution in a play. Billali was not good at crawling, I suppose his years stood in the way, and our progress up that apartment was a very long affair. I was immediately behind him, and several times I was sorely tempted to help him on with a good kick. It is so absurd to advance into the presence of savage royalty after the fashion of an Irishman driving a pig to market, for that is what we looked like, and the idea nearly made me burst out laughing then and there. I had to work off my dangerous tendency to unseemly merriment by blowing my nose, a proceeding which filled old Billali with horror, for he looked over his shoulder and made a ghastly face at me, and I heard him murmur, 'Oh, my poor Baboon!'

At last we reached the curtains, and here Billali collapsed flat on to his stomach, with his hands stretched out before him as though he were dead, and I, not knowing what to do, began to stare about the place. But presently I clearly felt that somebody was looking at me from behind the curtains. I could not see the person, but I could distinctly feel his or her gaze, and, what is more, it produced a very odd effect upon my nerves. I was frightened, I do not know why. The place was a strange one, it is true, and looked lonely, notwithstanding its rich hangings and the soft glow of the lamps—indeed, these accessories added to, rather than detracted from its loneliness, just as a lighted street at night has always a more solitary appearance than a dark one. It was so silent in the place, and there lay Billali like one dead before the heavy curtains, through which the odour of perfume seemed to float up towards the gloom of the arched roof above. Minute grew into minute, and still there was no sign of life, nor did the curtain move; but I felt the gaze of the unknown being sinking through and through me, and filling me with a nameless terror, till the perspiration stood in beads upon my brow.

At length the curtain began to move. Who could be behind it?—some naked savage queen, a languishing Oriental beauty, or a nineteenth-century young lady, drinking afternoon tea? I had not the slightest idea, and should not have been astonished at seeing any of the three. I was getting beyond astonishment. The curtain agitated itself a little, then suddenly between its folds there appeared a most beautiful white hand (white as snow), and with long tapering fingers, ending in the pinkest nails. The hand grasped the curtain, and drew it aside, and as it did so I heard a voice, I think the softest and yet most silvery voice I ever heard. It reminded me of the murmur of a brook.

'Stranger,' said the voice in Arabic, but much purer and more classical Arabic than the Amahagger talk—'stranger, wherefore art thou so much afraid?'

Now I flattered myself that in spite of my inward terrors I had kept a very fair command of my countenance, and was, therefore, a little astonished at this question. Before I had made up my mind how to answer it, however, the curtain was drawn, and a tall figure stood before us. I say a figure, for not only the body, but also the face was wrapped up in soft white, gauzy material in such a way as at first sight to remind me most forcibly of a corpse in its grave-clothes. And yet I do not know why it should have given me that idea, seeing that the wrappings were so thin that one could distinctly see the gleam of the pink flesh beneath them. I suppose it was owing to the way in which they were arranged, either accidentally, or more probably by design. Anyhow, I felt more frightened than ever at this ghost-like apparition, and my hair began to rise upon my head as the feeling crept over me that I was in the presence of something that was not canny. I could, however, clearly distinguish that the swathed mummy-like form before me was that of a tall and lovely woman, instinct with beauty in every part, and also with a certain snake-like grace which I had never seen anything to equal before. When she moved a hand or foot her entire frame seemed to undulate, and the neck did not bend, it curved.

'Why art thou so frightened, stranger?' asked the sweet voice again—a voice which seemed to draw the heart out of me, like the strains of softest music. 'Is there that about me that should affright a man? Then surely are men changed from what they used to be!' And with a little coquettish movement she turned herself, and held up one arm, so as to show all her loveliness and the rich hair of raven blackness that streamed in soft ripples down her snowy robes, almost to her sandalled feet.

'It is thy beauty that makes me fear, oh Queen,' I answered humbly, scarcely knowing what to say, and I thought that as I did so I heard old Billali, who was still lying prostrate on the floor, mutter, 'Good, my Baboon, good.'

'I see that men still know how to beguile us women with false words. Ah, stranger,' she answered, with a laugh that sounded like distant silver bells, 'thou wast afraid because mine eyes were searching out thine heart, therefore wast thou afraid. But being but a woman, I forgive thee for the lie, for it was courteously said. And now tell me how came ye hither to this land of the dwellers among caves—a land of swamps and evil things and dead old shadows of the dead? What came ye for to see? How is it that ye hold your lives so cheap as to place them in the hollow of the hand of *Hiya*, into the hand of "*She-who-must-be-obeyed*"? Tell me also how come ye to know the tongue I talk. It is an ancient tongue, that sweet child of the old Syriac. Liveth it yet in the world? Thou seest I dwell among the caves and the dead, and naught know I of the affairs of men, nor have I cared to know. I have lived, oh stranger, with my memories, and my memories are in a grave that mine own hands hollowed, for truly hath it been said that the child of man maketh his own path evil;' and her beautiful voice quivered, and broke in a note as soft as any wood-bird's. Suddenly her eye fell upon the sprawling frame of Billali, and she seemed to recollect herself.

'Ah! thou art there, old man. Tell me how it is that things have gone wrong in thine household. Forsooth, it seems that these my guests were set upon. Ay, and one was nigh to being slain by the hot pot to be eaten of those brutes, thy children, and had not the others fought gallantly they too had been slain, and not even I could have called back the life which had been loosed from the body. What means it, old man? What hast thou to say that I should not give thee over to those who execute my vengeance?'

Her voice had risen in her anger, and it rang clear and cold against the rocky walls. Also I thought I could see her eyes flash through the gauze that hid them. I saw poor Billali, whom I had believed to be a very fearless person, positively quiver with terror at her words.

'Oh "Hiya!" oh *She*!' he said, without lifting his white head from the floor. 'Oh *She*, as thou art great be merciful, for I am now as ever thy servant to obey. It was no plan or fault of mine, oh *She*, it was those wicked ones who are called my children. Led on by a woman whom thy guest the Pig had scorned, they would have followed the ancient custom of the land, and eaten the fat black stranger who came hither with these thy guests the Baboon and the Lion who is sick, thinking that no word had come from thee about the Black one. But when the Baboon and the Lion saw what they would do, they slew the woman, and slew also their servant to save him from the horror of the pot. Then those evil ones, ay, those children of the Wicked One who lives in the Pit, they went mad with the lust of blood, and flew at the throats of the Lion and the Baboon and the Pig. But gallantly they fought. Oh *Hiya*! they fought like very men, and slew many, and held their own, and then I came and saved them, and the evildoers have I sent on hither to Kôr to be judged of thy greatness, oh *She*! and here they are.'

'Ay, old man, I know it, and to-morrow will I sit in the great hall and do justice upon them, fear not. And for thee, I forgive thee, though hardly. See that thou dost keep thine household better. Go.'

Billali rose upon his knees with astonishing alacrity, bowed his head thrice, and, his white beard sweeping the ground, crawled down the apartment as he had crawled up it, till he finally vanished through the curtains, leaving me, not a little to my alarm, alone with this terrible but most fascinating person.

XIII

AYESHA UNVEILS

'There,' said *She*, 'he has gone, the white-bearded old fool! Ah, how little knowledge does a man acquire in his life. He gathereth it up like water, but like water it runneth through his fingers, and yet, if his hands be but wet as though with dew, behold a generation of fools call out, "See, he is a wise man!" Is it not so? But how call they thee? "Baboon," he says,' and she laughed; 'but that is the fashion of these savages who lack imagination, and fly to the beasts they resemble for a name. How do they call thee in thine own country,' stranger?'

'They call me Holly, oh Queen,' I answered.

'Holly,' she answered, speaking the word with difficulty, and yet with a most charming accent; 'and what is "Holly"?'

' "Holly" is a prickly tree,' I said.

'So. Well, thou hast a prickly and yet a tree-like look. Strong art thou, and ugly, but, if my wisdom be not at fault, honest at the core, and a staff to lean on. Also one who thinks. But stay, oh Holly, stand not there, enter with me and be seated by me. I would not see thee crawl before me like those slaves. I am aweary of their worship and their terror; sometimes when they vex me I could blast them for very sport, and to see the rest turn white, even to the heart.' And she held the curtain aside with her ivory hand to let me pass in.

I entered, shuddering. This woman was very terrible. Within the curtains was a recess, about twelve feet by ten, and in the recess was a couch and a table whereon stood fruit and sparkling water. By it, at its end, was a vessel like a font cut in carved stone, also full of pure water. The place was softly lit with lamps formed out of the beautiful vessels of which I have spoken, and the air and curtains were laden with a subtle perfume. Perfume too seemed to emanate from the glorious hair and white-clinging vestments of *She* herself. I entered the little room, and there stood uncertain.

'Sit,' said *She*, pointing to the couch. 'As yet thou hast no cause to fear me. If thou hast cause, thou shalt not fear for long, for I shall slay thee. Therefore let thy heart be light.'

I sat down on the end of the couch near to the font-like basin of water, and *She* sank down softly on to the other end.

'Now, Holly,' she said, 'how comest thou to speak Arabic? It is my
own dear tongue, for Arabian am I by my birth,* even "al Arab al
Ariba" (an Arab of the Arabs), and of the race of our father Yárab,
the son of Kâhtan, for in that fair and ancient city Ozal was I born,
in the province of Yaman the Happy. Yet dost thou not speak it as we
used to speak. Thy talk doth lack the music of the sweet tongue of
the tribes of Hamyar which I was wont to hear. Some of the words
too seemed changed, even as among these Amahagger, who have
debased and defiled its purity, so that I must speak with them in what
is to me another tongue.'[1]

'I have studied it,' I answered, 'for many years. Also the language
is spoken in Egypt and elsewhere.'

'So it is still spoken, and there is yet an Egypt? And what Pharaoh
sits upon the throne?* Still one of the spawn of the Persian Ochus, or
are the Achæmenians gone, for far is it to the days of Ochus.'

'The Persians have been gone from Egypt for nigh two thousand
years, and since then the Ptolemies, the Romans, and many others
have flourished and held sway upon the Nile, and fallen when their
time was ripe,' I said, aghast. 'What canst thou know of the Persian
Artaxerxes?'

She laughed, and made no answer, and again a cold chill went
through me. 'And Greece,' she said; 'is there still a Greece? Ah, I
loved the Greeks. Beautiful were they as the day, and clever, but
fierce at heart and fickle, notwithstanding.'

'Yes,' I said, 'there is a Greece; and, just now, is it once more a
people.* Yet the Greeks of to-day are not what the Greeks of the old
time were, and Greece herself is but a mockery of the Greece that
was.'

'So! The Hebrews, are they yet at Jerusalem? And does the Temple
that the wise king built* stand, and if so, what God do they worship
therein? Is their Messiah come, of whom they preached so much and
prophesied so loudly, and doth He rule the earth?'

'The Jews are broken and gone, and the fragments of their people

---

[1] Yárab the son of Kâhtan, who lived some centuries before the time of Abraham,
was the father of the ancient Arabs, and gave its name Araba to the country. In speaking
of herself as 'al Arab al Ariba,' *She* no doubt meant to convey that she was of the true
Arab blood as distinguished from the naturalised Arabs, the descendants of Ismael, the
son of Abraham and Hagar, who were known as 'al Arab al mostáreba.' The dialect of
the Koreish was usually called the clear or 'perspicuous' Arabic, but the Hamaritic
dialect approached nearer to the purity of the mother Syriac.—L. H. H.

strew the world, and Jerusalem is no more.* As for the temple that Herod built——'

'Herod!' she said. 'I know not Herod. But go on.'

'The Romans burnt it, and the Roman eagles flew across its ruins, and now Judæa is a desert.'

'So, so! They were a great people, those Romans, and went straight to their end—ay, they sped to it like Fate, or like their own eagles on their prey!—and left peace behind them.'

'Solitudinem faciunt, pacem appellant,'* I suggested.

'Ah, thou canst speak the Latin tongue, too!' she said, in surprise. 'It hath a strange ring in my ears after all these days, and it seems to me that thy accent does not fall as the Romans put it. Who was it wrote that? I know not the saying, but it is a true one of that great people. It seems that I have found a learned man—one whose hands have held the water of the world's knowledge. Knowest thou Greek also?'

'Yes, oh Queen, and something of Hebrew, but not to speak them well. They are all dead languages now.'

She clapped her hands in childish glee. 'Of a truth, ugly tree that thou art, thou growest the fruits of wisdom, oh, Holly,' she said, 'but of those Jews whom I hated, for they called me "heathen" when I would have taught them my philosophy. Did their Messiah come, and doth He rule the world?'

'Their Messiah came,' I answered with reverence; 'but He came poor and lowly, and they would have none of Him. They scourged Him, and crucified Him upon a tree, but yet His words and His works live on, for He was the Son of God, and now of a truth He doth rule half the world, but not with an Empire of the World.'

'Ah, the fierce-hearted wolves,' she said, 'the followers of Sense and of many gods—greedy of gain and faction-torn. I can see their dark faces yet. So they crucified their Messiah? Well can I believe it. That he was a Son of the Living Spirit would be naught to them, if indeed He was so, and of that we will talk afterwards. They would care naught for any God if he came not with pomp and power. They, a chosen people, a vessel of Him they call Jehovah, ay, and a vessel of Baal, and a vessel of Astoreth, and a vessel of the gods of the Egyptians—a high-stomached people, greedy of aught that brought them wealth and power. So they crucified their Messiah because He came in lowly guise—and now are they scattered about the earth.

Why, if I remember, so said one of their prophets that it should be.*
Well, let them go—they broke my heart, those Jews, and made me
look with evil eyes across the world, ay, and drove me to this wilderness, this place of a people that was before them. When I would have
taught them wisdom in Jerusalem they stoned me, ay, at the Gate of
the Temple those white-bearded hypocrites and Rabbis hounded the
people on to stone me! See, here is the mark of it to this day!' and
with a sudden move she pulled up the gauzy wrapping on her
rounded arm, and pointed to a little scar that showed red against its
milky beauty.

I shrank back horrified.

'Pardon me, oh Queen,' I said, 'but I am bewildered. Nigh upon
two thousand years have rolled across the earth since the Jewish
Messiah hung upon His cross at Golgotha. How then canst thou
have taught thy philosophy to the Jews before He was? Thou art a
woman, and no spirit. How can a woman live two thousand years?
Why dost thou befool me, oh Queen?'

She leaned back on the couch, and once more I felt the hidden
eyes playing upon me and searching out my heart.

'Oh man!' she said at last, speaking very slowly and deliberately, 'it
seems that there are still things upon the earth of which thou knowest naught. Dost thou still believe that all things die, even as those
very Jews believed? I tell thee that naught really dies. There is no
such thing as Death, though there be a thing called Change. See,'
and she pointed to some sculptures on the rocky wall. 'Three times
two thousand years have passed since the last of the great race that
hewed those pictures fell before the breath of the pestilence which
destroyed them, yet are they not dead. E'en now they live; perchance
their spirits are drawn toward us at this very hour,' and she glanced
round. 'Of a surety it sometimes seems to me that my eyes can see
them.'

'Yes, but to the world they are dead.'

'Ay, for a time; but even to the world are they born again and
again. I, yes I, Ayesha[1]—for that is my name, stranger—I say to thee
that I wait now for one I loved to be born again, and here I tarry till
he finds me, knowing of a surety that hither he will come, and that
here, and here only, shall he greet me. Why, dost thou suppose that I,

[1] Pronounced Assha.—L. H. H.

who am all powerful, I, whose loveliness is more than the loveliness of the Grecian Helen, of whom they used to sing, and whose wisdom is wider, ay, far more wide and deep than the wisdom of Solomon the Wise,—I, who know the secrets of the earth and its riches, and can turn all things to my uses,—I, who have even for a while overcome Change, that ye call Death,—why, I say, oh stranger, dost thou think that I herd here with barbarians lower than the beasts?'

'I know not,' I said humbly.

'Because I wait for him I love. My life has perchance been evil, I know not—for who can say what is evil and what good?—so I fear to die even if I could die, which I cannot until mine hour comes, to go and seek him where he is; for between us there might rise a wall I could not climb, at least, I dread it. Surely easy would it be also to lose the way in seeking in those great spaces wherein the planets wander on for ever. But the day will come, it may be when five thousand more years have passed, and are lost and melted into the vault of Time, even as the little clouds melt into the gloom of night, or it may be to-morrow, when he, my love, shall be born again, and then, following a law that is stronger than any human plan, he shall find me *here*, where once he knew me, and of a surety his heart will soften towards me though I sinned against him; ay, even though he know me not again, yet will he love me, if only for my beauty's sake.'

For a moment I was dumbfounded, and could not answer. The matter was too overpowering for my intellect to grasp.

'But even so, oh Queen,' I said at last, 'even if we men be born again and again, that is not so with thee, if thou speakest truly.' Here she looked up sharply, and once more I caught the flash of those hidden eyes; 'thou,' I went on hurriedly, 'who hast never died?'

'That is so,' she said; 'and it is so because I have, half by chance and half by learning, solved one of the great secrets of the world. Tell me, stranger: life is—why therefore should not life be lengthened for a while? What are ten or twenty or fifty thousand years in the history of life? Why in ten thousand years scarce will the rain and storms lessen a mountain top by a span in thickness? In two thousand years these caves have not changed, nothing has changed, but the beasts and man, who is as the beasts. There is naught that is wonderful about the matter, couldst thou but understand. Life is wonderful, ay, but that it should be a little lengthened is not wonderful. Nature hath her animating spirit as well as man, who is Nature's child, and he who can find that spirit, and let it breathe upon him, shall live with her life. He shall not live eternally, for Nature is not eternal, and she herself must die, even as the nature of the moon hath died. She herself must die, I say, or rather change and sleep till it be time for her to live again. But when shall she die? Not yet, I ween, and while she lives, so shall he who hath all her secret live with her. All I have it not, yet have I some, more perchance than any who were before me. Now, to thee I doubt not that this thing is a great mystery, therefore I will not overcome thee with it now. Another time will I tell thee more if the mood be on me, though perchance I shall never speak thereof again. Dost thou wonder how I knew that ye were coming to this land, and so saved your heads from the hot pot?'

'Ay, oh Queen,' I answered feebly.

'Then gaze upon that water,' and she pointed to the font-like vessel, and then, bending forward, held her hand over it.

I rose and gazed, and instantly the water darkened. Then it cleared, and I saw as distinctly as I ever saw anything in my life—I saw, I say, our boat upon that horrible canal. There was Leo lying at the bottom asleep in it, with a coat thrown over him to keep off the mosquitoes, in such a fashion as to hide his face, and myself, Job, and Mahomed towing on the bank.

I started back aghast, and cried out that it was magic, for I recognised the whole scene—it was one which had actually occurred.

'Nay, nay; oh, Holly,' she answered, 'it is no magic; that is a fiction of ignorance. There is no such thing as magic, though there is such a thing as a knowledge of the secrets of Nature. That water is my glass; in it I see what passes if I care to summon up the pictures, which is not often. Therein I can show thee what thou wilt of the past, if it be anything to do with this country and with what I have known, or anything that thou, the gazer, hast known. Think of a face if thou wilt, and it shall be reflected from thy mind upon the water. I know not all the secret yet—I can read nothing in the future. But it is an old secret; I did not find it. In Arabia and in Egypt the sorcerers knew it centuries ago. So one day I chanced to bethink me of that old canal—some twenty centuries ago I sailed upon it, and I was minded to look thereon again. And so I looked, and there I saw the boat and three men walking, and one, whose face I could not see, but a youth of a noble form, sleeping in the boat, and so I sent and saved ye. And now farewell. But stay, tell me of this youth—the Lion, as the old man calls him. I would look upon him, but he is sick, thou sayest— sick with the fever, and also wounded in the fray.'

'He is very sick,' I answered sadly; 'canst thou do nothing for him, oh Queen! who knowest so much?'

'Of a surety I can. I can cure him; but why speakest thou so sadly? Doth thou love the youth? Is he perchance thy son?'

'He is my adopted son, oh Queen! Shall he be brought in before thee?'

'Nay. How long hath the fever taken him?

'This is the third day.'

'Good; then let him lie another day. Then will he perchance throw it off by his own strength, and that is better than that I should cure him, for my medicine is of a sort to shake the life in its very citadel. If, however, by to-morrow night, at that hour when the fever first took him, he doth not begin to mend, then will I come to him and cure him. Stay, who nurses him?'

'Our white servant, him whom Billali names the Pig; also,' and here I spoke with some little hesitation, 'a woman named Ustane, a very handsome woman of this country, who came and embraced him when first she saw him, and hath stayed by him ever since, as I understand is the fashion of thy people, oh Queen.'

'My people! speak not to me of my people,' she answered, hastily; 'these slaves are no people of mine, they are but dogs to do my bidding till the day of my deliverance comes; and, as for their customs, naught have I to do with them. Also, call me not Queen—I am sick of flattery and titles—call me Ayesha, the name hath a sweet sound in mine ears, it is an echo from the past. As for this Ustane, I know not. I wonder if it be she against whom I was warned, and whom I in turn did warn? Hath she—stay, I will see;' and, bending forward, she passed her hand over the font of water and gazed intently into it. 'See,' she said quietly, 'is that the woman?'

I looked into the water, and there, mirrored upon its placid surface, was the silhouette of Ustane's stately face. She was bending forward, with a look of infinite tenderness upon her features, watching something beneath her, and with her chestnut locks falling on to her right shoulder.

'It is she,' I said, in a low voice, for once more I felt much disturbed at this most uncommon sight. 'She watches Leo asleep.'

'Leo!' said Ayesha, in an absent voice; 'why, that is "lion" in the Latin tongue. The old man hath named happily for once. It is very strange,' she went on speaking to herself, 'very. So like—but it is not possible!' With an impatient gesture she passed her hand over the water once more. It darkened, and the image vanished silently and mysteriously as it had risen, and once more the lamplight, and the lamplight only, shone on the placid surface of that limpid, living mirror.

'Hast thou aught to ask me before thou goest, oh Holly?' she said, after a few moments' reflection. 'It is but a rude life that thou must live here, for these people are savages, and know not the ways of cultivated man. Not that I am troubled thereby, for, behold my food,' and she pointed to the fruit upon the little table. 'Naught but fruit doth ever pass my lips—fruit and cakes of flour, and a little water. I have bidden my girls to wait upon thee. They are mutes thou knowest, deaf are they and dumb, and therefore the safest of servants, save to those who can read their faces and their signs. I bred them so—it hath taken many centuries and much trouble; but at last I have triumphed. Once I succeeded before, but the race was too ugly, so I let it die away; but now, as thou seest, they are otherwise. Once, too, I reared a race of giants, but after a while Nature would no more of it, and it died away. Hast thou aught to ask of me?'

'Ay, one thing, oh Ayesha,' I said boldly; but feeling by no means as bold as I trust I looked. 'I would gaze upon thy face.'

She laughed out in her bell-like notes. 'Bethink thee, Holly,' she answered; 'bethink thee. It seems that thou knowest the old myths of the gods of Greece. Was there not one Actæon* who perished miserably because he looked on too much beauty? If I show thee my face, perchance thou wouldst perish miserably also; perchance thou wouldst eat out thy heart in impotent desire; for know I am not for thee—I am for no man, save one, who hath been, but is not yet.'

'As thou wilt, Ayesha,' I said. 'I fear not thy beauty. I have put my heart away from such vanity as woman's loveliness, that passes like a flower.'

'Nay, thou errest,' she said; 'that does *not* pass. My beauty endures even as I endure; still if thou wilt, oh rash man, have thy will; but blame not me if passion mount thy reason, as the Egyptian breakers used to mount a colt, and guide it whither thou wilt not. Never may the man to whom my beauty hath been unveiled put it from his mind, and therefore even with these savages do I go veiled, lest they vex me, and I should slay them. Say, wilt thou see?'

'I will,' I answered, my curiosity overpowering me.

She lifted her white and rounded arms—never had I seen such arms before—and slowly, very slowly, withdrew some fastening beneath her hair. Then all of a sudden the long, corpse-like wrappings fell from her to the ground, and my eyes travelled up her form, now only robed in a garb of clinging white that did but serve to show its perfect and imperial shape, instinct with a life that was more than life, and with a certain serpent-like grace that was more than human. On her little feet were sandals, fastened with studs of gold. Then came ankles more perfect than ever sculptor dreamed of. About the waist her white kirtle was fastened by a double-headed snake of solid gold, above which her gracious form swelled up in lines as pure as they were lovely, till the kirtle ended on the snowy argent of her breast, whereon her arms were folded. I gazed above them at her face, and—I do not exaggerate—shrank back blinded and amazed. I have heard of the beauty of celestial beings, now I saw it; only this beauty, with all its awful loveliness and purity, was *evil*—at least, at the time, it struck me as evil. How am I to describe it? I cannot— simply, I cannot! The man does not live whose pen could convey a sense of what I saw. I might talk of the great changing eyes of deepest, softest black, of the tinted face, of the broad and noble brow, on which the hair grew low, and delicate, straight features. But, beautiful, surpassingly beautiful as they all were, her loveliness did not lie in them. It lay rather, if it can be said to have had any fixed abiding place, in a visible majesty, in an imperial grace, in a godlike stamp of softened power, which shone upon that radiant countenance like a living halo. Never before had I guessed what beauty made sublime could be—and yet, the sublimity was a dark one—the glory was not all of heaven—though none the less was it glorious. Though the face before me was that of a young woman of certainly not more than thirty years, in perfect health, and the first flush of ripened beauty, yet it had stamped upon it a look of unutterable experience, and of deep acquaintance with grief and passion. Not even the lovely smile that crept about the dimples of her mouth could hide this shadow of sin and sorrow. It shone even in the light of the glorious eyes, it was present in the air of majesty, and it seemed to say: 'Behold me, lovely as no woman was or is, undying and half-divine;

memory haunts me from age to age, and passion leads me by the hand—evil have I done, and with sorrow have I made acquaintance from age to age, and from age to age evil I shall do, and sorrow shall I know till my redemption comes.'

Drawn by some magnetic force which I could not resist, I let my eyes rest upon her shining orbs, and felt a current pass from them to me that bewildered and half-blinded me.

She laughed—ah, how musically! and nodded her little head at me with an air of sublimated coquetry that would have done credit to a Venus Victrix.*

'Rash man!' she said; 'like Actæon, thou hast had thy will; be careful lest, like Actæon, thou too dost perish miserably, torn to pieces by the ban-hounds* of thine own passions. I too, oh Holly, am a virgin goddess, not to be moved of any man, save one, and it is not thou. Say, hast thou seen enough!'

'I have looked on beauty, and I am blinded,' I said hoarsely, lifting my hand to cover up my eyes.

'So! what did I tell thee? Beauty is like the lightning; it is lovely, but it destroys—especially trees, oh Holly!' And again she nodded and laughed.

Suddenly she paused, and through my fingers I saw an awful change come over her countenance. Her great eyes suddenly fixed themselves into an expression in which horror seemed to struggle with some tremendous hope arising through the depths of her dark soul. The lovely face grew rigid, and the gracious, willowy form seemed to erect itself.

'Man,' she half whispered, half hissed, throwing back her head like a snake about to strike—'man, where didst thou get that scarab on thy hand? Speak, or by the Spirit of Life I will blast thee where thou standest!' and she took one light step towards me, and from her eyes there shone such an awful light—to me it seemed almost like a flame—that I fell, then and there, on the ground before her, babbling confusedly in my terror.

'Peace,' she said, with a sudden change of manner, and speaking in her former soft voice, 'I did affright thee! Forgive me! But at times, oh Holly, the almost infinite mind grows impatient of the slowness of the very finite, and I am tempted to use my power out of pure vexation—very nearly wast thou dead, but I remembered——. But the scarab—about the scarabæus!'

'I picked it up,' I gurgled feebly, as I got on to my feet again, and it is a solemn fact that my mind was so disturbed that at the moment I could remember nothing else about the ring except that I had picked it up in Leo's cave.

'It is very strange,' she said, with a sudden access of womanlike trembling and agitation which seemed out of place in this awful woman—'but once I knew a scarab like that. It—hung round the neck—of one I loved,' and she gave a little sob, and I saw that after all she was only a woman, although she might be a very old one.

'There,' she went on, 'it must be one like it, and yet never did I see one like it, for thereto hung a history, and he who wrote it prized it much.[1] But the scarab that I knew was not set thus in the bezel of a ring. Go now, Holly, go, and, if thou canst, try to forget that thou hast looked upon Ayesha's beauty,' and, turning from me, she flung herself on her couch, and buried her face in the cushions.

As for me, I stumbled from her presence, and I do not remember how I reached my own cave.

[1] I am informed* by a renowned and most learned Egyptologist, to whom I have submitted this very interesting and beautifully finished scarab, 'Suten se Rā,' that he has never seen one resembling it. Although it bears a title frequently given to Egyptian royalty, he is of opinion that it is not necessarily the cartouche of a Pharaoh, on which either the throne or personal name of the monarch is generally inscribed. What the history of this particular scarab may have been we can now, unfortunately, never know, but I have little doubt but that it played some part in the tragic story of the Princess Amenartas and her lover Kallikrates, the forsworn priest of Isis.—EDITOR.

XIV

IT was nearly ten o'clock at night when I cast myself down upon my bed, and began to gather my scattered wits, and reflect upon what I had seen and heard. But the more I reflected the less I could make of it. Was I mad, or drunk, or dreaming, or was I merely the victim of a gigantic and most elaborate hoax? How was it possible that I, a rational man, not unacquainted with the leading scientific facts of our history, and hitherto an absolute and utter disbeliever in all the hocus-pocus that in Europe goes by the name of the supernatural, could believe that I had within the last few minutes been engaged in conversation with a woman two thousand and odd years old? The thing was contrary to the experience of human nature, and absolutely and utterly impossible. It must be a hoax, and yet, if it were a hoax, what was I to make of it? What, too, was to be said of the figures on the water, of the woman's extraordinary acquaintance with the remote past, and her ignorance, or apparent ignorance, of any subsequent history? What, too, of her wonderful and awful loveliness? This, at any rate, was a patent fact, and beyond the experience of the world. No merely mortal woman could shine with such a supernatural radiance. About that she had, at any rate, been in the right—it was not safe for any man to look upon such beauty. I was a hardened vessel in such matters, having, with the exception of one painful experience of my green and tender youth, put the softer sex (I sometimes think that this is a misnomer) almost entirely out of my thoughts. But now, to my intense horror, I *knew* that I could never put away the vision of those glorious eyes; and, alas! the very *diablerie**
of the woman, whilst it horrified and repelled, attracted in even a greater degree. A person with the experience of two thousand years at her back, with the command of such tremendous powers and the knowledge of a mystery that could hold off death, was certainly worth falling in love with, if ever woman was. But, alas! it was not a question of whether or no she was worth it, for so far as I could judge, not being versed in such matters, I, a fellow of my college, noted for what my acquaintances are pleased to call my misogyny, and a respectable man now well on in middle life, had fallen absolutely and

hopelessly in love with this white sorceress. Nonsense; it must be nonsense! She had warned me fairly, and I had refused to take the warning. Curses on the fatal curiosity that is ever prompting man to draw the veil from woman, and curses on the natural impulse that begets it! It is the cause of half—ay, and more than half, of our misfortunes. Why cannot man be content to live alone and be happy, and let the women live alone and be happy too? But perhaps they would not be happy, and I am not sure that we should either. Here was a nice state of affairs. I, at my age, to fall a victim to this modern Circe!* But then she was not modern, at least she said not. She was almost as ancient as the original Circe.

I tore my hair, and jumped up from my couch, feeling that if I did not do something I should go off my head. What did she mean about the scarabæus too? It was Leo's scarabæus, and had come out of the old coffer that Vincey had left in my rooms nearly one-and-twenty years before. Could it be, after all, that the whole story was true, and the writing on the sherd was *not* a forgery, or the invention of some crack-brained, long-forgotten individual? And if so, could it be that *Leo* was the man that *She* was waiting for—the dead man who was to be born again! Impossible again! The whole thing was gibberish! Who ever heard of a man being born again?*

But if it were possible that a woman could exist for two thousand years, this might be possible also—anything might be possible. I myself might, for aught I knew, be a reincarnation of some other forgotten self, or perhaps the last of a long line of ancestral selves. Well, *vive la guerre!* why not? Only, unfortunately, I had no recollection of these previous conditions. The idea was so absurd to me that I burst out laughing, and, addressing the sculptured picture of a grim-looking warrior on the cave wall, called out to him aloud, 'Who knows, old fellow?—perhaps I was your contemporary. By Jove! perhaps I was you and you are I,' and then I laughed again at my own folly, and the sound of my laughter rang dismally along the vaulted roof, as though the ghost of the warrior had uttered the ghost of a laugh.

Next I bethought me that I had not been to see how Leo was, so, taking up one of the lamps which was burning at my bedside, I slipped off my shoes and crept down the passage to the entrance of his sleeping cave. The draught of the night air was lifting his curtain to and fro gently, as though spirit hands were drawing and redrawing

it. I slid into the vault-like apartment, and looked round. There was
a light by which I could see that Leo was lying on the couch, tossing
restlessly in his fever, but asleep. At his side, half-lying on the floor,
half-leaning against the stone couch, was Ustane. She held his hand
in one of hers, but she too was dozing, and the two made a pretty, or
rather a pathetic, picture. Poor Leo! his cheek was burning red, there
were dark shadows beneath his eyes, and his breath came heavily. He
was very, very ill; and again the horrible fear seized me that he might
die, and I be left alone in the world. And yet if he lived he would
perhaps be my rival with Ayesha; even if he were not the man, what
chance should I, middle-aged and hideous, have against his bright
youth and beauty? Well, thank Heaven! my sense of right was not
dead. *She* had not killed that yet; and, as I stood there, I prayed to the
Almighty in my heart that my boy, my more than son, might live—
ay, even if he proved to be the man.

Then I went back as softly as I had come, but still I could not
sleep; the sight and thought of dear Leo lying there so ill had but
added fuel to the fire of my unrest. My wearied body and over-
strained mind awakened all my imagination into preternatural activ-
ity. Ideas, visions, almost inspirations, floated before it with startling
vividness. Most of them were grotesque enough, some were ghastly,
some recalled thoughts and sensations that had for years been buried
in the *débris* of my past life. But, behind and above them all, hovered
the shape of that awful woman, and through them gleamed the
memory of her entrancing loveliness. Up and down the cave I
strode—up and down.

Suddenly I observed, what I had not noticed before, that there was
a narrow aperture in the rocky wall. I took up the lamp and examined it; the aperture led to a passage. Now, I was still sufficiently
sensible to remember that it is not pleasant, in such a situation as
ours was, to have passages running into one's bed-chamber from no
one knows where. If there are passages, people can come up them;
they can come up when one is asleep. Partly to see where it went to,
and partly from a restless desire to be doing something, I followed
the passage. It led to a stone stair, which I descended; the stair ended
in another passage, or rather tunnel, also hewn out of the bed-rock,
and running, so far as I could judge, exactly beneath the gallery that
led to the entrance of our rooms, and across the great central cave. I
went on down it: it was as silent as the grave, but still, drawn by some

sensation or attraction that I cannot describe, I followed on, my stockinged feet falling without noise on the smooth and rocky floor. When I had traversed some fifty yards of space, I came to another passage running at right angles, and here an awful thing happened to me: the sharp draught caught my lamp and extinguished it, leaving me in utter darkness in the bowels of that mysterious place. I took a couple of strides forward so as to clear the bisecting tunnel, being terribly afraid lest I should turn up it in the dark if once I got confused as to the direction, and then paused to think. What was I to do? I had no match; it seemed awful to attempt that long journey back through the utter gloom, and yet I could not stand there all night, and, if I did, probably it would not help me much, for in the bowels of the rock it would be as dark at midday as at midnight. I looked back over my shoulder—not a sight or a sound. I peered forward down the darkness: surely, far away, I saw something like the faint glow of fire. Perhaps it was a cave where I could get a light—at any rate, it was worth investigating. Slowly and painfully I crept along the tunnel, keeping my hand against its wall, and feeling at every step with my foot before I put it down, fearing lest I should fall into some pit. Thirty paces—there was a light, a broad light that came and went, shining through curtains! Fifty paces—it was close at hand! Sixty—oh, great heaven!

I was at the curtains, and they did not hang close, so I could see clearly into the little cavern beyond them. It had all the appearance of being a tomb, and was lit up by a fire that burnt in its centre with a whitish flame and without smoke. Indeed, there, to the left, was a stone shelf with a little ledge to it three inches or so high, and on the shelf lay what I took to be a corpse; at any rate, it looked like one, with something white thrown over it. To the right was a similar shelf, on which lay some broidered coverings. Over the fire bent the figure of a woman; she was sideways to me and facing the corpse, wrapped in a dark mantle that hid her like a nun's cloak. She seemed to be staring at the flickering flame. Suddenly, as I was trying to make up my mind what to do, with a convulsive movement that somehow gave an impression of despairing energy, the woman rose to her feet and cast the dark cloak from her.

It was *She* herself!

She was clothed, as I had seen her when she unveiled, in the kirtle of clinging white, cut low upon her bosom, and bound in at the waist with the barbaric double-headed snake, and, as before, her rippling black hair fell in heavy masses down her back. But her face was what caught my eye, and held me as in a vice, not this time by the force of its beauty, but by the power of fascinated terror. The beauty was still there, indeed, but the agony, the blind passion, and the awful vindictiveness displayed upon those quivering features, and in the tortured look of the upturned eyes, were such as surpass my powers of description.

For a moment she stood still, her hands raised high above her head, and as she did so the white robe slipped from her down to her golden girdle, baring the blinding loveliness of her form. She stood there, her fingers clenched, and the awful look of malevolence gathered and deepened on her face.

Suddenly, I thought of what would happen if she discovered me, and the reflection made me turn sick and faint. But even if I had known that I must die if I stopped, I do not believe that I could have moved, for I was absolutely fascinated. But still I knew my danger. Supposing she should hear me, or see me through the curtain, supposing I even sneezed, or that her magic told her that she was being watched—swift indeed would be my doom.

Down came the clenched hands to her sides, then up again above her head, and, as I am a living and honourable man, the white flame of the fire leapt up after them, almost to the roof, throwing a fierce and ghastly glare upon *She* herself, upon the white figure beneath the covering, and every scroll and detail of the rockwork.

Down came the ivory arms again, and as they did so she spoke, or rather hissed, in Arabic, in a note that curdled my blood, and for a second stopped my heart.

'Curse her, may she be everlastingly accursed.'

The arms fell and the flame sank. Up they went again, and the broad tongue of fire shot up after them; then again they fell.

'Curse her memory—accursed be the memory of the Egyptian.'

Up again, and again down.

'Curse her, the fair daughter of the Nile, because of her beauty.'

'Curse her, because her magic hath prevailed against me.'

'Curse her, because she kept my beloved from me.'

And again the flame dwindled and shrank.

She put her hands before her eyes, and, abandoning the hissing tone, cried aloud:—

'What is the use of cursing?—she prevailed, and she is gone.'

Then she recommenced with an even more frightful energy:—

'Curse her where she is. Let my curses reach her where she is and disturb her rest.

'Curse her through the starry spaces. Let her shadow be accursed.

'Let my power find her even there.

'Let her hear me even there. Let her hide herself in the blackness.

'Let her go down into the pit of despair, because I shall one day find her.'

Again the flame fell, and again she covered her eyes with her hands.

'It is no use—no use,' she wailed; 'who can reach those who sleep? Not even I can reach them.'

Then once more she began her unholy rites.

'Curse her when she shall be born again. Let her be born accursed.

'Let her be utterly accursed from the hour of her birth until sleep finds her.

'Yea, then, let her be accursed: for then shall I overtake her with my vengeance, and utterly destroy her.'

And so on. The flame rose and fell, reflecting itself in her agonised eyes; the hissing sound of her terrible maledictions, and no words of mine, especially on paper, can convey how terrible they were, ran round the walls and died away in little echoes, and the fierce light and deep gloom alternated themselves on the white and dreadful form stretched upon that bier of stone.

But at length she seemed to wear herself out, and ceased. She sat herself down upon the rocky floor, and shook the dense cloud of her beautiful hair over her face and breast, and began to sob terribly in the torture of a heartrending despair.

'Two thousand years,' she moaned—'two thousand years have I waited and endured; but though century doth still creep on to century, and time give place to time, the sting of memory hath not lessened, the light of hope doth not shine more bright. Oh! to have lived two thousand years, with my passion eating at my heart, and with my sin ever before me. Oh, that for me life cannot bring forget-fulness! Oh, for the weary years that have been and are yet to come, and evermore to come, endless and without end!

'My love! my love! my love! Why did that stranger bring thee back to me after this sort? For five hundred years I have not suffered thus. Oh, if I sinned against thee, have I not wiped away the sin? When wilt thou come back to me who have all, and yet without thee have naught? What is there that I can do? What? What? What? And perchance she—perchance that Egyptian doth abide with thee where thou art, and mock my memory. Oh, why could I not die with thee, I who slew thee? Alas, that I cannot die! Alas! Alas!' and she flung herself prone upon the ground, and sobbed and wept till I thought her heart must burst.

Suddenly she ceased, raised herself to her feet, rearranged her robe, and, tossing back her long locks impatiently, swept across to where the figure lay upon the stone.

'Oh Kallikrates,' she cried, and I trembled at the name, 'I must look upon thy face again, though it be agony. It is a generation since I looked upon thee whom I slew—slew with mine own hand,' and with trembling fingers she seized the corner of the sheet-like wrapping that covered the form upon the stone bier, and then paused. When she spoke again, it was in a kind of awed whisper, as though her idea were terrible even to herself.

'Shall I raise thee,' she said, apparently addressing the corpse, 'so that thou standest there before me, as of old? I *can* do it,' and she held out her hands over the sheeted dead, while her whole frame became rigid and terrible to see, and her eyes grew fixed and dull. I shrank in horror behind the curtain, my hair stood up upon my head, and whether it was my imagination or a fact I am unable to say, but I thought that the quiet form beneath the covering began to quiver, and the winding sheet to lift as though it lay on the breast of one who slept. Suddenly she withdrew her hands, and the motion of the corpse seemed to me to cease.

'What is the use?' she said gloomily. 'Of what use is it to recall the semblance of life when I cannot recall the spirit? Even if thou stoodest before me thou wouldst not know me, and couldst but do what I bid thee. The life in thee would be *my* life, and not *thy* life, Kallikrates.'

For a moment she stood there brooding, and then cast herself down on her knees beside the form, and began to press her lips against the sheet, and weep. There was something so horrible about the sight of this awe-inspiring woman letting loose her passion on the dead—so much more horrible even than anything that had gone before, that I could no longer bear to look at it, and, turning, began to creep, shaking as I was in every limb, slowly along the pitch-dark passage, feeling in my trembling heart that I had a vision of a Soul in Hell.

On I stumbled, I scarcely know how. Twice I fell, once I turned up the bisecting passage, but fortunately found out my mistake in time. For twenty minutes or more I crept along, till at last it occurred to me that I must have passed the little stair by which I descended. So, utterly exhausted, and nearly frightened to death, I sank down at length there on the stone flooring, and sank into oblivion.

When I came to I noticed a faint ray of light in the passage just behind me. I crept to it, and found it was the little stair down which the weak dawn was stealing. Passing up it I gained my chamber in safety, and, flinging myself on the couch, was soon lost in slumber or rather stupor.

XV

AYESHA GIVES JUDGMENT

THE next thing that I remember was opening my eyes and perceiving the form of Job, who had now practically recovered from his attack of fever. He was standing in the ray of light that pierced into the cave from the outer air, shaking out my clothes as a makeshift for brushing them, which he could not do because there was no brush, and then folding them up neatly and laying them on the foot of the stone couch. This done, he got my travelling dressing-case out of the Gladstone bag, and opened it ready for my use. First, he stood it on the foot of the couch also, then, being afraid, I suppose, that I should kick it off, he placed it on a leopard skin on the floor, and stood back a step or two to observe the effect. It was not satisfactory, so he shut up the bag, turned it on end, and, having rested it against the foot of the couch, placed the dressing-case on it. Next, he looked at the pots full of water, which constituted our washing apparatus. 'Ah!' I heard him murmur, 'no hot water in this beastly place. I suppose these poor creatures only use it to boil each other in,' and he sighed deeply.

'What is the matter, Job?' I said.

'Beg pardon, sir,' he said, touching his hair. 'I thought you were asleep, sir; and I am sure you look as though you want it. One might think from the look of you that you had been having a night of it.'

I only groaned by way of answer. I had, indeed, been having a night of it, such as I hope never to have again.

'How is Mr. Leo, Job?'

'Much the same, sir. If he don't soon mend, he'll end, sir; and that's all about it; though I must say that that there savage, Ustane, do do her best for him, almost like a baptised Christian. She is always hanging round and looking after him, and if I ventures to interfere, it's awful to see her; her hair seems to stand on end, and she curses and swears away in her heathen talk—at least I fancy she must be cursing from the look of her.'

'And what do you do then?'

'I make her a perlite bow, and I say, "Young woman, your position is one that I don't quite understand and can't recognise. Let me tell you that I has a duty to perform to my master as is incapacitated by illness, and that I am going to perform it until I am incapacitated too," but she don't take no heed, not she—only curses and swears away worse than ever. Last night she put her hand under that sort of nightshirt she wears and whips out a knife with a kind of a curl in the blade, so I whips out my revolver, and we walks round and round each other till at last she bursts out laughing. It isn't nice treatment for a Christian man to have to put up with from a savage, however handsome she may be, but it is what people must expect as is *fools* enough' (Job laid great emphasis on the 'fools') 'to come to such a place to look for things no man is meant to find. It's a judgment on us, sir—that's my opinion; and I, for one, is of opinion, that the judgment isn't half done yet, and when it is done, we shall be done too, and just stop in these beastly caves with the ghosts and the corpseses* for once and all. And now, sir, I must be seeing about Mr. Leo's broth, if that wild cat will let me; and, perhaps, you would like to get up, sir, because it's past nine o'clock.'

Job's remarks were not of an exactly cheering order to a man who had passed such a night as I had; and, what is more, they had the weight of truth. Taking one thing with another, it appeared to me to be an utter impossibility that we should escape from the place where we were. Supposing that Leo recovered, and supposing that *She* would let us go, which was exceedingly doubtful, and that she did not 'blast' us in some moment of vexation, and that we were not hot-potted by the Amahagger, it would be quite impossible for us to find our way across the network of marshes which, stretching for scores and scores of miles, formed a stronger and more impassable fortification round the various Amahagger households than any that could be built or designed by man. No, there was but one thing to do—face it out; and, speaking for my own part, I was so intensely interested in the whole weird story that, so far as I was concerned, notwithstanding the shattered state of my nerves, I asked nothing better, even if my life paid forfeit to my curiosity. What man for whom physiology has charms could forbear to study such a character as that of this Ayesha when the opportunity of doing so presented itself? The very terror of the pursuit added to its fascination, and besides, as I was forced to own to myself even now in the sober light of day, she herself had attractions that I could not forget. Not even the dreadful sight which I had witnessed during the night could drive that folly from my mind; and alas! that I should have to admit it, it has not been driven thence to this hour.

After I had dressed myself I passed into the eating, or rather embalming chamber, and had some food, which was as before brought to me by the girl mutes. When I had finished I went and saw poor Leo, who was quite off his head, and did not even know me. I asked Ustane how she thought he was; but she only shook her head and began to cry a little. Evidently her hopes were small; and I then and there made up my mind that, if it were in any way possible, I would get *She* to come and see him. Surely she would cure him if she chose—at any rate she said she could. While I was in the room, Billali entered, and also shook his head.

'He will die at night,' he said.

'God forbid, my father,' I answered, and turned away with a heavy heart.

'*She-who-must-be-obeyed* commands thy presence, my Baboon,' said the old man as soon as we got to the curtain; 'but, oh my dear son, be more careful. Yesterday I made sure in my heart that *She* would blast thee when thou didst not crawl upon thy stomach before her. She is sitting in the great hall even now to do justice upon those who would have smitten thee and the Lion. Come on, my son; come swiftly.'

I turned, and followed him down the passage, and when we reached the great central cave saw that many Amahagger, some robed, and some merely clad in the sweet simplicity of a leopard skin, were hurrying up it. We mingled with the throng, and walked up the enormous and, indeed, almost interminable cave. All the way its walls were elaborately sculptured, and every twenty paces or so passages opened out of it at right angles, leading, Billali told me, to tombs, hollowed in the rock by 'the people who were before.' Nobody visited those tombs now, he said; and I must say that my heart rejoiced when I thought of the opportunities of antiquarian research which opened out before me.

At last we came to the head of the cave, where there was a rock daïs almost exactly similar to the one on which we had been so furiously attacked, a fact that proved to me that these daïs must have been used as altars, probably for the celebration of religious ceremonies, and more especially of rites connected with the interment of the dead. On either side of this daïs were passages leading, Billali informed me, to other caves full of dead bodies. 'Indeed,' he added, 'the whole mountain is full of dead, and nearly all of them are perfect.'

In front of the daïs were gathered a great number of people of both sexes, who stood staring about in their peculiar gloomy fashion, which would have reduced Mark Tapley* himself to misery in about five minutes. On the daïs was a rude chair of black wood inlaid with ivory, having a seat made of grass fibre, and a footstool formed of a wooden slab attached to the framework of the chair.

Suddenly there was a cry of 'Hiya! Hiya!' (*'She! She!'*), and thereupon the entire crowd of spectators instantly precipitated itself upon the ground, and lay still as though it were individually and collectively stricken dead, leaving me standing there like some solitary survivor of a massacre. As it did so a long string of guards began to defile from a passage to the left, and ranged themselves on either side of the daïs. Then followed about a score of male mutes, then as many women mutes bearing lamps, and then a tall white figure, swathed from head to foot, in whom I recognised *She* herself. She mounted the daïs and sat down upon the chair, and spoke to me in *Greek*, I suppose because she did not wish those present to understand what she said.

'Come hither, oh Holly,' she said, 'and sit thou at my feet, and see me do justice on those who would have slain thee. Forgive me if my Greek doth halt like a lame man; it is so long since I have heard the sound of it that my tongue is stiff, and will not bend rightly to the words.'

I bowed, and, mounting the daïs, sat down at her feet.

'How didst thou sleep, my Holly?' she asked.

'I slept not well, oh Ayesha!' I answered with perfect truth, and with an inward fear that perhaps she knew how I had passed the heart of the night.

'So,' she said, with a little laugh, 'I, too, have not slept well. Last night I had dreams, and methinks that thou didst call them to me, oh Holly.'

'Of what didst thou dream, Ayesha?' I asked indifferently.

'I dreamed,' she answered quickly, 'of one I hate and one I love,' and then, as though to turn the conversation, she addressed the captain of her guard in Arabic: 'Let the men be brought before me.'

The captain bowed low, for the guard and her attendants did not prostrate themselves but had remained standing, and departed with his underlings down a passage to the right.

Then came a silence. *She* leant her swathed head upon her hand and appeared to be lost in thought, while the multitude before her continued to grovel upon their stomachs, only screwing their heads round a little so as to get a view of us with one eye. It seemed that their Queen so rarely appeared in public that they were willing to undergo this inconvenience, and even graver risks, to have the opportunity of looking on her, or rather on her garments, for no living man there except myself had ever seen her face. At last we caught sight of the waving of lights, and heard the tramp of men coming along the passage, and in filed the guard, and with them the survivors of our would-be murderers to the number of twenty or more, on whose countenances the natural expression of sullenness struggled with the terror that evidently filled their savage hearts. They were ranged in front of the daïs, and would have cast themselves down on the floor of the cave like the spectators, but *She* stopped them.

'Nay,' she said in her softest voice, 'stand; I pray you stand. Perchance the time will soon be when ye shall grow weary of being stretched out,' and she laughed melodiously.

I saw a cringe of terror run along the rank of the poor doomed wretches, and, wicked villains as they were, I felt sorry for them. Some minutes, perhaps two or three, passed before anything fresh occurred, during which *She* appeared from the movement of her head—for, of course, we could not see her eyes—to be slowly and carefully examining each delinquent. At last she spoke, addressing herself to me in a quiet and deliberate tone.

'Dost thou, oh my guest, who art known in thine own country by the name of the Prickly Tree, recognise these men?'

'Ay, oh Queen, nearly all of them,' I said, and I saw them glower at me as I said it.

'Then tell to me, and this great company, the tale whereof I have heard.'

Thus adjured, I, in as few words as I could, related the history of the cannibal feast, and of the attempted torture of our poor servant. The narrative was received in perfect silence, both by the accused and by the audience, and also by *She* herself. When I had done, Ayesha called upon Billali by name, and, lifting his head from the ground, but without rising, the old man confirmed my story. No further evidence was taken.

'Ye have heard,' said *She* at length, in a cold, clear voice, very different from her usual tones—indeed, it was one of the most remarkable things about this extraordinary creature that her voice had the power of suiting itself in a wonderful manner to the mood of the moment. 'What have ye to say, ye rebellious children, why vengeance should not be done upon you?'

For some time there was no answer, but at last one of the men, a fine, broad-chested fellow, well on in middle-life, with deep-graven features and an eye like a hawk's, spoke, and said that the orders that they had received were not to harm the white men; nothing was said of their black servant, so, egged on thereto by a woman who was now dead, they proceeded to try to hot-pot him after the ancient and honourable custom of their country, with a view of eating him in due course. As for their attack upon ourselves, it was made in an access of sudden fury, and they deeply regretted it. He ended by humbly praying that mercy might be extended to them; or, at least, that they might be banished into the swamps, to live or die as it might chance; but I saw it written on his face that he had but little hope of mercy.

Then came a pause, and the most intense silence reigned over the whole scene, which, illuminated as it was by the flicker of the lamps striking out broad patterns of light and shadow upon the rocky walls, was as strange as any I ever saw, even in that unholy land. Upon the ground before the daïs were stretched scores of the corpselike forms of the spectators, till at last the long lines of them were lost in the gloomy background. Before this outstretched audience were the knots of evil-doers, trying to cover up their natural terrors with a brave appearance of unconcern. On the right and left stood the silent guards, robed in white and armed with great spears and daggers, and men and women mutes watching with hard curious eyes. Then, seated in her barbaric chair above them all, with myself at her feet, was the veiled white woman, whose loveliness and awesome power seemed to visibly shine about her like a halo, or rather like the glow from some unseen light. Never have I seen her veiled shape look more terrible than it did in that space, while she gathered herself up for vengeance.

At last it came.

'Dogs and serpents,' *She* began in a low voice that gradually gathered power as she went on, till the place rang with it. 'Eaters of human flesh, two things have ye done. First, ye have attacked these strangers, being white men, and would have slain their servant, and for that alone death is your reward. But that is not all. Ye have dared to disobey me. Did I not send my word unto you by Billali, my servant, and the father of your household? Did I not bid you to hospitably entertain these strangers, whom now ye have striven to slay, and whom, had not they been brave and strong beyond the strength of men, ye would cruelly have murdered? Hath it not been taught to you from childhood that the law of *She* is an ever fixed law, and that he who breaketh it by so much as one jot or tittle* shall perish? And is not my lightest word a law? Have not your fathers taught you this, I say, whilst as yet ye were but children? Do ye not know that as well might ye bid these great caves to fall upon you, or the sun to cease its journeying, as to hope to turn me from my courses, or make my word light or heavy, according to your minds? Well do ye know it, ye Wicked Ones. But ye are all evil—evil to the core—the wickedness bubbles up in you like a fountain in the spring-time. Were it not for me, generations since had ye ceased to be, for of your own evil way had ye destroyed each other. And now, because ye have done this thing, because ye have striven to put these men, my guests, to death, and yet more because ye have dared to disobey my word, this is the doom that I doom you to. That ye be taken to the cave of torture,[1] and given over to the tormentors, and that on the going down of to-morrow's sun those of you who yet remain alive be slain, even as ye would have slain the servant of this my guest.'

She ceased, and a faint murmur of horror ran round the cave. As for the victims, as soon as they realised the full hideousness of their doom, their stoicism forsook them, and they flung themselves down upon the ground, and wept and implored for mercy in a way that was

[1] 'The cave of torture.' I afterwards saw this dreadful place, also a legacy from the prehistoric people who lived in Kôr. The only objects in the cave itself were slabs of rock arranged in various positions to facilitate the operations of the torturers. Many of these slabs, which were of a porous stone, were stained quite dark with the blood of ancient victims that had soaked into them. Also in the centre of the room was a place for a furnace, with a cavity wherein to heat the historic pot. But the most dreadful thing about the cave was that over each slab was a sculptured illustration of the appropriate torture being applied. These sculptures were so awful that I will not harrow the reader by attempting a description of them.—L. H. H.

dreadful to behold. I, too, turned to Ayesha, and begged her to spare them, or at least to mete out their fate in some less awful way. But she was hard as adamant about it.

'My Holly,' she said, again speaking in Greek, which, to tell the truth, although I have always been considered a better scholar of that language than most men, I found it rather difficult to follow, chiefly because of the change in the fall of the accent. Ayesha, of course, talked with the accent of her contemporaries, whereas we have only tradition and the modern accent to guide us as to the exact pro-nunciation—'My Holly, it cannot be. Were I to show mercy to those wolves, your lives would not be safe among this people for a day. Thou knowest them not. They are tigers to lap blood, and even now they hunger for your lives. How thinkest thou that I rule this people? I have but a regiment of guards to do my bidding, therefore it is not by force. It is by terror. My empire is of the imagination. Once in a generation mayhap I do as I have done but now, and slay a score by torture. Believe not that I would be cruel, or take vengeance on anything so low. What can it profit me to be avenged on such as these? Those who live long, my Holly, have no passions, save where they have interests. Though I may seem to slay in wrath, or because my mood is crossed, it is not so. Thou hast seen how in the heavens the little clouds blow this way and that without a cause, yet behind them is the great wind sweeping on its path whither it listeth. So is it with me, oh Holly. My moods and changes are the little clouds, and fitfully these seem to turn; but behind them ever blows the great wind of my purpose. Nay, the men must die; and die as I have said.' Then, suddenly turning to the captain of the guard—

'As my word is, so be it!'

XVI

THE TOMBS OF KÔR

AFTER the prisoners had been removed Ayesha waved her hand, and the spectators turned round, and began to crawl off down the cave like a scattered flock of sheep. When they were a fair distance from the daïs, however, they rose and walked away, leaving the Queen and myself alone, with the exception of the mutes and the few remaining guards, most of whom had departed with the doomed men. Thinking this a good opportunity, I asked *She* to come and see Leo, telling her of his serious condition; but she would not, saying that he certainly would not die before the night, as people never died of that sort of fever except at nightfall or dawn. Also she said that it would be better to let the sickness spend its course as much as possible before she cured it. Accordingly, I was rising to leave, when she bade me follow her, as she would talk with me, and show me the wonders of the caves.

I was too much involved in the web of her fatal fascinations to say her no, even if I had wished, which I did not. She rose from her chair, and, making some signs to the mutes, descended from the daïs. Thereon four of the girls took lamps, and ranged themselves two in front and two behind us, but the others went away, as also did the guards.

'Now,' she said, 'wouldst thou see some of the wonders of this place, oh Holly? Look upon this great cave. Sawest thou ever the like? Yet was it, and many more like it, hollowed by the hands of the dead race that once lived here in the city on the plain. A great and a wonderful people must they have been, those men of Kôr, but, like the Egyptians, they thought more of the dead than of the living. How many men, thinkest thou, working for how many years, did it need to the hollowing out this cave and all the galleries thereof?'

'Tens of thousands,' I answered.

'So, oh Holly. This people was an old people before the Egyptians were. A little can I read of their inscriptions, having found the key thereto—and, see thou here, this was one of the last of the caves that they hollowed,' and, turning to the rock behind her, she motioned the mutes to hold up the lamps. Carven over the daïs was the figure of an old man seated in a chair, with an ivory rod in his hand. It struck me at once that his features were exceedingly like those of the man who was represented as being embalmed in the chamber where we took our meals. Beneath the chair, which, by the way was shaped exactly like the one in which Ayesha had sat to give judgment, was a short inscription in the extraordinary characters of which I have already spoken, but which I do not remember sufficient of to illustrate. It looked more like Chinese writing than any other that I am acquainted with. This inscription Ayesha proceeded, with some difficulty and hesitation, to read aloud and translate. It ran as follows:—

'In the year four thousand two hundred and fifty-nine from the founding of the City of imperial Kôr was this cave (or burial place) completed by Tisno, King of Kôr, the people thereof and their slaves having laboured thereat for three generations, to be a tomb for their citizens of rank who shall come after. May the blessing of the heaven above the heaven rest upon their work, and make the sleep of Tisno, the mighty monarch, the likeness of whose features is graven above, a sound and happy sleep till the day of awakening,[1] and also the sleep of his servants, and of those of his race who, rising up after him, shall yet lay their heads as low.'

'Thou seest, oh Holly,' she said, 'this people founded the city, of which the ruins yet cumber the plain yonder, four thousand years before this cave was finished. Yet, when first mine eyes beheld it two thousand years ago, was it even as it is now. Judge, therefore, how old must that city have been! And now, follow thou me, and I will show thee after what fashion this great people fell when the time was come for it to fall,' and she led the way down to the centre of the cave, stopping at a spot where a round rock had been let into a kind of large manhole in the flooring, accurately filling it just as the iron plates fill the spaces in the London pavements down which the coals are thrown. 'Thou seest,' she said. 'Tell me, what is it?'

'Nay, I know not,' I answered; whereon she crossed to the left-hand side of the cave (looking towards the entrance) and signed to the mutes to hold up the lamps. On the wall was something painted with a red pigment in similar characters to those hewn beneath the

---

[1] This phrase is remarkable, as seeming to indicate a belief in a future state.— EDITOR.

sculpture of Tisno, King of Kôr. This inscription she proceeded to translate to me, the pigment still being quite fresh enough to show the form of the letters. It ran as follows:—

'*I, Junis, a priest of the Great Temple of Kôr, write this upon the rock of the burying-place in the year four thousand eight hundred and three from the founding of Kôr. Kôr is fallen! No more shall the mighty feast in her halls, no more shall she rule the world, and her navies go out to commerce with the world. Kôr is fallen! and her mighty works and all the cities of Kôr, and all the harbours that she built and the canals that she made, are for the wolf and the owl and the wild swan, and the barbarian who comes after. Twenty and five moons ago did a cloud settle upon Kôr, and the hundred cities of Kôr, and out of the cloud came a pestilence that slew her people, old and young, one with another, and spared not. One with another they turned black and died—the young and the old, the rich and the poor, the man and the woman, the prince and the slave. The pestilence slew and slew, and ceased not by day or by night, and those who escaped from the pestilence were slain of the famine. No longer could the bodies of the children of Kôr be preserved according to the ancient rites, because of the number of the dead, therefore were they hurled into the great pit beneath the cave through the hole in the floor of the cave. Then at last, a remnant of this the great people, the light of the whole world, went down to the coast and took ship and sailed northwards; and now am I, the Priest Junis, who write this, the last man left alive of this great city of men, but whether there be any yet left in the other cities I know not. This do I write in misery of heart before I die, because Kôr the Imperial is no more, and because there are none to worship in her temple, and all her palaces are empty, and her princes and her captains and her traders and her fair women have passed off the face of the earth.*'

I gave a sigh of astonishment—the utter desolation depicted in this rude scrawl was so overpowering. It was terrible to think of this solitary survivor of a mighty people recording its fate before he too went down into darkness. What must the old man have felt as, in ghastly terrifying solitude, by the light of one lamp feebly illumining a little space of gloom, he in a few brief lines daubed the history of his nation's death upon the cavern wall? What a subject for the moralist, or the painter, or indeed for any one who can think!

'Doth it not occur to thee, oh Holly,' said Ayesha, laying her hand upon my shoulder, 'that those men who sailed North may have been the fathers of the first Egyptians?'

'Nay, I know not,' I said; 'it seems that the world is very old.'

'Old? Yes, it is old indeed. Time after time have nations, ay, and rich and strong nations, learned in the arts, been and passed away and been forgotten, so that no memory of them remains. This is but one of several; for Time eats up the works of man, unless, indeed, he digs in caves like the people of Kôr, and then mayhap the sea swallows them, or the earthquake shakes them in. Who knows what hath been on the earth, or what shall be? There is no new thing under the sun, as the wise Hebrew wrote long ago.* Yet were not these people utterly destroyed, as I think. Some few remained in the other cities, for their cities were many. But the barbarians from the south, or perchance my people, the Arabs, came down upon them, and took their women to wife, and the race of the Amahagger that is now is a bastard brood of the mighty sons of Kôr, and behold it dwelleth in the tombs with its fathers' bones.[1] But I know not: who can know? My arts cannot pierce so far into the blackness of Time's night. A great people were they. They conquered till none were left to conquer, and then they dwelt at ease within their rocky mountain walls, with their man servants and their maid servants, their minstrels, their sculptors, and their concubines, and traded and quarrelled, and ate and hunted and slept and made merry till their time came. But come, I will show thee the great pit beneath the cave whereof the writing speaks. Never shall thine eyes witness such another sight.'

Accordingly I followed her to a side passage opening out of the main cave, then down a great number of steps, and along an underground shaft which cannot have been less than sixty feet beneath the surface of the rock, and was ventilated by curious borings that ran upward, I do not know where. Suddenly the passage ended, and she halted and bade the mutes hold up the lamps, and, as she had prophesied, I saw a scene such as I was not likely to see again. We were standing in an enormous pit, or rather on the edge of it, for it went down deeper—I do not know how much—than the level on which we stood, and was edged in with a low wall of rock. So far as I could judge, this pit was about the size of the space beneath the dome of St. Paul's in London, and when the lamps were held up I saw that it

---

[1] The name of the race Ama-hagger would seem to indicate a curious mingling of races such as might easily have occurred in the neighbourhood of the Zambesi. The prefix 'Ama' is common to the Zulu and kindred races, and signifies 'people,' while 'hagger' is an Arabic word meaning a stone.—EDITOR.

was nothing but one vast charnel-house, being literally full of thousands of human skeletons, which lay piled up in an enormous gleaming pyramid, formed by the slipping down of the bodies at the apex as fresh ones were dropped in from above. Anything more appalling than this jumbled mass of the remains of a departed race I cannot imagine, and what made it even more dreadful was that in this dry air a considerable number of the bodies had simply become desiccated with the skin still on them, and now, fixed in every conceivable position, stared at us out of the mountain of white bones, grotesquely horrible caricatures of humanity. In my astonishment I uttered an ejaculation, and the echoes of my voice ringing in the vaulted space disturbed a skull that had been accurately balanced for many thousands of years near the apex of the pile. Down it came with a run, bounding along merrily towards us, and of course bringing an avalanche of other bones after it, till at last the whole pit rattled with their movement, even as though the skeletons were getting up to greet us.

'Come,' I said, 'I have seen enough. These are the bodies of those who died of the great sickness, is it not so?' I added, as we turned away.

'Yes. The people of Kôr ever embalmed their dead, as did the Egyptians, but their art was greater than the art of the Egyptians, for whereas the Egyptians disembowelled and drew the brain, the people of Kôr injected fluid into the veins, and thus reached every part. But stay, thou shalt see,' and she halted at haphazard at one of the little doorways opening out of the passage along which we were walking, and motioned to the mutes to light us in. We entered into a small chamber similar to the one in which I had slept at our first stopping-place, only instead of one there were two stone benches or beds in it. On the benches lay figures covered with yellow linen,[1] on which a fine and impalpable dust had gathered in the course of ages but nothing like to the extent that one would have anticipated, for in these deep-hewn caves there is no material to turn to dust. About the bodies on the stone shelves and floor of the tomb were many painted vases, but I saw very few ornaments or weapons in any of the vaults.

'Uplift the cloths, oh Holly,' said Ayesha, but when I put out my

---

[1] All the linen that the Amahagger wore was taken from the tombs, which accounted for its yellow hue. If it was well washed, however, and properly rebleached, it acquired its former snowy whiteness, and was the softest and best linen I ever saw.—L. H. H.

hand to do so I drew it back again. It seemed like sacrilege, and to speak the truth I was awed by the dread solemnity of the place, and of the presences before us. Then, with a little laugh at my fears, she drew them herself, only to discover other and yet finer cloths lying over the forms upon the stone bench. These also she withdrew, and then for the first time for thousands upon thousands of years did living eyes look upon the face of that chilly dead. It was a woman; she might have been thirty-five years of age, or perhaps a little less, and had certainly been beautiful. Even now her calm clear-cut features, marked out with delicate eyebrows and long eyelashes which threw little lines of the shadow of the lamplight upon the ivory face, were wonderfully beautiful. There, robed in white, down which her blue-black hair was streaming, she slept her last long sleep, and on her arm, its face pressed against her breast, there lay a little babe. So sweet was the sight, although so awful, that—I confess it without shame—I could scarcely withhold my tears. It took me back across the dim gulf of the ages to some happy home in dead Imperial Kôr, where this winsome lady girt about with beauty had lived and died, and dying taken her last-born with her to the tomb. There they were before us, mother and babe, the white memories of a forgotten human history speaking more eloquently to the heart than could any written record of their lives. Reverently I replaced the grave-cloths, and, with a sigh that flowers so fair should, in the purpose of the Everlasting, have only bloomed to be gathered to the grave, I turned to the body on the opposite shelf, and gently unveiled it. It was that of a man in advanced life, with a long grizzled beard, and also robed in white, probably the husband of the lady who, after surviving her many years, came at last to sleep once more for good and all beside her.

We left the place and entered others. It would be too long to describe the many things I saw in them. Each one had its occupants, for the five hundred and odd years that had elapsed between the completion of the cave and the destruction of the race had evidently sufficed to fill these catacombs, numberless as they were, and all appeared to have been undisturbed since the day when they were placed there. I could fill a book with the description of them, but to do so would only be to repeat what I have said, with variations.

Nearly all the bodies, so masterly was the art with which they had been treated, were as perfect as on the day of death thousands of years before. Nothing came to injure them in the deep silence of the living rock: they were beyond the reach of heat and cold and damp, and the aromatic drugs with which they had been saturated were evidently practically everlasting in their effect. Here and there, however, we saw an exception, and in these cases, although the flesh looked sound enough externally, if one touched it it fell in, and revealed the fact that the figure was but a pile of dust. This arose, Ayesha told me, from these particular bodies having, either owing to haste in the burial or other causes, been soaked in the preservative,[1] instead of its being injected into the substance of the flesh.

About the last tomb we visited I must, however, say one word, for its contents spoke even more eloquently to the human sympathies than those of the first. It had but two occupants, and they lay together on a single shelf. I withdrew the grave-cloths, and there, clasped heart to heart, were a young man and a blooming girl. Her head rested on his arm, and his lips were pressed against her brow. I opened the man's linen robe, and there over his heart was a dagger-wound, and beneath the girl's fair breast was a like cruel stab, through which her life had ebbed away. On the rock above was an inscription in three words. Ayesha translated it. It was '*Wedded in Death.*'

What was the life-history of these two, who, of a truth, were beautiful in their lives, and in their death were not divided?*

I closed my eyelids, and imagination taking up the thread of thought shot its swift shuttle back across the ages, weaving a picture on their blackness so real and vivid in its detail that I could almost for a moment think that I had triumphed o'er the Past, and that my spirit's eyes had pierced the mystery of Time.

---

[1] Ayesha afterwards showed me the tree from the leaves of which this ancient preservative was manufactured. It is a low bush-like tree, that to this day grows in wonderful plenty upon the sides of the mountains, or rather upon the slopes leading up to the rocky walls. The leaves are long and narrow, a vivid green in colour, but turning a bright red in the autumn, and not unlike those of a laurel in general appearance. They have little smell when green, but if boiled the aromatic odour from them is so strong that one can hardly bear it. The best mixture, however, was made from the roots, and among the people of Kôr there was a law, which Ayesha showed me alluded to on some of the inscriptions, to the effect that under heavy penalties no one under a certain rank was to be embalmed with the drugs prepared from the roots. The object and effect of this was, of course, to preserve the trees from extermination. The sale of the leaves and roots was a Government monopoly, and from it the Kings of Kôr derived a large proportion of their private revenue.—L. H. H.

I seemed to see this fair girl form—the yellow hair streaming down her, glittering against her garments snowy white, and the bosom that was whiter than the robes, even dimming with its lustre her ornaments of burnished gold. I seemed to see the great cave filled with warriors, bearded and clad in mail, and, on the lighted daïs where Ayesha had given judgment, a man standing, robed, and surrounded by the symbols of his priestly office. And up the cave there came one clad in purple, and before him and behind him came minstrels and fair maidens, chanting a wedding song. White stood the maid against the altar, fairer than the fairest there—purer than a lily, and more cold than the dew that glistens in its heart. But as the man drew near she shuddered. Then out of the press and throng there sprang a dark-haired youth, and put his arm about this long-forgotten maid, and kissed her pale face in which the blood shot up like lights of the red dawn across the silent sky. And next there was turmoil and uproar, and a flashing of swords, and they tore the youth from her arms, and stabbed him, but with a cry she snatched the dagger from his belt, and drove it into her snowy breast, home to the heart, and down she fell, and then, with cries and wailing, and every sound of lamentation, the pageant rolled away from the arena of my vision, and once more the past shut to its book.

Let him who reads forgive the intrusion of a dream into a history of fact. But it came so home to me—I saw it all so clear in a moment, as it were; and, besides, who shall say what proportion of fact, past, present, or to come, may lie in the imagination? What is imagination? Perhaps it is the shadow of the intangible truth, perhaps it is the soul's thought.

In an instant the whole thing had passed through my brain, and *She* was addressing me.

'Behold the lot of man,' said the veiled Ayesha, as she drew the winding sheets back over the dead lovers, speaking in a solemn, thrilling voice, which accorded well with the dream that I had dreamed: 'to the tomb, and to the forgetfulness that hides the tomb, must we all come at last! Ay, even I who live so long. Even for me, oh Holly, thousands upon thousands of years hence; thousands of years after thou hast gone through the gate and been lost in the mists, a day will dawn whereon I shall die, and be even as thou art and these are. And then what will it avail that I have lived a little longer, holding off death by the knowledge I have wrung from Nature, since at last I too must die? What is a span of ten thousand years, or ten times ten thousand years, in the history of time? It is as naught—it is as the mists that roll up in the sunlight; it fleeth away like an hour of sleep or a breath of the Eternal Spirit. Behold the lot of man! Certainly it shall overtake us, and we shall sleep. Certainly, too, we shall awake, and live again and again shall sleep, and so on and on, through periods, spaces, and times, from æon unto æon, till the world is dead, and the worlds beyond the world are dead, and naught liveth save the Spirit that is Life. But for us twain and for these dead ones shall the end of ends be Life, or shall it be Death? As yet Death is but Life's Night, but out of the night is the Morrow born again, and doth again beget the Night. Only when Day and Night, and Life and Death, are ended and swallowed up in that from which they came, what shall be our fate, oh Holly? Who can see so far? Not even I!'

And then, with a sudden change of tone and manner—

'Hast thou seen enough, my stranger guest, or shall I show thee more of the wonders of these tombs that are my palace halls? If thou wilt, I can lead thee to where Tisno, the mightiest and most valorous King of Kôr, in whose day these caves were ended, lies in a pomp that seems to mock at nothingness, and bid the empty shadows of the past do homage to his sculptured vanity!'

'I have seen enough, oh Queen,' I answered. 'My heart is over-whelmed by the power of the present Death. Mortality is weak, and easily broken down by a sense of the companionship that waits upon its end. Take me hence, oh Ayesha!'

XVII

THE BALANCE TURNS

IN a few minutes, following the lamps of the mutes, which, held out from the body as a bearer holds water in a vessel, had the appearance of floating down the darkness by themselves, we came to a stair which led us to *She's* ante-room, the same that Billali had crept up upon all fours on the previous day. Here I would have bid the Queen adieu, but she would not.

'Nay,' she said, 'enter with me, oh Holly, for of a truth thy conversation pleaseth me. Think, oh Holly; for two thousand years have I had none to converse with save slaves and my own thoughts, and though of all this thinking hath much wisdom come, and many secrets been made plain, yet am I weary of my thoughts, and have come to loathe mine own society, for surely the food that memory gives to eat is bitter to the taste, and it is only with the teeth of hope that we can bear to bite it. Now though thy thoughts are green and tender, as becometh one so young, yet are they those of a thinking brain, and in truth thou dost bring back to my mind certain of those old philosophers with whom in days bygone I have disputed at Athens, and at Becca in Arabia, for thou hast the same crabbed air and dusty look, as though thou hadst passed thy days in reading ill-writ Greek, and been stained dark with the grime of manuscripts. So draw the curtain, and sit here by my side, and we will eat fruit, and talk of pleasant things. See, I will again unveil to thee. Thou hast brought it on thyself, oh Holly; fairly have I warned thee—and thou shalt call me beautiful as even those old philosophers were wont to do. Fie upon them, forgetting their philosophy!'

And without more ado she stood up and shook the white wrappings from her, and came forth shining and splendid like some glittering snake when she has cast her slough; ay, and fixed her wonderful eyes upon me—more deadly than any Basilisk's*—and pierced me through and through with their beauty, and sent her light laugh ringing through the air like chimes of silver bells.

A new mood was on her, and the very colour of her mind seemed to change beneath it. It was no longer torture-torn and hateful, as I had seen it when she was cursing her dead rival by the leaping

flames, no longer icily terrible as in the judgment-hall, no longer
rich, and sombre, and splendid, like a Tyrian cloth, as in the dwell-
ings of the dead. No, her mood now was that of Aphrodité* triumph-
ing. Life—radiant, ecstatic, wonderful—seemed to flow from her
and around her. Softly she laughed and sighed, and swift her glances
flew. She shook her heavy tresses, and their perfume filled the place;
she struck her little sandalled foot upon the floor, and hummed a
snatch of some old Greek epithalamium.* All the majesty was gone,
or did but lurk and faintly flicker through her laughing eyes, like
lightning seen through sunlight. She had cast off the terror of the
leaping flame, the cold power of judgment that was even now being
done, and the wise sadness of the tombs—cast them off and put
them behind her, like the white shroud she wore, and now stood out
the incarnation of lovely tempting womanhood, made more perfect—
and in a way more spiritual—than ever woman was before.

'There, my Holly, sit there where thou canst see me. It is by thine
own wish, remember—again I say, blame me not if thou dost spend
the rest of thy little span with such a sick pain at the heart that thou
wouldst fain have died before ever thy curious eyes were set upon
me. There, sit so, and tell me, for in truth I am inclined for praises—
tell me, am I not beautiful? Nay, speak not so hastily; consider well
the point; take me feature by feature, forgetting not my form, and my
hands and feet, and my hair, and the whiteness of my skin, and then
tell me truly hast thou ever known a woman who in aught, ay, in one
little portion of her beauty, in the curve of an eyelash even, or the
modelling of a shell-like ear, is justified to hold a light before my
loveliness? Now, my waist! Perchance thou thinkest it too large, but
of a truth it is not so; it is this golden snake that is too large, and
doth not bind it as it should. It is a wise snake, and knoweth that it is
ill to tie in the waist. But see, give me thy hands—so—now press
them round me, there, with but a little force, thy fingers touch, oh
Holly.'

I could bear it no longer. I am but a man, and she was more than a
woman. Heaven knows what she was—I do not! But then and there I
fell upon my knees before her, and told her in a sad mixture of languages—for such moments confuse the thoughts—that I worshipped her as never woman was worshipped, and that I would give
my immortal soul to marry her, which at that time I certainly would
have done, and so, indeed, would any other man, or all the race of

men rolled into one. For a moment she looked a little surprised, and then she began to laugh, and clap her hands in glee.

'Oh, so soon, oh Holly!' she said. 'I wondered how many minutes it would need to bring thee to thy knees. I have not seen a man kneel before me for so many days, and, believe me, to a woman's heart the sight is sweet, ay, wisdom and length of days take not from that dear pleasure which is our sex's only right.

'What wouldst thou?—what wouldst thou? Thou dost not know what thou doest. Have I not told thee that I am not for thee? I love but one, and thou art not the man. Ah Holly, for all thy wisdom— and in a way thou art wise—thou art but a fool running after folly. Thou wouldst look into mine eyes—thou wouldst kiss me! Well, if it pleaseth thee, *look*,' and she bent herself towards me, and fixed her dark and thrilling orbs upon my own; 'ay, and *kiss* too, if thou wilt, for, thanks be given to the scheme of things, kisses leave no marks, except upon the heart. But if thou dost kiss, I tell thee of a surety wilt thou eat out thy breast with love of me, and die!' and she bent yet further towards me till her soft hair brushed my brow, and her fragrant breath played upon my face, and made me faint and weak. Then of a sudden, even as I stretched out my arms to clasp, she straightened herself, and a quick change passed over her. Reaching out her hand, she held it over my head, and it seemed to me that something flowed from it that chilled me back to common sense, and a knowledge of propriety and the domestic virtues.

'Enough of this wanton play,' she said with a touch of sternness. 'Listen, Holly. Thou art a good and honest man, and I fain would spare thee; but, oh! it is so hard for a woman to be merciful. I have said I am not for thee, therefore let thy thoughts pass by me like an idle wind, and the dust of thy imagination sink again into the depths—well, of despair, if thou wilt. Thou dost not know me, Holly. Hadst thou seen me but ten hours past when my passion seized me, thou hadst shrunk from me in fear and trembling. I am a woman of many moods, and, like the water in that vessel, I reflect many things; but they pass, my Holly; they pass, and are forgotten. Only the water is the water still, and I still am I, and that which maketh the water maketh it, and that which maketh me maketh me, nor can my quality be altered. Therefore, pay no heed to what I seem, seeing that thou canst not know what I am. If thou troublest me again I will veil myself, and thou shalt behold my face no more.'

I rose, and sank on the cushioned couch beside her, yet quivering with emotion, though for a moment my mad passion had left me, as the leaves of a tree quiver still, although the gust be gone that stirred them. I did not dare to tell her that I *had* seen her in that deep and hellish mood, muttering incantations to the fire in the tomb.

'So,' she went on, 'now eat some fruit; believe me, it is the only true food for man. Oh, tell me of the philosophy of that Hebrew Messiah, who came after me, and whom thou sayest doth now rule Rome, and Greece, and Egypt, and the barbarians beyond. It must have been a strange philosophy that He taught, for in my day the peoples would have naught of our philosophies. Revel and lust and drink, blood and cold steel, and the shock of men gathered in the battle—these were the canons of their creeds.'

I had recovered myself a little by now, and, feeling bitterly ashamed of the weakness into which I had been betrayed, I did my best to expound to her the doctrines of Christianity, to which, however, with the single exception of our conception of Heaven and Hell, I found that she paid but faint attention, her interest being all directed towards the Man who taught them. Also I told her that among her own people, the Arabs, another prophet, one Mohammed, had arisen and preached a new faith to which many millions of mankind now adhered.

'Ah!' she said; 'I see—two new religions! I have known so many, and doubtless there have been many more since I knew aught beyond these caves of Kôr. Mankind asks ever of the skies to vision out what lies behind them. It is terror for the end, and but a subtler form of selfishness—this it is that breeds religions. Mark, my Holly, each religion claims the future for its followers; or, at the least, the good thereof. The evil is for those benighted ones who will have none of it; seeing the light the true believers worship, as the fishes see the stars, but dimly. The religions come and the religions pass, and the civilisations come and pass, and naught endures but the world and human nature. Ah! if man would but see that hope is from within and not from without—that he himself must work out his own salvation! He is there, and within him is the breath of life and a knowledge of good and evil as good and evil is to him. Thereon let him build and stand erect, and not cast himself before the image of some unknown God, modelled like his poor self, but with a bigger brain to think the evil thing; and a longer arm to do it.'

I thought to myself, which shows how old such reasoning is, being, indeed, one of the recurring quantities of theological discussion, that her argument sounded very like some that I have heard in the nineteenth century, and in other places than the caves of Kôr, and with which, by the way, I totally disagree, but I did not care to try and discuss the question with her. To begin with, my mind was too weary with all the emotions through which I had passed, and, in the second place, I knew that I should get the worst of it. It is weary work enough to argue with an ordinary materialist, who hurls statistics and whole strata of geological facts at your head, whilst you can only buffet him with deductions and instincts and the snowflakes of faith, that are, alas! so apt to melt in the hot embers of our troubles. How little chance, then, should I have against one whose brain was supernaturally sharpened, and who had two thousand years of experience, besides all manner of knowledge of the secrets of Nature at her command! Feeling that she would be more likely to convert me than I should to convert her, I thought it best to leave the matter alone, and so sat silent. Many a time since then have I bitterly regretted that I did so, for thereby I lost the only opportunity I can remember having had of ascertaining what Ayesha *really* believed, and what her 'philosophy' was.

'Well, my Holly,' she continued, 'and so those people of mine have also found a prophet, a false prophet thou sayest, for he is not thine own, and, indeed, I doubt it not. Yet in my day was it otherwise, for then we Arabs had many gods.* Allât there was, and Saba, the Host of Heaven, Al Uzza, and Manah the stony one, for whom the blood of victims flowed, and Wadd and Sawâ, and Yaghûth the Lion of the dwellers in Yaman, and Yäûk the Horse of Morad, and Nasr the Eagle of Hamyar; ay, and many more. Oh, the folly of it all, the shame and the pitiful folly! Yet when I rose in wisdom and spoke thereof, surely they would have slain me in the name of their outraged gods. Well, so hath it ever been;—but, my Holly, art thou weary of me already, that thou dost sit so silent? Or dost thou fear lest I should teach thee my philosophy?—for know I have a philosophy. What would a teacher be without her own philosophy? and if thou dost vex me overmuch beware! for I will have thee learn it, and thou shalt be my disciple, and we twain will found a faith that shall swallow up all others. Faithless man! And but half an hour since thou wast upon thy knees—the posture does not suit thee, Holly—

swearing that thou didst love me. What shall we do?—Nay, I have it. I will come and see this youth, the Lion, as the old man Billali calls him, who came with thee, and who is so sick. The fever must have run its course by now, and if he is about to die I will recover him. Fear not, my Holly, I shall use no magic. Have I not told thee that there is no such thing as magic, though there is such a thing as understanding and applying the forces which are in Nature? Go now, and presently when I have made the drug ready I will follow thee.'[1]

Accordingly I went, only to find Job and Ustane in a great state of grief, declaring that Leo was in the throes of death, and that they had been searching for me everywhere. I rushed to the couch, and glanced at him: clearly he was dying. He was senseless, and breathing heavily, but his lips were quivering, and every now and again a little shudder ran down his frame. I knew enough of doctoring to see that in another hour he would be beyond the reach of earthly help— perhaps in another five minutes. How I cursed my selfishness and the folly that had kept me lingering by Ayesha's side while my dear boy lay dying! Alas and alas! how easily the best of us are lighted down to evil by the gleam of a woman's eyes! What a wicked wretch was I! Actually, for the last half-hour I had scarcely thought of Leo, and this, be it remembered, of the man who for twenty years had been my dearest companion, and the chief interest of my existence. And now, perhaps, it was too late!

I wrung my hands, and glanced round. Ustane was sitting by the couch, and in her eyes burnt the dull light of despair. Job was blub- bering—I am sorry I cannot name his distress by any more delicate word—audibly in the corner. Seeing my eye fixed upon him he went outside to give way to his grief in the passage. Obviously the only hope lay in Ayesha. She, and she alone—unless, indeed, she was an impostor, which I could not believe—could save him. I would go and implore her to come. As I started to do so, however, Job came flying into the room, his hair literally standing on end with terror.

'Oh, God help us, sir!' he ejaculated in a frightened whisper, 'here's a corpse a-coming sliding down the passage!'

For a moment I was puzzled, but presently, of course, it struck me

[1] Ayesha was a great chemist, indeed chemistry appears to have been her only amusement and occupation. She had one of the caves fitted up as a laboratory, and, although her appliances were necessarily rude, the results that she attained were, as will become clear in the course of this narrative, sufficiently surprising.—L. H. H.

that he must have seen Ayesha, wrapped in her grave-like garment, and been deceived by the extraordinary undulating smoothness of her walk into a belief that she was a white ghost gliding towards him. Indeed, at that very moment the question was settled, for Ayesha herself was in the apartment, or rather cave. Job turned, and saw her sheeted form, and then, with a convulsive howl of 'Here it comes!' sprang into a corner, and jammed his face against the wall, and Ustane, guessing whose the dread presence must be, prostrated herself upon her face.

'Thou comest in a good time, Ayesha,' I said, 'for my boy lies at the point of death.'

'So,' she said softly; 'provided he be not dead, it is no matter, for I can bring him back to life, my Holly. Is that man there thy servant, and is that the method wherewith thy servants greet strangers in thy country?'

'He is frightened of thy garb—it hath a death-like air,' I answered. She laughed.

'And the girl? Ah, I see now. It is her of whom thou didst speak to me. Well, bid them both to leave us, and we will see to this sick Lion of thine. I love not that underlings should perceive my wisdom.'

Thereon I told Ustane in Arabic and Job in English both to leave the room; an order which the latter obeyed readily enough, and was glad to obey, for he could not in any way subdue his fear. But it was otherwise with Ustane.

'What does *She* want?' she whispered, divided between her fear of the terrible Queen and her anxiety to remain near Leo. 'It is surely the right of a wife to be near her husband when he dieth. Nay, I will not go, my lord, the Baboon.'

'Why doth not that woman leave us, my Holly?' asked Ayesha, from the other end of the cave, where she was engaged in carelessly examining some of the sculptures on the wall.

'She is not willing to leave Leo,' I answered, not knowing what to say. Ayesha wheeled round, and, pointing to the girl Ustane, said one word, and one only, but it was quite enough, for the tone in which it was said meant volumes.

'Go!'

And then Ustane crept past her on her hands and knees, and went.

'Thou seest, my Holly,' said Ayesha, with a little laugh, 'it was needful that I should give these people a lesson in obedience. That girl went nigh to disobeying me, but then she did not learn this morn how I treat the disobedient. Well, she has gone; and now let me see the youth,' and she glided towards the couch on which Leo lay, with his face in the shadow and turned toward the wall.

'He hath a noble shape,' she said, as she bent over him to look upon his face.

Next second her tall and willowy form was staggering back across the room, as though she had been shot or stabbed, staggering back till at last she struck the cavern wall, and then there burst from her lips the most awful and unearthly scream that I ever heard in all my life.

'What is it, Ayesha?' I cried. 'Is he dead?'

She turned, and sprang towards me like a tigress.

'Thou dog!' she said, in her terrible whisper, which sounded like the hiss of a snake, 'why didst thou hide this from me?' And she stretched out her arm, and I thought that she was about to slay me.

'What?' I ejaculated, in the most lively terror; 'what?'

'Ah!' she said, 'perchance thou didst not know. Learn, my Holly, learn: there lies—there lies my lost Kallikrates. Kallikrates, who has come back to me at last, as I knew he would, as I knew he would;' and she began to sob and to laugh, and generally to conduct herself like any other lady who is a little upset, murmuring 'Kallikrates, Kallikrates!'

'Nonsense,' thought I to myself, but I did not like to say it; and, indeed, at that moment I was thinking of Leo's life, having forgotten everything else in that terrible anxiety. What I feared now was that he should die while she was 'carrying on.'

'Unless thou art able to help him, Ayesha,' I put in, by way of a reminder, 'thy Kallikrates will soon be far beyond thy calling. Surely he dieth even now.'

'True,' she said, with a start. 'Oh, why did I not come before! I am unnerved—my hand trembles, even mine—and yet it is very easy. Here, thou Holly, take this phial,' and she produced a tiny jar of pottery from the folds of her garment, 'and pour the liquid in it down his throat. It will cure him if he be not dead. Swift, now! Swift! The man dies!'

I glanced towards him; it was true enough, Leo was in his death-struggle. I saw his poor face turning ashen, and heard the breath begin to rattle in his throat. The phial was stoppered with a little piece of wood. I drew it with my teeth, and a drop of the fluid within flew out upon my tongue. It had a sweet flavour, and for a second made my head swim, and a mist gather before my eyes, but happily the effect passed away as swiftly as it had arisen.

When I reached Leo's side he was plainly expiring—his golden head was slowly turning from side to side, and his mouth was slightly open. I called to Ayesha to hold his head, and this she managed to do, though the woman was quivering from head to foot, like an aspen-leaf or a startled horse. Then, forcing the jaw a little more open, I poured the contents of the phial into his mouth. Instantly a little vapour arose from it, as happens when one disturbs nitric acid, and this sight did not increase my hopes, already faint enough, of the efficacy of the treatment.

One thing, however, was certain, the death-throes ceased—at first I thought because he had got beyond them, and crossed the awful river. His face turned to a livid pallor, and his heart-beats, which had been feeble enough before, seemed to die away altogether—only the eyelid still twitched a little. In my doubt I looked up at Ayesha, whose head-wrapping had slipped back in her excitement when she went reeling across the room. She was still holding Leo's head, and, with a face as pale as his own, watching his countenance with such an expression of agonised anxiety as I have never seen before. Clearly she did not know if he would live or die. Five minutes slowly passed, and I saw that she was abandoning hope; her lovely oval face seemed to fall in and grow visibly thinner beneath the pressure of a mental agony whose pencil drew black lines about the hollows of her eyes. The coral faded even from her lips, till they were as white as Leo's face, and quivered pitifully. It was shocking to see her: even in my own grief I felt for hers.

'Is it too late?' I gasped.

She hid her face in her hands, and made no answer, and I too turned away. But as I did so I heard a deep-drawn breath, and looking down perceived a line of colour creeping up Leo's face, then another and another, and then, wonder of wonders, the man we had thought dead turned over on his side.

'Thou seest,' I said in a whisper.

'I see,' she answered hoarsely. 'He is saved. I thought we were too late—another moment—one little moment more—and he had been gone!' and she burst into an awful flood of tears, sobbing as though her heart would break, and yet looking lovelier than ever as she did it. At last she ceased.

'Forgive me, my Holly—forgive me for my weakness,' she said. 'Thou seest after all I am a very woman. Think—now think of it! This morning didst thou speak of the place of torment appointed by this new religion of thine. Hell or Hades thou didst call it—a place where the vital essence lives and retains an individual memory, and where all the errors and faults of judgment, and unsatisfied passions and the unsubstantial terrors of the mind wherewith it hath at any time had to do, come to mock and haunt and gibe and wring the heart for ever and for ever with the vision of its own hopelessness. Thus, even thus, have I lived for full two thousand years—for some six and sixty generations, as ye reckon time—in a Hell, as thou callest it—tormented by the memory of a crime, tortured day and night with an unfulfilled desire—without companionship, without comfort, without death, and led on only down my dreary road by the marsh lights of Hope, which though they flickered here and there, and now glowed strong, and now were not, yet, as my skill told me, would one day lead unto my deliverer.

'And then—think of it still, oh Holly, for never shalt thou hear such another tale, or see such another scene, nay, not even if I give thee ten thousand years of life—and thou shalt have it in payment if thou wilt—think: at last my deliverer came—he for whom I had watched and waited through the generations—at the appointed time he came to seek me, as I knew that he must come, for my wisdom could not err, though I knew not when or how. Yet see how ignorant I was! See how small my knowledge, and how faint my strength! For hours he lay here sick unto death, and I felt it not—I who had waited for him for two thousand years—I knew it not. And then at last I see him, and behold, my chance is gone but by a hair's breadth even before I have it, for he is in the very jaws of death; whence no power of mine can draw him. And if he die, surely must the Hell be lived through once more—once more must I face the weary centuries, and wait, and wait till the time in its fulness shall bring my beloved back to me. And then thou gavest him the medicine, and that five minutes dragged along before I knew if he would live or die, and I tell thee that all the sixty generations that are gone were not so long as that five minutes. But they passed at length, and still he showed no sign, and I knew that if the drug works not then, so far as I have had knowledge, it works not at all. Then thought I that he was once more dead, and all the tortures of all the years gathered themselves into a single venomed spear, and pierced me through and through, because once again I had lost Kallikrates! And then, when all was done, behold! he sighed, behold! he lived, and I knew that he would live, for none die on whom the drug takes hold. Think of it now, my Holly—think of the wonder of it! He will sleep for twelve hours, and then the fever will have left him!'

She stopped, and laid her hand upon the golden head, and then bent down and kissed the brow with a chastened abandonment of tenderness that would have been beautiful to behold had not the sight cut me to the heart—for I was jealous!

XVIII

GO, WOMAN!

THEN followed a silence of a minute or so, during which *She* appeared, if one might judge from the almost angelic rapture of her face—for she looked angelic sometimes—to be plunged in a happy ecstasy. Suddenly, however, a new thought struck her, and her expression became the very reverse of angelic.

'Almost had I forgotten,' she said, 'that woman, Ustane. What is she to Kallikrates—his servant, or——' and she paused, and her voice trembled.

I shrugged my shoulders. 'I understand that she is wed to him according to the custom of the Amahagger,' I answered; 'but I know not.'

Her face grew dark as a thunder-cloud. Old as she was, Ayesha had not outlived jealousy.

'Then there is an end,' she said; 'she must die, even now!'

'For what crime?' I asked, horrified. 'She is guilty of naught that thou art not guilty of thyself, oh Ayesha. She loves the man, and he has been pleased to accept her love: where, then, is her sin?'

'Truly, oh Holly, thou art foolish,' she answered, almost petulantly. 'Where is her sin? Her sin is that she stands between me and my desire. Well, I know that I can take him from her—for dwells there a man upon this earth, oh Holly, who could resist me if I put out my strength? Men are faithful for so long only as temptations pass them by. If the temptation be but strong enough, then will the man yield, for every man, like every rope, hath his breaking strain, and passion is to men what gold and power are to women—the weight upon their weakness. Believe me, ill will it go with mortal women in that heaven of which thou speakest, if only the spirits be more fair, for their lords will never turn to look upon them, and their heaven will become their hell. For man can be bought with woman's beauty, if it be but beautiful enough; and woman's beauty can be ever bought with gold, if only there be gold enough. So was it in my day, and so it will be to the end of time. The world is a great mart, my Holly, where all things are for sale to him who bids the highest in the currency of our desires.'

These remarks, which were as cynical as might have been expected from a woman of Ayesha's age and experience, jarred upon me, and I answered, testily, that in our heaven there was no marriage or giving in marriage.*

'Else would it not be heaven, dost thou mean?' she put in. 'Fie upon thee, Holly, to think so ill of us poor women! Is it, then, marriage that marks the line between thy heaven and thy hell? But enough of this. This is no time for disputing and the challenge of our wits. Why dost thou always dispute? Art thou also a philosopher of these latter days? As for this woman, she must die; for though I can take her lover from her, yet, while she lived, might he think tenderly of her, and that I cannot away with.* No other woman shall dwell in my Lord's thoughts; my empire shall be all my own. She hath had her day, let her be content; for better is an hour with love than a century of loneliness—now the night shall swallow her.'

'Nay, nay,' I cried, 'it would be a wicked crime; and from a crime naught comes but what is evil. For thine own sake do not this deed.'

'Is it, then, a crime, oh foolish man, to put away that which stands between us and our ends? Then is our life one long crime, my Holly; for day by day we destroy that we may live, since in this world none save the strongest can endure. Those who are weak must perish; the earth is to the strong, and the fruits thereof. For every tree that grows a score shall wither, that the strong ones may take their share. We run to place and power over the dead bodies of those who fail and fall; ay, we win the food we eat from out the mouths of starving babes. It is the scheme of things. Thou sayest, too, that a crime breeds evil, but therein thou dost lack experience; for out of crimes come many good things, and out of good grows much evil. The cruel rage of the tyrant may prove a blessing to thousands who come after him, and the sweet-heartedness of a holy man may make a nation slaves. Man doeth this and doeth that from the good or evil of his heart; but he knoweth not to what end his moral sense doth prompt him; for when he striketh he is blind to where the blow shall fall, nor can he count the airy threads that weave the web of circumstance. Good and evil, love and hate, night and day, sweet and bitter, man and woman, heaven above and the earth beneath—all these things are necessary, one to the other, and who knows the end of each? I tell thee that there is a hand of Fate that twines them up to bear the burden of its purpose, and all things are gathered in that great rope

to which all things are needful. Therefore doth it not become us to
say this thing is evil and this good, or the dark is hateful and the light
lovely; for to other eyes than ours the evil may be the good and the
darkness more beautiful than the day, or all alike be fair. Hearest
thou, my Holly?'

I felt it was hopeless to argue against casuistry of this nature,
which, if it were carried to its logical conclusion, would absolutely
destroy all morality, as we understand it. But her talk gave me a
fresh thrill of fear; for what may not be possible to a being who,
unconstrained by human law, is also absolutely unshackled by a
moral sense of right and wrong, which, however partial and conventional it may be, is yet based, as our conscience tells us, upon the
great wall of individual responsibility that marks off mankind from
the beasts?

But I was deeply anxious to save Ustane, whom I liked and
respected, from the dire fate that overshadowed her at the hands of
her mighty rival. So I made one more appeal.

'Ayesha,' I said, 'thou art too subtle for me; but thou thyself hast
told me that each man should be a law unto himself, and follow the
teaching of his heart. Hath thy heart no mercy towards her whose
place thou wouldst take? Bethink thee, as thou sayest—though to me
the thing is incredible—him whom thou desirest has returned to
thee after many ages, and but now thou hast, as thou sayest also,
wrung him from the jaws of death. Wilt thou celebrate his coming by
the murder of one who loved him, and whom perchance he loved—
one, at the least, who saved his life for thee when the spears of thy
slaves would have made an end thereof? Thou sayest also that in past
days thou didst grievously wrong this man, that with thine own hand
thou didst slay him because of the Egyptian Amenartas whom he
loved.'

'How knowest thou that, oh stranger? How knowest thou that
name? I spoke it not to thee,' she broke in with a cry, catching at my
arm.

'Perchance I dreamed it,' I answered; 'strange dreams do hover
about these caves of Kôr. It seems that the dream was, indeed, a
shadow of the truth. What came to thee of thy mad crime?—two
thousand years of waiting, was it not? And now wouldst thou repeat
the history? Say what thou wilt, I tell thee that evil will come of it;
for to him who doeth, at the least, good breeds good and evil evil,

even though in after days out of evil cometh good. Offences must needs come; but woe to him by whom the offence cometh. So said that Messiah* of whom I spoke to thee, and it was truly said. If thou slayest this innocent woman, I say unto thee that thou shalt be accursed, and pluck no fruit from thine ancient tree of love. Also, what thinkest thou? How will this man take thee red-handed from the slaughter of her who loved and tended him?'

'As to that,' she answered, 'I have already answered thee. Had I slain thee as well as her, yet should he love me, Holly, because he could not save himself therefrom any more than thou couldst save thyself from dying, if by chance I slew thee, oh Holly. And yet maybe there is truth in what thou dost say; for in some way it presseth on my mind. If it may be, I will spare this woman; for have I not told thee that I am not cruel for the sake of cruelty? I love not to see suffering, or to cause it. Let her come before me—quick now, before my mood changes,' and she hastily covered her face with its gauzy wrapping.

Well pleased to have succeeded even to this extent, I passed out into the passage and called to Ustane, whose white garment I caught sight of some yards away, huddled up against one of the earthenware lamps that were placed at intervals along the tunnel. She rose, and ran towards me.

'Is my lord dead? Oh, say not he is dead,' she cried, lifting her noble-looking face, all stained as it was with tears, up to me with an air of infinite beseeching that went straight to my heart.

'Nay, he lives,' I answered. '*She* hath saved him. Enter.'

She sighed deeply, entered, and fell upon her hands and knees, after the custom of the Amahagger people, in the presence of the dread *She*.

'Stand,' said Ayesha in her coldest voice, 'and come hither.'

Ustane obeyed, standing before her with bowed head.

Then came a pause, which Ayesha broke.

'Who is this man?' she said, pointing to the sleeping form of Leo.

'The man is my husband,' she answered in a low voice.

'Who gave him to thee for a husband?'

'I took him according to the custom of our country, oh *She*.'

'Thou hast done evil, woman, in taking this man, who is a stranger. He is not a man of thine own race, and the custom fails. Listen: perchance thou didst this thing through ignorance, therefore,

woman, do I spare thee, otherwise hadst thou died. Listen again.
Go from hence back to thine own place, and never dare to speak
to or set thine eyes upon this man again. He is not for thee. Listen
a third time. If thou breakest this my law, that moment thou
diest. Go.'

But Ustane did not move.

'Go, woman!'

Then she looked up, and I saw that her face was torn with passion.

'Nay, oh *She*, I will not go,' she answered in a choked voice: 'the
man is my husband, and I love him—I love him, and I will not leave
him. What right hast thou to command me to leave my husband?'

I saw a little quiver pass down Ayesha's frame, and shuddered
myself, fearing the worst.

'Be pitiful,' I said in Latin; 'it is but Nature working.'

'I am pitiful,' she answered coldly in the same language; 'had I not
been pitiful she had been dead even now.' Then addressing Ustane:
'Woman, I say to thee, go before I destroy thee where thou art!'

'I will not go! He is mine—mine!' she cried in anguish. 'I took
him, and I saved his life! Destroy me, then, if thou hast the power! I
will not give thee my husband—never—never!'

Ayesha made a movement so swift that I could scarcely follow it,
but it seemed to me that she lightly struck the poor girl upon the
head with her hand. I looked at Ustane, and then staggered back in
horror, for there upon her hair, right across her bronze-like tresses,
were three finger-marks *white as snow*. As for the girl herself, she had
put her hands to her head, and was looking dazed.

'Great heavens!' I said, perfectly aghast at this dreadful manifestation of inhuman power; but *She* did but laugh a little.

'Thou thinkest, poor ignorant fool,' she said to the bewildered
woman, 'that I have not power to slay. Stay, there lies a mirror,' and
she pointed to Leo's round shaving-glass that had been arranged by
Job with other things upon his portmanteau; 'give it to this woman,
my Holly, and let her see that which lies across her hair, and whether
or no I have power to slay.'

I picked up the glass, and held it before Ustane's eyes. She gazed,
then felt at her hair, then gazed again, and then sank upon the
ground with a sort of sob.

'Now, wilt thou go, or must I strike a second time?' asked Ayesha,
in mockery. 'Look, I have set my seal upon thee so that I may know

thee till thy hair is all as white as it. If I see thy face here again, be sure, too, that thy bones shall soon be whiter than my mark upon thy hair.'

Utterly awed and broken down, the poor creature rose, and, marked with that awful mark, crept from the room sobbing bitterly.

'Look not so frighted, my Holly,' said Ayesha, when she had gone. 'I tell thee I deal not in magic—there is no such thing. 'Tis only a force that thou dost not understand. I marked her to strike terror to her heart, else must I have slain her. And now I will bid my servants bear my Lord Kallikrates to a chamber near mine own, that I may watch over him, and be ready to greet him when he wakes; and thither, too, shalt thou come, my Holly, and the white man, thy servant. But one thing remember at thy peril. Naught shalt thou say to Kallikrates as to how this woman went, and as little as may be of me. Now, I have warned thee!' and she slid away to give her orders, leaving me more absolutely confounded than ever. Indeed, so bewildered was I, and racked and torn with such a succession of various emotions, that I began to think that I must be going mad. However, perhaps fortunately, I had but little time to reflect, for presently the mutes arrived to carry the sleeping Leo and our possessions across the central cave, so for a while all was bustle. Our new rooms were situated immediately behind what we used to call Ayesha's boudoir—the curtained space where I had first seen her. Where she herself slept I did not then know, but it was somewhere quite close.

That night I passed in Leo's room, but he slept through it like the dead, never once stirring. I also slept fairly well, as, indeed, I needed to do, but my sleep was full of dreams of all the horrors and wonders I had undergone. Chiefly, however, I was haunted by that frightful piece of *diablerie* by which Ayesha left her finger marks upon her rival's hair. There was something so terrible about the swift, snake-like movement, and the instantaneous blanching of that threefold line, that, if the results to Ustane had been much more tremendous, I doubt if they would have impressed me so deeply. To this day I often dream of that awful scene, and see the weeping woman, bereaved, and marked like Cain, cast a last look at her lover, and creep from the presence of her dread Queen.

Another dream that troubled me originated in the huge pyramid of bones. I dreamed that they all stood up and marched past me in thousands and tens of thousands—in squadrons, companies, and armies—with the sunlight shining through their hollow ribs. On they rushed across the plain to Kôr, their imperial home; I saw the drawbridges fall before them, and heard their bones clank through the brazen gates. On they went, up the splendid streets, on past fountains, palaces, and temples such as the eye of man never saw. But there was no man to greet them in the market-place, and no woman's face appeared at the windows—only a bodiless voice went before them, calling: '*Fallen is Imperial Kôr!**—fallen!—fallen! fallen!' On, right through the city, marched those gleaming phalanxes, and the rattle of their bony tread echoed through the silent air as they pressed grimly on. They passed through the city and climbed the wall, and marched along the great roadway that was made upon the wall, till at length they once more reached the drawbridge. Then, as the sun was sinking, they returned again towards their sepulchre, and luridly his light shone in the sockets of their empty eyes, throwing gigantie shadows of their bones, that stretched away, and crept and crept like huge spider's legs as their armies wound across the plain. Then they came to the cave, and once more one by one flung themselves in unending files through the hole into the pit of bones, and I awoke, shuddering, to see *She*, who had evidently been standing between my couch and Leo's, glide like a shadow from the room.

After this I slept again, soundly this time, till morning, when I awoke much refreshed, and got up. At last the hour drew near at which, according to Ayesha, Leo was to awake, and with it came *She* herself, as usual, veiled.

'Thou shalt see, oh Holly,' she said; 'presently shall he awake in his right mind, the fever having left him.'

Hardly were the words out of her mouth, when Leo turned round and stretched out his arms, yawned, opened his eyes, and, perceiving a female form bending over him, threw his arms round her and kissed her, mistaking her, perhaps, for Ustane. At any rate, he said, in Arabic, 'Hullo, Ustane, why have you tied your head up like that? Have you got the toothache?' and then, in English, 'I say, I'm awfully hungry. Why, Job, you old son of a gun, where the deuce have we got to now—eh?'

'I am sure I wish I knew, Mr. Leo,' said Job, edging suspiciously past Ayesha, whom he still regarded with the utmost disgust and horror, being by no means sure that she was not an animated corpse;

'but you mustn't talk, Mr. Leo, you've been very ill, and given us a great deal of hanxiety, and, if this lady,' looking at Ayesha, 'would be so kind as to move, I'll bring you your soup.'

This turned Leo's attention to the 'lady,' who was standing by in perfect silence. 'Hullo!' he said; 'that is not Ustane—where is Ustane?'

Then, for the first time, Ayesha spoke to him, and her first words were a lie. 'She has gone from hence upon a visit,' she said; 'and, behold, in her place am I here as thine handmaiden.'

Ayesha's silver notes seemed to puzzle Leo's half-awakened intellect, as also did her corpse-like wrappings. However, he said nothing at the time, but drank off his soup greedily enough, and then turned over and slept again till the evening. When he woke for the second time he saw me, and began to question me as to what had happened, but I had to put him off as best I could till the morrow, when he awoke almost miraculously better. Then I told him something of his illness and of my doings, but as Ayesha was present I could not tell him much except that she was the Queen of the country, and well disposed towards us, and that it was her pleasure to go veiled; for, though of course I spoke in English, I was afraid that she might understand what we were saying from the expression of our faces, and besides, I remembered her warning.

On the following day Leo got up almost entirely recovered. The flesh wound in his side was healed, and his constitution, naturally a vigorous one, had shaken off the exhaustion consequent on his terrible fever with a rapidity that I can only attribute to the effects of the wonderful drug which Ayesha had given to him, and also to the fact that his illness had been too short to reduce him very much. With his returning health came back full recollection of all his adventures up to the time when he had lost consciousness in the marsh, and of course of Ustane also, to whom I had discovered he had grown considerably attached. Indeed, he overwhelmed me with questions about the poor girl, which I did not dare to answer, for after Leo's first wakening *She* had sent for me, and again warned me solemnly that I was to reveal nothing of the story to him, delicately hinting that if I did it would be the worse for me. She also, for the second time, cautioned me not to tell Leo anything more than I was obliged about herself, saying that she would reveal herself to him in her own time.

Indeed, her whole manner changed. After all that I had seen I had expected that she would take the earliest opportunity of claiming the man she believed to be her old-world lover, but this, for some reason of her own, which was at the time quite inscrutable to me, she did not do. All that she did was to attend to his wants quietly, and with a humility which was in striking contrast with her former imperious bearing, addressing him always in a tone of something very like respect, and keeping him with her as much as possible. Of course his curiosity was as much excited about this mysterious woman as my own had been, and he was particularly anxious to see her face, which I had, without entering into particulars, told him was as lovely as her form and voice. This in itself was enough to raise the expectations of any young man to a dangerous pitch, and had it not been that he had not as yet completely shaken off the effects of illness, and was much troubled in his mind about Ustane, of whose affection and brave devotion he spoke in touching terms, I have no doubt that he would have entered into her plans, and fallen in love with her by anticipation. As it was, however, he was simply wildly curious, and also, like myself, considerably awed, for though no hint had been given to him by Ayesha of her extraordinary age, he not unnaturally came to identify her with the woman spoken of on the potsherd. At last, quite driven into a corner by his continual questions, which he showered on me while he was dressing on this third morning, I referred him to Ayesha, saying, with perfect truth, that I did not know where Ustane was. Accordingly, after Leo had eaten a hearty breakfast, we adjourned into *She's* presence, for her mutes had orders to admit us at all hours.

She was, as usual, seated in what, for want of a better term, we called her boudoir, and on the curtains being drawn she rose from her couch and, stretching out both hands, came forward to greet us, or rather Leo; for I, as may be imagined, was now quite left in the cold. It was a pretty sight to see her veiled form gliding towards the sturdy young Englishman, dressed in his grey flannel suit; for though he is half a Greek in blood, Leo is, with the exception of his hair, one of the most English-looking men I ever saw. He has nothing of the supple form or slippery manner of the modern Greek about him, though I presume that he got his remarkable personal beauty from his foreign mother, whose portrait he resembles not a little. He is very tall and big-chested, and yet not awkward, as so many big men are, and his head is set upon him in such a fashion as to give him a proud and vigorous air, which was well translated in his Amahagger name of the 'Lion.'

'Greeting to thee, my young stranger lord,' she said in her softest voice. 'Right glad am I to see thee upon thy feet. Believe me, had I not saved thee at the last, never wouldst thou have stood upon those feet again. But the danger is done, and it shall be my care'—and she flung a world of meaning into the words—'that it doth return no more.'

Leo bowed to her, and then, in his best Arabic, thanked her for all her kindness and courtesy in caring for one unknown to her.

'Nay,' she answered softly, 'ill could the world spare such a man. Beauty is too rare upon it. Give me no thanks, who am made happy by thy coming.'

'Humph! old fellow,' said Leo aside to me in English, 'the lady is very civil. We seem to have tumbled into clover. I hope that you have made the most of your opportunities. By Jove! what a pair of arms she has got!'

I nudged him in the ribs to make him keep quiet, for I caught sight of a gleam from Ayesha's veiled eyes, which were regarding me curiously.

'I trust,' went on Ayesha, 'that my servants have attended well upon thee; if there can be comfort in this poor place, be sure it waits on thee. Is there aught that I can do for thee more?'

'Yes, oh *She*,' answered Leo hastily. 'I would fain know whither the young lady who was looking after me has gone to.'

'Ah,' said Ayesha: 'the girl—yes, I saw her. Nay, I know not; she said that she would go, I know not whither. Perchance she will return, perchance not. It is wearisome waiting on the sick, and these savage women are fickle.'

Leo looked both sulky and distressed at this intelligence.

'It's very odd,' he said to me in English; and then addressing *She*, 'I cannot understand,' he said; 'the young lady and I—well—in short, we had a regard for each other.'

Ayesha laughed a little very musically, and then turned the subject.

THE conversation after this was of such a desultory order that I do not quite recollect it. For some reason, perhaps from a desire to keep her identity and character in reserve, Ayesha did not talk freely, as she usually did. Presently, however, she informed Leo that she had arranged a dance that night for our amusement. I was astonished to hear this, as I fancied that the Amahagger were much too gloomy a folk to indulge in any such frivolity; but, as will presently more clearly appear, it turned out that an Amahagger dance has little in common with such fantastic festivities in other countries, savage or civilised. Then, as we were about to withdraw, she suggested that Leo might like to see some of the wonders of the caves, and as he gladly assented thither we departed, accompanied by Job and Billali. To describe our visit would only be to repeat a great deal of what I have already said. The tombs we entered were indeed different, for the whole rock was a honeycomb of sepulchres,[1] but the contents were nearly always similar. Afterwards we visited the pyramid of bones that had haunted my dreams on the previous night, and from thence went down a long passage to one of the great vaults occupied by the bodies of the poorer citizens of Imperial Kôr. These bodies were not nearly so well preserved as were those of the wealthier classes. Many of them had no linen covering on them, also they were buried from five hundred to one thousand in a single large vault, the corpses in some instances being thickly piled one upon another, like a heap of slain.

Leo was of course intensely interested in this stupendous and unequalled sight, which was, indeed, enough to awake all the imagination a man had in him into the most active life. But to poor Job it did not prove attractive. His nerves—already seriously shaken by what he had undergone since we had arrived in this terrible country—were, as may be imagined, still further disturbed by the spectacle

---

[1] For a long while it puzzled me to know what could have been done with the enormous quantities of rock that must have been dug out of these vast caves; but I afterwards discovered that it was for the most part built into the walls and palaces of Kôr, and also used to line the reservoirs and sewers.—L. H. H.

of these masses of departed humanity, whereof the forms still remained perfect before his eyes, though their voices were for ever lost in the eternal silence of the tomb. Nor was he comforted when old Billali, by way of soothing his evident agitation, informed him that he should not be frightened of these dead things, as he would soon be like them himself.

'There's a nice thing to say of a man, sir,' he ejaculated, when I translated this little remark; 'but there, what can one expect of an old man-eating savage? Not but what I dare say he's right,' and Job sighed.

When we had finished inspecting the caves, we returned and had our meal, for it was now past four in the afternoon, and we all— especially Leo—needed some food and rest. At six o'clock we, together with Job, waited on Ayesha, who set to work to terrify our poor servant still further by showing him pictures on the pool of water in the font-like vessel. She learnt from me that he was one of seventeen children, and then bid him think of all his brothers and sisters, or as many of them as he could, gathered together in his father's cottage. Then she told him to look in the water, and there, reflected from its stilly surface, was that dead scene of many years gone by, as it was recalled to our retainer's brain. Some of the faces were clear enough, but some were mere blurrs and splotches, or with one feature grossly exaggerated; the fact being that, in these instances, Job had been unable to recall the exact appearances of the individuals, or remembered them only by a peculiarity of his tribe, and the water could only reflect what he saw with his mind's eye. For it must be remembered that *She's* power in this matter was strictly limited; she could apparently, except in very rare instances, only photograph upon the water what was actually in the mind of some one present, and then only by his will. But if she was personally acquainted with a locality, she could, as in the case of ourselves and the whale-boat, throw its reflection upon the water, and also it seems the reflection of anything extraneous that was passing there at the time. This power, however, did not extend to the minds of others. For instance, she could show me the interior of my college chapel, as I remembered it, but not as it was at the moment of reflection; for, where other people were concerned, her art was strictly limited to the facts or memories present to *their* consciousness at the moment. So much was this so, that when we tried, for her amusement, to show her pictures of noted buildings, such as St. Paul's or the Houses of Parliament, the result was most imperfect; for, of course, though we had a good general idea of their appearance, we could not recall all the architectural details, and therefore the minutiæ necessary to a perfect reflection were wanting. But Job could not be got to understand this, and so far from accepting a natural explanation of the matter, which was after all, though strange enough in all conscience, nothing more than an instance of glorified and perfected telepathy, he set the whole thing down as a manifestation of the blackest magic. I shall never forget the howl of terror which he uttered when he saw the more or less perfect portraits of his long-scattered brethren staring at him from the quiet water, or the merry peal of laughter with which Ayesha greeted his consternation. As for Leo, he did not altogether like it either, but ran his fingers through his yellow curls, and remarked that it gave him the creeps.

After about an hour of this amusement, in the latter part of which Job did *not* participate, the mutes by signs indicated that Billali was waiting for an audience. Accordingly he was told to 'crawl up,' which he did as awkwardly as usual, and announced that the dance was ready to begin if *She* and the white strangers would be pleased to attend. Shortly afterwards we all rose, and Ayesha having thrown a dark cloak (the same, by the way, that she had worn when I saw her cursing by the fire) over her white wrappings, we started. The dance was to be held in the open air, on the smooth rocky plateau in front of the great cave, and thither we made our way. About fifteen paces from the mouth of the cave we found three chairs placed, and here we sat and waited, for as yet no dancers were to be seen. The night was almost, but not quite, dark, the moon not having risen as yet, which made us wonder how we should be able to see the dancing.

'Thou wilt presently understand,' said Ayesha, with a little laugh, when Leo asked her; and we certainly did. Scarcely were the words out of her mouth when from every point we saw dark forms rushing up, each bearing with him what we at first took to be an enormous flaming torch. Whatever they were they were burning furiously, for the flames stood out a yard or more behind each bearer. On they came, fifty or more of them, carrying their flaming burdens and looking like so many devils from hell. Leo was the first to discover what these burdens were.

'Great heaven!' he said, 'they are corpses on fire!'

I stared and stared again—he was perfectly right—the torches that were to light our entertainment were human mummies from the caves!

On rushed the bearers of the flaming corpses, and, meeting at a spot about twenty paces in front of us, built their ghastly burdens crossways into a huge bonfire. Heavens! how they roared and flared! No tar barrel could have burnt as those mummies did. Nor was this all. Suddenly I saw one great fellow seize a flaming human arm that had fallen from its parent frame, and rush off into the darkness. Presently he stopped, and a tall streak of fire shot up into the air, illumining the gloom, and also the lamp from which it sprang. That lamp was the mummy of a woman tied to a stout stake let into the rock, and he had fired her hair. On he went a few paces and touched a second, then a third, and a fourth, till at last we were surrounded on all three sides by a great ring of bodies flaring furiously, the material with which they were preserved having rendered them so inflammable that the flames would literally spout out of the ears and mouth in tongues of fire a foot or more in length.

Nero* illuminated his gardens with live Christians soaked in tar, and we were now treated to a similar spectacle, probably for the first time since his day, only happily our lamps were not living ones.

But although this element of horror was fortunately wanting, to describe the awful and hideous grandeur of the spectacle thus presented to us is, I feel, so absolutely beyond my poor powers, that I scarcely dare attempt it. To begin with, it appealed to the moral as well as the physical susceptibilities. There was something very terrible, and yet very fascinating, about the employment of the remote dead to illumine the orgies of the living; in itself the thing was a satire, both on the living and the dead. Cæsar's dust—or is it Alexander's?—may stop a bunghole, but the functions of these dead Cæsars of the past was to light up a savage fetish dance. To such base uses may we come,* of so little account may we be in the minds of the eager multitudes that we shall breed, many of whom, so far from revering our memory, will live to curse us for begetting them into such a world of woe.

Then there was the physical side of the spectacle, and a weird and splendid one it was. Those old citizens of Kôr burnt as, to judge from their sculptures and inscriptions, they had lived, very fast, and with the utmost liberality. What is more, there were plenty of them. As soon as ever a mummy had burnt down to the ankles, which it did in about twenty minutes, the feet were kicked away, and another one put in its place. The bonfire was kept going on the same generous scale, and its flames shot up, with a hiss and a crackle, twenty or thirty feet into the air, throwing great flashes of light far out into the gloom, through which the dark forms of the Amahagger flitted to and fro like devils replenishing the infernal fires. We all stood and stared aghast—shocked, and yet fascinated at so strange a spectacle, and half-expecting to see the spirits those flaming forms had once enclosed come creeping from the shadows to work vengeance on their desecrators.

'I promised thee a strange sight, my Holly,' laughed Ayesha, whose nerves alone did not seem to be affected; 'and, behold, I have not failed thee. Also, it hath its lesson. Trust not to the future, for who knows what the future may bring! Therefore, live for the day, and endeavour not to escape the dust which seems to be man's end. What thinkest thou those long-forgotten nobles and ladies would have felt had they known that they should one day flare to light the dance or boil the pot of savages? But see, here come the dancers; a merry crew—are they not? The stage is lit—now for the play.'

As she spoke, we perceived two lines of figures, one male and the other female, to the number of about a hundred, each advancing round the human bonfire, arrayed only in the usual leopard and buck skins. They formed up, in perfect silence, in two lines, facing each other between us and the fire, and then the dance—a sort of infernal and fiendish cancan—began. To describe it is quite impossible, but, though there was a good deal of tossing of legs and double-shuffling, it seemed to our untutored minds to be more of a play than a dance, and, as usual with this dreadful people, whose minds seem to have taken their colour from the caves in which they live, and whose jokes and amusements are drawn from the inexhaustible stores of pre-served mortality with which they share their homes, the subject appeared to be a most ghastly one. I know that it represented an attempted murder first of all, and then the burial alive of the victim and his struggling from the grave; each act of the abominable drama, which was carried on in perfect silence, being rounded off and fin-ished with a furious and most revolting dance round the supposed victim, who writhed upon the ground in the red light of the bonfire.

Presently, however, this pleasing piece was interrupted. Suddenly there was a slight commotion, and a large powerful woman, whom I had noted as one of the most vigorous of the dancers, came, made mad and drunken with unholy excitement, bounding and staggering towards us, shrieking out as she came:—

'I want a black goat, I must have a black goat, bring me a black goat!' and down she fell upon the rocky floor foaming and writhing, and shrieking for a black goat, about as hideous a spectacle as can well be conceived.

Instantly most of the dancers came up and got round her, though some still continued their capers in the background.

'She has got a Devil,' called out one of them. 'Run and get a black goat. There, Devil, keep quiet! keep quiet! You shall have the goat presently. They have gone to fetch it, Devil.'

'I want a black goat, I must have a black goat!' shrieked the foaming rolling creature again.

'All right, Devil, the goat will be here presently; keep quiet, there's a good Devil!'

And so on till the goat taken from a neighbouring kraal did at last arrive, being dragged bleating on to the scene by its horns.

'Is it a black one, is it a black one?' shrieked the possessed.

'Yes, yes, Devil, as black as night;' then aside, 'keep it behind thee, don't let the Devil see that it has got a white spot on its rump and another on its belly. In one minute, Devil. There, cut his throat quick. Where is the saucer?'

'The goat! the goat! the goat! Give me the blood of my black goat! I must have it, don't you see I must have it? Oh! oh! oh! give me the blood of the goat.'

At this moment a terrified *bah!* announced that the poor goat had been sacrificed, and the next minute a woman ran up with a saucer full of the blood. This the possessed creature, who was then raving and foaming her wildest, seized and *drank*, and was instantly recovered, and without a trace of hysteria, or fits, or being possessed, or whatever dreadful thing it was she was suffering from. She stretched her arms, smiled faintly, and walked quietly back to the dancers, who presently withdrew in a double line as they had come, leaving the space between us and the bonfire deserted.

I thought that the entertainment was now over, and, feeling rather queer, was about to ask *She* if we could rise, when suddenly what at first I took to be a baboon came hopping round the fire, and was instantly met upon the other side by a lion, or rather a human being dressed in a lion's skin. Then came a goat, then a man wrapped in an ox's hide, with the horns wobbling about in a ludicrous way. After him followed a blesbok, then an impala, then a koodoo,* then more goats, and many other animals, including a girl sewn up in the shining scaly hide of a boa constrictor, several yards of which trailed along the ground behind her. When all the beasts had collected they began to dance about in a lumbering, unnatural fashion, and to imitate the sounds produced by the respective animals they represented, till the whole air was alive with roars and bleating and the hissing of snakes. This went on for a long time, till, getting tired of the pantomime, I asked Ayesha if there would be any objection to Leo and myself walking round to inspect the human torches, and, as she had nothing to say against it, we started, striking round to the left. After looking at one or two of the flaming bodies, we were about to return, thoroughly disgusted with the grotesque weirdness of the spectacle, when our attention was attracted by one of the dancers, a particularly active leopard, that had separated itself from its fellow-beasts, and was whisking about in our immediate neighbourhood, but gradually drawing into a spot where the shadow was darkest, equidistant between two of the flaming mummies. Drawn by curiosity, we followed it, when suddenly it darted past us into the shadows beyond, and as it did so erected itself and whispered, 'Come,' in a voice that we both recognised as that of Ustane. Without waiting to consult me Leo turned and followed her into the outer darkness, and I, feeling sick enough at heart, went after them. The leopard crawled on for about fifty paces—a sufficient distance to be quite beyond the light of the fire and torches—and then Leo came up with it, or, rather, with Ustane.

'Oh, my lord,' I heard her whisper, 'so I have found thee! Listen. I am in peril of my life from "*She-who-must-be-obeyed*." Surely the Baboon has told thee how she drove me from thee? I love thee, my lord, and thou art mine according to the custom of the country. I saved thy life! My Lion, wilt thou cast me off now?'

'Of course not,' ejaculated Leo; 'I have been wondering whither thou hadst gone. Let us go and explain matters to the Queen.'

'Nay, nay, she would slay us. Thou knowest not her power—the Baboon there, he knoweth, for he saw. Nay, there is but one way: if thou wilt cleave to me, thou must flee with me across the marshes even now, and then perchance we may escape.'

'For Heaven's sake, Leo,' I began, but she broke in—

'Nay, listen not to him. Swift—be swift—death is in the air we breathe. Even now, mayhap, *She* heareth us,' and without more ado she proceeded to back her arguments by throwing herself into his arms. As she did so the leopard's head slipped from her hair, and I saw the three white finger-marks upon it, gleaming faintly in the starlight. Once more realising the desperate nature of the position, I was about to interpose, for I knew that Leo was not too strong-minded where women were concerned, when—oh! horror!—I heard a little silvery laugh behind me. I turned round, and there was *She* herself, and with her Billali and two male mutes. I gasped and nearly sank to the ground, for I knew that such a situation must result in some dreadful tragedy, of which it seemed exceedingly probable to me that I should be the first victim. As for Ustane, she untwined her arms and covered her eyes with her hands, while Leo, not knowing the full terror of the position, merely coloured up, and looked as foolish as a man caught in such a trap would naturally do.

XX

TRIUMPH

THEN followed a moment of the most painful silence that I ever endured. It was broken by Ayesha, who addressed herself to Leo.

'Nay, now my lord and guest,' she said in her softest tones, which yet had the ring of steel about them, 'look not so bashful. Surely the sight was a pretty one—the leopard and the lion!'

'Oh, hang it all!' said Leo in English.

'And thou, Ustane,' she went on, 'surely I should have passed thee by had not the light fallen on the white across thy hair,' and she pointed to the bright edge of the rising moon which was now appearing above the horizon. 'Well! well! the dance is done—see, the tapers have burnt down, and all things end in silence and in ashes. So thou thoughtest it a fit time for love, Ustane, my servant—and I, dreaming not that I could be disobeyed, thought thee already far away.'

'Play not with me,' moaned the wretched woman; 'slay me, and let there be an end.'

'Nay, why? It is not well to go so swift from the hot lips of love down to the cold mouth of the grave,' and she made a motion to the mutes, who instantly stepped up and caught the girl by either arm. With an oath Leo sprang upon the nearest, and hurled him to the ground, and then stood over him with his face set, and his fist ready.

Again Ayesha laughed. 'It was well thrown, my guest; thou hast a strong arm for one who so late was sick. But now out of thy courtesy I pray thee let that man live and do my bidding. He shall not harm the girl; the night air grows chill, and I would welcome her in mine own place. Surely she whom thou dost favour shall be favoured of me also.'

I took Leo by the arm, and pulled him from the prostrate mute, and he, half bewildered, obeyed the pressure. Then we all set out for the cave across the plateau, where a pile of white human ashes was all that remained of the fire that had lit the dancing, for the dancers had vanished.

In due course we gained Ayesha's boudoir—all too soon it seemed to me, having a sad presage of what was to come lying heavy on my heart.

Ayesha seated herself upon her cushions, and, having dismissed Job and Billali, by signs bade the mutes tend the lamps and retire, all save one girl, who was her favourite personal attendant. We three remained standing, the unfortunate Ustane a little to the left of the rest of us.

'Now, oh Holly,' Ayesha began, 'how came it that thou who didst hear my words bidding this evil-doer'—and she pointed to Ustane— 'to go from hence—thou at whose prayer I did weakly spare her life—how came it, I say, that thou wast a sharer in what I saw to-night? Answer, and for thine own sake, I say, speak all the truth, for I am not minded to hear lies upon this matter!'

'It was by accident, oh Queen,' I answered. 'I knew naught of it.'

'I do believe thee, oh Holly,' she answered coldly, 'and well it is for thee that I do—then does the whole guilt rest upon her.'

'I do not find any guilt therein,' broke in Leo. 'She is not another man's wife, and it appears that she has married me according to the custom of this awful place, so who is the worse? Any way, madam,' he went on, 'whatever she has done I have done too, so if she is to be punished let me be punished also; and I tell thee,' he went on, working himself up into a fury, 'that if thou biddest one of those deaf and dumb villains to touch her again I will tear him to pieces!' And he looked as though he meant it.

Ayesha listened in icy silence, and made no remark. When he had finished, however, she addressed Ustane.

'Hast thou aught to say, woman? Thou silly straw, thou feather, who didst think to float towards thy passion's petty ends, even against the great wind of my will! Tell me, for I fain would understand. Why didst thou this thing?'

And then I think I saw the most tremendous exhibition of moral courage and intrepidity that it is possible to conceive. For the poor doomed girl, knowing what she had to expect at the hands of her terrible Queen, knowing, too, from bitter experience how great was her adversary's power, yet gathered herself together, and out of the very depths of her despair drew materials to defy her.

'I did it, oh *She*,' she answered, drawing herself up to the full of her stately height, and throwing back the panther skin from her head, 'because my love is stronger than the grave. I did it because my life without this man whom my heart chose would be but a living death. Therefore did I risk my life, and now that I know that it is forfeit to thine anger, yet am I glad that I did risk it, and pay it away in the risking, ay, because he embraced me once, and told me that he loved me yet.'

Here Ayesha half rose from her couch, and then sank down again.

'I have no magic,' went on Ustane, her rich voice ringing strong and full, 'and I am not a Queen, nor do I live for ever, but a woman's heart is heavy to sink through waters, however deep, oh Queen! and a woman's eyes are quick to see, even through thy veil, oh Queen!

'Listen: I know it, thou dost love this man thyself, and therefore wouldst thou destroy me who stand across thy path. Ay, I die—I die, and go into the darkness, nor know I whither I go. But this I know. There is a light shining in my breast, and by that light, as by a lamp, I see the truth, and the future that I shall not share unroll itself before me like a scroll. When first I knew my lord,' and she pointed to Leo, 'I knew also that death would be the bridal gift he gave me—it rushed upon me of a sudden, but I turned not back, being ready to pay the price, and, behold, death is here! And now, even as I knew that, so do I, standing on the steps of doom, know that thou shalt not reap the profits of thy crime. Mine he is, and, though thy beauty shine like a sun among the stars, mine shall he remain for thee. Never here in this life shall he look thee in the eyes and call thee spouse. Thou too art doomed, I see'—and her voice rang like the cry of an inspired prophetess; 'ah, I see——'

Then came an answering cry of mingled rage and terror. I turned my head. Ayesha had risen, and was standing with her outstretched hand pointing at Ustane, who had suddenly stopped speaking. I gazed at the poor woman, and as I gazed there came upon her face that same woful, fixed expression of terror that I had seen once before when she had broken out into her wild chant. Her eyes grew large, her nostrils dilated, and her lips blanched.

Ayesha said nothing, she made no sound, she only drew herself up, stretched out her arm, and, her tall veiled frame quivering like an aspen leaf, appeared to look fixedly at her victim. Even as she did so Ustane put her hands to her head, uttered one piercing scream, turned round twice, and then fell backwards with a thud— prone upon the floor. Both Leo and myself rushed to her—she was stone dead—blasted into death by some mysterious electric agency or overwhelming will-force whereof the dread *She* had command.

For a moment Leo did not quite realise what had happened. But when he did, his face was awful to see. With a savage oath he rose from beside the corpse, and, turning, literally sprang at Ayesha. But she was watching, and, seeing him come, stretched out her hand again, and he went staggering back towards me, and would have fallen, had I not caught him. Afterwards he told me that he felt as though he had suddenly received a violent blow in the chest, and, what is more, utterly cowed, as if all the manhood had been taken out of him.

Then Ayesha spoke. 'Forgive me, my guest,' she said softly, addressing him, 'if I have shocked thee with my justice.'

'Forgive thee, thou fiend,' roared poor Leo, wringing his hands in his rage and grief. 'Forgive thee, thou murdress! By Heaven I will kill thee if I can!'

'Nay, nay,' she answered, in the same soft voice, 'thou dost not understand—the time has come for thee to learn. *Thou* art my love, my Kallikrates, my Beautiful, my Strong! For two thousand years, Kallikrates, have I waited for *thee*, and now at length thou hast come back to me; and as for this woman,' pointing to the corpse, 'she stood between me and thee, and therefore have I removed her, Kallikrates.'

'It is an accursed lie!' said Leo. 'My name is not Kallikrates! I am Leo Vincey; my ancestor was Kallikrates—at least, I believe he was.'

'Ah, thou sayest it—thine ancestor was Kallikrates, and thou, even thou, art Kallikrates reborn, come back—and mine own dear lord!'

'I am not Kallikrates, and as for being thy lord, or having aught to do with thee, I had sooner be the lord of a fiend from hell, for she would be better than thou.'

'Sayest thou so—sayest thou so, Kallikrates? Nay, but thou hast not seen me for so long a time that no memory remains. Yet am I very fair, Kallikrates!'

'I hate thee, murdress, and I have no wish to see thee. What is it to me how fair thou art? I hate thee, I say.'

'Yet within a very little space shalt thou creep to my knee, and swear that thou dost love me,' answered Ayesha, with a sweet, mocking laugh. 'Come, there is no time like the present time, here before this dead girl who loved thee, let us put it to the proof.

'Look now on me, Kallikrates!' and with a sudden motion she

shook her gauzy covering from her, and stood forth in her low kirtle and her snaky zone,* in her glorious radiant beauty and her imperial grace, rising from her wrappings, as it were, like Venus from the wave, or Galatea from her marble, or a beatified spirit from the tomb. She stood forth, and fixed her deep and glowing eyes upon Leo's eyes, and I saw his clenched fists unclasp, and his set and quivering features relax beneath her gaze. I saw his wonder and astonishment grow into admiration, and then into fascination, and the more he struggled the more I saw the power of her dread beauty fasten on him and take possession of his senses, drugging them, and drawing the heart out of him. Did I not know the process? Had not I, who was twice his age, gone through it myself? Was I not going through it afresh even then, although her sweet and passionate gaze was not for me? Yes, alas, I was! Alas, that I should have to confess that at that very moment I was rent by mad and furious jealousy. I could have flown at him, shame upon me! The woman had confounded and almost destroyed my moral sense, as she was bound to confound all who looked upon her superhuman loveliness. But—I do not quite know how—I got the better of myself, and once more turned to see the climax of the tragedy.

'Oh, great Heaven!' gasped Leo, 'art thou a woman?'

'A woman in truth—in very truth—and thine own spouse, Kallikrates!' she answered, stretching out her rounded ivory arms towards him, and smiling, ah, so sweetly!

He looked and looked, and slowly I perceived that he was drawing nearer to her. Suddenly his eye fell upon the corpse of poor Ustane, and he shuddered and stopped.

'How can I?' he said hoarsely. 'Thou art a murdress; she loved me.'

Observe, he was already forgetting that he had loved her.

'It is naught,' she murmured, and her voice sounded sweet as the night-wind passing through the trees. 'It is naught at all. If I have sinned, let my beauty answer for my sin. If I have sinned, it is for love of thee: let my sin, therefore, be put away and forgotten;' and once more she stretched out her arms and whispered '*Come*,' and then in another few seconds it was over. I saw him struggle—I saw him even turn to fly; but her eyes drew him more strongly than iron bonds, and the magic of her beauty and concentrated will and passion entered into him and overpowered him—ay, even there, in the

presence of the body of the woman who had loved him well enough
to die for him. It sounds horrible and wicked enough, but he cannot
be blamed too much, and be sure his sin will find him out. The
temptress who drew him into evil was more than human, and her
beauty was greater than the loveliness of the daughters of men.

I looked up again, and now her perfect form lay in his arms, and
her lips were pressed against his own; and thus, with the corpse of
his dead love for an altar, did Leo Vincey plight his troth to her red-
handed murdress—plight it for ever and a day. For those who sell
themselves into a like dominion, paying down the price of their own
honour, and throwing their soul into the balance to sink the scale to
the level of their lusts, can hope for no deliverance here or hereafter.
As they have sown, so shall they reap and reap, even when the poppy
flowers of passion have withered in their hands, and their harvest is
but bitter tares, garnered in satiety.

Suddenly, with a snake-like motion, she seemed to slip from his
embrace, and then again broke out into her low laugh of triumphant
mockery.

'Did I not tell thee that within a little space thou wouldst creep to
my knee, oh Kallikrates? And surely the space has not been a great
one!'

Leo groaned in shame and misery; for though he was overcome
and stricken down, he was not so lost as to be unaware of the depth
of the degradation to which he had sunk. On the contrary, his better
nature rose up in arms against his fallen self, as I saw clearly enough
later on.

Ayesha laughed again, and then quickly veiled herself, and made a
sign to the girl mute, who had been watching the whole scene with
curious startled eyes. The girl left, and presently returned, followed
by two male mutes, to whom the Queen made another sign. Thereon
they all three seized the body of poor Ustane by the arms, and
dragged it heavily down the cavern and away through the curtains at
the end. Leo watched it for a little while, and then covered his eyes
with his hand, and it too, to my excited fancy, seemed to watch us as
it went.

'There passes the dead past,' said Ayesha, solemnly, as the curtains
shook and fell back into their places, when the ghastly procession
had vanished behind them. And then, with one of those extraordinary transitions of which I have already spoken, she again threw off

her veil, and broke out, after the ancient and poetic fashion of the dwellers in Arabia,[1] into a pæan of triumph or epithalamium, which, wild and beautiful as it was, is exceedingly difficult to render into English, and ought by rights to be sung to the music of a cantata, rather than written and read. It was divided into two parts—one descriptive or definitive, and the other personal; and, as nearly as I can remember, ran as follows:—

Love is like a flower in the desert.

It is like the aloe of Arabia that blooms but once and dies; it blooms in the salt emptiness of Life, and the brightness of its beauty is set upon the waste as a star is set upon a storm.

It hath the sun above that is the spirit, and above it blows the air of its divinity.

At the echoing of a step, Love blooms, I say; I say Love blooms, and bends her beauty down to him who passeth by.

He plucketh it, yea, he plucketh the red cup that is full of honey, and beareth it away; away across the desert, away till the flower be withered, away till the desert be done.

There is only one perfect flower in the wilderness of Life.

That flower is Love!

There is only one fixed star in the mists of our wandering.

That star is Love!

There is only one hope in our despairing night.

That hope is Love!

All else is false. All else is shadow moving upon water. All else is wind and vanity.

Who shall say what is the weight or the measure of Love?

It is born of the flesh, it dwelleth in the spirit. From each doth it draw its comfort.

For beauty it is as a star.

---

[1] Among the ancient Arabians the power of poetic declamation, either in verse or prose, was held in the highest honour and esteem, and he who excelled in it was known as 'Khâteb,' or Orator. Every year a general assembly was held at which the rival poets repeated their compositions, when those poems which were judged to be the best were, so soon as the knowledge of the art of writing became general, inscribed on silk in letters of gold, and publicly exhibited, being known as 'Al Modhahabât,' or golden verses. In the poem given above by Mr. Holly, Ayesha evidently followed the traditional poetic manner of her people, which was to embody their thoughts in a series of somewhat disconnected sentences, each remarkable for its beauty and the grace of its expression.—EDITOR.

Many are its shapes, but all are beautiful, and none know where the star rose, or the horizon where it shall set.

Then, turning to Leo, and laying her hand upon his shoulder, she went on in a fuller and more triumphant tone, speaking in balanced sentences that gradually grew and swelled from idealised prose into pure and majestic verse:—

Long have I loved thee, oh, my love; yet has my love not lessened.

Long have I waited for thee, and behold my reward is at hand—is here!

Far away I saw thee once, and thou wast taken from me.

Then in a grave sowed I the seed of patience, and shone upon it with the sun of hope, and watered it with tears of repentance, and breathed on it with the breath of my knowledge. And now, lo! it hath sprung up, and borne fruit. Lo! out of the grave hath it sprung. Yea, from among the dry bones and ashes of the dead.

I have waited and my reward is with me.

I have overcome Death, and Death brought back to me him that was dead.

Therefore do I rejoice, for fair is the future.

Green are the paths that we shall tread across the everlasting meadows.

The hour is at hand. Night hath fled away into the valleys.

The dawn kisseth the mountain tops.

Soft shall we lie, my love, and easy shall we go.

Crowned shall we be with the diadem of Kings.

Worshipping and wonder struck all peoples of the world,

Blinded shall fall before our beauty and our might.

From time unto times shall our greatness thunder on,

Rolling like a chariot through the dust of endless days.

Laughing shall we speed in our victory and pomp,

Laughing like the Daylight as he leaps along the hills.

Onward, still triumphant to a triumph ever new!

Onward, in our power to a power unattained!

Onward, never weary, clad with splendour for a robe!

Till accomplished be our fate, and the night is rushing down.

She paused in her strange and most thrilling allegorical chant, of which I am, unfortunately, only able to give the burden,* and that feebly enough, and then said—

'Perchance thou dost not believe my word, Kallikrates—perchance thou thinkest that I do delude thee, and that I have not lived these

many years, and that thou hast not been born again to me. Nay, look
not so—put away that pale cast of doubt, for oh be sure herein can
error find no foothold! Sooner shall the suns forget their course and
the swallow miss her nest, than my soul shall swear a lie and be led
astray from thee, Kallikrates. Blind me, take away mine eyes, and let
the darkness utterly fence me in, and still mine ears would catch the
tone of thine unforgotten voice, striking more loud against the
portals of my sense than can the call of brazen-throated clarions:—
stop up mine hearing also, and let a thousand touch me on the brow,
and I would name thee out of all:—yea, rob me of every sense, and
see me stand deaf and blind, and dumb, and with nerves that cannot
weigh the value of a touch, yet would my spirit leap within me like a
quickening child and cry unto my heart, behold Kallikrates! behold,
thou watcher, the watches of thy night are ended! behold thou who
seekest in the night season, thy morning Star ariseth.'*

She paused awhile and then continued, 'But stay, if thy heart is
yet hardened against the mighty truth and thou dost require a further pledge of that which thou dost find too deep to understand,
even now shall it be given to thee, and to thee also, oh my Holly.
Bear each one of you a lamp, and follow after me whither I shall
lead you.'

Without stopping to think—indeed, speaking for myself, I had
almost abandoned the function in circumstances under which to
think seemed to be absolutely useless, since thought fell hourly helpless against a black wall of wonder—we took the lamps and followed
her. Going to the end of her 'boudoir,' she raised a curtain and
revealed a little stair of the sort that was so common in these dim
caves of Kôr. As we hurried down the stair I observed that the steps
were worn in the centre to such an extent that some of them had
been reduced from seven and a half inches, at which I guessed their
original height, to about three and a half. Now, all the other steps
that I had seen in the caves had been practically unworn, as was to be
expected, seeing that the only traffic which ever passed upon them
was that of those who bore a fresh burden to the tomb. Therefore
this fact struck my notice with that curious force with which little
things do strike us when our minds are absolutely overwhelmed by a
sudden rush of powerful sensations; beaten flat, as it were, like a sea
beneath the first burst of a hurricane, so that every little object on
the surface starts into an unnatural prominence.

At the bottom of the staircase I stood and stared at the worn steps, and Ayesha, turning, saw me.

'Wonderest thou whose are the feet that have worn away the rock, my Holly?' she asked. 'They are mine—even mine own light feet! I can remember when these stairs were fresh and level, but for two thousand years and more have I gone down hither day by day, and see, my sandals have worn out the solid rock!'

I made no answer, but I do not think that anything that I had heard or seen brought home to my limited understanding so clear a sense of this being's overwhelming antiquity as that hard rock hollowed out by her soft white feet. How many millions of times must she have passed up and down that stair to bring about such a result?

The stair led to a tunnel, and a few paces down the tunnel was one of the usual curtain-hung doorways, a glance at which told me that it was the same where I had been a witness of that terrible scene by the leaping flame. I recognised the pattern of the curtain, and the sight of it brought the whole event vividly before my eyes, and made me tremble even at its memory. Ayesha entered the tomb (for it was a tomb), and we followed her—I, for one, rejoicing that the mystery of the place was about to be cleared up, and yet afraid to face its solution.

XXI

THE DEAD AND LIVING MEET

'SEE now the place where I have slept for these two thousand years,' said Ayesha, taking the lamp from Leo's hand and holding it above her head. Its rays fell upon a little hollow in the floor, where I had seen the leaping flame, but the fire was out now. They fell upon the white form stretched there beneath its wrappings upon its bed of stone, upon the fretted carving of the tomb, and upon another shelf of stone opposite the one on which the body lay, and separated from it by the breadth of the cave.

'Here,' went on Ayesha, laying her hand upon the rock—'here have I slept night by night for all these generations, with but a cloak to cover me. It did not become me that I should lie soft when my spouse yonder,' and she pointed to the rigid form, 'lay stiff in death. Here night by night have I slept in his cold company—till, thou seest, this thick slab, like the stairs down which we passed, has worn thin with the tossing of my form—so faithful have I been to thee even in thy space of sleep, Kallikrates. And now, mine own, thou shalt see a wonderful thing—living, thou shalt behold thyself dead—for well have I tended thee during all these years, Kallikrates. Art thou prepared?'

We made no answer, but gazed at each other with frightened eyes, the whole scene was so dreadful and so solemn. Ayesha advanced, and laid her hand upon the corner of the shroud, and once more spoke.

'Be not affrighted,' she said; 'though the thing seem wonderful to thee—all we who live have thus lived before; nor is the very shape that holds us a stranger to the sun! Only we know it not, because memory writes no record, and earth hath gathered in the earth she lent us, for none have saved our glory from the grave. But I, by my arts and by the arts of those dead men of Kôr which I have learned, have held thee back, oh Kallikrates, from the dust, that the waxen stamp of beauty on thy face should ever rest before mine eye. 'Twas a mask that memory might fill, serving to fashion out thy presence from the past, and give it strength to wander in the habitations of my thought, clad in a mummery of life that stayed my appetite with visions of dead days.

'Behold now, let the Dead and Living meet! Across the gulf of Time they still are one. Time hath no power against Identity, though sleep the merciful hath blotted out the tablets of our mind, and with oblivion sealed the sorrows that else would hound us from life to life, stuffing the brain with gathered griefs till it burst in the madness of uttermost despair. Still are they one, for the wrappings of our sleep shall roll away as thunder clouds before the wind; the frozen voices of the past shall melt in music like mountain snows beneath the sun; and the weeping and the laughter of the lost hours shall be heard once more most sweetly echoing up the cliffs of immeasurable time.

'Ay, the sleep shall roll away, and the voices shall be heard, when down the completed chain, whereof our each existence is a link, the lightning of the Spirit hath passed to work out the purpose of our being; quickening and fusing those separated days of life, and shaping them to a staff whereon we may safely lean as we wend to our appointed fate.

'Therefore, have no fear, Kallikrates, when thou—living, and but lately born—shalt look upon thine own departed self, who breathed and died so long ago. I do but turn one page in thy Book of Being, and show thee what is writ thereon.

'*Behold!*'

With a sudden motion she drew the shroud from the cold form, and let the lamplight play upon it. I looked, and then shrank back terrified; since, say what she might in explanation, the sight was an uncanny one—for her explanations were beyond the grasp of our finite minds, and when they were stripped from the mists of vague esoteric philosophy, and brought into conflict with the cold and horrifying fact, did not do much to break its force. For there, stretched upon the stone bier before us, robed in white and perfectly preserved, was what appeared to be the body of Leo Vincey. I stared from Leo, standing *there* alive, to Leo lying *there* dead, and could see no difference; except, perhaps, that the body on the bier looked older. Feature for feature they were the same, even down to the crop of little golden curls, which was Leo's most uncommon beauty. It even seemed to me, as I looked, that the expression on the dead man's face resembled that which I had sometimes seen upon Leo's when he was plunged into profound sleep. I can only sum up the closeness of the resemblance by saying that I never saw twins so exactly similar as that dead and living pair.

I turned to see what effect was produced upon Leo by this sight of his dead self, and found it to be one of partial stupefaction. He stood for two or three minutes staring and said nothing, and when at last he spoke it was only to ejaculate—

'Cover it up and take me away.'

'Nay, wait, Kallikrates,' said Ayesha, who, standing with the lamp raised above her head, flooding with its light her own rich beauty and the cold wonder of the death-clothed form upon the bier, resembled an inspired Sibyl* rather than a woman, as she rolled out her majestic sentences with a grandeur and a freedom of utterance which I am, alas! quite unable to reproduce.

'Wait; I would show thee something, that no tittle of my crime may be hidden from thee. Do thou, oh Holly, open the garment on the breast of the dead Kallikrates, for perchance my lord may fear to touch himself.'

I obeyed with trembling hands. It seemed a desecration and an unhallowed thing to touch that sleeping image of the live man by my side. Presently his broad chest was bare, and there upon it, right over the heart, was a wound, evidently inflicted with a spear.

'Thou seest, Kallikrates,' she said. 'Know then that it was *I* who slew thee: in the Place of Life *I* gave thee death. I slew thee because of the Egyptian Amenartas, whom thou didst love, for by her wiles she held thy heart, and her I could not smite as but now I smote the woman, for she was too strong for me. In my haste and bitter anger I slew thee, and now for all these days have I lamented thee, and waited for thy coming. And thou hast come, and none can stand between thee and me, and of a truth now for death I will give thee life—not life eternal, for that none can give, but life and youth that shall endure for thousands upon thousands of years, and with it pomp, and power, and wealth, and all things that are good and beautiful, such as have been to no man before thee, nor shall be to any man who comes after. And now one thing more, and thou shalt rest and make ready for the day of thy new birth. Thou seest this body, which was thine own. For all these centuries it hath been my cold comfort and my companion, but now I need it no more, for I have thy living presence, and it can but serve to stir up memories of that which I would fain forget. Let it therefore go back to the dust from which I held it.

'Behold! I have prepared against this happy hour!' and going to the other shelf, or stone ledge, which, she said, had served her for a bed, she took from it a large vitrified* double-handed vase, the mouth of which was tied up with a bladder. This she loosed, and then, having bent down and gently kissed the white forehead of the dead man, she undid the vase, and sprinkled its contents carefully over the form, taking, I observed, the greatest precautions against any drop of them touching us or herself, and then poured out what remained of the liquid upon the chest and head. Instantly a dense vapour arose, and the cave was filled with choking fumes that prevented us from seeing anything while the deadly acid (for I presume it was some tremendous preparation of that sort) did its work. From the spot where the body lay came a fierce fizzing and cracking sound, which ceased, however, before the fumes had cleared away. At last they were all gone, except a little cloud that still hung over the corpse. In a couple of minutes more this too had vanished, and, wonderful as it may seem, it is a fact that on the stone bench that had supported the mortal remains of the ancient Kallikrates for so many centuries there was now nothing to be seen but a few handfuls of smoking white powder. The acid had utterly destroyed the body, and even in places eaten into the stone. Ayesha stooped down, and, taking a handful of this powder in her grasp, threw it into the air, saying at the same time, in a voice of calm solemnity—

'Dust to dust!*—the past to the past!—the dead to the dead!— Kallikrates is dead, and is born again!'

The ashes floated noiselessly to the rocky floor, and we stood in awed silence and watched them fall, too overcome for words.

'Now leave me,' she said, 'and sleep if ye may. I must watch and think, for to-morrow night we go hence, and the time is long since I trod the path that we must follow.'

Accordingly we bowed, and left her.

As we passed to our own apartment I peeped into Job's sleeping place, to see how he fared, for he had gone away just before our interview with the murdered Ustane, quite prostrated by the terrors of the Amahagger festivity. He was sleeping soundly, good honest fellow that he was, and I rejoiced to think that his nerves, which, like those of most uneducated people, were far from strong, had been spared the closing scenes of this dreadful day. Then we entered our own chamber, and here at last poor Leo, who, ever since he had looked upon that frozen image of his living self, had been in a state not far removed from stupefaction, burst out into a torrent of grief. Now that he was no longer in the presence of the dread *She*, his sense of the awfulness of all that had happened, and more especially of the wicked murder of Ustane, who was bound to him by ties so close, broke upon him like a storm, and lashed him into an agony of remorse and terror which was painful to witness. He cursed himself—he cursed the hour when we had first seen the writing on the sherd, which was being so mysteriously verified, and bitterly he cursed his own weakness. Ayesha he dared not curse—who dared speak evil of such a woman, whose consciousness for aught we knew was watching us at the very moment?

'What am I to do, old fellow?' he groaned, resting his head against my shoulder in the extremity of his grief. 'I let her be killed—not that I could help that, but within five minutes I was kissing her murdress over her body. I am a degraded brute, but I cannot resist that' (and here his voice sank)—'that awful sorceress. I know I shall do it again to-morrow; I know that I am in her power for always; if I never saw her again I should never think of anybody else during all my life; I must follow her as a needle follows a magnet; I would not go away now if I could; I could not leave her, my legs would not carry me, but my mind is still clear enough, and in my mind I hate her—at least, I think so. It is all so horrible; and that—that body! What can I make of it? It was *me*! I am sold into bondage, old fellow, and she will take my soul as the price of herself!'

Then, for the first time, I told him that I was in a but very little better position; and I am bound to say that, notwithstanding his own infatuation, he had the decency to sympathise with me. Perhaps he did not think it worth while being jealous, realising that he had no cause so far as the lady was concerned. I went on to suggest that we should try to run away, but we soon rejected the project as futile, and, to be perfectly honest, I do not believe that either of us would really have left Ayesha even if some superior power had suddenly offered to convey us from these gloomy caves and set us down in Cambridge. We could no more have left her than a moth can leave the light that destroys it. We were like confirmed opium-eaters: in our moments of reason we well knew the deadly nature of our pursuit, but we certainly were not prepared to abandon its terrible delights.

No man who once had seen *She* unveiled, and heard the music of her voice, and drunk in the bitter wisdom of her words, would willingly give up the sight for a whole sea of placid joys. How much more, then, was this likely to be so when, as in Leo's case, to put myself out of the question, this extraordinary creature declared her utter and absolute devotion, and gave what appeared to be proofs of its having lasted for some two thousand years?

No doubt she was a wicked person, and no doubt she had murdered Ustane when she stood in her path, but then she was very faithful, and by a law of nature man is apt to think but lightly of a woman's crimes, especially if that woman be beautiful, and the crime be committed for the love of him.

And then for the rest, when had such a chance ever come to a man before as that which now lay in Leo's hand? True, in uniting himself to this dread woman, he would place his life under the influence of a mysterious creature of evil tendencies,[1] but then that would be likely enough to happen to him in any ordinary marriage. On the other hand, however, no ordinary marriage could bring him such awful beauty—for awful is the only word that can describe it—such divine devotion, such wisdom, and command over the secrets of nature, and

---

[1] After some months of consideration of this statement I am bound to confess that I am not quite satisfied of its truth. It is perfectly true that Ayesha committed a murder, but I shrewdly suspect that, were we endowed with the same absolute power, and if we had the same tremendous interest at stake, we should be very apt to do likewise under parallel circumstances. Also, it must be remembered that she looked on it as an execution for disobedience under a system which made the slightest disobedience punishable by death. Putting aside this question of the murder, her evil-doing resolves itself into the expression of views and the acknowledgment of motives which are contrary to our preaching if not to our practice. Now at first sight this might be fairly taken as a proof of an evil nature, but when we come to consider the great antiquity of the individual it becomes doubtful if it was anything more than the natural cynicism which arises from age and bitter experience, and the possession of extraordinary powers of observation. It is a well-known fact that very often, putting the period of boyhood out of the question, the older we grow the more cynical and hardened we get, indeed many of us are only saved by timely death from utter moral petrifaction if not moral corruption. No one will deny that a young man is on the average better than an old one, for he is without that experience of the order of things that in certain thoughtful dispositions can hardly fail to produce cynicism, and that disregard of acknowledged methods and established custom which we call evil. Now the oldest man upon the earth was but a babe compared to Ayesha, and the wisest man upon the earth was not one-third as wise. And the fruit of her wisdom was this, that there was but one thing worth living for, and that was Love in its highest sense, and to gain that good thing she was not prepared to stop at trifles. This is really the sum of her evil doings, and it must be remembered on the other hand that whatever may be thought of them she had some virtues developed to a degree very uncommon in either sex—constancy, for instance.—L. H. H.

the place and power that they must win, or lastly the royal crown of unending youth, if indeed she could give that. No, on the whole, it is not wonderful that though Leo was plunged in bitter shame and grief, such as any gentleman would have felt under the circumstances, he was not ready to entertain the idea of running away from his extraordinary fortune.

My own opinion is that he would have been mad if he had done so. But then I confess that my statement on the matter must be accepted with qualifications. I am in love with Ayesha myself to this day, and I would rather have been the object of her affection for one short week than that of any other woman in the world for a whole lifetime. And let me add that if anybody who doubts this statement, and thinks me foolish for making it, could have seen Ayesha draw her veil and flash out in beauty on his gaze, his view would exactly coincide with my own. Of course, I am speaking of any *man*. We never had the advantage of a lady's opinion of Ayesha, but I think it quite possible that she would have regarded the Queen with dislike, would have expressed her disapproval in some more or less pointed manner, and ultimately have got herself blasted.

For two hours or more Leo and. I sat with shaken nerves and frightened eyes, and talked over the miraculous events through which we were passing. It seemed like a dream or a fairy tale, instead of the solemn, sober fact. Who would have believed that the writing on the potsherd was not only true, but that we should live to verify its truth, and that we two seekers should find her who was sought, patiently awaiting our coming in the tombs of Kôr? Who would have thought that in the person of Leo this mysterious woman should, as she believed, discover the being whom she awaited from century to century, and whose former earthly habitation she had till this very night preserved? But so it was. In the face of all we had seen it was difficult for us as ordinary reasoning men any longer to doubt its truth, and therefore at last, with humble hearts and a deep sense of the impotence of human knowledge, and the insolence of its assumption that denies that which it has no experience of to be possible, we laid ourselves down to sleep, leaving our fates in the hands of that watching Providence which had thus chosen to allow us to draw the veil of human ignorance, and reveal to us for good or evil some glimpse of the possibilities of life.

XXII

JOB HAS A PRESENTIMENT

It was nine o'clock on the following morning when Job, who still looked scared and frightened, came in to call me, and at the same time breathe his gratitude at finding us alive in our beds, which it appeared was more than he had expected. When I told him of the awful end of poor Ustane he was even more grateful at our survival, and much shocked, though Ustane had been no favourite of his, or he of hers, for the matter of that. She called him 'pig' in bastard Arabic, and he called her 'hussy' in good English, but these amenities were forgotten in the face of the catastrophe that had overwhelmed her at the hands of her Queen.

'I don't want to say anything as mayn't be agreeable, sir,' said Job, when he had finished exclaiming at my tale, 'but it's my opinion that that there *She* is the old gentleman himself, or perhaps his wife, if he has one, which I suppose he has, for he couldn't be so wicked all by himself. The Witch of Endor* was a fool to her, sir: bless you, she would make no more of raising every gentleman in the Bible out of these here beastly tombs than I should of growing cress on an old flannel. It's a country of devils, this is, sir, and she's the master one of the lot; and if ever we get out of it it will be more than I expect to do. I don't see no way out of it. That witch isn't likely to let a fine young man like Mr. Leo go.'

'Come,' I said, 'at any rate she saved his life.'

'Yes, and she'll take his soul to pay for it. She'll make him a witch, like herself. I say it's wicked to have anything to do with those sort of people. Last night, sir, I lay awake and read in my little Bible that my poor old mother gave me about what is going to happen to sorceresses and them sort* till my hair stood on end. Lord, how the old lady would stare if she saw where her Job had got to!'

'Yes,' it's a queer country, and a queer people too, Job,' I answered, with a sigh, for, though I am not superstitious like Job, I admit to a natural shrinking (which will not bear investigation) from the things that are above Nature.

'You are right, sir,' he answered, 'and if you won't think me very foolish, I should like to say something to you now that Mr. Leo is out

of the way'—(Leo had got up early and gone for a stroll)—'and that
is that I know it is the last country as ever I shall see in this world. I
had a dream last night, and I dreamed that I saw my old father with a
kind of night-shirt on him, something like these folks wear when
they want to be in particular full-dress, and a bit of that feathery
grass in his hand, which he may have gathered on the way, for I saw
lots of it yesterday about three hundred yards from the mouth of this
beastly cave.

' "Job," he said to me, solemn like, and yet with a kind of satisfaction shining through him, more like a Methody* parson when he has
sold a neighbour a marked horse for a sound one and cleared twenty
pounds by the job than anything I can think on—"Job, time's up,
Job; but I never did expect to have to come and hunt you out in this
'ere place, Job. Such ado as I have had to nose you up; it wasn't
friendly to give your poor old father such a run, let alone that a
wonderful lot of bad characters hail from this place Kôr." '

'Regular cautions,' I suggested.

'Yes, sir—of course, sir, that's just what he said they was—
"cautions, downright scorchers"—sir, and I'm sure I don't doubt it,
seeing what I know of them and their hot-potting ways,' went on Job,
sadly. 'Anyway, he was sure that time was up, and went away saying
that we should see more than we cared for of each other soon, and I
suppose he was a-thinking of the fact that father and I never could
hit it off together for longer nor three days, and I dare say that things
will be similar when we meet again.'

'Surely,' I said, 'you don't think that you are going to die because
you dreamed you saw your old father; if one dies because one dreams
of one's father, what happens to a man who dreams of his mother-in-
law?'

'Ah, sir, you're laughing at me,' said Job; 'but, you see, you didn't
know my old father. If it had been anybody else—my Aunt Mary, for
instance, who never made much of a job—I should not have thought
so much of it; but my father was that idle, which he shouldn't have
been with seventeen children, that he would never have put himself
out to come here just to see the place. No, sir; I know that he meant
business. Well, sir, I can't help it; I suppose every man must go some
time or other, though it is a hard thing to die in a place like this,
where Christian burial isn't to be had for its weight in gold. I've tried
to be a good man, sir, and do my duty honest, and if it wasn't for the

supercilus* kind of way in which father carried on last night—a sort of sniffing at me as it were, as though he hadn't no opinion of my references and testimonials—I should feel easy enough in my mind. Any way, sir, I've been a good servant to you and Mr. Leo, bless him! Why, it seems but the other day that I used to lead him about the streets with a penny whip; and if ever you get out of this place—which, as father didn't allude to you, perhaps you may—I hope you will think kindly of my whitened bones, and never have anything more to do with Greek writing on flower-pots, sir, if I may make so bold as to say so.'

'Come, come, Job,' I said seriously, 'this is all nonsense, you know. You mustn't be silly enough to go getting such ideas into your head. We've lived through some queer things, and I hope that we may go on doing so.'

'No, sir,' answered Job, in a tone of conviction that jarred on me unpleasantly, 'it isn't nonsense. I'm a doomed man, and I feel it, and a wonderful uncomfortable feeling it is, sir, for one can't help wondering how it's going to come about. If you are eating your dinner you think of poison and it goes against your stomach, and if you are walking along these dark rabbit-burrows you think of knives, and Lord, don't you just shiver about the back! I ain't particular, sir, provided it's sharp, like that poor girl, who, now that she's gone, I am sorry to have spoke hard on, though I don't approve of her morals in getting married, which I consider too quick to be decent. Still, sir,' and poor Job turned a shade paler as he said it, 'I do hope it won't be that hot-pot game.'

'Nonsense,' I broke in angrily, 'nonsense!'

'Very well, sir,' said Job, 'it isn't my place to differ from you, sir, but if you happen to be going anywhere, sir, I should be obliged if you could manage to take me with you, seeing that I shall be glad to have a friendly face to look at when the time comes, just to help one through, as it were. And now, sir, I'll be getting the breakfast,' and he went, leaving me in a very uncomfortable state of mind. I was deeply attached to old Job, who was one of the best and honestest men I have ever had to do with in any class of life, and really more of a friend than a servant, and the mere idea of anything happening to him brought a lump into my throat. Beneath all his ludicrous talk I could see that he himself was quite convinced that something was going to happen, and though in most cases these convictions turn

out to be utter moonshine—and this particular one especially was to
be amply accounted for by the gloomy and unaccustomed surroundings in which its victim was placed—still it did more or less carry a
chill to my heart, as any dread that is obviously a genuine object of
belief is apt to do, however absurd the belief may be. Presently the
breakfast arrived, and with it Leo, who had been taking a walk outside the cave—to clear his mind, he said—and very glad I was to
see both, for they gave me a respite from my gloomy thoughts.
After breakfast we went for another walk, and watched some of the
Amahagger sowing a plot of ground with the grain from which they
make their beer. This they did in scriptural fashion—a man with a
bag made of goat's-hide fastened round his waist walking up and
down the plot and scattering the seed as he went. It was a positive
relief to see one of these dreadful people do anything so homely and
pleasant as sow a field, perhaps because it seemed to link them, as it
were, with the rest of humanity.

As we were returning Billali met us, and informed us that it was
She's pleasure that we should wait upon her, and accordingly we
entered her presence, not without trepidation, for Ayesha was certainly an exception to the rule. Familiarity with her might and did
breed passion and wonder and horror, but it certainly did *not* breed
contempt.

We were as usual shown in by the mutes, and after these had
retired Ayesha unveiled, and once more bade Leo embrace her,
which, notwithstanding his heart-searchings of the previous night,
he did with more alacrity and fervour than in strictness courtesy
required.

She laid her white hand on his head, and looked him fondly in the
eyes. 'Dost thou wonder, my Kallikrates,' she said, 'when thou shalt
call me all thine own, and when we shall of a truth be for one another
and to one another? I will tell thee. First, must thou be even as I am,
not immortal indeed, for that I am not, but so cased and hardened
against the attacks of Time that his arrows shall glance from the
armour of thy vigorous life as the sunbeams glance from water. As
yet I may not mate with thee, for thou and I are different, and the
very brightness of my being would burn thee up, and perchance
destroy thee. Thou couldst not even endure to look upon me for too
long a time lest thine eyes should ache, and thy senses swim, and
therefore (with a little coquettish nod) shall I presently veil myself

again.' (This by the way she did not do.) 'No: listen, thou shalt not be tried beyond endurance, for this very evening, an hour before the sun goes down, shall we start hence, and by tomorrow's dark, if all goes well, and the road is not lost to me, which I pray it may not be, shall we stand in the place of Life, and thou shalt bathe in the fire, and come forth glorified, as no man ever was before thee, and then, Kallikrates, shalt thou call me wife, and I will call thee husband.'

Leo muttered something in answer to this astonishing statement, I do not know what, and she laughed a little at his confusion, and went on.

'And thou, too, oh Holly; on thee also will I confer this boon, and then of a truth shalt thou be an evergreen tree, and this will I do—well, because thou hast pleased me, Holly, for thou art not altogether a fool, like most of the sons of men, and because, though thou hast a school of philosophy as full of nonsense as those of the old days, yet hast thou not forgotten how to turn a pretty phrase about a lady's eyes.'

'Hulloa, old fellow!' whispered Leo, with a return of his old cheerfulness, 'have you been paying compliments? I should never have thought it of you!'

'I thank thee, oh Ayesha,' I replied, with as much dignity as I could command, 'but if there be such a place as thou dost describe, and if in this strange place there may be found a fiery virtue that can hold off Death when he comes to pluck us by the hand, yet would I none of it. For me, oh Ayesha, the world has not proved so soft a nest that I would lie in it for ever. A stony-hearted mother is our earth, and stones are the bread she gives her children* for their daily food. Stones to eat and bitter water for their thirst, and stripes for tender nurture. Who would endure this for many lives? Who would so load up his back with memories of lost hours and loves, and of his neighbour's sorrows that he cannot lessen, and wisdom that brings not consolation? Hard is it to die, because our delicate flesh doth shrink back from the worm it will not feel, and from that unknown which the winding-sheet doth curtain from our view. But harder still, to my fancy, would it be to live on, green in the leaf and fair, but dead and rotten at the core, and feel that other secret worm of recollection gnawing ever at the heart.'

'Bethink thee, Holly,' she said; 'yet doth long life and strength and beauty beyond measure mean power and all things that are dear to man.'

'And what, oh Queen,' I answered, 'are those things that are dear to man? Are they not bubbles? Is not ambition but an endless ladder by which no height is ever climbed till the last unreachable rung is mounted? For height leads on to height, and there is no resting-place upon them, and rung doth grow upon rung, and there is no limit to the number. Doth not wealth satiate and become nauseous, and no longer serve to satisfy or pleasure, or to buy an hour's ease of mind? And is there any end to wisdom that we may hope to reach it? Rather, the more we learn shall we not thereby be able only to better compass out our ignorance? Did we live ten thousand years could we hope to solve the secrets of the suns, and of the space beyond the suns, and of the Hand that hung them in the heavens? Would not our wisdom be but as a gnawing hunger calling our consciousness day by day to a knowledge of the empty craving of our souls? Would it not be but as a light in one of these great caverns, that though bright it burn, and brighter yet, doth but the more serve to show the depths of the gloom around it? And what good thing is there beyond that we may gain by length of days?'

'Nay, my Holly, there is love—love which makes all things beautiful, and doth breathe divinity into the very dust we tread. With love shall life roll gloriously on from year to year, like the voice of some great music that hath power to hold the hearer's heart poised on eagle's wings above the sordid shame and folly of the earth.'

'It may be so,' I answered; 'but if the loved one prove a broken reed to pierce us, or if the love be loved in vain—what then? Shall a man grave his sorrows upon a stone when he hath but need to write them on the water? Nay, oh *She*, I will live my day and grow old with my generation, and die my appointed death, and be forgotten. For I do hope for an immortality to which the little span that perchance thou canst confer will be but as a finger's length laid against the measure of the great world; and, mark this! the immortality to which I look, and which my faith doth promise to me, shall be free from the bonds that here must tie my spirit down. For, while the flesh endures, sorrow and evil and the scorpion whips of sin* must endure also; but when the flesh hath fallen from us, then shall the spirit shine forth clad in the brightness of eternal good, and for its common air shall breathe so rare an ether of most noble thoughts, that the highest aspiration of our manhood, or the purest incense of a maiden's prayer, would prove too earthly gross to float therein.'

'Thou lookest high,' answered Ayesha, with a little laugh, 'and speakest clearly as a trumpet and with no uncertain sound. And yet methinks that but now didst thou talk of "that Unknown" from which the winding-sheet doth curtain us. But perchance, thou seest with the eye of Faith, gazing on this brightness that is to be, through the painted-glass of thy imagination. Strange are the pictures of the future that mankind can thus draw with this brush of faith and this many-coloured pigment of imagination! Strange, too, that no one of them doth agree with another! I could tell thee—but there, what is the use? why rob a fool of his bauble? Let it pass, and I pray, oh Holly, that when thou dost feel old age creeping slowly toward thyself, and the confusion of senility making havoc in thy brain, thou mayest not bitterly regret that thou didst cast away the imperial boon I would have given to thee. But so it hath ever been; man can never be content with that which his hand can pluck. If a lamp be in his reach to light him through the darkness, he must needs cast it down because it is no star. Happiness danceth ever a pace before him, like the marsh-fires in the swamps, and he must catch the fire, and he must hold the star! Beauty is naught to him, because there are lips more honey-sweet; and wealth is naught, because others can weigh him down with heavier shekels; and fame is naught, because there have been greater men than he. Thyself thou saidst it, and I turn thy words against thee. Well, thou dreamest that thou shalt pluck the star. I believe it not, and I think thee a fool, my Holly, to throw away the lamp.'

I made no answer, for I could not—especially before Leo—tell her that since I had seen her face I knew that it would always be before my eyes, and that I had no wish to prolong an existence which must always be haunted and tortured by her memory, and by the last bitterness of unsatisfied love. But so it was, and so, alas, is it to this hour!

'And now,' went on *She*, changing her tone and the subject together, 'tell me, my Kallikrates, for as yet I know it not, how came ye to seek me here? Yesternight thou didst say that Kallikrates—him whom thou sawest—was thine ancestor. How was it? Tell me—thou dost not speak overmuch!'

Thus adjured, Leo told her the wonderful story of the casket and of the potsherd that, written on by his ancestress, the Egyptian Amenartas, had been the means of guiding us to her. Ayesha listened intently, and, when he had finished, spoke to me.

'Did I not tell thee one day, when we did talk of good and evil, oh Holly—it was when my beloved lay so ill—that out of good came evil, and out of evil good—that they who sowed knew not what the crop should be, nor he who struck where the blow should fall? See, now: this Egyptian Amenartas, this royal child of the Nile who hated me, and whom even now I hate, for in a way she did prevail against me—see, now, she herself hath been the very means to bring her lover to mine arms! For her sake I slew him, and now, behold, through her he hath come back to me! She would have done me evil, and sowed her seeds that I might reap tares, and behold she hath given me more than all the world can give, and there is a strange square for thee to fit into thy circle of good and evil, oh Holly!

'And so,' she went on after a pause—'and so she bade her son destroy me if he might, because I slew his father. And thou, my Kallikrates, art the father, and in a sense thou art likewise the son; and wouldst thou avenge thy wrong, and the wrong of that far-off mother of thine upon me, oh Kallikrates? See,' and she slid to her knees, and drew the white corsage still farther down her ivory bosom—'see, here beats my heart, and there by thy side is a knife, heavy, and long, and sharp, the very knife to slay an erring woman with. Take it now, and be avenged. Strike, and strike home!—so shalt thou be satisfied, Kallikrates, and go through life a happy man, because thou hast paid back the wrong, and obeyed the mandate of the past.'

He looked at her, and then stretched out his hand and lifted her to her feet.

'Rise, Ayesha,' he said sadly; 'well thou knowest that I cannot strike thee, no, not even for the sake of her whom thou slewest but last night. I am in thy power, and a very slave to thee. How can I kill thee?—sooner should I slay myself.'

'Almost dost thou begin to love me, Kallikrates,' she answered, smiling. 'And now tell me of thy country—'tis a great people, is it not? with an empire like that of Rome! Surely thou wouldst return thither, and it is well, for I mean not that thou shouldst dwell in these caves of Kôr. Nay, when once thou art even as I am, we will go hence—fear not but that I shall find a path—and then shall we cross to this England of thine, and live as it becometh us to live. Two thousand years have I waited for the day when I should see the last of these hateful caves and this gloomy-visaged folk, and now it is at hand, and my heart bounds up to meet it like a child's towards its holiday. For thou shalt rule this England——'

'But we have a queen already,' broke in Leo, hastily.

'It is naught, it is naught,' said Ayesha; 'she can be overthrown.'

At this we both broke out into an exclamation of dismay, and explained that we should as soon think of overthrowing ourselves.

'But here is a strange thing,' said Ayesha, in astonishment; 'a queen whom her people love! Surely the world must have changed since I dwelt in Kôr.'

Again we explained that it was the character of monarchs that had changed, and that the one under whom we lived was venerated and beloved by all right-thinking people in her vast realms.* Also, we told her that real power in our country rested in the hands of the people, and that we were in fact ruled by the votes of the lower and least educated classes of the community.*

'Ah,' she said, 'a democracy—then surely there is a tyrant, for I have long since seen that democracies, having no clear will of their own, in the end set up a tyrant, and worship him.'

'Yes,' I said, 'we have our tyrants.'

'Well,' she answered resignedly, 'we can at any rate destroy these tyrants, and Kallikrates shall rule the land.'

I instantly informed Ayesha that in England 'blasting' was not an amusement that could be indulged in with impunity, and that any such attempt would meet with the consideration of the law and probably end upon a scaffold.

'The law,' she laughed with scorn—'the law! Canst thou not understand, oh Holly, that I am above the law, and so shall my Kallikrates be also? All human law will be to us as the north wind to a mountain. Does the wind bend the mountain, or the mountain the wind?

'And now leave me, I pray thee, and thou too, my own Kallikrates, for I would get me ready against our journey, and so must ye both, and your servant also. But bring no great quantity of things with thee, for I trust that we shall be but three days gone. Then shall we return hither, and I will make a plan whereby we can bid farewell for ever to these sepulchres of Kôr. Yes, surely thou mayst kiss my hand!'

So we went, I, for one, meditating deeply on the awful nature of the problem that now opened out before us. The terrible *She* had evidently made up her mind to go to England, and it made me absolutely shudder to think what would be the result of her arrival there. What her powers were I knew, and I could not doubt but that she would exercise them to the full. It might be possible to control her for a while, but her proud, ambitious spirit would be certain to break loose and avenge itself for the long centuries of its solitude. She would, if necessary, and if the power of her beauty did not unaided prove equal to the occasion, blast her way to any end she set before her, and as she could not die, and for aught I knew could not even be killed,[1] what was there to stop her? In the end she would, I had little doubt, assume absolute rule over the British dominions, and probably over the whole earth, and, though I was sure that she would speedily make ours the most glorious and prosperous empire that the world has ever seen, it would be at the cost of a terrible sacrifice of life.

The whole thing sounded like a dream or some extraordinary invention of a speculative brain, and yet it was a fact—a wonderful fact—of which the whole world would soon be called on to take notice. What was the meaning of it all? After much thinking I could only conclude that this wonderful creature, whose passion had kept her for so many centuries chained as it were, and comparatively harmless, was now about to be used by Providence as a means to change the order of the world, and possibly, by the building up of a power that could no more be rebelled against or questioned than the decrees of Fate, to change it materially for the better.

[1] I regret to say that I was never able to ascertain if *She* was invulnerable against the accidents of life. Presumably this was so, else some misadventure would have been sure to put an end to her in the course of so many centuries. True, she offered to let Leo slay her, but very probably this was only an experiment to try his temper and mental attitude towards her. Ayesha never gave way to impulse without some valid object.—L. H. H.

XXIII

THE TEMPLE OF TRUTH

OUR preparations did not take us very long. We put a change of clothing apiece and some spare boots into my Gladstone bag, also we took our revolvers and an express rifle each, together with a good supply of ammunition, a precaution to which, under Providence, we subsequently owed our lives over and over again. The rest of our gear, together with our heavy rifles, we left behind us.

A few minutes before the appointed time we once more attended in Ayesha's boudoir, and found her also ready, her dark cloak thrown over her winding-sheet like wrappings.

'Are ye prepared for the great venture?' she said.

'We are,' I answered, 'though for my part, Ayesha, I have no faith in it.'

'Ah, my Holly,' she said, 'thou art of a truth like those old Jews— of whom the memory vexes me so sorely—unbelieving, and hard to accept that which they have not known. But thou shalt see; for unless my mirror yonder lies,' and she pointed to the font of crystal water, 'the path is yet open as it was of old time. And now let us start upon the new life which shall end—who knoweth where?'

'Ah,' I echoed, 'who knoweth where?' and we passed down into the great central cave, and out into the light of day. At the mouth of the cave we found a single litter with six bearers, all of them mutes, waiting, and with them I was relieved to see our old friend Billali, for whom I had conceived a sort of affection. It appeared that, for reasons not necessary to explain at length, Ayesha had thought it best that, with the exception of herself, we should proceed on foot, and this we were nothing loth to do, after our long confinement in these caves, which, however suitable they might be for sarcophagi—a singularly inappropriate word, by the way, for these particular tombs, which certainly did not consume the bodies given to their keep- ing*—were depressing habitations for breathing mortals like our- selves. Either by accident or by the orders of *She*, the space in front of the cave where we had beheld that awful dance was perfectly clear of spectators. Not a soul was to be seen, and consequently I do not believe that our departure was known to anybody, except perhaps the mutes who waited on *She*, and they were, of course, in the habit of keeping what they saw to themselves.

In a few minutes' time we were stepping out sharply across the great cultivated plain or lake bed, framed like a vast emerald in its setting of frowning cliff, and had another opportunity of wondering at the extraordinary nature of the site chosen by these old people of Kôr for their capital, and at the marvellous amount of labour, ingenuity, and engineering skill that must have been brought into requisition by the founders of the city to drain so huge a sheet of water, and to keep it clear of subsequent accumulations. It is, indeed, so far as my experience goes, an unequalled instance of what man can do in the face of nature, for in my opinion such achievements as the Suez Canal or even the Mont Cenis Tunnel do not approach this ancient undertaking in magnitude and grandeur of conception.

When we had been walking for about half an hour, enjoying ourselves exceedingly in the delightful cool which about this time of the day always appeared to descend upon the great plain of Kôr, and which in some degree atoned for the want of any land or sea breeze—for all wind was kept off by the rocky mountain wall—we began to get a clear view of what Billali had informed us were the ruins of the great city. And even from that distance we could see how wonderful those ruins were, a fact which with every step we took became more evident. The city was not very large if compared to Babylon or Thebes, or other cities of remote antiquity; perhaps its outer wall contained some twelve square miles of ground, or a little more. Nor had the walls, so far as we could judge when we reached them, been very high, probably not more than forty feet, which was about their present height where they had not through the sinking of the ground, or some such cause, fallen into ruin. The reason of this, no doubt, was that the people of Kôr, being protected from any outside attack by far more tremendous ramparts than any that the hand of man could rear, only required them for show and to guard against civil discord. But on the other hand they were as broad as they were high, built entirely of dressed stone, hewn, no doubt, from the vast caves, and surrounded by a great moat about sixty feet in width, some reaches of which were still filled with water. About ten minutes before the sun finally sank we reached this moat, and passed down and through it, clambering across what evidently were the piled-up fragments of a great bridge in order to do so, and then with some little difficulty up the slope of the wall to its summit. I wish that it lay within the power of my pen to give some idea of the grandeur of the sight that then met our view. There, all bathed in the red glow of the sinking sun, were miles upon miles of ruins—columns, temples, shrines, and the palaces of kings, varied with patches of green bush. Of course, the roofs of these buildings had long since fallen into decay and vanished, but owing to the extreme massiveness of the style of building, and to the hardness and durability of the rock employed, most of the party walls and great columns still remained standing.[1]

Straight before us stretched away what had evidently been the main thoroughfare of the city, for it was very wide, wider than the Thames Embankment, and regular. Being, as we afterwards discovered, paved, or rather built, throughout of blocks of dressed stone, such as were employed in the walls, it was but little overgrown even now with grass and shrubs that could get no depth of soil to live in. What had been the parks and gardens, on the contrary, were now dense jungle. Indeed, it was easy even from a distance to trace the course of the various roads by the burnt-up appearance of the scanty grass that grew upon them. On either side of this great thoroughfare were vast blocks of ruins, each block, generally speaking, being separated from its neighbour by a space of what had once, I suppose, been garden-ground, but was now dense and tangled bush. They were all built of the same coloured stone, and most of them had pillars, which was as much as we could make out in the fading light as we passed swiftly up the main road, that I believe I am right in saying no living foot had pressed for thousands of years.[2]

---

[1] In connection with the extraordinary state of preservation of these ruins after so vast a lapse of time—at least six thousand years—it must be remembered that Kôr was not burnt or destroyed by an enemy or an earthquake, but deserted, owing to the action of a terrible plague. Consequently the houses were left unharmed; also the climate of the plain is remarkably fine and dry, and there is very little rain or wind; as a result of which these relics have only to contend against the unaided action of time, that works but slowly upon such massive blocks of masonry.—L. H. H.

[2] Billali told me that the Amahagger believe that the site of the city is haunted, and could not be persuaded to enter it upon any consideration. Indeed, I could see that he himself did not at all like doing so, and was only consoled by the reflection that he was under the direct protection of *She*. It struck Leo and myself as very curious that a people which has no objection to living amongst the dead, with whom their familiarity has perhaps bred contempt, and even using their bodies for purposes of fuel, should be terrified at approaching the habitations that these very departed had occupied when alive. After all, however, it is only a savage inconsistency.—L. H. H.

Presently we came to an enormous pile, which we rightly took to be a temple covering at least four acres of ground, and apparently arranged in a series of courts, each one enclosing another of smaller size, on a principle of a Chinese nest of boxes, which were separated one from the other by rows of huge columns. And, whilst I think of it, I may as well state a remarkable thing about the shape of these columns, which resembled none that I have ever seen or heard of, being fashioned with a kind of waist in the centre, and swelling out above and below. At first we thought that this shape was meant to roughly symbolise or suggest the female form, as was a common habit amongst the ancient religious architects of many creeds. On the following day, however, as we went up the slopes of the mountain, we discovered a large quantity of the most stately looking palms, of which the trunks grew exactly in this shape, and I have now no doubt but that the first designer of those columns drew his inspiration from the graceful bends of those very palms, or rather of their ancestors, which then, some eight or ten thousand years ago, as now, beautified the slopes of the mountain that had once formed the shores of the volcanic lake.

At the *façade* of this huge temple, which, I should imagine, is almost as large as that of El-Karnac, at Thebes, some of the largest columns, which I measured, being between eighteen to twenty feet in diameter at the base, by about seventy feet in height, our little procession was halted, and Ayesha descended from her litter.

'There used to be a spot here, Kallikrates,' she said to Leo, who had run up to help her down, 'where one might sleep. Two thousand years ago did thou and I and that Egyptian asp rest therein, but since then have I not set foot here, nor any man, and perchance it has fallen,' and, followed by the rest of us, she passed up a vast flight of broken and ruined steps into the outer court, and looked round into the gloom. Presently she seemed to recollect, and, walking a few paces along the wall to the left, halted.

'It is here,' she said, and at the same time beckoned to the two mutes, who were loaded with provisions and our little belongings, to advance. One of them came forward, and, producing a lamp, lit it from his brazier (for the Amahagger when on a journey nearly always carried with them a little lighted brazier, from which to provide fire). The tinder of this brazier was made of broken fragments of mummy carefully damped, and, if the admixture of moisture was properly managed, this unholy compound would smoulder away for hours.[1] As soon as the lamp was lit we entered the place before which Ayesha had halted. It turned out to be a chamber hollowed in the thickness of the wall, and, from the fact of there still being a massive stone table in it, I should think that it had probably served as a living-room, perhaps for one of the door-keepers of the great temple.

Here we stopped, and after cleaning the place out and making it as comfortable as circumstances and the darkness would permit, we ate some cold meat, at least Leo, Job, and I did, for Ayesha, as I think I have said elsewhere, never touched anything except cakes of flour, fruit, and water. While we were still eating, the moon, which was at her full, rose above the mountain-wall, and began to flood the place with silver.

'Wot ye why I have brought you here to-night, my Holly?' said Ayesha, leaning her head upon her hand and watching the great orb as she rose, like some heavenly queen, above the solemn pillars of the temple. 'I brought you—nay, it is strange, but knowest thou, Kallikrates, that thou liest at this moment upon the very spot where thy dead body lay when I bore thee back to those caves of Kôr so many years ago? It all returns to my mind now. I can see it, and horrible is it to my sight!' and she shuddered.

Here Leo jumped up and hastily changed his seat. However the reminiscence might affect Ayesha, it clearly had few charms for him.

'I brought you,' went on Ayesha presently, 'that ye might look upon the most wonderful sight that ever the eye of man beheld—the full moon shining over ruined Kôr. When ye have done your eating—I would that I could teach thee to eat naught but fruit, Kallikrates, but that will come after thou hast laved in the fire. Once I, too, ate flesh like a brute beast. When ye have done we will go out, and I will show you this great temple and the God whom men once wor-shipped therein.'

Of course we got up at once, and started. And here again my pen fails me. To give a string of measurements and details of the various courts of the temple would only be wearisome, supposing that I had them, and yet I know not how I am to describe what we saw,

---

[1] After all we are not much in advance of the Amahagger in these matters. 'Mummy,' that is pounded ancient Egyptian, is, I believe, a pigment much used by artists, and especially by those of them who direct their talents to the reproduction of the works of the old masters.—EDITOR.

magnificent as it was even in its ruin, almost beyond the power of realisation. Court upon dim court, row upon row of mighty pillars—some of them (especially at the gateways) sculptured from pedestal to capital—space upon space of empty chambers that spoke more eloquently to the imagination than any crowded streets. And over all, the dead silence of the dead, the sense of utter loneliness, and the brooding spirit of the Past! How beautiful it was, and yet how drear! We did not dare to speak aloud. Ayesha herself was awed in the presence of an antiquity compared to which even her length of days was but a little thing; we only whispered, and our whispers seemed to run from column to column, till they were lost in the quiet air. Bright fell the moonlight on pillar and court and shattered wall, hiding all their rents and imperfections in its silver garment, and clothing their hoar majesty with the peculiar glory of the night. It was a wonderful sight to see the full moon looking down on the ruined fane* of Kôr. It was a wonderful thing to think for how many thousands of years the dead orb above and the dead city below had gazed thus upon each other, and in the utter solitude of space poured forth each to each the tale of their lost life and long-departed glory. The white light fell, and minute by minute the quiet shadows crept across the grass-grown courts like the spirits of old priests haunting the habitations of their worship—the white light fell, and the long shadows grew till the beauty and grandeur of the scene and the untamed majesty of its present Death seemed to sink into our very souls, and speak more loudly than the shouts of armies concerning the pomp and splendour that the grave had swallowed, and even memory had forgotten.

'Come,' said Ayesha, after we had gazed and gazed, I know not for how long, 'and I will show you the stony flower of Loveliness and Wonder's very crown, if yet it stands to mock time with its beauty and fill the heart of man with longing for that which is behind the veil,' and, without waiting for an answer, she led us through two more pillared courts into the inner shrine of the old fane.

And there, in the centre of the inmost court, that might have been some fifty yards square, or a little more, we stood face to face with what is perhaps the grandest allegorical work of Art that the genius of her children has ever given to the world. For in the exact centre of the court, placed upon a thick square slab of rock, was a huge round ball of dark stone, some forty feet in diameter, and standing on the ball was a colossal winged figure of a beauty so entrancing and divine that when I first gazed upon it, illuminated and shadowed as it was by the soft light of the moon, my breath stood still, and for an instant my heart ceased its beating.

The statue was hewn from marble so pure and white that even now, after all those ages, it shone as the moonbeams danced upon it, and its height was, I should say, a trifle under twenty feet. It was the winged figure of a woman of such marvellous loveliness and delicacy of form that the size seemed rather to add to than to detract from its so human and yet more spiritual beauty. She was bending forward and poising herself upon her half-spread wings as though to preserve her balance as she leant. Her arms were outstretched like those of some woman about to embrace one she dearly loved, while her whole attitude gave an impression of the tenderest beseeching. Her perfect and most gracious form was naked, save—and here came the extra-ordinary thing—the face, which was thinly veiled, so that we could only trace the marking of her features. A gauzy veil was thrown round and about the head, and of its two ends one fell down across her left breast, which was outlined beneath it, and one, now broken, streamed away upon the air behind her.

'Who is she?' I asked, as soon as I could take my eyes off the statue.

'Canst thou not guess, oh Holly?' answered Ayesha. 'Where then is thy imagination? It is Truth standing on the World, and calling to its children to unveil her face. See what is writ upon the pedestal. Without doubt it is taken from the book of the Scriptures of these men of Kôr,' and she led the way to the foot of the statue, where an inscription of the usual Chinese-looking hieroglyphics was so deeply graven as to be still quite legible, at least to Ayesha. According to her translation it ran thus:—

'Is there no man that will draw my veil and look upon my face, for it is very fair? Unto him who draws my veil shall I be, and peace will I give him, and sweet children of knowledge and good works.'

And a voice cried, 'Though all those who seek after thee desire thee, behold! Virgin art thou, and Virgin shalt thou go till Time be done. No man is there born of woman who may draw thy veil and live, nor shall be. By Death only can thy veil be drawn, oh Truth!'

And Truth stretched out her arms and wept, because those who sought her might not find her, nor look upon her face to face.

'Thou seest,' said Ayesha, when she had finished translating, 'Truth was the Goddess of the people of old Kôr, and to her they built their shrines, and her they sought; knowing that they should never find, still sought they.'

'And so,' I added sadly, 'do men seek to this very hour, but they find not; and, as this scripture saith, nor shall they; for in Death only is Truth found.'

Then with one more look at this veiled and spiritualised loveliness—which was so perfect and so pure that one might almost fancy that the light of a living spirit shone through the marble prison to lead man on to high and ethereal thoughts—this poet's dream of beauty frozen into stone, which I never shall forget while I live, though I find myself so helpless when I attempt to describe it, we turned and went back through the vast moonlit courts to the spot whence we had started. I never saw the statue again, which I the more regret, because on the great ball of stone representing the World whereon the figure stood, lines were drawn, that probably, had there been light enough, we should have discovered to be a map of the Universe as it was known to the people of Kôr. It is at any rate suggestive of some scientific knowledge that these long-dead worshippers of Truth had recognised the fact that the globe is round.

XXIV

WALKING THE PLANK

NEXT day the mutes woke us before the dawn; and by the time that we had got the sleep out of our eyes, and gone through a perfunctory wash at a spring which still welled up into the remains of a marble basin in the centre of the North quadrangle of the vast outer court, we found *She* standing by the litter ready to start, while old Billali and the two bearer mutes were busy collecting the baggage. As usual, Ayesha was veiled like the marble Truth (by the way, I wonder if she originally got the idea of covering up her beauty from that statue?) I noticed, however, that she seemed very depressed, and had none of that proud and buoyant bearing which would have betrayed her among a thousand women of the same stature, even if they had been veiled like herself. She looked up as we came—for her head was bowed—and greeted us. Leo asked her how she had slept.

'Ill, my Kallikrates,' she answered, 'ill. This night have strange and hideous dreams come creeping through my brain, and I know not what they may portend. Almost do I feel as though some evil overshadowed me; and yet how can evil touch me? I wonder,' she went on with a sudden outbreak of womanly tenderness, 'I wonder if, should aught happen to me, so that I slept awhile and left thee waking, wouldst thou think gently of me? I wonder, my Kallikrates, if thou wouldst tarry till I came again, as for so many centuries I have tarried for thy coming?'

Then, without waiting for an answer, she went on: 'Come, let us be setting forth, for we have far to go, and before another day is born in yonder blue should we stand in the place of Life.'

In another five minutes we were once more on our way through the vast ruined city, which loomed at us on either side in the grey dawning in a way that was at once grand and oppressive. Just as the first ray of the rising sun shot like a golden arrow athwart this storied desolation we gained the further gateway of the outer wall, and having given one more glance at the hoar and pillared majesty through which we had passed, and (with the exception of Job, for whom ruins had no charms) breathed a sigh of regret that we had not had more time to explore it, passed through the great moat, and on to the plain beyond.

As the sun rose so did Ayesha's spirits, till by breakfast-time they had regained their normal level, and she laughingly set down her previous depression to the associations of the spot where she had slept.

'These barbarians declare that Kôr is haunted,' she said, 'and of a truth I do believe their saying, for never did I know so ill a night save once. I remember it now. It was on that very spot when thou didst lie dead at my feet, Kallikrates. Never will I visit it again; it is a place of evil omen.'

After a very brief halt for breakfast we pressed on with such good will that by two o'clock in the afternoon we were at the foot of the vast wall of rock that formed the lip of the volcano, and which at this point towered up precipitously above us for fifteen hundred or two thousand feet. Here we halted, certainly not to my astonishment, for I did not see how it was possible that we should go any farther.

'Now,' said Ayesha, as she descended from her litter, 'doth our labour but commence, for here do we part with these men, and henceforward must we bear ourselves; and then, addressing Billali, 'do thou and these slaves remain here, and abide our coming. By to-morrow at the midday shall we be with thee—if not, wait.'

Billali bowed humbly, and said that her august bidding should be obeyed if they stopped there till they grew old.

'And this man, oh Holly,' said *She*, pointing to Job; 'best is it that he should tarry also, for if his heart be not high and his courage great, perchance some evil might overtake him. Also, the secrets of the place whither we go are not fit for common eyes.'

I translated this to Job, who instantly and earnestly entreated me, almost with tears in his eyes, not to leave him behind. He said he was sure that he could see nothing worse than he had already seen, and that he was terrified to death at the idea of being left alone with those 'dumb folk,' who, he thought, would probably take the opportunity to hot-pot him.

I translated what he said to Ayesha, who shrugged her shoulders, and answered, 'Well, let him come, it is naught to me; on his own head be it, and he will serve to bear the lamp and this,' and she pointed to a narrow plank, some sixteen feet in length, which had been bound above the long bearing-pole of her hammock, as I had thought to make curtains spread out better, but, as it now appeared, for some unknown purpose connected with our extraordinary undertaking.

Accordingly, the plank, which, though tough, was very light, was given to Job to carry, and also one of the lamps. I slung the other on to my back, together with a spare jar of oil, while Leo loaded himself with the provisions and some water in a kid's skin. When this was done *She* bade Billali and the six bearer mutes to retreat behind a grove of flowering magnolias about a hundred yards away, and remain there under pain of death till we had vanished. They bowed humbly, and went, and, as he departed, old Billali gave me a friendly shake of the hand, and whispered that he had rather that it was I than he who was going on this wonderful expedition with '*She-who-must-be-obeyed*,' and upon my word I felt inclined to agree with him. In another minute they were gone, and then, having briefly asked us if we were ready, Ayesha turned, and gazed up the towering cliff.

'Goodness me, Leo,' I said, 'surely we are not going to climb that precipice!'

Leo shrugged his shoulders, being in a condition of half fascinated, half expectant mystification, and as he did so, Ayesha with a sudden move began to climb the cliff, and of course we had to follow her. It was perfectly marvellous to see the ease and grace with which she sprang from rock to rock, and swung herself along the ledges. The ascent was not, however, so difficult as it seemed, although there were one or two nasty places where it did not do to look behind you, the fact being that the rock still sloped here, and was not absolutely precipitous as it was higher up. In this way we, with no great labour, mounted to the height of some fifty feet above our last standing place, the only really troublesome thing to manage being Job's board, and in doing so drew some fifty or sixty paces to the left of our starting point, for we went up like a crab, sideways. Presently we reached a ledge, narrow enough at first, but which widened as we followed it, and moreover sloped inwards like the petal of a flower, so that as we followed it we gradually got into a kind of rut or fold of rock that grew deeper and deeper, till at last it resembled a Devonshire lane in stone, and hid us perfectly from the gaze of anybody on the slope below, if there had been anybody to gaze. This lane (which appeared to be a natural formation) continued for some fifty or sixty paces, and then suddenly ended in a cave, also natural, running at right angles to it. I am sure that it was a natural cave, and not hollowed by the hand of man, because of its irregular and contorted shape and course, which gave it the appearance of having been blown bodily in the mountain by some frightful eruption of gas following the line of the least resistance. All the caves hollowed by the ancients of Kôr, on the contrary, were cut out with the most perfect regularity and symmetry. At the mouth of this cave Ayesha halted, and bade us light the two lamps, which I did, giving one to her and keeping the other myself. Then, taking the lead, she advanced down the cavern, picking her way with great care, as indeed it was necessary to do, for the floor was most irregular—strewn with boulders like the bed of a stream, and in some places pitted with deep holes, in which it would have been easy to break one's leg.

This cavern we pursued for twenty minutes or more, it being, so far as I could form a judgment—owing to its numerous twists and turns no easy task—about a quarter of a mile long.

At last, however, we halted at its farther end, and whilst I was still trying to pierce the gloom a great gust of air came tearing down it, and extinguished both the lamps.

Ayesha called to us, and we crept up to her, for she was a little in front, and were rewarded with a view that was positively appalling in its gloom and grandeur. Before us was a mighty chasm in the black rock, jagged and torn and splintered through it in a far past age by some awful convulsion of Nature, as though it had been cleft by stroke upon stroke of the lightning. This chasm, which was bounded by a precipice on the hither, and presumably, though we could not see it, on the farther side also, may have measured any width across, but from its darkness I do not think that it can have been very broad. It was impossible to make out much of its outline, or how far it ran, for the simple reason that the point where we were standing was so far from the upper surface of the cliff, at least fifteen hundred or two thousand feet, that only a very dim light struggled down to us from above. The mouth of the cavern that we had been following gave on to a most curious and tremendous spur of rock, which jutted out in mid air into the gulf before us, for a distance of some fifty yards, coming to a sharp point at its termination, and resembling nothing that I can think of so much as the spur upon the leg of a cock in shape. This huge spur was attached only to the parent precipice at its base, which was, of course, enormous, just as the cock's spur is attached to its leg. Otherwise it was utterly unsupported.

'Here must we pass,' said Ayesha. 'Be careful lest giddiness overcome you, or the wind sweep you into the gulf beneath, for of a truth
it hath no bottom;' and, without giving us any further time to get
scared, she started walking along the spur, leaving us to follow her as
best we might. I was next to her, then came Job, painfully dragging
his plank, while Leo brought up the rear. It was a wonderful sight to
see this intrepid woman gliding fearlessly along that dreadful place.
For my part, when I had gone but a very few yards, what between the
pressure of the air and the awful sense of the consequences that a slip
would entail, I found it necessary to go down on my hands and knees
and crawl, and so did the other two.

But Ayesha never condescended to this. On she went, leaning her
body against the gusts of wind, and never seeming to lose her head or
her balance.

In a few minutes we had crossed some twenty paces of this awful
bridge, which got narrower at every step, and then all of a sudden a
great gust came tearing along the gorge. I saw Ayesha lean herself
against it, but the strong draught got under her dark cloak, and tore
it from her, and away it went down the wind flapping like a wounded
bird. It was dreadful to see it go, till it was lost in the blackness. I
clung to the saddle of rock, and looked round, while the great spur
vibrated with a humming sound beneath us, like a living thing. The
sight was a truly awesome one. There we were poised in the gloom
between earth and heaven. Beneath us were hundreds upon hundreds
of feet of emptiness that gradually grew darker, till at last it was
absolutely black, and at what depth it ended is more than I can guess.
Above were space upon space of giddy air, and far, far away a line of
blue sky. And down this vast gulf upon which we were pinnacled the
great draught dashed and roared, driving clouds and misty wreaths
of vapour before it, till we were nearly blinded, and utterly confused.

The whole position was so tremendous and so absolutely
unearthly, that I believe it actually lulled our sense of terror, but to
this hour I often see it in my dreams, and wake up covered with cold
perspiration at its mere phantasy.

'On! on!' cried the white form before us, for now the cloak had gone
She was robed in white, and looked more like a spirit riding down the
gale than a woman; 'On, or ye will fall and be dashed to pieces. Keep
your eyes fixed upon the ground, and closely hug the rock.'

We obeyed her, and crept painfully along the quivering path, against which the wind shrieked and wailed as it shook it, causing it to murmur like a vast tuning-fork. On we went, I do not know for how long, only gazing round now and again, when it was absolutely necessary, until at last we saw that we were on the very tip of the spur, a slab of rock, little larger than an ordinary table, and that throbbed and jumped like any over-engined steamer. There we lay on our stomachs, clinging to the ground, and looked about us, while Ayesha stood leaning out against the wind, down which her long hair streamed, and, absolutely heedless of the hideous depth that yawned beneath, pointed before her. Then we saw why the narrow plank, which Job and I had painfully dragged along between us, had been provided. Before us was an empty space, on the other side of which was something, as yet we could not see what, for here—either owing to the shadow of the opposite cliff, or from some other cause—the gloom was that of night.

'We must wait awhile,' called Ayesha; 'soon there will be light.'

At the moment I could not imagine what she meant. How could more light than there was ever come to this dreadful spot? Whilst I was still debating in my mind, suddenly, like a great sword of flame, a beam from the setting sun pierced the Stygian gloom, and smote upon the point of rock whereon we lay, illumining Ayesha's lovely form with an unearthly splendour. I only wish that I could describe the wild and marvellous beauty of that sword of fire, laid across the darkness and rushing mist-wreaths of the gulf. How it got there I do not to this moment know, but I presume that there was some cleft or hole in the opposing cliff, through which it pierced when the setting orb was in a direct line therewith. All I can say is, that the effect was the most wonderful that I ever saw. Right through the heart of the darkness that flaming sword was stabbed, and where it lay there was the most surpassingly vivid light, so vivid that even at a distance one could see the grain of the rock, while, outside of it—yes, within a few inches of its keen edge—was naught but clustering shadows.

And now, by this ray of light, for which *She* had been waiting, and timed our arrival to meet, knowing that at this season for thousands of years it had always struck thus at sunset, we saw what was before us. Within eleven or twelve feet of the very tip of the tongue-like rock whereon we stood there arose, presumably from the far bottom of the gulf, a sugarloaf-shaped cone, of which the summit was exactly opposite to us. But had there been a summit only it would not have helped us much, for the nearest point of its circumference was some forty feet from where we were. On the lip of this summit, however, which was circular and hollow, rested a tremendous flat stone, something like a glacier stone—perhaps it was one, for all I know to the contrary—and the end of this stone approached to within twelve feet or so of us. This huge boulder was nothing more or less than a gigantic rocking-stone, accurately balanced upon the edge of the cone or miniature crater, like a half-crown on the rim of a wine-glass; for, in the fierce light that played upon it and us, we could see it oscillating in the gusts of wind.

'Quick!' said Ayesha; 'the plank—we must cross while the light endures; presently it will be gone.'

'Oh, Lord, sir!' groaned Job, 'surely she don't mean us to walk across that there place on that there thing,' as in obedience to my direction he pushed the long board towards me.

'That's it, Job,' I halloaed in ghastly merriment, though the idea of walking the plank was no pleasanter to me than to him.

I pushed the board on to Ayesha, who deftly ran it across the gulf so that one end of it rested on the rocking-stone, the other remaining on the extremity of the trembling spur. Then placing her foot upon it to prevent it from being blown away, she turned to me.

'Since last I was here, oh Holly,' she called, 'the support of the moving stone hath lessened somewhat, so that I am not sure if it will bear our weight and fall or no. Therefore will I cross the first, because no harm will come unto me,' and, without further ado, she trod lightly but firmly across the frail bridge, and in another second was standing safe upon the heaving stone.

'It is safe,' she called. 'See, hold thou the plank! I will stand on the farther side of the stone so that it may not overbalance with your greater weights. Now come, oh Holly, for presently the light will fail us.'

I struggled to my knees, and if ever I felt sick in my life I felt sick then, and I am not ashamed to say that I hesitated and hung back.

'Surely thou art not afraid,' called this strange creature in a lull of the gale, from where she stood, poised like a bird on the highest point of the rocking-stone. 'Make then way for Kallikrates.'

This settled me; it is better to fall down a precipice and die than be laughed at by such a woman; so I clenched my teeth, and in another instant I was on that horrible, narrow, bending plank, with bottomless space beneath and around me. I have always hated a great height, but never before did I realise the full horrors of which such a position is capable. Oh, the sickening sensation of that yielding board resting on the two moving supports. I grew dizzy, and thought that I must fall; my spine *crept*; it seemed to me that I was falling, and my delight at finding myself sprawling upon that stone, which rose and fell beneath me like a boat in a swell, cannot be expressed in words. All I know is that briefly, but earnestly enough, I thanked Providence for preserving me so far.

Then came Leo's turn, and, though he looked rather queer, he came across like a rope-dancer. Ayesha stretched out her hand to clasp his own, and I heard her say, 'Bravely done, my love—bravely done! The old Greek spirit lives in thee yet!'

And now only poor Job remained on the farther side of the gulf. He crept up to the plank, and yelled out, 'I can't do it, sir. I shall fall into that beastly place.'

'You must,' I remember saying with inappropriate facetiousness—'you must, Job, it's as easy as catching flies.' I suppose that I said it to satisfy my conscience, because although the expression conveys a wonderful idea of facility, as a matter of fact I know no more difficult operation in the whole world than catching flies—that is, in warm weather, unless, indeed, it is catching mosquitoes.

'I can't, sir—I can't, indeed.'

'Let the man come, or let him stop and perish there. See, the light is dying! In a moment it will be gone!' said Ayesha.

I looked. She was right. The sun was passing below the level of the hole or cleft in the precipice through which the ray reached us.

'If you stop there, Job, you will die alone,' I called; 'the light is going.'

'Come, be a man, Job,' roared Leo; 'it's quite easy.'

Thus adjured, the miserable Job, with a most awful yell, precipitated himself face downwards on the plank—he did not dare, small blame to him, to try to walk it, and commenced to draw himself across in little jerks, his poor legs hanging down on either side into the nothingness beneath.

His violent jerks at the frail board made the great stone, which was only balanced on a few inches of rock, oscillate in a most sickening manner, and, to make matters worse, when he was half-way across the flying ray of lurid light suddenly went out, just as though a lamp had been extinguished in a curtained room, leaving the whole howling wilderness of air black with darkness.

'Come on, Job, for God's sake!' I shouted in an agony of fear, while the stone, gathering motion with every swing, rocked so violently that it was difficult to hang on to it. It was a truly awful position.

'Lord have mercy on me!' cried poor Job from the darkness. 'Oh, the plank's slipping!' and I heard a violent struggle, and thought that he was gone.

But at that moment his outstretched hand, clasping in agony at the air, met my own, and I hauled—ah, how I did haul, putting out all the strength that it has pleased Providence to give me in such abundance—and to my joy in another minute Job was gasping on the rock beside me. But the plank! I felt it slip, and heard it knock against a projecting knob of rock, and it was gone.

'Great heavens!' I exclaimed. 'How are we going to get back?'

'I don't know,' answered Leo, out of the gloom. ' "Sufficient to the day is the evil thereof." I am thankful enough to be here.'

But Ayesha merely called to me to take her hand and creep after her.

XXV

THE SPIRIT OF LIFE

I DID as I was bid, and in fear and trembling felt myself guided over the edge of the stone. I sprawled my legs out, but could touch nothing.

'I am going to fall!' I gasped.

'Nay, let thyself go, and trust to me,' answered Ayesha.

Now, if the position is considered, it will be easily understood that this was a greater demand upon my confidence than was justified by my knowledge of Ayesha's character. For all I knew she might be in the very act of consigning me to a horrible doom. But in life we sometimes have to lay our faith upon strange altars, and so it was now.

'Let thyself go!' she cried, and, having no choice, I did.

I felt myself slide a pace or two down the sloping surface of the rock, and then pass into the air, and the thought flashed through my brain that I was lost. But no! In another instant my feet struck against a rocky floor, and I felt that I was standing on something solid, and out of reach of the wind, which I could hear singing away overhead. As I stood there thanking Heaven for these small mercies, there was a slip and a scuffle, and down came Leo alongside of me.

'Hulloa, old fellow!' he called out, 'are you there? This is getting interesting, is it not?'

Just then, with a terrific yell, Job arrived right on the top of us, knocking us both down. By the time that we had struggled to our feet again Ayesha was standing among us, and bidding us light the lamps, which fortunately remained uninjured, as also did the spare jar of oil.

I got out my box of Bryant and May's wax matches, and they struck as merrily, there, in that awful place, as they could have done in a London drawing-room.

In a couple of minutes both the lamps were alight; and a curious scene they revealed. We were huddled together in a rocky chamber, some ten feet square, and scared enough we looked; that is, except Ayesha, who was standing calmly with her arms folded, and waiting for the lamps to burn up. The chamber appeared to be partly natural, and partly hollowed out of the top of the cone. The roof of the natural part was formed of the swinging stone, and that of the back part of the chamber, which sloped downwards, was hewn from the live rock. For the rest, the place was warm and dry—a perfect haven of rest compared to the giddy pinnacle above, and the quivering spur that shot out to meet it in mid-air.

'So!' said *She*, 'safely have we come, though once I feared that the rocking-stone would fall with you, and precipitate you into the bottomless deeps beneath, for I do believe that the cleft goeth down to the very womb of the world. The rock whereon the stone resteth hath crumbled beneath the swinging weight. And now that he,' nodding towards Job, who was sitting on the floor, feebly wiping his forehead with a red cotton pocket-handkerchief, 'whom they rightly call the "Pig," for as a pig is he stupid, hath let fall the plank, it will not be easy to return across the gulf, and to that end must I make a plan. But now rest a while, and look upon this place. What think ye that it is?'

'We know not,' I answered.

'Wouldst thou believe, oh Holly, that once a man did choose this airy nest for a daily habitation, and did here endure for many years; leaving it only but one day in every twelve to seek food and water and oil that the people brought, more than he could carry, and laid as an offering in the mouth of the tunnel through which we passed hither?'

We looked up wonderingly, and she continued—

'Yet so it was. There was a man—Noot, he named himself—who, though he lived in the latter days, had of the wisdom of the sons of Kôr. A hermit was he, and a philosopher, and skilled in the secrets of Nature, and he it was who discovered the Fire that I shall show you, which is Nature's blood and life, and also that he who bathed therein, and breathed thereof, should live while Nature lives. But like unto thee, oh Holly, this man, Noot, would not turn his knowledge to account. "Ill," he said, "was it for man to live, for man was born to die." Therefore did he tell his secret to none, and therefore did he come and live here, where the seeker after Life must pass, and was revered of the Amahagger of the day as holy, and a hermit. And when first I came to this country—knowest thou how I came, Kallikrates? Another time will I tell thee, it is a strange tale—I heard of this philosopher, and waited for him when he came to fetch his food, and returned with him hither, though greatly did I fear to tread the gulf. Then did I beguile him with my beauty and my wit, and flatter him with my tongue, so that he led me down and showed me the Fire, and told me the secrets of the Fire, but he would not suffer me to step therein,* and, fearing lest he should slay me, I refrained, knowing that the man was very old, and soon would die. And I returned, having learned from him all that he knew of the wonderful Spirit of the World, and that was much, for the man was wise and very ancient, and by purity and abstinence, and the contemplations of his innocent mind, had worn thin the veil between that which we see and the great invisible truths, the whisper of whose wings at times we hear as they sweep through the gross air of the world. Then—it was but a very few days after, I met thee, my Kallikrates, who hadst wandered hither with the beautiful Egyptian Amenartas, and I learned to love for the first and last time, once and for ever, so that it entered into my mind to come hither with thee, and receive the gift of Life for thee and me. Therefore came we, with that Egyptian who would not be left behind, and, behold, we found the old man Noot lying but newly dead. *There* he lay, and his white beard covered him like a garment,' and she pointed to a spot near where I was sitting; 'but surely he hath long since crumbled into dust, and the wind hath borne his ashes hence.'

Here I put out my hand and felt in the dust, and presently my fingers touched something. It was a human tooth, very yellow, but sound. I held it up and showed it to Ayesha, who laughed.

'Yes,' she said, 'it is his without a doubt. Behold what remaineth of Noot and the wisdom of Noot—one little tooth! And yet that man had all life at his command, and for his conscience' sake would have none of it. Well, he lay there newly dead, and we descended whither I shall lead you, and then, gathering up all my courage, and courting death that I might perchance win so glorious a crown of life, I stepped into the flames, and behold! life such as ye can never know until ye feel it also, flowed into me, and I came forth undying, and lovely beyond imagining. Then did I stretch out mine arms to thee, Kallikrates, and bid thee take thine immortal bride, and behold, as I spoke, thou, blinded by my beauty, didst turn from me, and throw thine arms about the neck of Amenartas. And then a great fury filled me, and made me mad, and I seized the javelin that thou didst bear, and stabbed thee, so that there, at my very feet, in the place of Life, thou didst groan and go down into death. I knew not then that I had strength to slay with mine eyes and by the power of my will, therefore in my madness slew I with the javelin.[1]

'And when thou wast dead, ah! I wept, because I was undying and thou wast dead. I wept there in the place of Life so that had I been mortal any more my heart had surely broken. And she, the swart Egyptian—she cursed me by her gods.* By Osiris did she curse me and by Isis, by Nephthys and by Hekt, by Sekhet, the lion-headed, and by Set, calling down evil on me, evil and everlasting desolation. Ah! I can see her dark face now lowering o'er me like a storm, but she could not hurt me, and I—I know not if I could hurt her. I did not try; it was naught to me then; so together we bore thee hence. And afterwards I sent her—the Egyptian—away through the swamps, and it seems that she lived to bear a son and to write the tale that should lead thee, her husband, back to me, her rival and thy murdress.

'Such is the tale, my love, and now is the hour at hand that shall set a crown upon it. Like all things on the earth, it is compounded of evil and of good—more of evil than of good, perchance; and writ in letters of blood. It is the truth; naught have I hidden from thee, Kallikrates. And now one thing before the final moment of thy trial. We go down into the presence of Death, for Life and Death are very near together, and—who knoweth?—that might happen which should separate us for another space of waiting. I am but a woman, and no prophetess, and I cannot read the future. But this I know—for I learnt it from the lips of the wise man Noot—that my life is but prolonged and made more bright. It cannot live for aye. Therefore, before we go, tell me, oh Kallikrates, that of a truth thou dost forgive me, and dost love me from thy heart. See, Kallikrates: much evil have I done—perchance it was evil but two nights gone to strike that

[1] It will be observed that Ayesha's account of the death of Kallikrates differs materially from that written on the potsherd by Amenartas. The writing on the sherd says, 'Then in her rage did she smite him *by her magic*, and he died.' We never ascertained which was the correct version, but it will be remembered that the body of Kallikrates had a spear-wound in the breast, which seems conclusive, unless, indeed, it was inflicted after death. Another thing that we never ascertained was *how* the two women—*She* and the Egyptian Amenartas—managed to bear the corpse of the man they both loved across the dread gulf and along the shaking spur. What a spectacle the two distracted creatures must have presented in their grief and loveliness as they toiled along that awful place with the dead man between them! Probably however the passage was easier then.— L. H. H.

girl who loved thee cold in death—but she disobeyed me and angered me, prophesying misfortune to me, and I smote. Be careful when power comes to thee also, lest thou too shouldst smite in thine anger or thy jealousy, for unconquerable strength is a sore weapon in the hands of erring man. Yea, I have sinned—out of the bitterness born of a great love have I sinned—but yet do I know the good from the evil, nor is my heart altogether hardened.* Thy love, oh Kallikrates, shall be the gate of my redemption, even as aforetime my passion was the path down which I ran to evil. For deep love unsatisfied is the hell of noble hearts and a portion for the accursed, but love that is mirrored back more perfect from the soul of our desired doth fashion wings to lift us above ourselves, and make us what we might be. Therefore, Kallikrates, take me by the hand, and lift my veil with no more fear than though I were some peasant girl, and not the wisest and most beauteous woman in this wide world; and look me in the eyes, and tell me that thou dost forgive me with all thine heart, and that with all thine heart thou dost worship me.'

She paused, and the strange tenderness in her voice seemed to hover round us like a memory. I know that the sound of it moved me more even than her words, it was so very human—so very womanly. Leo, too, was strangely touched. Hitherto he had been fascinated against his better judgment, something as a bird is fascinated by a snake, but now I think that all this passed away, and he realised that he really loved this strange and glorious creature, as, alas! I loved her also. At any rate, I saw his eyes fill with tears, and he stepped swiftly to her and undid the gauzy veil, and then took her by the hand, and, gazing into her deep eyes, said aloud—

'Ayesha, I love thee with all my heart, and so far as forgiveness is possible I forgive thee the death of Ustane. For the rest, it is between thee and thy Maker; I know naught of it. I only know that I love thee as I never loved before, and that I will cleave to thee to the end.'

'Now,' answered Ayesha, with proud humility—'now when my lord doth speak thus royally and give with so free a hand, it cannot become me to lag behind in words, and be beggared of my generosity. Behold!' and she took his hand and placed it upon her shapely head, and then bent herself slowly down till one knee for an instant touched the ground—'Behold! in token of submission do I bow me to my lord! Behold!' and she kissed him on the lips, 'in token of my wifely love do I kiss my lord. Behold!' and she laid her hand upon his heart, 'by the sin I sinned, by my lonely centuries of waiting where-with it was wiped out, by the great love wherewith I love, and by the Spirit—the Eternal Thing that doth beget all life, from whom it ebbs, to whom it doth return again—I swear:—

'I swear, even in this first most holy hour of completed Woman-hood, that I will abandon Evil and cherish Good. I swear that I will be ever guided by thy voice in the straightest path of Duty. I swear that I will eschew Ambition, and through all my length of endless days set Wisdom over me as a guiding star to lead me unto Truth and a knowledge of the Right. I swear also that I will honour and will cherish thee, Kallikrates, who hast been swept by the wave of time back into my arms, ay, till the very end, come it soon or late. I swear—nay, I will swear no more, for what are words? Yet shalt thou learn that Ayesha hath no false tongue.

'So I have sworn, and thou, my Holly, art witness to my oath. Here, too, are we wed, my husband, with the gloom for bridal canopy—wed till the end of all things; here do we write our marriage vows upon the rushing winds which shall bear them up to heaven, and round and continually round this rolling world.

'And for a bridal gift I crown thee with my beauty's starry crown, and enduring life, and wisdom without measure, and wealth that none can count. Behold! the great ones of the earth shall creep about thy feet, and their fair women shall cover up their eyes because of the shining glory of thy countenance, and their wise ones shall be abased before thee. Thou shalt read the hearts of men as an open writing, and hither and thither shalt thou lead them as thy pleasure listeth. Like that old Sphinx of Egypt shalt thou sit aloft from age to age, and ever shall they cry to thee to solve the riddle of thy greatness that doth not pass away, and ever shalt thou mock them with thy silence!

'Behold! once more I kiss thee, and by that kiss I give to thee dominion over sea and earth,* over the peasant in his hovel, over the monarch in his palace halls, and cities crowned with towers, and those who breathe therein. Where'er the sun shakes out his spears, and the lonesome waters mirror up the moon, where'er storms roll, and Heaven's painted bows arch in the sky—from the pure North clad in snows, across the middle spaces of the world, to where the amorous South, lying like a bride upon her blue couch of seas, breathes in sighs made sweet with the odour of myrtles—there shall thy power pass and thy dominion find a home. Nor sickness, nor icy-fingered fear, nor sorrow, and pale waste of form and mind hovering ever o'er humanity, shall so much as shadow thee with the shadow of their wings. As a God shalt thou be, holding good and evil in the hollow of thy hand, and I, even I, I humble myself before thee. Such is the power of Love, and such is the bridal gift I give unto thee, Kallikrates, beloved of Rā, my Lord and Lord of All.

'And now it is done, and come storm, come shine, come good, come evil, come life, come death, it never, never can be undone. For, of a truth, that which is, is, and, being done, is done for aye, and cannot be altered. I have said—Let us hence, that all things may be accomplished in their order;' and, taking one of the lamps, she advanced towards the end of the chamber that was roofed in by the swaying stone, where she halted.

We followed her, and perceived that in the wall of the cone there was a stair, or, to be more accurate, that some projecting knobs of rock had been so shaped as to form a good imitation of a stair. Down this Ayesha began to climb, springing from step to step, like a chamois, and after her we followed with less grace. When we had descended some fifteen or sixteen steps we found that they ended in a tremendous rocky slope, running first outwards and then inwards—like the slope of an inverted cone, or tunnel. The slope was very steep, and often precipitous, but it was nowhere impassable, and by the light of the lamps we went down it with no great difficulty, though it was gloomy work enough travelling on thus, no one of us knew whither, into the dead heart of a volcano. As we went, however, I took the precaution of noting our route as well as I could; and this was not difficult, owing to the extraordinary and most fantastic shape of the rocks that were strewn about, many of which in that dim light looked more like the grim faces carven upon mediæval gargoyles than ordinary boulders.

For a long period we travelled on thus, half an hour I should say, till, after we had descended for many hundreds of feet, I perceived that we were reaching the point of the inverted cone. In another minute we were there, and found that at the very apex of the funnel was a passage, so low and narrow that we had to stoop as we crept along it in indian file. After some fifty yards of this creeping, the passage suddenly widened into a cave, so huge that we could see neither the roof nor the sides. We only knew that it was a cave by the echo of our tread and the perfect quiet of the heavy air. On we went for many minutes in absolute awed silence, like lost souls in the depths of Hades, Ayesha's white and ghost-like form flitting in front of us, till once more the cavern ended in a passage which opened into a second cavern much smaller than the first. Indeed, we could clearly make out the arch and stony banks of this seond cave, and, from their rent and jagged appearance, discovered that, like the first long passage down which we had passed through the cliff before we reached the quivering spur, it had to all appearance been torn in the bowels of the rock by the terrific force of some explosive gas. At length this cave ended in a third passage, through which gleamed a faint glow of light.

I heard Ayesha give a sigh of relief as this light dawned upon us.

'It is well,' she said; 'prepare to enter the very womb of the Earth, wherein she doth conceive the Life that ye see brought forth in man and beast—ay, and in every tree and flower.'

Swiftly she sped along, and after her we stumbled as best we might, our hearts filled like a cup with mingled dread and curiosity. What were we about to see? We passed down the tunnel; stronger and stronger the light beamed, reaching us in great flashes like the rays from a lighthouse, as one by one they are thrown wide upon the darkness of the waters. Nor was this all, for with the flashes came a soul-shaking sound like that of thunder and of crashing trees. Now we were through it, and—oh, heavens!

We stood in a third cavern, some fifty feet in length by perhaps as great a height, and thirty wide. It was carpeted with fine white sand, and its walls had been worn smooth by the action of I know not what. The cavern was not dark like the others, it was filled with a soft glow of rose-coloured light, more beautiful to look on than anything that can be conceived. But at first we saw no flashes, and heard no more of the thunderous sound. Presently, however, as we stood in amaze, gazing at the wonderful sight, and wondering whence the rosy radiance flowed, a dread and beautiful thing happened. Across the far end of the cavern, with a grinding and crashing noise—a noise so dreadful and awe-inspiring that we all trembled, and Job actually sank to his knees—there flamed out an awful cloud or pillar of fire, like a rainbow many-coloured, and like the lightning bright. For a space, perhaps forty seconds, it flamed and roared thus, turning slowly round and round, and then by degrees the terrible noise ceased, and with the fire it passed away—I know not where—leaving behind it the same rosy glow that we had first seen.

'Draw near, draw near!' cried Ayesha, with a voice of thrilling exultation. 'Behold the very Fountain and Heart of Life as it beats in the bosom of the great world. Behold the substance from which all things draw their energy, the bright Spirit of the Globe, without which it cannot live, but must grow cold and dead as the dead moon. Draw near, and wash you in the living flames, and take their virtue into your poor frames in all its virgin strength—not as it now feebly glows within your bosoms, filtered thereto through all the fine strainers of a thousand intermediate lives, but as it is here in the very fount and seat of earthly Being.'

We followed her through the rosy glow up to the head of the cave, till at last we stood before the spot where the great pulse beat and the great flame passed. And as we went we became sensible of a wild and splendid exhilaration, of a glorious sense of such a fierce intensity of Life that the most buoyant moments of our strength seemed flat and tame and feeble beside it. It was the mere effluvium of the flame, the subtle ether that it cast off as it passed, working on us, and making us feel strong as giants and swift as eagles.

We reached the head of the cave, and gazed at each other in the glorious glow, and laughed aloud—even Job laughed, and he had not laughed for a week—in the lightness of our hearts and the divine intoxication of our brains. I know that I felt as though all the varied genius of which the human intellect is capable had descended upon me. I could have spoken in blank verse of Shakespearean beauty, all sorts of great ideas flashed through my mind; it was as though the bonds of my flesh had been loosened, and left the spirit free to soar to the empyrean of its native power. The sensations that poured in upon me are indescribable. I seemed to live more keenly, to reach to a higher joy, and sip the goblet of a subtler thought than ever it had been my lot to do before. I was another and most glorified self, and all the avenues of the Possible were for a space laid open to the footsteps of the Real.

Then, suddenly, whilst I rejoiced in this splendid vigour of a new-found self, from far, far away there came a dreadful muttering noise, that grew and grew to a crash and a roar, which combined in itself all that is terrible and yet splendid in the possibilities of sound. Nearer it came, and nearer yet, till it was close upon us, rolling down like all the thunder-wheels of heaven behind the horses of the lightning. On it came, and with it came the glorious blinding cloud of many-coloured light, and stood before us for a space, turning, as it seemed to us, slowly round and round, and then, accompanied by its attendant pomp of sound, passed away I know not whither.

So astonishing was the wondrous sight that one and all of us, save *She*, who stood up and stretched her hands towards the fire, sank down before it, and hid our faces in the sand.

When it was gone, Ayesha spoke.

'Now, Kallikrates,' she said, 'the mighty moment is at hand. When the great flame comes again thou must stand in it. First throw aside thy garments, for it will burn them, though thee it will not hurt. Thou must stand in the flame while thy senses will endure, and when it embraces thee suck the fire down into thy very heart, and let it leap and play around thy every part, so that thou lose no moiety of its virtue. Hearest thou me, Kallikrates?'

'I hear thee, Ayesha,' answered Leo, 'but, of a truth—I am no coward—but I doubt me of that raging flame. How know I that it will not utterly destroy me, so that I lose myself and lose thee also? Nevertheless will I do it,' he added.

Ayesha thought for a minute, and then said—

'It is not wonderful that thou shouldst doubt. Tell me, Kallikrates: if thou seest me stand in the flame and come forth unharmed, wilt thou enter also?'

'Yes,' he answered, 'I will enter even if it slay me. I have said that I will enter now.'

'And that will I also,' I cried.

'What, my Holly!' she laughed aloud; 'methought that thou wouldst naught of length of days. Why, how is this?'

'Nay, I know not,' I answered, 'but there is that in my heart that calleth to me to taste of the flame, and live.'

'It is well,' she said. 'Thou art not altogether lost in folly. See now, I will for the second time bathe me in this living bath. Fain would I add to my beauty and my length of days if that be possible. If it be not possible, at the least it cannot harm me.

'Also,' she continued, after a momentary pause, 'is there another and a deeper cause why I would once again dip me in the flame. When first I tasted of its virtue full was my heart of passion and of hatred of that Egyptian Amenartas, and therefore, despite my strivings to be rid thereof, have passion and hatred been stamped upon my soul from that sad hour to this. But now it is otherwise. Now is my mood a happy mood, and filled am I with the purest part of thought, and so would I ever be. Therefore, Kallikrates, will I once more wash and make me pure and clean, and yet more fit for thee. Therefore also, when thou dost in turn stand in the fire, empty all thy heart of evil, and let sweet contentment hold the balance of thy mind. Shake loose thy spirit's wings, and take thy stand upon the utter verge of holy contemplation; ay, dream upon thy mother's kiss, and turn thee towards the vision of the highest good that hath ever swept on silver wings across the silence of thy dreams. For from the germ of what thou art in that dread moment shall grow the fruit of what thou shalt be for all unreckoned time.

'Now prepare thee, prepare! even as though thy last hour were at hand, and thou wast about to cross to the land of shadows, and not through the gates of glory into the realms of Life made beautiful. Prepare, I say!'

XXVI

WHAT WE SAW

THEN came a few moments' pause, during which Ayesha seemed to be gathering up her strength for the fiery trial, while we clung to each other, and waited in utter silence.

At last, from far far away, came the first murmur of sound, that grew and grew till it began to crash and bellow in the distance. As she heard it, Ayesha swiftly threw off her gauzy wrapping, loosened the golden snake from her kirtle, and then, shaking her lovely hair about her like a garment, beneath its cover slipped the kirtle off and replaced the snaky belt around her and outside the masses of falling hair. There she stood before us as Eve might have stood before Adam, clad in nothing but her abundant locks, held round her by the golden band; and no words of mine can tell how sweet she looked— and yet how divine. Nearer and nearer came the thunder wheels of fire, and as they came she pushed one ivory arm through the dark masses of her hair and flung it round Leo's neck.

'Oh, my love, my love!' she murmured, 'wilt thou ever know how I have loved thee?' and she kissed him on the forehead, and then went and stood in the pathway of the flame of Life.

There was, I remember, to my mind something very touching about her words and that embrace upon the forehead. It was like a mother's kiss, and seemed to convey a benediction with it.

On came the crashing, rolling noise, and the sound thereof was as the sound of a forest being swept flat by a mighty wind, and then tossed up by it like so much grass, and thundered down a mountain-side. Nearer and nearer it came; now flashes of light, forerunners of the revolving pillar of flame, were passing like arrows through the rosy air; and now the edge of the pillar itself appeared. Ayesha turned towards it, and stretched out her arms to greet it. On it came very slowly, and lapped her round with flame. I saw the fire run up her form. I saw her lift it with both hands as though it were water, and pour it over her head. I even saw her open her mouth and draw it down into her lungs, and a dread and wonderful sight it was.

Then she paused, and stretched out her arms, and stood there quite still, with a heavenly smile upon her face, as though she were the very Spirit of the Flame.

The mysterious fire played up and down her dark and rolling locks, twining and twisting itself through and around them like threads of golden lace; it gleamed upon her ivory breast and shoulder, from which the hair had slipped aside; it slid along her pillared throat and delicate features, and seemed to find a home in the glorious eyes that shone and shone, more brightly even than the spiritual essence.

Oh, how beautiful she looked there in the flame! No angel out of heaven could have worn a greater loveliness. Even now my heart faints before the recollection of it, as she stood and smiled at our awed faces, and I would give half my remaining time upon this earth to see her once like that again.

But suddenly—more suddenly than I can describe—a kind of change came over her face, a change which I could not define or explain on paper, but none the less a change. The smile vanished, and in its place there came a dry, hard look; the rounded face seemed to grow pinched, as though some great anxiety were leaving its impress upon it. The glorious eyes, too, lost their light, and, as I thought, the form its perfect shape and erectness.

I rubbed my eyes, thinking that I was the victim of some hallucination, or that the refraction from the intense light produced an optical delusion; and, as I did so, the flaming pillar slowly twisted and thundered off whithersoever it passes to in the bowels of the great earth, leaving Ayesha standing where it had been.

As soon as it was gone, she stepped forward to Leo's side—it seemed to me that there was no spring in her step—and stretched out her hand to lay it on his shoulder. I gazed at her arm. Where was its wonderful roundness and beauty? It was getting thin and angular. And her face—by Heaven!—*her face was growing old before my eyes!* I suppose that Leo saw it also; certainly he recoiled a step or two.

'What is it, my Kallikrates?' she said, and her voice—what was the matter with those deep and thrilling notes? They were quite high and cracked.

'Why, what is it—what is it?' she said confusedly. 'I feel dazed. Surely the quality of the fire hath not altered. Can the principle of Life alter? Tell me, Kallikrates, is there aught wrong with my eyes? I see not clear,' and she put her hand to her head and touched her hair—and oh, *horror of horrors!*—it all fell upon the floor.

'Oh, *look!—look!—look!*' shrieked Job, in a shrill falsetto of terror, his eyes nearly dropping out of his head, and foam upon his lips. '*Look!—look!—look!* she's shrivelling up! she's turning into a monkey!' and down he fell upon the ground, foaming and gnashing in a fit.

True enough—I faint even as I write it in the living presence of that terrible recollection—she *was* shrivelling up; the golden snake that had encircled her gracious form slipped over her hips and to the ground; smaller and smaller she grew; her skin changed colour, and in place of the perfect whiteness of its lustre it turned dirty brown and yellow, like an old piece of withered parchment. She felt at her head: the delicate hand was nothing but a claw now, a human talon like that of a badly-preserved Egyptian mummy, and then she seemed to realise what kind of change was passing over her, and she shrieked—ah, she shrieked!—she rolled upon the floor and shrieked!

Smaller she grew, and smaller yet, till she was no larger than a baboon. Now the skin was puckered into a million wrinkles, and on the shapeless face was the stamp of unutterable age. I never saw anything like it; nobody ever saw anything like the frightful age that was graven on that fearful countenance, no bigger now than that of a two-months' child, though the skull remained the same size, or nearly so, and let all men pray to God they never may, if they wish to keep their reason.

At last she lay still, or only feebly moving. She, who but two minutes before had gazed upon us the loveliest, noblest, most splendid woman the world has ever seen, she lay still before us, near the masses of her own dark hair, no larger than a big monkey, and hideous—ah, too hideous for words. And yet, think of this—at that very moment I thought of it—it was the *same* woman!

She was dying: we saw it, and thanked God—for while she lived she could feel, and what must she have felt? She raised herself upon her bony hands, and blindly gazed around her, swaying her head slowly from side to side as a tortoise does. She could not see, for her whitish eyes were covered with a horny film. Oh, the horrible pathos of the sight! But she could still speak.

'Kallikrates,' she said in husky, trembling notes. 'Forget me not, Kallikrates. Have pity on my shame; I shall come again, and shall once more be beautiful, I swear it—it is true! *Oh—h—h—*' and she fell upon her face, and was still.

On the very spot where more than twenty centuries before she had slain Kallikrates the priest, she herself fell down and died.

Overcome with the extremity of horror, we too fell on the sandy floor of that dread place, and swooned away.

*   *   *   *   *   *   *

I know not how long we remained thus. Many hours, I suppose. When at last I opened my eyes, the other two were still outstretched upon the floor. The rosy light yet beamed like a celestial dawn, and the thunder-wheels of the Spirit of Life yet rolled upon their accustomed track, for as I awoke the great pillar was passing away. There, too, lay the hideous little monkey frame, covered with crinkled yellow parchment, that once had been the glorious *She*. Alas! it was no hideous dream—it was an awful and unparalleled fact!

What had happened to bring this shocking change about? Had the nature of the life-giving Fire changed? Did it, perhaps, from time to time send forth an essence of Death instead of an essence of Life? Or was it that the frame once charged with its marvellous virtue could bear no more, so that were the process repeated—it mattered not at what lapse of time—the two impregnations neutralised each other, and left the body on which they acted as it was before it ever came into contact with the very essence of life? This, and this alone, would account for the sudden and terrible ageing of Ayesha, as the whole length of her two thousand years took effect upon her. I have not the slightest doubt myself but that the frame now lying before me was just what the frame of a woman would be if by any extraordinary means life could be preserved in her till she at length died at the age of two-and-twenty centuries.

But who can tell what had happened? There was the fact. Often since that awful hour I have reflected that it requires no great stretch of imagination to see the finger of Providence in the matter. Ayesha locked up in her living tomb waiting from age to age for the coming of her lover worked but a small change in the order of the World. But Ayesha strong and happy in her love, clothed in immortal youth and godlike beauty, and the wisdom of the centuries, would have revolutionised society, and even perchance have changed the destiny of Mankind. Thus she opposed herself against the eternal Law, and, strong though she was, by it was swept back to nothingness—swept back with shame and hideous mockery!

For some minutes I lay faintly turning these terrors over in my mind, while my physical strength came back to me, which it quickly did in that buoyant atmosphere. Then I bethought me of the others, and staggered to my feet, to see if I could arouse them. But first I took up Ayesha's kirtle and the gauzy scarf with which she had been wont to hide her dazzling loveliness from the eyes of men, and, averting my head so that I might not look upon it, covered up that dreadful relic of the glorious dead, that shocking epitome of human beauty and human life. I did this hurriedly, fearing lest Leo should recover, and see it again.

Then, stepping over the perfumed masses of dark hair that lay upon the sand, I stooped down by Job, who was lying upon his face, and turned him over. As I did so his arm fell back in a way that I did not like, and which sent a chill through me, and I glanced sharply at him. One look was enough. Our old and faithful servant was dead. His nerves, already shattered by all he had seen and undergone, had utterly broken down beneath this last dire sight, and he had died of terror, or in a fit brought on by terror. One had only to look at his face to see it.

It was another blow; but perhaps it may help people to understand how overwhelmingly awful was the experience through which we had passed—we did not feel it much at the time. It seemed quite natural that the poor old fellow should be dead. When Leo came to himself, which he did with a groan and trembling of the limbs about ten minutes afterwards, and I told him that Job was dead, he merely said, 'Oh!' And, mind you, this was from no heartlessness, for he and Job were much attached to each other; and he often talks of him now with the deepest regret and affection. It was only that his nerves would bear no more. A harp can give out but a certain quantity of sound, however heavily it is smitten.

Well, I set myself to recovering Leo, who, to my infinite relief, I found was not dead, but only fainting, and in the end I succeeded, as I have said, and he sat up; and then I saw another dreadful thing. When we entered that awful place his curling hair had been of the ruddiest gold, now it was turning grey, and by the time we gained the outer air it was snow white. Besides, he looked twenty years older.

'What is to be done, old fellow?' he said in a hollow, dead sort of voice, when his mind had cleared a little, and a recollection of what had happened forced itself upon it.

'Try and get out, I suppose,' I answered; 'that is, unless you would like to go in there,' and I pointed to the column of fire that was once more rolling by.

'I would go in if I were sure that it would kill me,' he said with a little laugh. 'It was my cursed hesitation that did this. If I had not been doubtful she might never have tried to show me the road. But I am not sure. The fire might have the opposite effect upon me. It might make me immortal; and, old fellow, I have not the patience to wait a couple of thousand years for her to come back again as she did for me. I had rather die when my hour comes—and I should fancy that it isn't far off either—and go my ways to look for her. Do you go in if you like.'

But I merely shook my head, my excitement was as dead as ditchwater, and my distaste for the prolongation of my mortal span had come back upon me more strongly than ever. Besides, we neither of us knew what the effects of the fire might be. The result upon *She* had not been of an encouraging nature, and of the exact causes that produced that result we were, of course, ignorant.

'Well, my boy,' I said, 'we cannot stop here till we go the way of those two,' and I pointed to the little heap under the white garment and to the stiffening corpse of poor Job. 'If we are going we had better go. But, by the way, I expect that the lamps have burnt out,' and I took one up and looked at it, and sure enough it had.

'There is some more oil in the vase,' said Leo indifferently—'if it is not broken, at least.'

I examined the vessel in question—it was intact. With a trembling hand I filled the lamps—luckily there was still some of the linen wick unburnt. Then I lit them with one of our wax matches. While I did so we heard the pillar of fire approaching once more as it went on its never-ending journey, if, indeed, it was the same pillar that passed and repassed in a circle.

'Let's see it come once more,' said Leo; 'we shall never look upon its like again in this world.'

It seemed a bit of idle curiosity, but somehow I shared it, and so we waited till, turning slowly round upon its own axis, it had flamed and thundered by; and I remember wondering for how many thousands of years this same phenomenon had been taking place in the bowels of the earth, and for how many more thousands it would continue to take place. I wondered also if any mortal eyes would ever again mark its passage, or any mortal ears be thrilled and fascinated by the swelling volume of its majestic sound. I do not think that they will. I believe that we are the last human beings who will ever see that unearthly sight. Presently it had gone, and we too turned to go.

But before we did so we each took Job's cold hand in ours and shook it. It was a rather ghastly ceremony, but it was the only means in our power of showing our respect to the faithful dead and of celebrating his obsequies. The heap beneath the white garment we did not uncover. We had no wish to look upon that terrible sight again. But we went to the pile of rippling hair that had fallen from her in the agony of that hideous change which was worse than a thousand natural deaths, and each of us drew from it a shining lock, and these locks we still have, the sole memento that is left to us of Ayesha as we knew her in the fulness of her grace and glory. Leo pressed the perfumed hair to his lips.

'She called to me not to forget her,' he said hoarsely; 'and swore that we should meet again. By Heaven! I never will forget her. Here I swear that, if we live to get out of this, I will not for all my days have anything to say to another living woman, and that wherever I go I will wait for her as faithfully as she waited for me.'

'Yes,' I thought to myself, 'if she comes back as beautiful as we knew her. But supposing she came back like that!'[1]

Well, and then we went. We went, and left those two in the presence of the very well and spring of Life, but gathered to the cold company of Death. How lonely they looked as they lay there, and how ill assorted! That little heap had been for two thousand years the wisest, loveliest, proudest creature—I can hardly call her woman— in the whole universe. She had been wicked, too, in her way; but, alas! such is the frailty of the human heart, her wickedness had not detracted from her charm. Indeed, I am by no means certain that it did not add to it. It was after all of a grand order, there was nothing mean or small about Ayesha.

And poor Job, too! His presentiment had come true, and there was an end of him. Well, he has a strange burial-place—no Norfolk hind*

---

[1] What a terrifying reflection it is, by the way, that nearly all our deep love for women who are not our kindred depends—at any rate, in the first instance—upon their personal appearance. If we lost them, and found them again dreadful to look on, though otherwise they were the very same, should we still love them?—L. H. H.

ever had a stranger, or ever will; and it is something to lie in the same sepulchre with the poor remains of the imperial *She*.

We looked our last upon them and the indescribable rosy glow in which they lay, and then with hearts far too heavy for words we left them, and crept thence broken-down men—so broken down that we even renounced the chance of practically immortal life, because all that made life valuable had gone from us, and we knew even then that to prolong our days indefinitely would only be to prolong our sufferings. For we felt—yes, both of us—that having once looked Ayesha in the eyes, we could not forget her for ever and ever while memory and identity remained. We both loved her now and for always, she was stamped and carven on our hearts, and no other woman or interest could ever raze that splendid die. And I—there lies the sting—I had and have no right to think thus of her. As she told me, I was naught to her, and never shall be through the unfathomed depth of Time, unless, indeed, conditions alter, and a day comes at last when two men may love one woman, and all three be happy in the fact. It is the only hope of my broken-heartedness, and a rather faint one. Beyond it I have nothing. I have paid down this heavy price, all that I am worth here and hereafter, and that is my sole reward. With Leo it is different, and often and often I bitterly envy him his happy lot, for if *She* was right, and her wisdom and know-ledge did not fail her at the last, which, arguing from the precedent of her own case, I think most unlikely, he has some future to look forward to. But I have none, and yet—mark the folly and the weak-ness of the human heart, and let him who is wise learn wisdom from it—yet I would not have it otherwise. I mean that I am content to give what I have given and must always give, and take in payment those crumbs that fall from my mistress's table, the memory of a few kind words, the hope one day in the far undreamed future of a sweet smile or two of recognition, a little gentle friendship, and a little show of thanks for my devotion to her—and Leo.

If that does not constitute true love, I do not know what does, and all I have to say is that it is a very bad state of mind for a man on the wrong side of middle age to fall into.

XXVII

WE passed through the caves without trouble, but when we came to the slope of the inverted cone two difficulties stared us in the face. The first of these was the laborious nature of the ascent, and the next the extreme difficulty of finding our way. Indeed, had it not been for the mental notes that I had fortunately taken of the shape of various rocks, etc., I am sure that we never should have managed it at all, but have wandered about in the dreadful womb of the volcano—for I suppose it must once have been something of the sort—until we died of exhaustion and despair. As it was we went wrong several times, and once nearly fell into a huge crack or crevasse. It was terrible work creeping about in the dense gloom and awful stillness from boulder to boulder, and examining it by the feeble light of the lamps to see if I could recognise its shape. We rarely spoke, our hearts were too heavy for speech, we simply stumbled about, falling sometimes and cutting ourselves, in a rather dogged sort of way. The fact was that our spirits were utterly crushed, and we did not greatly care what happened to us. Only we felt bound to try and save our lives whilst we could, and indeed a natural instinct prompted us to it. So for some three or four hours, I should think—I cannot tell exactly how long, for we had no watch left that would go—we blundered on. During the last two hours we were completely lost, and I began to fear that we had got into the funnel of some subsidiary cone, when at last I suddenly recognised a very large rock which we had passed in descending but a little way from the top. It is a marvel that I should have recognised it, and, indeed, we had already passed it going at right angles to the proper path, when something about it struck me, and I turned back and examined it in an idle sort of way, and, as it happened, this proved our salvation.

After this we gained the rocky natural stair without much further trouble, and in due course found ourselves back in the little chamber where the benighted Noot had lived and died.

But now a fresh terror stared us in the face. It will be remembered that owing to Job's fear and awkwardness, the plank upon which we had crossed from the huge spur to the rocking-stone had been whirled off into the tremendous gulf below.

How were we to cross without the plank?

There was only one answer—we must try and *jump* it, or else stop there till we starved. The distance in itself was not so very great, between eleven and twelve feet I should think, and I have seen Leo jump over twenty when he was a young fellow at college; but then, think of the conditions. Two weary, worn-out men, one of them on the wrong side of forty, a rocking-stone to take off from, a trembling point of rock some few feet across to land upon, and a bottomless gulf to be cleared in a raging gale! It was bad enough, God knows, but when I pointed out these things to Leo, he put the whole matter in a nutshell by replying that, merciless as the choice was, we must choose between the certainty of a lingering death in the chamber and the risk of a swift one in the air. Of course, there was no arguing against this, but one thing was clear, we could not attempt that leap in the dark; the only thing to do was to wait for the ray of light which pierced through the gulf at sunset. How near to or how far from sunset we might be, neither of us had the faintest notion; all we did know was, that when at last the light came it would not endure more than a couple of minutes at the outside, so that we must be prepared to meet it. Accordingly, we made up our minds to creep on to the top of the rocking-stone and lie there in readiness. We were the more easily reconciled to this course by the fact that our lamps were once more nearly exhausted—indeed, one had gone out bodily, and the other was jumping up and down as the flame of a lamp does when the oil is done. So, by the aid of its dying light, we hastened to crawl out of the little chamber and clamber up the side of the great stone.

As we did so the light went out.

The difference in our position was a sufficiently remarkable one. Below, in the little chamber, we had only heard the roaring of the gale overhead—here, lying on our faces on the swinging stone, we were exposed to its full force and fury, as the great draught drew first from this direction and then from that, howling against the mighty precipice and through the rocky cliffs like ten thousand despairing souls. We lay there hour after hour in terror and misery of mind so deep that I will not attempt to describe it, and listened to the wild storm-voices of that Tartarus,* as, set to the deep undertone of the spur opposite against which the wind hummed like some awful harp, they called to each other from precipice to precipice. No nightmare dreamed by man, no wild invention of the romancer, can ever equal the living horror of that place, and the weird crying of those voices of the night, as we clung like shipwrecked mariners to a raft, and tossed on the black, unfathomed wilderness of air. Fortunately the temperature was not a low one; indeed, the wind was warm, or we should have perished. So we clung and listened, and while we were stretched out upon the rock a thing happened which was so curious and suggestive in itself, though doubtless a mere coincidence, that, if anything, it added to, rather than deducted from, the burden on our nerves.

It will be remembered that when Ayesha was standing on the spur, before we crossed to the stone, the wind tore her cloak from her, and whirled it away into the darkness of the gulf, we could not see whither. Well—I hardly like to tell the story; it is so strange. As we lay there upon the rocking-stone, this very cloak came floating out of the black space, like a memory from the dead, and fell on Leo—so that it covered him nearly from head to foot. We could not at first make out what it was, but soon discovered by its feel, and then poor Leo, for the first time, gave way, and I heard him sobbing there upon the stone. No doubt the cloak had been caught upon some pinnacle of the cliff, and was thence blown hither by a chance gust; but still, it was a most curious and touching incident.

Shortly after this, suddenly, without the slightest previous warning, the great red knife of light came stabbing the darkness through and through—struck the swaying stone on which we were, and rested its sharp point upon the spur opposite.

'Now for it,' said Leo, 'now or never.'

We rose and stretched ourselves, and looked at the cloud-wreaths stained the colour of blood by that red ray as they tore through the sickening depths beneath, and then at the empty space between the swaying stone and the quivering rock, and, in our hearts, despaired, and prepared for death. Surely we could not clear it—desperate though we were.

'Who is to go first?' said I.

'Do you, old fellow,' answered Leo. 'I will sit upon the other side of the stone to steady it. You must take as much run as you can, and jump high; and God have mercy on us, say I.'

I acquiesced with a nod, and then I did a thing I had never done since Leo was a little boy. I turned and put my arm round him, and kissed him on the forehead. It sounds rather French, but as a fact I was taking my last farewell of a man whom I could not have loved more if he had been my own son twice over.

'Good-bye, my boy,' I said, 'I hope that we shall meet again, wherever it is that we go to.'

The fact was I did not expect to live another two minutes.

Next I retreated to the far side of the rock, and waited till one of the chopping gusts of wind got behind me, and then, commending my soul to God, I ran the length of the huge stone, some three or four and thirty feet, and sprang wildly out into the dizzy air. Oh! the sickening terrors that I felt as I launched myself at that little point of rock, and the horrible sense of despair that shot through my brain as I realised that I had *jumped short*! But so it was, my feet never touched the point, they went down into space, only my hands and body came in contact with it. I gripped at it with a yell, but one hand slipped, and I swung right round, holding by the other, so that I faced the stone from which I had sprung. Wildly I stretched up with my left hand, and this time managed to grasp a knob of rock, and there I hung in the fierce red light, with thousands of feet of empty air beneath me. My hands were holding to either side of the under part of the spur, so that its point was touching my head. Therefore, even if I could have found the strength, I could not pull myself up. The most that I could do would be to hang for about a minute, and then drop down, down into the bottomless pit. If any man can imagine a more hideous position, let him speak! All I know is that the torture of that half-minute nearly turned my brain.

I heard Leo give a cry, and then suddenly saw him in mid air springing up and out like a chamois. It was a splendid leap that he took under the influence of his terror and despair, clearing the horrible gulf as though it were nothing, and, landing well on to the rocky point, he threw himself upon his face, to prevent his pitching off into the depths. I felt the spur above me shake beneath the shock of his impact, and as it did so I saw the huge rocking-stone, that had been violently depressed by him as he sprang, fly back when relieved of his weight till, for the first time during all these centuries, it got beyond its balance, and fell with a most awful crash right into the rocky chamber which had once served the philosopher Noot for a hermitage, as I have no doubt, for ever hermetically sealing the passage that leads to the Place of Life with some hundreds of tons of rock.

All this happened in a second, and curiously enough, notwithstanding my terrible position, I noted it involuntarily, as it were. I even remember thinking that no human being would go down that dread path again.

Next instant I felt Leo seize me by the right wrist with both hands. By lying flat on the point of rock he could just reach me.

'You must let go and swing yourself clear,' he said in a calm and collected voice, 'and then I will try and pull you up, or we will both go together. Are you ready?'

By way of answer I let go, first with my left hand and then with the right, and swayed out as a consequence clear of the overshadowing rock, my weight hanging upon Leo's arms. It was a dreadful moment. He was a very powerful man, I knew, but would his strength be equal to lifting me up till I could get a hold on the top of the spur, when owing to his position he had so little purchase?

For a few seconds I swung to and fro, while he gathered himself for the effort, and then I heard his sinews cracking above me, and felt myself lifted up as though I were a little child, till I got my left arm round the rock, and my chest was resting on it. The rest was easy; in two or three more seconds I was up, and we were lying panting side by side, trembling like leaves, and with the cold perspiration of terror pouring from our skins.

And then, as before, the light went out like a lamp.

For some half-hour we lay thus without speaking a word, and then at length began to creep along the great spur as best we might in the dense gloom. As we drew towards the face of the cliff, however, from which the spur sprang out like a spike from a wall, the light increased, though only a very little, for it was night overhead. After that the gusts of wind decreased, and we got along rather better, and at last reached the mouth of the first cave or tunnel. But now a fresh trouble stared us in the face: our oil was gone, and the lamps were, no doubt, crushed to powder beneath the fallen rocking-stone. We were even without a drop of water to stay our thirst, for we had drunk the last in the chamber of Noot. How were we to see to make our way through this last boulder-strewn tunnel?

Clearly all that we could do was to trust to our sense of feeling, and attempt the passage in the dark, so in we crept, fearing that if we delayed to do so our exhaustion would overcome us, and we should probably lie down and die where we were.

Oh, the horrors of that last tunnel! The place was strewn with rocks, and we fell over them, and knocked ourselves up against them till we were bleeding from a score of wounds. Our only guide was the side of the cavern, which we kept touching, and so bewildered did we grow in the darkness that we were several times seized with the terrifying thought that we had turned, and were travelling the wrong way. On we went, feebly, and still more feebly, for hour after hour, stopping every few minutes to rest, for our strength was spent. Once we fell asleep, and, I think, must have slept for some hours, for, when we woke, our limbs were quite stiff, and the blood from our blows and scratches had caked, and was hard and dry upon our skin. Then we dragged ourselves on again, till at last, when despair was entering into our hearts, we once more saw the light of day, and found ourselves outside the tunnel in the rocky fold on the outer surface of the cliff that, it will be remembered, led into it.

It was early morning—that we could tell by the feel of the sweet air and the look of the blessed sky, which we had never hoped to see again. It was, so near as we knew, an hour after sunset when we entered the tunnel, so it followed that it had taken us the entire night to crawl through that dreadful place.

'One more effort, Leo,' I gasped, 'and we shall reach the slope where Billali is, if he hasn't gone. Come, don't give way,' for he had cast himself upon his face. He got up, and, leaning on each other, we got down that fifty feet or so of cliff—somehow, I have not the least notion how. I only remember that we found ourselves lying in a heap at the bottom, and then once more began to drag ourselves along on our hands and knees towards the grove where *She* had told Billali to wait her re-arrival, for we could not walk another foot. We had not gone fifty yards in this fashion when suddenly one of the mutes emerged from some trees on our left, through which, I presume, he had been taking a morning stroll, and came running up to see what sort of strange animals we were. He stared, and stared, and then held up his hands in horror, and nearly fell to the ground. Next, he started off as hard as he could for the grove some two hundred yards away. No wonder that he was horrified at our appearance, for we must have been a shocking sight. To begin, Leo, with his golden curls turned a snowy white, his clothes nearly rent from his body, his worn face and his hands a mass of bruises, cuts, and blood-encrusted filth, was a sufficiently alarming spectacle, as he painfully dragged himself along the ground, and I have no doubt that I was little better to look on. I know that two days afterwards when I looked at my face in some water I scarcely recognised myself. I have never been famous for beauty, but there was something beside ugliness stamped upon my features that I have never got rid of until this day, something resembling that wild look with which a startled person wakes from deep sleep more than anything else that I can think of. And really it is not to be wondered at. What I do wonder at is that we escaped at all with our reason.

Presently, to my intense relief, I saw old Billali hurrying towards us, and even then I could scarcely help smiling at the expression of consternation on his dignified countenance.

'Oh, my Baboon! my Baboon!' he cried, 'my dear son, is it indeed thee and the Lion? Why, his mane that was ripe as corn is white like the snow. Whence come ye? and where is the Pig, and where too *She-who-must-be-obeyed*?'

'Dead, both dead,' I answered; 'but ask no questions; help us, and give us food and water, or we too shall die before thine eyes. Seest thou not that our tongues are black for want of water? How can we talk then?'

'Dead!' he gasped. 'Impossible. *She* who never dies—dead, how can it be?,' and then, perceiving, I think, that his face was being watched by the mutes who had come running up, he checked himself, and motioned to them to carry us to the camp, which they did.

Fortunately when we arrived some broth was boiling on the fire, and with this Billali fed us, for we were too weak to feed ourselves, thereby I firmly believe saving us from death by exhaustion. Then he bade the mutes wash the blood and grime from us with wet cloths, and after that we were laid down upon piles of aromatic grass, and instantly fell into the dead sleep of absolute exhaustion of mind and body.

XXVIII

OVER THE MOUNTAIN

THE next thing I recollect is a feeling of the most dreadful stiffness, and a sort of vague idea passing through my half-awakened brain that I was a carpet that had just been beaten. I opened my eyes, and the first thing they fell on was the venerable countenance of our old friend Billali, who was seated by the side of the improvised bed upon which I was sleeping, and thoughtfully stroking his long beard. The sight of him at once brought back to my mind a recollection of all that we had recently passed through, which was accentuated by the vision of poor Leo lying opposite to me, his face knocked almost to a jelly, and his beautiful crowd of curls turned from yellow to white,[1] and I shut my eyes again and groaned.

'Thou has slept long, my Baboon,' said old Billali.

'How long, my father?' I asked.

'A round of the sun and a round of the moon, a day and a night hast thou slept, and the Lion also. See, he sleepeth yet.'

'Blessed is sleep,' I answered, 'for it swallows up recollection.'

'Tell me,' he said, 'what hath befallen ye, and what is this strange story of the death of Her who dieth not. Bethink thee, my son: if this be true, then is thy danger and the danger of the Lion very great—nay, almost is the pot red wherewith ye shall be potted, and the stomachs of those who shall eat ye are already hungry for the feast. Knowest thou not that these Amahagger, my children, these dwellers in the caves, hate ye? They hate ye as strangers, they hate ye more because of their brethren whom *She* put to the torment for your sake. Assuredly, if once they learn that there is naught to fear from Hiya, from the terrible One-who-must-be-obeyed, they will slay ye by the pot. But let me hear thy tale, my poor Baboon.'

Thus adjured, I set to work and told him—not everything, indeed, for I did not think it desirable to do so, but sufficient for my purpose, which was to make him understand that *She* was really no more, having fallen into some fire, and, as I put it—for the real thing would

---

[1] Curiously enough, Leo's hair has lately been to some extent regaining its colour—that is to say, it is now a yellowish grey, and I am not without hopes that it will in time come quite right.—L. H. H

have been incomprehensible to him—been burnt up. I also told him some of the horrors we had undergone in effecting our escape, and these produced a great impression on him. But I clearly saw that he did not believe in the report of Ayesha's death. He believed indeed that we thought that she was dead, but his explanation was that it had suited her to disappear for a while. Once, he said, in his father's time, she had done so for twelve years, and there was a tradition in the country that many centuries back no one had seen her for a whole generation, when she suddenly reappeared, and destroyed a woman who had assumed the position of Queen. I said nothing to this, but only shook my head sadly. Alas! I knew too well that Ayesha would appear no more, or at any rate that Billali would never see her again.

'And now,' concluded Billali, 'what wouldst thou do, my Baboon?'

'Nay,' I said, 'I know not, my father. Can we not escape from this country?'

He shook his head.

'It is very difficult. By Kôr ye cannot pass, for ye would be seen, and as soon as those fierce ones found that ye were alone, well,' and he smiled significantly, and made a movement as though he were placing a hat on his head. 'But there is a way over the cliff whereof I once spake to thee, where they drive the cattle out to pasture. Then beyond the pastures are three days' journey through the marshes, and after that I know not, but I have heard that seven days' journey from thence is a mighty river, which floweth to the black water. If ye could come thither, perchance ye might escape, but how can ye come thither?'

'Billali,' I said, 'once, thou knowest, I did save thy life. Now pay back the debt, my father, and save me mine and my friend's, the Lion's. It shall be a pleasant thing for thee to think of when thine hour comes, and something to set in the scale against the evil doing of thy days, if perchance thou hast done any evil. Also, if thou be right, and if *She* doth but hide herself, surely when she comes again she shall reward thee.'

'My son the Baboon,' answered the old man, 'think not that I have an ungrateful heart. Well do I remember how thou didst rescue me when those dogs stood by to see me drown. Measure for measure will I give thee, and if thou canst be saved, surely I will save thee. Listen: by dawn to-morrow be prepared, for litters shall be here to bear ye away across the mountains, and through the marshes beyond. This will I do, saying that it is the word of *She* that it be done, and he who obeyeth not the word of *She* food is he for the hyænas. Then when ye have crossed the marshes, ye must strike with your own hands, so that perchance, if good fortune go with you, ye may live to come to that black water whereof ye told me. And now, see, the Lion wakes, and ye must eat the food I have made ready for you.'

Leo's condition when once he was fairly aroused proved not to be so bad as might have been expected from his appearance, and we both of us managed to eat a hearty meal, which indeed we needed sadly enough. After this we limped down to the spring and bathed, and then came back and slept again till evening, when we once more ate enough for five. Billali was away all that day, no doubt making arrangements about litters and bearers, for we were awakened in the middle of the night by the arrival of a considerable number of men in the little camp.

At dawn the old man himself appeared, and told us that he had by using *She's* dreaded name, though with some difficulty, succeeded in getting the necessary men and two guides to conduct us across the swamps, and that he urged us to start at once, at the same time announcing his intention of accompanying us so as to protect us against treachery. I was much touched by this act of kindness on the part of that wily old barbarian towards two utterly defenceless strangers. A three—or in his case, for the would have to return, six—days' journey through those deadly swamps was no light undertaking for a man of his age, but he consented to do it cheerfully in order to promote our safety. It shows that even among those dreadful Amahagger—who are certainly with their gloom and their devilish and ferocious rites by far the most terrible savages that I ever heard of—there are people with kindly hearts. Of course self-interest may have had something to do with it. He may have thought that *She* would suddenly reappear and demand an account of us at his hands, but still, allowing for all deductions, it was a great deal more than we could expect under the circumstances, and I can only say that I shall for as long as I live cherish a most affectionate remembrance of my nominal parent, old Billali.

Accordingly, after swallowing some food, we started in the litters, feeling, so far as our bodies went, wonderfully like our old selves after our long rest and sleep. I must leave the condition of our minds to the imagination.

Then came a terrible pull up the cliff. Sometimes the ascent was natural, more often it was a zig-zag roadway cut, no doubt, in the first instance by the old inhabitants of Kôr. The Amahagger say they drive their spare cattle over it once a year to pasture outside; all I know is that those cattle must be uncommonly active on their feet. Of course the litters were useless here, so we had to walk.

By midday, however, we reached the great flat top of that mighty wall of rock, and grand enough the view was from it, with the plain of Kôr, in the centre of which we could clearly make out the pillared ruins of the Temple of Truth to the one side, and the boundless and melancholy marsh on the other. This wall of rock, which had no doubt once formed the lip of the crater, was about a mile and a half thick, and still covered with clinker. Nothing grew there, and the only thing to relieve our eyes were occasional pools of rain-water (for rain had lately fallen) wherever there was a little hollow. Over the flat crest of this mighty rampart we went, and then came the descent, which, if not so difficult a matter as the getting up, was still sufficiently break-neck, and took us till sunset. That night, however, we camped in safety upon the mighty slopes that rolled away to the marsh beneath.

On the following morning, about eleven o'clock, began our dreary journey across those awful seas of swamps which I have already described.

For three whole days, through stench and mire, and the all-prevailing flavour of fever, did our bearers struggle along, till at length we came to open rolling ground quite uncultivated, and mostly treeless, but covered with game of all sorts, which lies beyond that most desolate, and without guides utterly impracticable, district. And here on the following morning we bade farewell, not without some regret, to old Billali, who stroked his white beard and solemnly blessed us.

'Farewell, my son the Baboon,' he said, 'and farewell to thee too, oh Lion. I can do no more to help you. But if ever ye come to your country, be advised, and venture no more into lands that ye know not, lest ye come back no more, but leave your white bones to mark the limit of your journeyings. Farewell once more; often shall I think of you, nor wilt thou forget me, my Baboon, for though thy face is ugly thy heart is true.' And then he turned and went, and with him went the tall and sullen-looking bearers, and that was the last that we saw of the Amahagger. We watched them winding away with the empty litters like a procession bearing dead men from a battle, till the mists from the marsh gathered round them and hid them, and then, left utterly desolate in the vast wilderness, we turned and gazed around us and at each other.

Three weeks or so before four men had entered the marshes of Kôr, and now two of us were dead, and the other two had gone through adventures and experiences so strange and terrible that death himself hath not a more fearful countenance. Three weeks— and only three weeks! Truly time should be measured by events, and not by the lapse of hours. It seemed like thirty years since we saw the last of our whale-boat.

'We must strike out for the Zambesi, Leo,' I said, 'but God knows if we shall ever get there.'

Leo nodded. He had become very silent of late, and we started with nothing but the clothes we stood in, a compass, our revolvers and express rifles, and about two hundred rounds of ammunition, and so ended the history of our visit to the ancient ruins of mighty and imperial Kôr.

As for the adventures that subsequently befell us, strange and varied as they were, I have, after deliberation, determined not to record them here. In these pages I have only tried to give a short and clear account of an occurrence which I believe to be unprecedented, and this I have done, not with a view to immediate publication, but merely to put on paper while they are yet fresh in our memories the details of our journey and its result, which will, I believe, prove interesting to the world if ever we determine to make them public. This, as at present advised, we do not intend should be done during our joint lives.

For the rest, it is of no public interest, resembling as it does the experience of more than one Central African traveller. Suffice it to say, that we did, after incredible hardships and privations, reach the Zambesi, which proved to be about a hundred and seventy miles south of where Billali left us. There we were for six months imprisoned by a savage tribe, who believed us to be supernatural beings, chiefly on account of Leo's youthful face and snow-white hair. From these people we ultimately escaped, and, crossing the Zambesi, wandered off southwards, where, when on the point of starvation, we were sufficiently fortunate to fall in with a half-caste Portuguese elephant-hunter who had followed a troop of elephants farther inland than he had ever been before. This man treated us most hospitably, and ultimately through his assistance we, after innumerable sufferings and adventures, reached Delagoa Bay, more than eighteen months from the time when we emerged from the marshes of Kôr, and the very next day managed to catch one of the steamboats that run round the Cape to England. Our journey home was a prosperous one, and we set our foot on the quay at Southampton exactly two years from the date of our departure upon our wild and seemingly ridiculous quest, and I now write these last words with Leo leaning over my shoulder in my old room in my college, the very same into which some two-and-twenty years ago my poor friend Vincey came stumbling on the memorable night of his death, bearing the iron chest with him.

And that is the end of this history so far as it concerns science and the outside world. What its end will be as regards Leo and myself is more than I can guess at. But we feel that is not reached yet. A story that began more than two thousand years ago may stretch a long way into the dim and distant future.

Is Leo really a reincarnation of the ancient Kallikrates of whom the inscription tells? Or was Ayesha deceived by some strange hereditary resemblance? The reader must form his own opinion on this as on many other matters. I have mine, which is that she made no such mistake.

Often I sit alone at night, staring with the eyes of the mind into the blackness of unborn time, and wondering in what shape and form the great drama will be finally developed, and where the scene of its next act will be laid. And when that *final* development ultimately occurs, as I have no doubt it must and will occur, in obedience to a fate that never swerves and a purpose that cannot be altered, what will be the part played therein by that beautiful Egyptian Amenartas, the Princess of the royal race of the Pharaohs, for the love of whom the Priest Kallikrates broke his vows to Isis, and, pursued by the inexorable vengeance of the outraged Goddess, fled down the coast of Libya to meet his doom at Kôr?

FINIS.

EXPLANATORY NOTES

7 *Dedication*: Andrew Lang (1844–1912), prolific writer in many fields (poetry, fiction, criticism, classical scholarship, anthropology, etc.). His interest in folklore and myth (*Custom and Myth*, 1884; *Myth, Ritual and Religion*, 1887) made him an apt dedicatee of *She*, as did his preference for romance-writing over realism. He admired Haggard's work, and later collaborated with him in *The World's Desire* (1891).

11 *vir doctissimus et amicus meus*: 'a most learned man and my friend'. Adapting Cicero, *Ad Atticum* (*Letters to Atticus*), VII vii. i: 'vir optimus . . . et doctissimus tuique amantissimus', 'an excellent fellow . . . a good scholar and your very staunch friend' (trans. E. O. Winstedt, Loeb Library, 1928). In the *Graphic* version, the 'friend' is his brother, and the Latin tag is omitted.

Apollo: Greek sun-god, the classical type of male beauty.

Charon: in Greek myth, the ferryman who conducted the souls of the dead across the river Styx to the underworld.

13 *a book of yours describing a Central African adventure*: *King Solomon's Mines* (1885).

Central Asia: anticipating the sequel to *She, Ayesha: The Return of She* (1905).

16 *Like Cain, I was branded*: Genesis 4: 15.

17 *the monkey theory*: in the *Graphic* version, 'Darwin's theory'. The change is to the more colloquial term; but see also Introduction, p. xx.

18 *Isis*: Egyptian goddess of fertility, sister and consort of Osiris.

Hak-Hor: or Achoris, third Pharaoh of the 29th Dynasty (399–380 BC) which came from Mendes, a city in the eastern part of the Nile Delta (hence 'Mendesian'). He raised an army of Greek mercenaries to combat the threat of a Persian invasion. See also note to p. 36 below.

Herodotus: the Greek historian (*c*.480–*c*.425 BC), whose *History* of the struggle between Greece and Persia is alluded to in Holly's footnote.

Lacedæmonians: another name for the Spartans.

19 *Delagoa Bay*: now the bay of Lourenço Marques, off the coast of southern Mozambique in the Indian Ocean. 'Lorenzo Marquez' is mentioned in one of the inscriptions on the sherd (see p. 45), but in his letter to Leo, Vincey places the scene further north: see p. 34 and note.

about 770 A.D., when Charlemagne invaded Lombardy: Charlemagne (= Carolus Magnus, Charles the Great, 742–814), king of the Franks (768) and Emperor of the West (800).

in the reign of Edward the Confessor: 1043–66. Haggard carefully distinguishes the Vinceys from those French families who came to England *with* William the Conqueror in 1066.

21 *Chancery*: a division of the High Court, presided over by the Lord Chancellor, responsible for safeguarding the interests of orphaned heirs until they came of age; see the lawyers' letter in Chapter II, p. 25.

the sport of which you are so fond: game hunting; see p. 28.

though I am dead and forgotten, yet shall I live: John 11: 25–6: 'Jesus said unto her, I am the resurrection and the life: he that believeth in me, though he were dead, yet shall he live: and whosoever liveth and believeth in me shall never die.' Vincey however refers not to resurrection through faith, but to reincarnation.

There is no such thing as death, Holly, only a change: Job 14: 14: 'If a man die, shall he live again? all the days of my appointed time will I wait, till my change come.' Also 1 Corinthians 15: 51–2: 'Behold, I shew you a mystery; We shall not all sleep, but we shall all be changed . . . at the last trump; for the trumpet shall sound, and the dead shall be raised incorruptible, and we shall be changed.'

22 *with the word 'Remember' on his lips, was gone*: this, together with the fact that Vincey makes Holly swear an oath, and the mention of a ghost at the end of the chapter, suggests an echo of the Ghost in *Hamlet* and his injunction 'Remember me' (I. v. 91).

23 *gyp*: Cambridge term for a college servant.

25 *Consols*: short for Consolidated Annuities, Government securities yielding 3 per cent per annum; a standard 'safe' investment.

26 *a most respectable round-faced young man*: the character of Job was based on that of Stephen Lanham, a young groom from Bradenham in Norfolk who accompanied Haggard and his wife on their trip to Africa in 1880.

28 *a great strapping butcher's man*: the combat between genteel boy and butcher has a famous literary antecedent in Dickens's *David Copperfield*, ch. 18.

29 *reading at Cambridge, and only going up to London to eat his dinners*: that is, studying law in Cambridge, and going to London three times a term to eat dinner at one of the Inns of Court, a formal requirement for trainee barristers.

31 *fire a mine*: set off an explosion (to undermine a fortification).

32 *Uncial Greek*: a script comprising large rounded letters (not joined to each other) characteristic of early classical manuscripts.

black-letter: also called 'Gothic', a script which developed from Carolingian Minuscule in the twelfth century and on which black-letter type was based. The sherd itself has an inscription in black-letter: see frontispiece and p. 43.

undoubtedly ancient potsherd: Haggard's close friend and sister-in-law, Agnes Barber, manufactured and inscribed the sherd. According to

Haggard, it was shown to Sir John Evans, the antiquary, who commented: 'All I can say is that it might *possibly* have been forged' (*The Days of My Life*, i. 248). The facsimile which formed the frontispiece for the first edition does not appear in the *Graphic* version: see note to p. 41 below. In later editions the colours on the facsimile of the sherd are not reproduced.

32 *amphora*: a two-handled vase or jar.

in some remote age: see the black-letter inscription on the sherd and its translation, pp. 44–5.

together with the writings on the parchments: not in the *Graphic* version; see below.

33 *composition scarabæus*: a ceramic gem in the form of the scarab beetle worshipped by the Egyptians. For the significance of the hieroglyphics, see 'Editor's' note on p. 40.

beloved wife: the *Graphic* version has 'beloved wife, died May, 1856'.

I stretch out my hand to you across the gulf of death: Virgil, *Aeneid*, vi. 313: 'Tendebantque manus ripae ulterioris amore', but referring there to the dead pleading with Charon to cross the Styx: 'and they reached out their hands in longing for the further shore'. Haggard may have been influenced by the final words of Anthony Trollope's *Autobiography*, published posthumously in 1883: 'Now I stretch out my hand, and from the further shore I bid adieu to all who have cared to read any among the many words that I have written.'

34 *where the Zambesi falls into the sea*: near Chinde in central Mozambique; over 500 miles in a straight line from Delagoa Bay (see p. 19).

dhow: small one-masted trading vessel.

"Omnia vincit amor": 'love conquers all things', a tag from Virgil (*Eclogues*, x. 69).

35 *The unknown is generally taken to be terrible*: adapting Tacitus (*Agricola*, 30): 'omne ignotum pro magnifico est', 'everything unknown is held to be glorious'.

thus far shalt thou go: God sets the boundaries of the ocean, Job 18: 11: 'Hitherto shalt thou come, but no further: and here shall thy proud waves be stayed.' The whole chapter concerns the limitations of human as opposed to divine knowledge.

36 *Nectanebes*: the 'Editor's' footnote is substantially accurate; Nekhtnebf was the last Pharaoh of the 30th Dynasty, which succeeded the 'Mendesian' Dynasty in 380 BC (see note to p. 18 above). 'Ochus' is the Persian Emperor Artaxerxes III: see p. 136.

the people who place pots upon the heads of strangers: readers who wish to anticipate the meaning of this phrase should turn to p. 94.

37 *very good Greek of the period it is*: the inscription was composed by Dr Hubert Holden, Haggard's former headmaster at Queen Elizabeth School, Ipswich.

40 *cartouche*: in Egyptian hieroglyphics, the oval or oblong figure which encloses characters expressing divine names or titles. See 'Editor's' footnote, which was not in the *Graphic* version; presumably someone pointed out the error to Haggard, who, ingeniously but rather meanly, attributed it to Holly.

HOG FECIT | DOROTHEA VINCEY: 'Dorothea Vincey made (i.e. wrote) this' (Latin). The orthography of the English couplet above suggests the fifteenth or sixteenth century. Dorothea Vincey's monogram is mentioned on p. 43. Her name may have been suggested by George Eliot's *Middlemarch*, whose heroine, Dorothea, marries the learned mythographer Mr Casaubon, and in which the Vincey family appears.

41 *'Ætate sua 17'*: 'in his seventeenth year' (Latin).

carelessly executed: not in the *Graphic* version; this and other changes (see below) suggest that the sherd itself was made between the serialization and the publication of the first edition.

with the exception of its termination (cvi): not in the *Graphic* version.

twelve: in the *Graphic* version, 'a dozen or more of'.

with three exceptions only: in the *Graphic* version, 'almost without exception'.

the name 'Vindex': Andrew Lang (see above, Dedication) confirmed the possibility of this as the original of 'Vincey': 'Vindex, Vindici, Vincey would knit' (D. S. Higgins, *Rider Haggard: The Great Storyteller*, London, 1981, p. 91).

42 *The following list*: this list is not in the *Graphic* version.

CONIVX: wife.

43 *a rather neat*: in the *Graphic* version, 'an almost obliterated'.

To the left . . . a date, 1800: this sentence is not in the *Graphic* version.

a fair mediæval Latinist: the medieval Latin and its black-letter English translation were done by the archaeologist and campanologist John Raven (1833–1906). Dr Raven was a committee member of the Norfolk and Norwich Archaeological Society.

44 *Modernised Version*: 'ye whyche' = the which; 'aunceteres' = ancestors; 'Armoryke . . . Britaine ye Lesse' = Brittany; 'should . . . honde' = was always urging my father; 'frusshe' = smash, destroy; 'tobrast' = broke; 'topeecyd' = joined.

45 *pinnance*: this should be 'pinnace' ('pinnance' is not recorded in the *Oxford English Dictionary* as an alternative form), a small light sailing vessel of the period, mostly used for scouting and messenger duties.

galleon: a ship of war of the period, larger and more heavily armed than a pinnace.

the well-known lines in Hamlet: I. v. 166–7. See note to p. 195 below for another quotation from *Hamlet*; both are addressed by Hamlet to Horatio, suggesting a link with Holly's first name, Horace.

45 *And now there remained but one more document*: this final flourish of learning was not in the *Graphic* version, which goes straight from the end of the previous paragraph to the one beginning ' "Well," I said' on p. 48.

Edmund Pratt: unlike Grocyn, an invented character.

Grocyn: William Grocyn (?1446–1519). See 'Editor's' footnote.

46 *the passage . . . 'advenaslasaniscoronantium'*: in the English version (p. 36), 'they brought us to the Queen of the people who place pots upon the heads of strangers'; it is on the 'mediæval learning and latinity' of this latter phrase that Haggard is complimenting Dr Raven (alias Edmund Pratt).

48 *Hec . . . MCCCCLXXXXV^n*: 'the learned man Edmund Pratt, licentiate in canon law, of Exeter College, Oxford, formerly one of the pupils of the most learned Grocyn, translated this Greek writing into Latin, on the Ides of April 1495.' The Ides of April fall on the 13th of the month.

53 *The whale-boat . . . Scotland*: modelled on the boat ordered from Messrs John Brown of Dundee by Haggard's friend Frederick Jackson for a journey to Lamu, on the coast of Kenya; its use to save the heroes' lives in a storm is also drawn directly from Jackson's experience: see Higgins, *Rider Haggard*, pp. 67, 93.

54 *parrel*: the rope or chain by which the yard is fastened to the mast.

55 *pooped*: the wave has broken over the dhow's poop (stern), filling her with water.

56 *the homely Cam*: the stream after which Cambridge is named.

58 *time to get up for chapel*: attendance at early morning service was compulsory for undergraduates at Oxford and Cambridge in this period.

61 *the old gentleman*: the devil.

an unbelieving Jew . . . Those who live will see: 'unbelieving Jews' (Acts 14: 2); 'There be some standing here, which shall not taste of death, till they see the Son of man coming in his kingdom' (Matthew 16: 28).

64 *vast flocks . . . see the sky*: although none of the characters remarks on it, this accords with Amenartas's description of 'wastes and marshes, where the sea fowl hid the sky' (p. 36).

66 *express rifle*: a high-velocity, low-trajectory weapon.

71 *Zanzibar coast*: the coast of East Africa (not that of the island of Zanzibar itself, which is several hundred miles south of Mombasa in Kenya).

75 *cup-shaped hill*: as with the waterfowl, this detail, confirming Vincey's account ('far inland are great mountains, shaped like cups', p. 34), goes unremarked by any of the characters.

76 *Mammon of Unrighteousness*: following the advice in Luke 16: 9 (the parable of the unjust steward): 'Make to yourselves friends of the mammon of unrighteousness.'

78 *oribé*: or 'oribi', a species of antelope native to South Africa and inhabiting the open plains.

79 *the customs of the early Christians*: alluding to the 'holy kiss' or 'kiss of charity', enjoined by Paul and Peter in their epistles (e.g. Romans 16: 16, 1 Peter 5: 14).

85 *at Jericho*: euphemism for 'at the devil'.

86 *the Norfolk red-pole strain*: red-haired hornless cattle; for Haggard's *A Farmer's Year* (1899) and *Rural England* (1902). Later editions have 'red-poll', the usual spelling.

91 *another Scriptural character*: Joseph, who rejects the advances of Potiphar's wife, Genesis 39: 7–12.

92 *Kafir corn*: Indian millet, *Sorghum vulgare*.

93 *Barmecide*: from the Arabian Nights tale (the Barber's Sixth Brother) in which Barmecide asks a poor man to dinner and offers him an imaginary banquet.

95 *struggling. He fought ... For a moment*: the attempted hot-potting of Mahomed is a revised version of the incident as it originally stood in the *Graphic*:

> struggling, and then—even now I can scarcely bear to write it—there was one awful, heartrending shriek, ending and smothered in a hissing sound, and the next thing that I saw was the poor wretch, broken loose from his captors, in the despairing effort of a hideous death, and rushing and rolling into the darkness beyond the lamps, *the red hot pot jammed upon his head*, completely covering it from view.
>
> I sprang to my feet with a yell of horror, and, drawing my revolver, fired it by a sort of instinct at the diabolical woman who had been caressing Mahomed, and was now gripping him in her arms. The bullet struck her in the back and killed her, and to this day I am glad that it did, for, as it afterwards transpired, she had availed herself of the anthropophagous customs of the Amahagger to organize the whole thing in revenge of the slight put upon her by Job.
>
> For a moment ... (30 Oct. 1886, p. 470; italics Haggard's)

This incident had been criticized for excessive violence; the feeling may have been exacerbated by the fact that it was the subject of one of the illustrations which headed the *Graphic* serial. This illustration—whether by mistake or not is uncertain—had already appeared, in the issue of the preceding week (23 Oct.), with a note at the end informing readers that the episode to which it applied would appear in the following issue. Someone may also have drawn Haggard's attention to the inconsistency of Mahomed 'rushing and rolling into the darkness' in one paragraph while being gripped by the 'diabolical woman' in the next.

anthropophagous: man-eating.

118 *honeysuckers*: small birds that feed on nectar.

119 *quagga*: a kind of zebra; it had become extinct in 1883.

119 *Martini*: short for Martini-Henry; the military version was standard issue in the British Army 1871–91. It was named after Friedrich von Martini, who invented the breech-mechanism, and Benjamin Tyler Henry, who devised the .45-calibre barrel.

130 *'kootooing'*: variant of 'kowtowing', i.e. prostrating oneself as a mark of obeisance.

136 *Arabian am I by my birth*: the origin of the Arab people given here and in Holly's footnote corresponds to what was popularly believed until relatively late in the century, though it was going out of date at the time of writing. Kâhtan was identified with the Old Testament Joktan, the son of Eber (Genesis 10: 25); Ishmael and his mother Hagar were cast out into the wilderness by Abraham at the insistence of Sarah (Genesis 21: 9–21).

what Pharaoh sits upon the throne?: see note to p. 36 above. The Achaemenid dynasty ruled Persia, 558–330 BC.

just now, is it once more a people: Greece had gained its independence from Turkey in 1829. Holly's low opinion of the modern Greeks as opposed to their classical ancestors was a Victorian commonplace.

the Temple that the wise king built: Ayesha refers to the temple built by Solomon (1 Kings 6); Holly mistakenly refers to the temple built by Herod the Great (the one referred to in the New Testament).

137 *Jerusalem is no more*: i.e. no longer a centre of power.

Solitudinem faciunt, pacem appellant: 'they make a wilderness and call it peace', a tag from Tacitus, *Agricola*, 30.

138 *so said one of their prophets that it should be*: more than one: e.g. Jeremiah 13: 24: 'Therefore will I scatter them as the stubble that passeth away by the wind of the wilderness'; Ezekiel 5: 10: 'I will execute judgments in thee, and the whole remnant of thee will I scatter into all the winds.'

142 *Actæon*: while out hunting, he came across Artemis bathing; she turned him into a stag, and he was killed by his own hounds. Ayesha draws the moral on p. 144.

144 *Venus Victrix*: the name of a celebrated statue by the Italian sculptor Antonio Canova.

ban-hounds: hounds which execute a 'ban' or curse.

145 *I am informed*: for the scarab, see p. 33.

146 *diablerie*: dealings with the devil: devil-likeness or devil-like behaviour.

147 *Circe*: the enchantress who turned men into pigs in Homer's *Odyssey*, x.

Who ever heard of a man being born again?: Like Nicodemus (John 3: 3–5) Holly takes the phrase literally, meaning physical reincarnation, ignoring the sense of spiritual rebirth: 'Jesus answered . . . Except a man be born again, he cannot see the kingdom of God. Nicodemus saith unto him, How can a man be born when he is old? can he enter the second time into his mother's womb, and be born? Jesus answered . . . Except a man be born of water and of the Spirit, he cannot enter into the kingdom of God.' The phrase is used by Ayesha on p. 208.

155 *corpseses*: not a misprint, but Job's dialect; cf. 'Methody' (p. 218) and 'supercilus' (p. 219).

157 *Mark Tapley*: the indomitably cheerful character in Dickens's *Martin Chuzzlewit*.

160 *jot or tittle*: Matthew 5: 18: 'Till heaven and earth pass, one jot or one tittle shall in no wise pass from the law.'

165 *as the wise Hebrew wrote long ago*: Solomon, in Ecclesiastes 1: 9.

168 *beautiful . . . not divided*: 2 Samuel 1: 23: 'Saul and Jonathan were lovely and pleasant in their lives, and in their death they were not divided.'

171 *more deadly than any Basilisk's*: the basilisk, also called the cockatrice, is a mythical reptile, hatched by a serpent from a cock's egg, whose glance is fatal.

172 *Aphrodité*: Greek goddess of love.

epithalamium: marriage-song.

175 *we Arabs had many gods*: Haggard's information on the many naturalistic and animistic deities of pre-Islamic Arabia is basically correct, taking into account the older forms of the names and the fact that the deities are not differentiated according to their regions.

183 *no marriage or giving in marriage*: Mark 12: 25; Jesus's answer to the Sadducees' riddle of whose wife in the afterlife would a woman be who had married seven brothers: 'For when they shall rise from the dead, they neither marry, nor are given in marriage; but are as the angels which are in heaven.'

away with: remove, overcome. Later revised to 'suffer'.

185 *So said that Messiah*: Matthew 18: 7.

188 *Fallen is Imperial Kôr!* Echoing Revelation 18: 2: 'And he cried mightily with a strong voice, saying, Babylon the great is fallen, is fallen, and is become the habitation of devils.'

195 *Nero*: Roman Emperor, 54–68; he persecuted the Christians in the aftermath of the great fire of 64, for which he made them the scapegoats.

Cæsar's dust . . . may we come: from *Hamlet*, v. i. 197–208: 'To what base uses we may return, Horatio! Why may not imagination trace the noble dust of Alexander till 'a find it stopping a bung-hole? . . . Imperious Caesar, dead and turn'd to clay, | Might stop a hole to keep the wind away.' See also note to p. 45 above.

198 *blesbok . . . impala . . . koodoo*: kinds of southern African antelope.

204 *zone*: girdle.

207 *the burden*: the general idea.

208 *yet would . . . ariseth*: drawing on a number of biblical texts: Luke 1: 44: 'For, lo, as soon as the voice of thy salutation sounded in mine ears, the

babe leaped in my womb for joy'; Song of Solomon 3: 1–3: 'By night on my bed I sought him whom my soul loveth: I sought him, but I found him not. . . . The watchmen that go about the city found me: to whom I said, Saw ye him whom my soul loveth?'; Isaiah 21: 11–12: 'Watchman, what of the night? The watchman said, The morning cometh, and also the night'; Revelation 22: 16: 'I am . . . the bright and morning star'.

212 *an inspired Sibyl*: a classical Greek or Roman prophetess. The two most celebrated Sibyls were those of Delphi and Cumae; their ecstatic utterances were attributed to divine possession, as in Virgil's description of the Cumaean Sibyl (*Aeneid*, vi): 'As she spoke the words, there, before the double doors, suddenly her countenance and her colour changed and her hair fell in disarray. Her breast heaved and her bursting heart was wild and mad; she appeared taller and spoke in no mortal tones, for the God was nearer and the breath of his power was upon her' (trans. W. F. Jackson Knight, Harmondsworth, 1958).

213 *vitrified*: glazed.

Dust to dust!: From the Anglican burial service: 'earth to earth, ashes to ashes, dust to dust; in sure and certain hope of the Resurrection to eternal life, through our lord Jesus Christ; who shall change our vile body, that it may be like unto his glorious body.'

217 *Witch of Endor*: she raised the ghost of the prophet Samuel for King Saul, 1 Samuel 28: 7–20.

what is going to happen to sorceresses and them sort: as in Revelation 21: 8: 'But the fearful, and unbelieving, and the abominable, and murderers, and whore-mongers, and sorcerers, and idolaters, and all liars, shall have their part in the lake which burneth with fire and brimstone: which is the second death.'

218 *Methody*: a vulgar or dialect form of 'Methodist'; but Haggard probably means Job to refer to the whole class of Evangelical or Dissenting clergy, whose image in Victorian fiction (e.g. Mr Chadband in Dickens's *Bleak House*) was often that of cant and deceit.

219 *supercilus*: Job's contraction of 'supercilious'.

221 *stones are the bread she gives her children*: contrast Matthew 7: 9–11 (the Sermon on the Mount): 'Or what man is there of you, whom if his son ask bread, will he give him a stone? . . . If ye then, being evil, know how to give good gifts unto your children, how much more shall your Father which is in heaven give good gifts to them that ask him?'

222 *scorpion whips of sin*: from 1 Kings 12: 11: 'my father hath chastised you with whips, but I will chastise you with scorpions.'

225 *the one under whom we lived . . . vast realms*: 1887, the year when *She* was published, was an especially apt year for this compliment: it was Queen Victoria's Jubilee, the fiftieth year of her reign.

we were in fact ruled . . . community: Haggard, the gentleman farmer, probably has in mind the third Reform Act (1884), which had extended the franchise to agricultural labourers (i.e. men of Job's class). Ayesha, of course, along with other women, would not have had the vote until 1918.

227 *sarcophagi . . . given to their keeping*: 'Sarcophagus' comes from the Greek meaning 'flesh-eating'; it appears in Holland's translation of Pliny (1601) as the name of a kind of limestone thought to consume flesh, and therefore used for coffins.

232 *fane*: temple.

246 *would not suffer me to step therein*: this does not accord with the inscription on the sherd, in which Amenartas implies that Ayesha already possessed 'life and loveliness that does not die' when she and Kallikrates first encountered her.

247 *her gods*: Osiris was the consort of Isis, the goddess whose priest Kallikrates had been; Nephthys was the sister of Osiris and his dark twin, Set; Hekt (Heket) was a goddess associated with childbirth; Sekhet (Sekhmet) was the goddess of war.

248 *Yea, I have sinned . . . hardened*: taking account of the episode in Chapter XX in which Ayesha compels Leo to pay homage to her over the corpse of the murdered Ustane, Haggard may here be recalling the scene in Browning's *Pippa Passes* (1841) between Ottima and her lover Sebald, who have just murdered Ottima's husband. Just as Sebald, in response to Ottima's demand that they glory in their crime, says 'I crown you | My great white queen, my spirit's arbitress, | Magnificent . . .', he is saved by Pippa's song from pronouncing the final words, 'in sin', and instead reaffirms his moral awareness: 'Though I be lost, | I know which is the better, never fear, | Of vice or virtue, purity or lust, | Nature or trick!' (Part I, ll. 218–20, 262–4).

249 *I give to thee dominion over sea and earth*: Genesis 1: 28: 'And God blessed them, and God said unto them, Be fruitful, and multiply, and replenish the earth, and subdue it: and have dominion over the fish of the sea, and over the fowl of the air, and over every living thing that moveth upon the earth.'

261 *hind*: peasant.

264 *Tartarus*: in classical mythology, the region of the Underworld where wrongdoers were tormented.

American Literature

British and Irish Literature

Children's Literature

Classics and Ancient Literature

Colonial Literature

Eastern Literature

European Literature

History

Medieval Literature

Oxford English Drama

Poetry

Philosophy

Politics

Religion

The Oxford Shakespeare

A complete list of Oxford Paperbacks, including Oxford World's Classics, Oxford Shakespeare, Oxford Drama, and Oxford Paperback Reference, is available in the UK from the Academic Division Publicity Department, Oxford University Press, Great Clarendon Street, Oxford OX2 6DP.

In the USA, complete lists are available from the Paperbacks Marketing Manager, Oxford University Press, 198 Madison Avenue, New York, NY 10016.

Oxford Paperbacks are available from all good bookshops. In case of difficulty, customers in the UK can order direct from Oxford University Press Bookshop, Freepost, 116 High Street, Oxford OX1 4BR, enclosing full payment. Please add 10 per cent of published price for postage and packing.